From This Day Forward

By Beryl Matthews

Hold on to Your Dreams
The Forgotten Family
Battles Lost and Won
Diamonds in the Dust
A Flight of Golden Wings
The Uncertain Years
The Day Will Come
When the Music Stopped
When Midnight Comes
Friends and Enemies
From This Day Forward
Together Under the Stars

a&b

From This Day Forward

BERYL MATTHEWS

Allison & Busby Limited
11 Wardour Mews
London W1F 8AN
allisonandbusby.com

First published in Great Britain by Allison & Busby in 2020.
This paperback edition published by Allison & Busby in 2021.

A CIP catalogue record for this book is available from the British Library.

10 9 8 7 6 5 4 3 2 1

ISBN 978-0-7490-2538-0

Typeset in 11/16 pt Sabon LT Pro by Allison & Busby Ltd.

The paper used for this Allison & Busby publication has been produced from trees that have been legally sourced from well-managed and credibly certified forests.

Printed and bound by
CPI Group (UK) Ltd, Croydon, CR0 4YY

Chapter One

Lambeth, London, 1880

In desperation Jane Roberts tried to wrestle her purse away from her husband. 'That's all I've got to feed us. If you take everything then you won't get any dinner tonight.'

Bert Roberts pushed her roughly away and slipped the money in his pocket. 'I don't care, cos I won't be here, so you'll have to find another way to get money. I'm fed up with you and the kids and I'm leaving.'

Her son Charlie rushed to catch her before she fell, and then rounded on his father. 'Don't you dare treat Mum like that!'

'You shut up, kid, or I'll give you a hiding you won't forget.'

She held her son's shoulders to stop him from getting into a fight with his father. 'Where are you going?'

He smirked. 'Found myself another woman, and she's real handsome. You ain't nothing like the smart girl I married.'

'Is that surprising after sixteen years of worrying about keeping a roof over our heads and food on the table? I've never known if you were going to give me any money or if you were gambling it away at the dogs. That is enough to break anyone's spirit.' Jane studied the man in front of her with disgust. 'You're not the dashing man who persuaded me to defy my parents and marry you, either.'

'And what a bloody mistake that was. They disowned you and threw us both out.'

She almost gasped, surprised just how much that hurt after all these years. 'You hadn't expected that, and it ruined all your schemes for an easy life, didn't it?'

'Too right, and I was stuck with you, but I ain't putting up with it no more.'

'Who is this woman? I suppose she's got money.' Jane was stunned by what she was hearing. She knew her husband hadn't been faithful to her, but she had put up with it for the sake of the children.

'She's got enough.' He tipped her handbag upside down to make sure there wasn't anything of value there.

'How can you do this, not only to me, but to your children? Don't you care what happens to us?'

Bert shook his head, then threw the house keys on the table and headed for the door. Before leaving he looked back. 'You are going to have to manage on your own. It ain't no good creeping back to your high-and-mighty family, cos they haven't even bothered to find you after all these years. There's always the workhouse if you can't pay the rent.'

With that he slammed the door behind him and she stared at it in disbelief. He really had gone, and dread rushed in and hit her like a tidal wave.

'Mum?'

She looked down at her youngest son's worried face and gathered him close, dismayed that Joe had witnessed that unpleasant scene.

'What did Dad mean? We haven't got to go to the workhouse, have we? That isn't a nice place.' His bottom lip trembled as he gazed imploringly at his mother.

'No, no, we won't let that happen.'

'We certainly won't!' Charlie ruffled his younger brother's hair and dredged up a smile in an effort to reassure the eight-year-old boy. He stood behind Joe so the youngster couldn't see his expression, and looked at their mother, his hazel eyes blazing with fury. 'What was that all about? What did he mean about your parents?'

Jane shook her head, worry and disbelief etched on her face. 'He was talking nonsense in an effort to hurt me as much as he could before leaving. He's taken every penny we had, Charlie.'

'Is there anyone we can go to for help?'

She shook her head. 'Everyone in this slum has enough trouble feeding their own families. We can't ask them to help us.'

Little Joe was gazing from his mother and then back to his older brother. 'Helen will help.'

Jane took a deep, silent breath in an effort to steady herself, knowing she had to stay strong in front of her children. 'I was hoping not to trouble her with this.'

'She's got a right to know,' Charlie stated. 'She'll be furious if we don't tell her.'

'You're right, of course. I'm not thinking straight at the moment.'

'I'll go and see her now.' Charlie shot out of the door and ran up the street at speed.

'Helen will know what to do,' Joe declared, seeming more at ease now Charlie had gone for their big sister. 'She's clever.'

'Yes, she is.' She looked lovingly at her youngest son. He was clearly frightened and she had to get control of her feelings in order to calm his fears. 'I need to go into the other room for a while, so why don't you do those arithmetic lessons I gave you.'

He nodded and sat at the table to do the work she had set him. Jane hurried out of the scullery, determined to clear her mind, because the last thing she must do was panic.

She sat down and closed her eyes, allowing her mind to go back to that time sixteen years ago. Most of her young life she had lived in different countries as her father had moved around. It had been a life of luxury, with servants on hand to meet her every need. Being an only child, she had been spoilt and denied very little. They had returned to this country when she was eighteen and London was exciting. She had slipped out one day on her own and stopped by the river to watch some swans. A young man had come up to her and given her a crust of bread to feed the birds and they had laughed at their antics. That's how it had started, and from then on she met him every time she was able to get out on her own. One day, without telling her what he was going to do, he had come to her house and introduced himself to her parents. Her father had immediately seen what he was and had forbidden her to ever see him again. She had defied him and continued to meet Bert, believing herself to be in love.

Jane moaned in disbelief. How could she not have seen what he was really after? He had seen a young girl of good class on her own, and spotting an opportunity for gain had courted her with charm and laughter. After her father's rejection of him he had set about to persuade her that if they were married he would be accepted into her family. He had made all the arrangements and she had gone along with them, completely fooled by his declarations of love.

Jane allowed the tears to run freely down her face as she recalled that terrible time. Furious that she had defied him, her father had disowned her and turned them both away. It was devastating and she'd looked to her new husband for support, but it wasn't there. He was in a rage that frightened her, and he brought her to this slum, telling her that she must get used to it because it was all they could afford. It was the first time she had seen where he lived and, disgusted with the squalor, she had scrubbed to remove the filth until her hands were raw. She soon found out he expected her to meet his needs, cook and do as she was told. The sensible thing would have been to leave him immediately, but she had no money and nowhere to go.

Since she had been in this disgusting place she'd had three children. Helen was now fifteen, Charlie thirteen and Joe eight. Helen was a determined girl and would fight her way through any obstacle. Charlie also had the same spirit. He was tall and strong in body and mind, but Joe was the one she worried about the most. He was gentle and kind to everyone, always wanting to help, and he was the most vulnerable of her children. That didn't mean he wasn't intelligent, because behind those clear eyes there was a sharp mind that didn't miss much. At least something good had come out of these nightmare years, and she would never regret that. She was prepared to do anything needed to keep them safe, but at the moment she was reeling with shock and the disaster facing them seemed insurmountable. *Helen*, she prayed silently, *I need your clear thinking and positive attitude.*

'Psst . . .'

Helen Roberts put the bucket down and turned her head to see who was making that hissing sound, and then gasped in surprise when she saw her brother's head peering round the kitchen door. She rushed over to him. 'What are you doing here?'

'That is what I was going to ask.' The housekeeper, Mrs Tarrant, swept over to them. 'Come inside, child, and close the door.'

Charlie stepped inside hesitantly and wiped the perspiration from his brow with the back of his hand, but held the stern housekeeper's gaze without flinching. 'I need to see my sister, please. It's urgent.'

'From the state you are in that is apparent. You may talk to her.' She stepped back a pace but didn't move away.

'Thank you, ma'am,' he replied politely.

Helen caught hold of her brother's arm, very concerned. Something bad must have happened or Charlie would never have come here for her. 'How did you get here?'

'I ran all the way.'

'What? It must be five miles or more. Why didn't you take the bus?'

'Couldn't. Didn't have any money, and I had to get here. We need you, sis.'

Then she asked the question she had been avoiding. 'What's happened?'

'Dad's gone,' he told her.

'What do you mean, "gone"?'

He cast a quick glance at the housekeeper and the rest of the staff who were all listening intently, and with a shrug he turned his attention back to Helen. 'He left. He took all his things, the money out of Mum's purse and the rent money out of the jar, threw his door key on the table and stormed out.' Charlie lowered his voice for a moment and then said in a quiet voice, 'Said he'd found himself a better woman.'

Furious now, Helen erupted. 'What the daft bugger

means is he's found a woman with a bit of money he can gamble with. How's Mum?'

'Worried sick. There's no food in the place, the rent man is due in two days' time and we can't pay him.' He looked at his big sister imploringly. 'We need your help, sis. Dad said if we get chucked out, they'll take us to the workhouse.'

'Oh no they won't!' Helen clenched her work-worn hands into fists. 'That's not going to happen to my family.'

Charlie breathed an audible sigh of relief when he saw his big sister's determined expression. 'Tell me what I can do.'

Mrs Tarrant made an angry sound of disgust and turned to Cook. 'Make up a basket of food for Helen's family.'

'Thank you, Mrs Tarrant. I must go home.'

'Of course you must. You can have a week to deal with this crisis. I will hold your job open for you that long, but no longer. You are a good worker and I hope you will return before the week runs out.'

'That is kind of you, and I will be back as quickly as possible.'

The lady gave one of her rare smiles. 'How old is little Joe?'

'He's eight and Charlie is thirteen.'

'Quite a difference in your ages. Just the three of you?'

'Yes,' Helen told her. 'Mum didn't think she was going to have any more after me and Charlie, but she did eventually have Joe.'

While they had been talking, Cook had given Charlie a meat pie and a large cup of tea, which he devoured rapidly, muttering thanks in between mouthfuls.

'Good heavens, child,' Cook exclaimed. 'How long is it since you've had something to eat?'

'A while,' was all he said, watching as his cup was refilled. When that was quickly emptied, he smiled at Cook. 'It was a long run.'

The butler pulled a coin out of his pocket and gave it to Charlie. 'You and your sister are to take a ride home.'

'Oh, thank you, sir.'

He patted the boy on the shoulder and said to Helen, 'Your brother is like you, polite and well spoken.'

'That is kind of you to say so, Mr Gregson. Mum taught us to read and write before we went to school, and insisted we had good manners.'

'Very wise of her. Now off you go and see what you can do for your family, and hurry back.'

She rushed upstairs to collect her things, and then ran back to her waiting brother. 'Come on, Charlie, let's sort this mess out.'

Cook handed her a basket full of food. 'That should keep you going for a couple of days.'

Helen hugged her, her eyes misting over with gratitude. With a heavy heart she walked out of the door, wondering if she really would be able to return. She was only a lowly maid, but the staff treated her kindly and she was grateful for the job.

Once outside, Charlie took the basket from her. 'Sorry I had to come for you, sis, but I didn't know what else to do.'

'You did the right thing. I've been saving up for a new pair of shoes, so I've got enough money to pay the rent man this week. That will give us some breathing space, but we need to find a way to earn some money – and quickly.'

He linked his arm through his sister's, confident that she would find a way. Helen could do anything. 'Dad said some peculiar things before he left.'

Helen snorted in disgust. 'That doesn't surprise me.'

'I know, but he talked as if Mum comes from a wealthy family and they threw her out when she married him. I asked her about it, but she said he was just talking nonsense.'

'Well, we know she has had a good education, but he probably thinks that anyone with a couple of shillings in their pocket is wealthy.'

'I expect you're right.'

On the journey home Helen's mind was racing, trying to find a way for them to survive, and she was also curious about their father's remarks.

The moment they walked in the house little Joe rushed up and threw his arms around her, holding on with all of his might. He gazed up at her, his bottom lip trembling. 'Don't let them throw us out on the street, Helen – please!'

She ruffled his curly brown hair and smiled. 'No one is going to do that. I'm not going to let anything hurt our family, Joe.'

He grasped her hands, holding on tight. 'I'm hungry.'

'I know, sweetheart. I've brought a basket of food with me and Charlie's unpacking it now. We'll eat as soon as I've seen Mum, so you set the table while I do that. Where is she?'

'She just went in the front room.'

Joe rushed off to carry out his task and Charlie said quietly, 'She's doing her best to hide it but she's in shock and needs shaking out of it or we are going to be in a real mess.'

'I'll do that.' She gazed affectionately at her brothers, both looking happier now, and determination surged through her. Charlie was old enough to understand the situation, but the terrified look in Joe's eyes had upset her.

Jane Roberts was sitting in a chair and staring into space, her eyes red from crying. Helen stood in front of her and spoke sharply. 'Mum, pull yourself together – and why the blazes are you crying over that man?'

Her daughter's reprimand made her jump in surprise, unaware she had come into the room. 'He's left us.'

'About time too. You are too good for him – always have been.'

'That's what my parents said, and I wouldn't listen to them.'

Ah, that was the first time her mother had ever mentioned them. Helen pulled up a chair and sat in front of her mother. 'You are educated and he's an ignorant man who can't read or write. All he can do is bet on the dogs and drink beer with his friends.'

'I tried to teach him just like I have the three of you, but he wasn't interested.'

'All he cares about is the pub and the dogs. As long as he could make out the numbers in the races, that was enough for him. That man has dragged you down to his level, but now that is going to stop.'

She stared at her daughter in disbelief. 'He's taken every penny I had. I can't pay the rent or buy food for any of us. We're at rock bottom.'

'That's true. There is only one way we can go now and that is up!'

'That is a good thought, but how on earth are we going to do that?'

The spark was back in her mother's eyes and Helen drew in a silent breath of relief. 'I've got a plan, but it is going to need every one of us to pitch in and make it work.' She stood up. 'I've got enough to pay the rent this week and I've brought food for all of us. Go and wash your face and join us for a meal. You mustn't let the boys see how upset you are.'

Jane hauled herself out of the chair, drained of all energy by this sudden turn of events. 'I'm sorry about that but it hit me hard and I let it show, so I came in here for a moment to try and get my thinking straight. Thank you for coming, Helen. I hope you haven't lost your job because of this?'

'They've given me a week to sort this mess out.'

Her mother straightened up. 'Then we had better see what this plan of yours is.'

'I'll explain when we have all had something to eat. Joe is starving.'

Jane gave a slight smile at the mention of her youngest son, and then walked out of the room, her step sure and her head up.

Good, Helen thought. That was the first hurdle over.

Cook had filled the basket to overflowing, and when they had all eaten their fill there was still enough left over for the next day. As an extra surprise the kind woman had even put in one of her famous large fruit cakes.

Joe's eyes opened wide when he saw it and exclaimed excitedly, 'It's so big! Can I take Granny Jarvis a slice? She doesn't get many treats.'

'Do you still go and see her?' Helen asked. Charlie had told her all about Joe's determination to look out for the elderly woman who had moved in next door two months ago.

He nodded. 'Every day. She hasn't got any family left and no one bothers to visit her. I get her shopping and make sure she has enough to eat.'

Her youngest brother was such a kind boy, and Helen loved him dearly. 'Does she have enough money to pay her rent and buy the food?'

'I'm not sure, but she must have, or they would have turned her out before now. She can't have much, so I wait until the shops are about to shut and I get the best bargains I can for her.' He grinned at his mother. 'Like you do, Mum. Can I take her a slice of that cake, please?'

'Of course you can. We must share our bounty.' Jane cut a large slice, wrapped it in a napkin from the basket and handed it to her son.

With a huge smile on his face he jumped to his feet and raced out to the elderly woman's house.

Charlie gave a quiet laugh. 'He really cares about that old lady. I went with him once just to check that everything was all right, but there's nothing to worry about. He chats away to her and there is noticeable affection in her eyes as she watches him trotting around doing any odd jobs for her. She tries to give him a penny at the end of each week for what he does, but he won't take it. When I asked him why, he said he doesn't do it for money. He likes her and she needs someone to make her smile and help in small ways.'

'He's an extraordinary little boy,' Jane remarked. 'I knew from the moment he was born that there was something different about him. I am desperately sorry I frightened him.'

'Don't worry, Mum, he's fine now. Anyone else want a piece of cake before Joe decides everyone in the street should have a slice?'

They all laughed and Charlie patted his stomach. 'I couldn't, but I will manage a piece later on.'

'We'll save it for then.' Jane stood up and began to clear the table.

By the time the washing-up was done, Joe burst back into the house.

'Granny said that was the best cake she had ever

tasted. I made her a pot of tea to go with it.' The smile faded from his animated face. 'I told her that Dad had left us and she said I wasn't to worry because everything was going to be all right. It will be, won't it, Mum?'

Jane smiled down at him. 'Everything is going to be just fine. I was shocked that your father should even think about leaving us, but Helen's here now and she has a plan.'

He nodded, the bright smile back. 'Helen's clever.'

'She is, so there is nothing to worry about. Now, we have decided to keep the cake for tea, but would you like a small piece now?'

'I can wait. I'm full up after that lovely meat pie we had.' He ran to his sister. 'What is your plan? Can I help?'

'It will need every one of us. Let's sit down and I'll explain.' Once they were seated, Helen handed round paper and pencils. 'I'll want you all to write down what you are good at. It doesn't matter what it is, just put down anything that comes to your mind. For instance, I'm good at scrubbing floors.'

That made them all laugh and turn their attention to the task.

Helen watched to see they were all busy writing before starting her own list. She had no idea what the outcome of this would be, but a way had to be found for the family to survive. The situation was desperate and the meagre amount of money she was earning at the house would nowhere near cover their needs. If they failed, then the spectre of them living on the streets begging for food was frightening, and the final humiliation would be the workhouse. She wouldn't let that happen to those she loved. She wouldn't!

For a moment the desperate situation they were in tried to overwhelm her, but she pushed it away. The last thing she must do is let in fear and doubt. It was obvious her mother was shocked and not thinking clearly, so they were all depending on her to find a solution and give them hope. She wouldn't let them down.

When everyone had stopped writing she looked up and smiled. 'All right, let me see what you've written.'

Joe handed his over first, looking rather dejected. 'I couldn't think of much.'

He'd only put down that he could read and write, and run fast in the school races. 'Oh, we can add quite a few things to your list,' she told him gently. 'You are good at looking after people, like you do with Granny Jarvis. You are good at figures and know how to get the best value for money. You are kind and care about people.'

The boy straightened up as he watched his sister add to his list.

Helen tapped him playfully. 'But you, young man, have forgotten the most important thing. Not many people can write as beautifully as you can. In fact, quite a few around here can't even sign their own name.'

'Mum taught me,' he said proudly. 'I'm the best in school at reading, writing and adding up. But how can that help us?'

'I have an idea, but we'll go through that when I've read all the lists.'

Charlie had put down quite a few things. He was tall for his age and strong. If anything needed fixing, he was the one to go to. He was good with his hands and would tackle any job.

Her mother's list was short, but Helen already had an idea for her. That left her contribution. She had learnt a lot from the staff where she worked about the running of a large household. It took planning to make everything run smoothly and the attention to detail fascinated her. She would use those organising skills to drag her family out of this mess. After writing on a fresh piece of paper for a while, she sat back and looked around at the expectant faces watching her. 'Right, this family is going into business. We are going to put cards in the corner shop window advertising our services.'

They all stared at her in disbelief.

'What services?' her mother asked.

'Joe will write letters for people who can't do it for themselves. The charge will be a halfpenny for a short note and a penny for a long letter. If it is for the authorities, then I will help with the wording.'

He wriggled in his chair excitedly. 'I can do that.'

'I know you can. Now, Charlie, you will offer to take on any building or repairs, for a price to be agreed between you and the customer.' When her older brother smiled agreement, she turned to her mother. 'You are educated and have given us lessons in many subjects, so you are going to set up classes for those who need to learn how to read and write – whatever their age.'

Jane's expression was one of astonishment. 'But the people round here can't afford to pay for something like that.'

'To begin with you will take anything they can offer. If it's a farthing or a cabbage that will do. We are going into business to survive. However, we mustn't forget that the people in these slum areas are desperately poor, so if we see a very needy person, you can relax the rules and teach them at no cost. Everyone around here must be aware of what we are trying to do, and above all they need to be able to respect and trust us. I want people to come to us with their concerns, knowing we will not take advantage of them. Do you understand what I'm saying?'

'You mean we are going to have to go slowly at first and build up a reputation for being honest and caring,' her mother stated.

'Exactly.' She glanced round at each person, her expression serious. 'It isn't going to be easy and there will be times when we want to give up, but that mustn't be allowed to happen. We keep going, whatever the difficulties.'

When they nodded, Helen sat back and sighed deeply. It was a plan, but it remained to be seen if it would work.

Chapter Two

When the boys were in bed, Helen and her mother sat in the front room enjoying a quiet cup of cocoa.

Jane was staring at the empty fireplace, a worried expression on her face. 'Winter's coming and I should have ordered the coal by now, but your father kept saying there was plenty of time and wouldn't give me the money. There's only one sack in the shed, and we must keep that for the stove so we can cook and heat water.'

'We'll get some as soon as we have made enough money. As long as you can keep the stove alight it will be warm in the scullery.'

'I know.' She sighed wearily and looked at her daughter. 'You have done well to cheer up the boys and give them hope, but you must know that making enough money to survive on our own is going to be impossible. I love your idea about me teaching people from deprived areas to read and write, but it won't bring in any money, you must know that.'

'It's going to be hard but not impossible, Mum.' She saw her mother's dejected expression and her heart ached for her. She mustn't allow her to sink too low, so she spoke firmly. 'It is going to take the determination of each one of us, and doubt mustn't creep in. If we fail, then the alternatives are too awful to contemplate. We've got to be positive, and by setting our minds on success we could get out of the slums and give us all a better life.'

Jane smiled then. 'My goodness, you have set your sights high. We are at the bottom of the heap and not many manage to scramble their way out.'

'We will!'

'I don't know where you've got your strength of character and determination from. It certainly hasn't come from me or your father.'

'I must have inherited it from a past relative.' She studied her mother intently for a moment. She was such a kind and gentle woman who loved her children and Helen wondered just how much she had endured over the years in order to protect them from an uncaring father. 'You know, I'd love to hear more about where you were born and your family.'

A look of utter sadness crossed her mother's face, but she didn't reply.

Helen probed, still intrigued by what Charlie had told

her. Her mother's past had always been a mystery and she would dearly love to know why that was. 'I've always felt that you weren't born to this life, Mum. Will you tell me how you ended up married to a man like Bert Roberts?'

'Where I came from and why I am living like this is unimportant. It is in the past and cannot be changed. The only thing that matters now is our survival.' Jane took a deep breath. 'We are on our own, darling, and that's a frightening situation to be in.'

It was evident that her mother wasn't going to talk about her life before she married, and Helen sensed it was too painful for her. That made her even more curious. There was evidently a big secret here and she was determined to uncover it one day.

'Well, whatever happened, you've done well,' Helen told her gently. 'But you don't belong here – I've always known that – and neither do your children. It has made me even more determined to get us all out of here.'

'I used to have dreams too, but they have faded over time.'

'Then it is time they were resurrected. You have shown enormous strength of character by surviving these years. You had to face them on your own, but that isn't the case this time – there are four of us now.' Helen stood up and pulled her mother out of the chair, giving her a hug and determined to see a spark of hope in her eyes again. 'Come on – laugh, dance, you are free now. This can be a new beginning for all of us and it's up to us to make it a fantastic one!'

Jane studied her daughter for a moment, and then a slow smile of realisation crossed her face. 'You're right, I am free at last, and we can move on and try to make a better life for all of us.'

They were both laughing and dancing around the small room, shouting, 'The only way is up!'

'What are you doing?'

They stopped and saw the two boys standing by the door, both grinning widely.

'Can we join in?' Joe asked, giggling at their antics.

Helen held out her arms. 'Come on, boys. It has been too long since laughter was heard in this house. Tomorrow we begin a new life. It isn't going to be easy, but by golly we'll make it work. When we have problems and setbacks we will talk them over, laugh about it, and then move on. From now on there are two words that will not appear in our vocabulary – "can't" and "discouraged".'

The boys shouted agreement and joined in the boisterous moment, spinning round and round in excitement.

'There's another word,' Charlie suggested, slightly out of breath from jumping around. '"Failure".'

'Agreed.' Jane stopped, and gathered her children towards her, smiling down at them. 'I think we should all have a cup of cocoa and another slice of cake.'

There were shouts of pleasure as the boys dashed off to the scullery, eager to enjoy the late-night treat.

Their mother watched them leave and then hugged her daughter. 'Thank you, my darling girl. You have given us all hope and something to work towards – our independence.'

'The cocoa's ready,' Joe hollered.

Sleep was illusive that night as Helen's mind continued to go over and over the plans. She had emphasised the fact that this was going to be a fight for survival, but it was more than that. Much more. Most people in the deprived areas never got past the continual struggle to pay the rent and put food on the table. They lived their entire lives like that, but working at the big house had opened her eyes, and she had begun to yearn for a better life for her family. It had seemed impossible, though, with that man ruling everything they did, and that was why she had gone into service. She just had to get away, and it had been a hard decision to leave her mum and the boys. Now he was out of their lives this was their chance to make a better future for themselves, and they had to grasp it with all their might. They all deserved better, and the way to get what they wanted was by hard work and determination. Failure must not be considered, no matter how tough the road in front of them was.

Aware of the enormity of the task facing them she drifted into a troubled sleep. It was still dark when she woke up and the worry for her family rushed in like a tidal wave. She had arrived back putting on a show of confidence and assuring them everything was going to be all right. It had been quite a performance so perhaps she should go on to the stage as an actress! Sitting on the edge of the bed she covered her face with her hands, allowing her fears to surface for a moment. Little Joe was causing her the most worry. Charlie was a bright boy and wouldn't go down without a fight, but their darling Joe was a different matter. He was young, needing protection, and they must all pull together to see he didn't suffer.

Drawing in a deep, ragged breath, she dressed and walked quietly down the stairs. Rising early to carry out her duties at the big house was a habit now, and she knew that returning to her job at the end of the week was going to cause her much heart searching. In this crisis her place was here, and yet she had a job. The pay was paltry, but it would help her family, and she might be able to get leftovers from Cook. Also, she would have her meals there and that meant one less person to feed here. Somehow, in a few short days, they had to make enough money for rent so she could return to her job.

While waiting for the kettle to boil she heard a movement behind her and turned to see a sleepy Charlie. 'Did I wake you?'

He shook his head. 'I heard you come downstairs and I want to talk to you before the others wake up.'

Helen made a pot of tea, cut slices of bread for their breakfast and, after pouring them both a cup, she smiled at her brother. 'All right, I'm listening.'

'I'm going to leave school and try to get a job. I'm the man of the house now and we can't leave everything to you, sis. I'm way ahead of the other kids, and they are not teaching me anything new. Mum isn't going to like it, though, so I need your help.' He gave her an imploring look. 'You went into service when you were fourteen, and I'll soon be fourteen. I know Mum wants me to stay at school for as long as they will let me, but things are different now.'

'Yes, they are.' Helen sipped her tea while she thought this through. After a moment she said, 'Don't say anything to Mum at the moment, but start looking for a job straight away. If you can find something, then that will be the time to let her know. What would you like to do?'

'Perhaps a carpenter. I love working with wood and could learn how to make useful things like furniture.' His eyes gleamed with enthusiasm, and then he shrugged. 'But I'll take anything I can get.'

'No, you won't,' she told him firmly. 'This isn't just a case of making enough money to survive on, it's about making a better life for ourselves, and that means doing things we love.' She reached across the table and took hold of his hands. 'If you want to be a carpenter then be one. Don't settle for anything less.'

'You're right, and by golly I'll do it!' He tipped his head to one side and studied his big sister. 'What about you? You are too clever to be a maid, so what do you really want to do?'

When she hesitated, Charlie grinned. 'Come on, sis, I've told you my dream.'

'All right, but I've never told anyone this before. Instead of scrubbing floors and cleaning out fire grates I want to do something more demanding, but I really don't know what yet.'

'Then keep searching. There's no point having dreams if we don't even try to make them come true.'

Joe arrived at that moment and hugged them both. 'What are you talking about?'

She poured him a cup of tea and put a slice of bread on a plate for him. 'We were saying what jobs we would like to do. What are you going to do when you grow up?'

'I'm going to be a policeman.'

They stared at their young brother in astonishment.

'Cricky, Joe,' Charlie exclaimed. 'You walk down this street dressed as a copper and you'll get bashed up.'

'We won't be living here then.' The young boy spread a little butter on the bread and took a bite.

'Er . . . where will we be?' Helen asked.

'In a nice house overlooking Clapham Common.'

Charlie shook his head, trying not to laugh at such an impossible idea. 'How do you know this?'

'I saw it in a dream.'

'Darling,' Helen said gently, 'we all have dreams at night, but they aren't real.'

'That's right,' Charlie agreed. 'Sometimes I have the weirdest dreams, but they aren't true.'

The young boy finished his bread and drained his cup, not at all troubled by their remarks. Then he grinned at his sister. 'This one is. You've got to have dreams, and Helen is going to make it happen.'

The weight on her shoulders suddenly became heavier. This lovely, gentle child believed she could do anything, and she wondered how it was going to be possible to live up to such high expectations.

'I've finished my breakfast, so can I go and see Granny now, please? It's Sunday and she goes to church. I help her because her legs are not too good now.'

'Of course.'

He jumped down and headed for the door, then spun round and rushed back. 'Is there any cake left? She'd like a piece with her cup of tea before going to church.'

'I think we can spare a little slice.' Helen picked up a knife and opened the tin.

Joe peered inside. 'Oh, not much there, so she can have my piece.'

'There's just enough for all of us.' She placed a slice in a napkin and handed it to her brother.

He took it and hugged her, then tore out of the house.

She watched silently for a moment and then looked at her other brother. 'What an extraordinary conversation. Does he often say things like that?'

'Like what?' Jane walked in looking more relaxed and rested.

She told her mother what Joe had said. 'He really believes it.'

Their mother smiled. 'I took him to Clapham Common once and he loved it. He's got a vivid imagination – but don't worry, he'll soon grow out of it.'

Chapter Three

There was a rap on the door and a face appeared wearing a huge grin. 'It's me, Granny.'

Dora smiled back. 'Good morning, Joe.'

He bounded in. 'It's a dry day, so you won't get wet when you go to church. Have you had your cup of tea yet?'

'I've just made a pot. Do you want one?'

He shook his head and held out his gift. 'I've brought you another piece of that cake you liked.'

'It was lovely, but are you sure your family can spare it?'

'There's enough for us to have one more slice each and then it's gone.' He poured her a cup of tea and then bustled about tidying up while she enjoyed her treat.

Dora watched him with affection shining in her eyes, but there was also concern for the young boy. That callous, selfish brute of a father had left them without any money. How could any man walk away from such a lovely family? 'Are you upset about your father going?' she asked gently.

He turned around, a thoughtful expression on his face. 'I ought to be, I suppose. Mum was upset and afraid of what was going to happen to us when we couldn't pay the rent, and that frightened me because Dad mentioned the workhouse. I don't want that to happen. We didn't have any food either, so Charlie ran and got Helen. She came back with him and had a big basket of food.'

'What about the rent money, Joe?'

'Sis had been saving up for a new pair of shoes, so we've got the rent for this week and a bit left over for food.'

'How are you going to manage after that?'

'Helen has a plan.' He broke into a gleeful grin. 'The Robertses are going into business.'

'My goodness, that sounds interesting.'

The young boy nodded. 'Helen's clever, like Mum, and they'll see we are all right. Now, are you ready for church? You don't want to be late.'

With her walking cane in one hand and the other one resting on his shoulder they left the house. The church was only ten minutes away and she listened to Joe chatting away. His sister had obviously done her best to put her young brother's mind at rest, but he wasn't a fool. It hadn't taken her long to discover that behind the bright smile was a sharp mind, and she hadn't missed the brief flashes of concern in his eyes.

'Shall I wait for you?' he asked when they reached the church door.

'No, you run off home. Someone will walk me back after the service.'

'All right. I'll pop in later to see you are all right.'

'Thank you, Joe.' As she went to enter the church, he caught hold of her sleeve and she looked down to see what he wanted.

His expression was serious now and he asked softly, 'Will you pray for us?'

'I always do, but I'll make a special prayer for all of you today.'

The smile was back as he turned and ran for home.

She watched him for a while and then went in to take her seat. Yes, she thought, she had been right. He was well aware of the perilous situation his family were in, and Dora was determined to watch carefully to see they didn't suffer.

She relaxed, enjoying the peaceful atmosphere before the service started, a slight smile on her face as she remembered how she had first met Joe. After finishing her shopping, she was on her way home when she tripped and fell. Her purchases were scattered everywhere and her handbag had flown quite a way from her. While she was trying to get up a young boy ran over and picked up the handbag. She had expected to see him turn and run away with it, but instead he rushed up to help her, asking all the time if she was all right. Once back on her feet again, he handed her the bag and then set about retrieving all of her shopping. He had insisted on helping her back home, and when they arrived he had immediately made her a pot of strong tea, explaining that his mother said it was the best remedy for a shock. Then he'd watched her drink two cups, washed up and told her he would come back later to check she was all right. That was just after she had moved into Fallon Street, and he had been coming every day since, insisting on doing her shopping and any other odd jobs. She had tried and tried to get him to take a small payment, but he wouldn't, declaring he didn't want money from her. He came because he liked her, he'd told her, and she needed someone to help her.

Jane Roberts was a good mother to her three children who were all the image of her, and nothing like their father, thank goodness. She didn't know the daughter well because she was in service and only came home on her free time, which was very little. The other boy had come in one day, obviously checking to see what his young brother was up to, and no doubt making sure he was quite safe when he visited her. Charlie was a fine lad, in fact all three children were polite, well spoken and a credit to their mother. Dora often wondered what such a cultured woman was doing married to a man like Bert Roberts and living in this dump.

The service began and she stood with everyone else for the opening hymn, determined to send up a special prayer for that darling boy and his family.

At the end of the service Dora was speaking to the rector and a few other people, when a man approached her.

'Allow me to walk you home, Mrs Jarvis.'

She smiled at him and rested her hand on his arm. 'Thank you, Mr Preston.'

They walked out of the churchyard talking politely, but as soon as they were away from everyone else they lowered their voices.

'Do you have any news yet?'

Dora shook her head. 'Nothing definite, but I'm sure he's the man responsible. He fits the description perfectly and lives in the last house at the end of the street. The neighbours talk openly about his criminal activities.'

'We need proof before approaching the police again.' He cast the elderly woman a concerned look. 'I've said it before, and I'll say it again, it is not wise to stay there. They are a rough lot, and even the police will only go down there in pairs.'

Dora gave an inelegant snort. 'And that is why the man is still free. I will not let him get away with what he did.'

'I understand how you feel, but you could be in danger if they find out who you really are. Quite frankly, I'm worried about you and wish you would leave this to the police.'

'I know what I am doing, and you mustn't be concerned. I give the impression of being an old woman who is not in good health, and neighbours talk to me. I've heard a lot about the people who live on that street, and everyone tells me that man is a criminal and a bully.'

'Hearsay is not enough,' he pointed out.

'I am well aware of that, but I'll get proof against him for something, even if not for the crime he committed against us.'

They turned into Fallon Street and Ian Preston grimaced. 'How long do you intend to stay in this disgusting place?'

'As long as it takes.'

'Please be careful, and you must send for me at the slightest hint of trouble.'

'I will.' She smiled and patted his arm. 'Don't worry; I'll be fine. The people here are not all bad; in fact, I want you to do something for me. I want you to look into the history of Mrs Roberts, who lives next door to me. Her family is in dire trouble and I long to help them, but can't do so openly.'

'Certainly not! That will make everyone here suspicious about you. What do you know about her?'

'Nothing, really, but she is well educated and clearly doesn't belong here. She has brought her three children up to be well spoken and polite. I would like to know where she came from.'

'I'll do some checking. Is that young boy who helps you one of her children?'

'Joe, yes.' She smiled up at him. 'He is such a caring little boy and has taken it upon himself to look after me.'

'Well, I'm pleased someone has. If I find out anything, I will tell you next Sunday.'

'Thank you, Ian. I am so pleased you have taken over my husband's firm. He always spoke very highly of you.'

'He is sorely missed.'

'Yes, he is,' she said quietly. 'Do any of the others know what I am doing?'

'No, I am the only one, and with regard to Mrs Roberts, all they will know is that a client has asked us to look into her past. What is her first name?'

'Jane, and the children are Helen, Charlie and Joe.'

'I'll see what I can find out.'

They stopped outside the house and she shook his hand politely. 'Your kindness is much appreciated, Mr Preston.'

He bowed slightly. 'My pleasure, Mrs Jarvis.'

She watched him stride away. He was a tall man in his forties with dark brown hair and gentle blue eyes. Her husband always told her that Ian had a fine mind and would take over the firm of solicitors when he retired. They hadn't been blessed with children and Alfred had looked upon him as a son.

Giving a deep sigh of sadness she settled back in the armchair and closed her eyes for a moment. How she missed her dear husband. They had been married for forty-two years, and he was the kindest man you could ever hope to meet. He hadn't deserved to suffer such an ordeal, and it broke her heart to imagine how afraid he must have been, knowing he was too frail to defend himself. Somehow, she would bring that nasty villain to justice before she died.

There was a gentle knock on the door and a familiar little voice called out, 'It's only me.'

She hadn't realised that tears had wet her cheeks

and quickly wiped them away. 'Come in, Joe.'

He was immediately there, his bright smile in place. 'Did you enjoy the service?'

'I did, and I prayed for you and your family.'

'Thank you. I'm sure your prayers are heard because you are a good person. I haven't told my sister I asked you to say a prayer for us.' He sat on a chair beside her, an earnest expression on his face. 'Helen worries about us, but especially me because I'm the youngest. She's the strongest, and we are all looking to her for help, so I don't want to be a burden to her.'

'My dear boy, you couldn't be a burden to anyone, and certainly not to a family who love you.'

The smile appeared again. 'I like talking to you. You are very wise, and I feel I can tell you things.'

Dora couldn't help giving a quiet laugh. This child never ceased to amaze her with some of the things he said. 'How I wish I were wise. What makes you think that?'

He shrugged. 'I just know. I'm going to be a policeman when I grow up, and they have to be able to tell what someone is like.'

'A policeman? Why choose that profession, Joe?'

'So I can help people be safe. Some steal and do things to hurt others, and that isn't right.'

'No, it isn't. The neighbours tell me that the man who lives at the end of this street is always up to no good.'

'That would be Fred Baker. Mum warned us to keep away from him. Charlie says he kept pestering our sister and she didn't like him. He won't do that now, though, because my brother's older and bigger now and he won't let anyone hurt any of us.' He jumped off the chair. 'I'm chatting away again and forgetting why I came. Mum wants to know if you've got enough for your dinner today. She's made a big pot of stew and dumplings from the food Helen brought home with her. Would you like some?'

'That is very kind of your mother, but I have a piece of mutton in the oven.' She smiled at the boy. 'You got it from the butcher for me, remember, and there's enough vegetables left to put with it.'

'Shall I peel the potatoes for you?'

'I did that before I went to church. I have everything I need, so you run off home and enjoy your dinner. And don't forget to thank your mother for me. I appreciate her kindness.'

'I will. See you tomorrow. I'll do your shopping after school.'

Dora watched him leave the house, a frown on her face. Living in this street was certainly showing her another side of life. At one end was a nasty criminal who needed to be put in prison and at the other end a family in dire trouble who were willing to share what little they had with a neighbour. Perhaps coming to live here hadn't been such a crazy idea, after all. It was certainly giving her a different perspective on life.

Chapter Four

'Granny said thank you, Mum, but she's got her dinner.'

'You've been a long time.'

'Ah, well, we had a nice chat. She likes to have someone to talk to.'

'What do you talk about?' Helen asked her youngest brother.

'All sorts of things. Shall I lay the table, Mum?'

When she nodded, he dashed off and Helen looked at her other brother. 'What can he find to talk about with an elderly woman?'

Charlie chuckled. 'I wondered that, so I went with him one day. He just bustles around doing odd jobs and chatting away about school and anything else he's done.'

'And she doesn't mind?'

'She seems quite happy and joins in asking him questions. While I was there I noticed she has loads of books. I had a quick look and they were the kind of subjects only someone with a good education would have.'

'Oh, such as?' This caught Helen's attention.

'The likes of Shakespeare and other authors I've never heard of. A few seemed to be on law.'

'Really? How interesting. I'll ask Joe to take me to see her sometime.'

'What's that?' The boy appeared again.

'I was just saying I would like to meet Granny Jarvis sometime.'

'You can come with me tomorrow. She'd like that. Dinner's ready.'

'Why do you call her "Granny"?' Helen asked as they settled themselves at the table.

'A man helped me pick her up when she fell down and he called her that. I haven't got a granny and I thought she was nice. She doesn't mind.'

'So you've adopted her, then.'

Joe nodded. 'You'll like her. She speaks like us so doesn't tease me like some of the others around here.'

'Don't let that worry you,' Charlie told him. 'We all have to put up with that.'

'I don't mind.' He grinned at his mother. 'You taught us properly, didn't you, Mum?'

'I did indeed, and what did I tell you about the people who make fun of us?'

Joe frowned in concentration for a moment, and then

said, 'What others think is their problem, not ours.'

'Exactly.' She smiled at her young son and gave him an extra dumpling. 'Eat up, now, because you've got some growing to do if you want to be a policeman.'

Charlie was grinning at the thought of his young brother wanting to become a policeman and gave Joe a gentle push. 'A copper living round here will cause a sensation. We should be called the misfits.'

Helen saw her mother's expression change from amusement to sorrow in an instant, and knew how much it hurt her to have to bring her children up in the slums. People born to this life accepted it, but anyone could see she had come from a very different background and clearly yearned for a better life for her children. Helen was even more determined to help drag them all out of this place.

The large pot of stew and dumplings was enjoyed with enough left over for another meal. They cleared the table and Helen got out paper and pencils. 'Right, let's get the notices done and on display at the corner shop. Joe, this is your job. I've written out what to say, but you are the neatest writer in the family.'

He immediately began on the task and Helen put the kettle on to make a pot of tea.

Jane stood beside her daughter and spoke quietly. 'We are facing a crossroad and our future depends on which road we now take.'

'And have you decided?'

Jane nodded. 'Whether it is the right road or not I

can't tell you, but I must start travelling along it and see where it leads. I want to do something I should have had the courage to do a long time ago, and that is seek a divorce from your father. I'll sell my wedding ring and another one I've kept hidden, and hope that will meet the cost. I know the money should be used for rent and food, but this is something I must do. Bert will kick up a fuss, but I won't allow him to intimidate me this time.'

'I understand and agree with you, so go ahead, Mum. Break the ties and be free of him.'

She hugged her daughter. 'Thank you, darling. A woman divorcing her husband is looked upon with disapproval and I couldn't have gone ahead without your support. I soon realised I had made a great mistake when I married Bert, but I've never had the courage to do anything about it. I'm such a weak person.'

'How can you think that?' Helen gasped. 'You have struggled with an uncaring man, dreadful conditions, and fought for your children. You are one of the strongest people I have ever come across, so don't believe for one moment that you are weak. It just isn't true!'

Jane thought about this for a moment, and then nodded. 'You are right. I am not a weak-willed girl any longer. I've brought up three strong, kind and sensible children against all the odds.' She smiled at her daughter. 'The four of us working together will get through this crisis no matter how difficult. No one is going to make a doormat of us again!'

'Absolutely.' Helen laughed, relieved to see determination in her mother now.

'I've finished,' Joe called, and they all gathered round to examine his work.

'They are excellent,' Jane praised. 'Clear and beautifully written. Well done.'

The boy beamed as Helen smiled approval and gathered the notices up. 'I'll take these to the shop in the morning. Now, it will probably take a while before we can earn any money, so we must decide how to survive in the meantime.'

'We might be able to find some things to pawn,' Jane suggested.

'Good idea, but what can we do without?' Helen frowned. Their possessions were meagre and they didn't have anything of value.

At the end of their search they had only found one cooking pot and a pair of Joe's old shoes, which were now too small for him.

'That won't raise much money.' Jane stared at the items in dismay. 'I'll have to add my wedding ring.'

'You mustn't do that, Mum, because you are going to need the money from that later.' She didn't mention the proposed divorce because the boys hadn't been told about that yet. 'I'll put in my big coat, and it should raise enough for another week's rent.'

Jane shook her head. 'Winter's nearly here and you are going to need your coat. Perhaps we can spare a blanket or two.'

'Out of the question,' Helen declared. 'You've all got to keep warm or you'll be sick, and then we will be in real trouble.'

Her mother and older brother stared at her in amazement and Charlie shook his head. 'I would say we are already in real trouble.'

'Then we've got to find a way out of it!' Helen tossed her coat on top of the meagre items. 'No more arguing. I'll visit the pawnbroker tomorrow and get the best price I can.'

Joe had been on his own search and came into the scullery clutching something. 'You can have these, sis. I don't need them any more.'

A lump came into Helen's throat when she saw what he was holding out to her. There was a picture book he had treasured from a baby, and a wooden model of a sailboat. She knew they were treasured items.

'Oh, darling,' Jane said huskily, tears in her eyes. 'You don't need to part with those. We'll manage without them.'

'I'm too old for them now.' He placed them with the other items and gave his sister a big smile. 'You get a good price for them.'

She knew he would be upset if they refused to take the precious toys because he would be desperate to help. 'I will, sweetheart, and when we have enough money, I'll get them back for you.'

He nodded. 'Granny's got loads of books and I expect she'll let me have a look at them.'

'I'm sure she will.' Helen dredged up a smile. 'Now, I suggest we get some sleep because we have a busy time ahead of us.'

Later that night, when Helen couldn't sleep, she made her way downstairs and found her mother in the scullery sobbing quietly as if her heart would break. She sat next to her and put her arm around her shoulders, saying nothing.

After a while Jane looked up and wiped her eyes. 'I can't take this, Helen. I am so frightened for all of us. This isn't right. No one should have to live like this.'

'I agree, and that is why we are going to try and do something about it. You know the saying: "It's always darkest before the dawn". Well, this is our darkest moment, but we'll make it through to the dawn – we must, there isn't any alternative. Don't let your fear for any of us make you doubt that. We are all aware of the struggle facing us, even Joe, and we've all got to pull together.'

Jane nodded. 'All the fears seem to rush in at night, but the dawn always comes, doesn't it?'

'Yes, and we mustn't forget that.' Helen stood up. 'Let's try to get some rest.'

The next morning, after the boys had gone to school, Helen gathered together the items for the pawnbroker. 'We are not going to get much for these, Mum, but I'll do my best.'

'I'm coming with you.' Jane gave a tired smile. 'The two of us might be able to squeeze a bit more out of him, and I want to see how much my rings will bring. If we can raise enough money to pay the rent for a couple of weeks, then that will give us some breathing space.'

'But you need that money for a divorce. That is important as well.'

'Yes, it is, but not as important as keeping a roof over our heads. If necessary, I'll find another way to pay the legal fees.' When Jane saw the frown on her daughter's face, she said, 'Don't look so concerned, darling. I will divorce him, even if I have to scrub floors to get the money. I have thought long and hard about everything and the security of my family must come first. Being free of your father is something I am determined about, and your positive attitude has woken up a fighting spirit in me. I am ready to battle like hell to get us out of this mess.'

Helen laughed. 'That's what I like to hear. Let the fight begin!'

They grinned at each other and Jane picked up Helen's coat. 'You keep that. It's a cold day.'

Heads held high and smiles on their faces they left the house and walked up the street, knowing many curious eyes were watching them. News travelled like lightning around here and everyone would know they had been abandoned to survive on their own. They were not going to show any sign of weakness.

They put the notices in the corner shop window

before making their way to the pawnbrokers. The shop was busy, as it always was in this area, and when their turn came they negotiated fiercely, especially over Joe's precious items. It took some time, but they left with enough for another week's rent and some food. Helen insisted her mother kept aside the money from the rings. That was only to be used in a desperate emergency.

'You'll need a solicitor, Mum, so let's have a look in the high street for one.'

'I'll do that later. I doubt there will be one in this deprived area.'

Helen shook her head, knowing just how important this was, not only to her mother but to all of them. She stopped by a door with a gold nameplate on it. 'You're wrong, there is one, so do it now. As it's situated in this street it might not be too expensive.'

Jane joined her. 'J and P Solicitors. Established 1860,' she read. 'I've never noticed that before and there's no harm in asking, I suppose.'

'I'll come with you.'

'I'd rather do this on my own.' She smiled gently at her daughter. 'Do you mind?'

'Of course not.'

'Thank you, darling. I'll see you back at the house.'

Helen watched her enter the building and stood there for a moment, then headed for home, deep in thought. It was understandable her mother didn't want her there, because she would most likely have to reveal things about herself she didn't want her children to know. She ought to be aware, though, that they all loved her too much to let anything in her past upset them.

It was a secret that had always intrigued Helen, and this unexpected turn of events had made her even more curious. She knew it would keep prodding her until she found out where her mother had come from and who she really was.

Chapter Five

'Can I help you, madam?' A young man asked the moment she walked into the offices.

'I would like to see a solicitor, please.'

'Do you have an appointment?'

'No, I saw your sign outside and came in hoping someone would be able to see me. I won't take up much of their time,' she added.

He smiled. 'Please take a seat for a moment and I'll check if Mr Preston is free.'

'Thank you.' Jane sat down and looked around the tastefully decorated office, very conscious of her shabby clothing. It was very doubtful she would be able to afford their services, even though it was in a deprived area, but determined now to find a way to end her disastrous marriage.

She stood when a tall, distinguished man entered the room and came towards her. He was about her age, she guessed, or maybe a little older, and when he smiled and introduced himself, she immediately felt at ease with him.

'Come to my office and tell me how we can help you, Mrs . . . ?'

'Roberts, Jane Roberts.' For a moment something seemed to flash through his eyes, and then it was gone. He held the door open for her and she walked into his office with him.

Once they were settled, she said, 'Thank you for seeing me without an appointment, sir.'

'One of my clients cancelled, so you came in at the right time.' He sat back and smiled again. 'What can I do for you, Mrs Roberts?'

'I want to divorce my husband,' she stated plainly.

'On what grounds?' he asked, his expression showing no sign of disapproval at her request.

'He has left us and gone to live with another woman.'

'Us?'

'I have three children, sir.'

'Do you know where he is living now?'

Jane shook her head. 'I'm afraid not.'

'Never mind. We will find him. It will be necessary to prove adultery and desertion before a divorce will be granted.'

'Before we continue, I must tell you the only money I have is from the sale of my rings, and I doubt it will cover your fees.' She took a desperate glance around at the spotlessly clean office, looking for a way to get over that problem. 'I know this is highly irregular, but I would be prepared to clean your premises until the debt is paid off.'

She expected to be shown out after such an outrageous offer, but he didn't move.

'Do you know how long that might take you?' he asked softly.

'No, sir, but I don't care if it takes me the rest of my life. I want us to be free of him.'

'Is he abusive to you or your children?'

She thought for a moment. 'He has pushed me a few times when he's had too much to drink or lost too much at the dogs, and shouts at the children for nothing at all, but I would call it mental abuse, rather than physical.'

'And he blames you for his losses?'

Her smile was grim. 'He blames me for everything.'

He passed a pen and paper over to her. 'Write down everything, Mrs Roberts. I need to know where and when you were married, the names and ages of your children, together with your address. Do you have your marriage certificate with you? I will need to see that as well.'

'I don't have it with me. Why do you need it?'

'It will contain necessary information.'

'I can tell you everything you need to know.' She shifted uncomfortably in her seat. This conversation was heading in a direction she didn't want to go.

A slight nod of his head showed he understood. 'For the moment, write down all the relevant details and we will start the process of obtaining you a divorce.'

'You still haven't told me what the cost will be.'

'It has always been the policy of this firm to take worthy cases even if the client is unable to pay the fees.'

'And you consider me a worthy case?' she asked, astonished by this turn of events.

'I do, and once the divorce has been granted we will discuss payment, and agree upon an amount you can easily afford.'

'That seems a strange way to run a business.'

'It is our way,' he told her with a smile. 'But I can see you have doubts.'

'I do. How do I know you won't present me with a bill I have no way of paying?'

'You have my word, Mrs Roberts. We take on two or three cases a year from clients such as yourself. Our founder insisted that the law was for everyone, no matter what their circumstances. Sadly, he is no longer with us, but we carry on in the way he would wish. You can trust us,' he told her gently.

She was silent for a moment as she thought this through. Years ago, she had been a foolhardy, trusting girl, but that had been knocked out of her by the constant struggle to keep her children fed and clothed. This man was offering her the opportunity to finally do something she had only dreamt about. She had to take the chance – she just had to. She looked him straight in the eyes and said, 'Trust is not something that comes easily to me, sir, but I must do this for us, so I will take you at your word.'

'We will not let you down or take advantage of your situation, and to put you more at ease we will send you a letter confirming our agreement and conditions.'

'Thank you. I would appreciate that.' She began to write down the details he had asked for and then handed the paper back to him.

He rose to his feet and shook her hand. 'Leave everything to us and we will be in touch to let you know how things are progressing.'

Ian Preston watched her leave the building and walk up the road. What an extraordinary thing to happen. Dora had asked him to find out about her neighbour, Mrs Jane Roberts, and the very woman had just walked into the offices. He studied the information she had given him, and one thing was apparent. She hadn't given her maiden name and was reluctant to let him see the marriage certificate.

'Is she a new client?' His assistant, Oscar, came and stood beside him.

'Yes, but she will come under the scheme Mr Jarvis set up.'

'Can't pay, then?'

'No, she lives in Fallon Street.'

'Really? I wouldn't have thought that. Her clothes have seen better days, but she was clean, well spoken and holds herself like a lady. What is she doing in a place like that?'

'My guess is she made a disastrous marriage choice and now needs a divorce. Her husband has left her and gone to live with another woman. She doesn't know where he is, so we must find him.'

'I'll get to it.'

Ian handed him the information he had. 'Fast as you can, Oscar. That poor woman is carrying a heavy burden so let's try to remove some of it for her as quickly as possible.'

'I'll give it top priority, sir.' Oscar glanced at the paper in his hands and frowned. 'Roberts? Isn't that the woman we are researching for someone?'

'I'm sure it is, but we will leave that for the moment and concentrate on helping her. I'll let the client know about this.'

'She hasn't given us her maiden name.'

'That is something she was reluctant to divulge, and she doesn't want me to see her marriage certificate.'

'Any chance there is something dodgy about the marriage? If it is illegal, then that is a different situation altogether.'

'I don't think it is, but we will have to check that, of course. I got the feeling she doesn't want anyone to know who she really is, so we will proceed with the information she has given us.'

'Quite a mystery.'

'Indeed, and if you do uncover anything, I want you to

come straight to me. No one else is to know what we find until we are able to proceed with a divorce for her. No one is better than you at unearthing useful information.'

The young man smiled at the praise. 'Thank you, sir.'

Ian returned the smile and went back to his office, deep in thought. It was only Monday and he would have to wait until Sunday before he could tell Dora about Jane Roberts' visit. He was tempted to go and see her straight away, but that wouldn't be wise. Walking her politely home after church was acceptable, but he mustn't be seen calling on her socially, and now there was another reason. Mrs Roberts mustn't see him visiting her neighbour either. His thoughts wandered back to Jane Roberts. He had noticed that she could be a lovely woman if she wasn't so bowed down with worry. Perhaps they could wipe some of that care from her face and reveal more of the woman she really was.

'How did you get on?' Helen asked her mother the moment she walked in.

'Better than I could have hoped for – at least I think it is good.' Jane then told her daughter about the meeting with the solicitor.

'How extraordinary,' Helen declared. 'You haven't paid him anything yet?'

'No, he didn't ask for a retaining fee, but there was something about him that made me feel he was trustworthy. I do hope he's as good as his word.'

'Well, if he sends you the letter setting out the

conditions you have agreed upon, that will be proof of his integrity.'

'I agree.' Jane grasped Helen's hand. 'This could lead to unpleasantness when your father finds out.'

'Mum, he's forfeited any rights he has with us by leaving to live with another woman. The only thing that matters here is that you really want to do this.'

'Yes, I want to be free of this disastrous marriage.'

'Then go ahead. We will support you and get through this together.'

'I hope the boys will feel as you do.'

'They will, but you must tell them what is being planned.'

Jane sighed wearily. 'Not just yet. Once I get confirmation that the divorce is going ahead that will be the time to tell them. Now, if we are very careful, we should be able to manage for three weeks on the money we raised today. We are going to need a response from the notices in the shop, but to be perfectly honest I don't hold out much hope. If I did get a pupil or two, I would have to bring them here and it wouldn't give a very good impression.'

'I know this is a bad area, but you've always kept our house clean, and it will have to do for the time being.'

'You're right, of course, but I'm sick with worry. I'll miss you so much when you go back at the end of the week.'

'You can always send Charlie for me if necessary, but I'll stay home if you need me all the time.'

'No, you mustn't leave your job. I shouldn't have said that, darling, because I have no right to put all of this on your shoulders. It is my mess and my responsibility to see we survive. The boys will be with me and Charlie is almost a man now. We will be fine.'

Helen smiled. 'Charlie has shot up, hasn't he, and he's quite a tough youngster.'

'I've been blessed with three lovely, intelligent children, and for that I am very grateful. It has made this squalid existence bearable.'

There was a light knock on the door and Jane opened it to see Joe's granny standing there.

'I thought it was time I introduced myself properly.' She held out her hand. 'I'm Dora Jarvis. I've just made a large pot of tea and wondered if you and your daughter would join me?'

'That's very kind of you, Mrs Jarvis.'

'Dora.' She smiled at Helen. 'Your delightful brother is so kind to me and I would like us to become better acquainted.'

Jane glanced at her daughter who nodded, so she said, 'We would be happy to share a pot of tea with you.'

'Splendid.'

They followed Dora back to her house and were surprised to find not only tea but a plate of sandwiches waiting for them as well.

'You shouldn't have gone to all this trouble and expense,' Jane told her.

'Of course I should. Please allow me to show my

appreciation for what your son does for me.'

'Joe has adopted you as his granny,' Helen told her. 'Shall I pour the tea?'

'Thank you, my dear.' Dora smiled at Jane. 'Joe told me the Robertses are going into business.'

'Well, we are going to try. It is Helen's idea for a way to earn enough money to survive on.'

'Not just survive, Mum,' Helen corrected. 'It is to make a better life for our family.'

'Splendid! Set your sights higher than just making ends meet.' Dora sipped her tea and studied her guests. 'What are you planning?'

'Mum's a good teacher, so we have put a notice in the corner shop advertising for pupils of any age. Charlie is good with wood and can turn his hand to almost any task. I'll keep my job for the time being because that will be one less mouth to feed, and then we will find some way for Joe to be involved so he doesn't feel left out.'

Dora nodded. 'That's important. He's a caring child and will be desperate to help. Helen, pull that small table out of the corner for me.'

She did so and found one of the legs was split and another loose. 'What a shame. This is a beautiful piece of furniture.'

'Do you think Charlie could repair it for me?'

'I'm sure he could, Mrs Jarvis.'

'Excellent. It is a useful table and I would like to be able to use it again.'

'Charlie's helping to repair a fence at the moment, but shall I ask him to come and see you?'

'Yes, please, dear, and tell him there's no rush. He must charge me a correct price for the work.'

'You can discuss that with him, but as you are a neighbour and friend, I expect he will only want to charge you for any materials used.'

'That is kind, but you are in need of money and must run your business with that in mind,' Dora admonished. 'I am willing to pay a fair price for the work. Now, Jane, tell me your plans for the school.'

'"School" is rather an ambitious word. If I get any pupils I will have to teach them here, which will limit who comes.'

'Hmm, there is a great need for education in this area, but you won't make much from the residents here. The church has a hut where it holds the Sunday school, but is little used during the week. Why don't you see if you can use that?'

'We couldn't afford to do that.'

'Not yet, of course, but why don't you let me have a word with the vicar. He is an understanding man and might be willing to help with such an excellent undertaking.'

'There's no harm in asking, I suppose.' Jane looked doubtful.

Dora smiled and held out the plate of rapidly disappearing sandwiches. 'Leave it with me. I'll see him after the service on Sunday.'

They spent another hour talking about many things, and when they returned to their own house, Jane and Helen stared at each other in surprise.

'Well,' Jane declared, quite lost for words.

'I know. That was extraordinary. Not only have we found Charlie a job, but she's going to see if you can use the church hut. That would be perfect if the vicar will allow it.'

'It certainly would.' She smiled at her daughter. 'It's been quite a day, and let's pray it continues in this way. It's a promising start, anyway.'

Chapter Six

By the end of the week Jane's hopes began to plummet. Charlie was helping a neighbour to fix a fence that had been blown down in the wind, and he had the offer to repair Dora's table, but they hadn't received any enquiries about teaching. Much to Joe's disappointment there hadn't been any requests for letters either. The most encouraging thing had been the letter from Mr Preston setting out the terms of the agreement for the divorce. With the prospect of that going ahead, Jane told the boys and was relieved to see they were not at all upset; in fact, they declared that it was the right thing for her to do.

On Saturday morning she watched her daughter walking up the road on her way back to her job at the house – back to scrubbing floors. That thought was followed by a surge of anger so intense she had to hold on to the windowsill to stop herself falling. This wasn't right! Why had she allowed this to continue for so long? She had been a spoilt, wilful girl and had made a stupid mistake by not listening to her parents sixteen years ago, and she had paid a high price for that. All right, she had got what she deserved, but the children were innocent and should not have to suffer because of her. They deserved better, and by heaven she would see they had what was rightfully theirs, regardless of the humiliation to her. She would somehow claim the heritage they were due!

Turning away from the window a sense of calm settled on her. It didn't matter what happened to her now – she had paid for her stupidity – and it was time to regain what she had lost. It wasn't going to be easy, but for the first time in years she knew she was strong enough for what had to be faced.

There was a sharp rap on the door and she opened it with a smile of confidence on her face. Standing there was a woman holding the hand of a girl about Joe's age.

'Are you Mrs Roberts?'

'Yes, I am.'

'I saw your notice in the shop and thought I'd come and see if you can help our Daisy. She's eight and can't seem to learn how to read and write. I tell you I'm at my wits' end to know what to do. I got three more kids and they don't have no trouble.'

'I'm sure I can help. Please come in, Mrs . . . ?'

'Bowler.'

She took them into the front room and the woman glanced around the spotlessly clean room, nodding to herself before fixing her attention on Jane.

'I don't have much money, but I can't let Daisy grow up like this. What do you charge?'

The woman's face was grey with worry and Jane's heart went out to her. 'I charge whatever you can afford, Mrs Bowler. Could you manage a penny an hour?'

There was a pause while this was considered, and Jane smiled at the young girl, who returned the smile. 'Would you like to come to me and learn how to read and write?'

Daisy nodded. 'I can't, though, because they say I'm stupid.'

'I'm sure that isn't true. Who says such unkind things?'

'Me brothers and at school.'

She reached out and held the girl's hands when she saw the hurt in her eyes. 'I can tell straight away that you are not stupid, Daisy. There is just something stopping you from learning, and we will find out what it is.'

The girl looked hopefully at her mother. 'Can I come here, Mum?'

'We'll give it a try, shall we?' The mother nodded to Jane. 'I can give you sixpence. How many lessons can you give for that?'

'Two hours a day from Monday to Friday,' she replied without hesitation.

The mother looked surprised. 'That is generous of you, Mrs Roberts.'

'Not at all. It will give me great pleasure to help Daisy. When would you like her to start?'

'Would Monday at ten o'clock be all right?'

'That will be fine.' Jane stood up and shook hands to seal the arrangement. 'The sooner we start, the better.'

Mrs Bowler opened her purse and took out the money. 'I'll pay you for the week now.'

'Thank you.' Jane walked out with them and waved to the girl as they walked up the road. Her first pupil and that was something to be happy about. All right, the child obviously had problems, but she didn't mind that, and was determined to find out what was stopping her from learning.

The boys were excited when she told them she had her first pupil, and it was an enormous relief to Jane.

Dora smiled politely when Ian entered the church and nodded as he took his usual seat. He didn't agree with what she was doing, but he was giving her his support by coming here each Sunday so they could keep in touch. It made her feel less alone.

After the service she lingered until there was an opportunity to speak to the vicar. She explained about Jane's scheme to start a school for anyone who needed extra help. The vicar was well aware of many in this area who lacked even the basic skills of reading and writing and readily agreed the hut could be used for that purpose during the week, without payment. Her gesture of a generous donation to church funds had no doubt helped, but he also appeared enthusiastic about the idea by promising to spread the word. She thanked him and turned to see Ian waiting for her.

Placing her hand on his arm, she immediately asked, 'Have you any news?'

'Something extraordinary has happened.' He told her about Jane's visit and the agreement they had come to.

'I'm so pleased you have taken the case. What are her chances of obtaining a divorce?'

'Her husband has deserted her to live with another woman, so if we can prove adultery as well, then that will help her cause. I've approached Culver to take the case.'

Dora gave him a startled look. 'He's a tough lawyer and one of the best, as well as expensive. Will he do it?'

'He's already agreed. I think the mystery of her origins intrigued him, and she stands a much better chance with him representing her.'

'There's no doubt about that, but can the business stand the expense?'

'I'll contribute to the cost myself.'

She stopped walking. 'Why?'

'There was something about her I liked, and I want us to help her.'

'I feel the same. If the expenses mount up, you must come to me and I will gladly help financially.' She began walking again. 'Thank you for doing this, Ian. I have become fond of this family and would like to see them climb out of the mess that man has left them in.'

'We'll do everything we can for them. Can you tell me

why you had such a long conversation with the vicar?' he asked, changing the subject.

'I have managed to get him to agree to Jane using the Sunday school hut during the week for a school she intends to set up. Her idea is to take pupils of any age who need special help with reading and writing.'

'My word, that is a splendid idea and much needed. I hope she succeeds.'

They had reached the top of the street and she smiled up at him. 'Don't come any further. Now Jane has met you it wouldn't do for her to see us together. Thank you for walking me back, Mr Preston,' she said politely as someone walked by.

'My pleasure, Mrs Jarvis.' Then he said quietly, 'I'll try and get any news to you.'

'Thank you.' She watched him stride away, a thoughtful expression on her face. He must have seen something special in Jane for him to go to so much trouble, but she was delighted he was taking an interest in the welfare of the Robertses.

Before going indoors, she went to give Jane the good news about the church hut.

Jane was excited about being able to use the church Sunday school hut, and without payment. Joe made out a new notice for the corner shop with a huge smile on his face.

'You'll have a proper school,' Charlie exclaimed. 'It might attract more pupils.'

'Let's hope so.' She read the notice Joe had finished giving the new address. 'That's perfect, darling. I'll take it to the shop tomorrow, but I will have to wait here until Daisy and her mother arrive in the morning.'

Jane had a restless night as plans rushed through her mind. Using the church hut could make all the difference and she couldn't wait to start. At last she was going to do something she had trained for all those years ago. Her parents hadn't agreed with her choice of work, of course, because they had wanted her to stay with them, but she had been adamant about teaching. She gave a deep sigh of remorse. And then she had thrown it all away, but now she had a chance to start again and she was going to take it.

The next morning, she kept looking out of the window waiting to see Daisy and her mother. The first lesson would be here, and then she would go to the hut to make sure everything was ready for the next day.

They arrived right on time and Mrs Bowler told Daisy to be a good girl and listen to Mrs Roberts and then left.

'Let's go to the scullery,' she told the girl. 'We can work on the table there.'

Paper and pencils were already on the table, and her first task would be to find out what Daisy knew. It didn't take her long to realise something was very wrong.

'Can you tell the time?'

The girl nodded.

Jane pointed to a clock on the mantelpiece. 'What does it say?'

'Just past ten o'clock,' she replied immediately.

She pointed to a letter in the book and asked, 'And what is that?'

Daisy squinted and shook her head. 'Dunno.'

Jane then drew a much larger letter. 'What about that?'

'It's a "B".'

She let out an exasperated breath. The child couldn't see close up. Why hadn't anyone noticed that?

'Didn't you tell your mother or teacher that you couldn't see properly?'

'I can see,' she exclaimed indignantly. 'Books are all blurry – that's all. They said I was stupid and that's why I can't read.'

'You are not stupid! All you need is help to be able to read close up.' Jane stood up. 'Come with me.'

The pawnshop wasn't busy when they arrived, so Jane went straight to the owner, Mr Higgins, know locally as Higgy. 'Have you got any spectacles?'

He wandered down the shop, took a box from a shelf and dumped it on the counter. 'Plenty.'

'Ah, good. May we have a look through them?'

He nodded and went off to serve another customer.

She opened the book she had brought with her. 'Now, Daisy, I want you to try on the spectacles and see if you can read the letters on this page.'

The girl tried on one pair and giggled, obviously thinking this was fun. She peered at the page and shook her head.

'Try another pair, and keep going until you find something that helps.'

Jane watched and it wasn't until they were halfway down the box that Daisy stopped, her finger running over the alphabet in the book. 'Can you read that now?'

The child nodded and grinned up at her before turning back to the book. She then began reading out the letters, running her finger along the page.

'You know the alphabet, then.'

'I learnt it, but then it became too fuzzy.'

'Why didn't you tell your mother or teacher?'

She shrugged. 'I tried but they just didn't believe me. They said I was too stupid to learn.'

'That isn't so, and now you know the truth. Your long sight is excellent, but you need spectacles for close work.'

Daisy took off the spectacles and gazed at them with longing. 'Can I keep these?'

Jane called Higgy over. 'How much do you want for the spectacles?'

He examined them. 'Hmm, nice pair, and gold.'

Jane laughed. 'Don't try that on me. Believe me I know the difference between gold and brass. How much?'

He smirked. 'Ah, well, I have to try. Five pence.'

'What! They are useless to you. I'll give you a penny, and that is being generous.'

'Tuppence, and that is my last offer.'

Secretly pleased with that, she rummaged in the box until she found a case. 'That price is worth the case as well.'

'Not likely. That will cost you another halfpenny.'

'Come on, Higgy, you know I haven't got any money, and the poor girl needs them because she can't read properly without some help.'

Raising his hands in surrender he put the spectacles in the case and handed them over to Daisy, who took them eagerly. Then he leant close to Jane and whispered, 'Don't tell anyone about this. I don't want word to get around that I'm a soft touch. You know what I mean?'

'Indeed I do,' she whispered back. 'It wouldn't be good for your business.'

'Too right,' he chuckled and winked at the child. 'Now you can learn to read, and I've got plenty of books here if you ever want them.'

Jane took hold of Daisy's hand. 'Come on, we have lessons to get back to.'

By the time Mrs Bowler arrived to collect her child, Daisy could print her name. 'Look, Mum, I can write letters.'

Her mother took the paper but continued to stare at her child who was smiling proudly. Then she looked at the neatly printed alphabet and her daughter's name at the end of the page.

'Mrs Roberts said I was good,' Daisy remarked, looking disappointed when her mother didn't say anything.

She smiled then at her daughter. 'You've done well; much better than I could have hoped. Good girl.'

'It's easy now I can see the letters properly.'

'What has happened?' Mrs Bowler asked Jane quietly. 'And where did those spectacles come from?'

'I got them from the pawnshop. Daisy has excellent long sight, but she couldn't see close up very well, and that has been holding her back. Your daughter is bright and only needs spectacles for reading and writing.'

The mother's relief was clear to see. 'Why didn't the teacher see that instead of labelling her stupid?'

'I don't know, but it would be wise to have her sight tested at some time, if you can afford it, of course. In the meantime, she appears quite happy with those.'

'How much did they cost you?'

'Don't worry about that. I took the money out of the sixpence you gave me.' Jane handed her the case. 'Daisy only needs to wear them for close work, so you can keep them safe in there.'

The mother grasped Jane's hand and shook it enthusiastically. 'I can't thank you enough. We didn't know. She never told us. Why didn't you tell us, Daisy?'

The girl shrugged. 'I tried to say it was all fuzzy, but everyone said I was stupid, so I thought they must be right.'

'You now know the reason why you couldn't read,' Jane told her, 'so don't you believe anyone who tries to say you are too stupid to learn. It isn't true, Daisy.'

After a slight hesitation she rushed up and threw her arms around Jane. 'You're nice.'

Jane laughed. 'So are you. I'll see you tomorrow. Oh, Mrs Bowler, the vicar is kindly allowing me to use the church hut for the lessons, so could you bring Daisy there tomorrow?'

'Of course. Ten o'clock?'

'Yes, please.'

After they left, Jane smiled, delighted she had been able to help the child. This was what she was meant to do, and for the first time in sixteen years she was beginning to feel as if there was some purpose to her life.

She spent the afternoon at the church hut making sure it was in order and ready for the next day. After that she returned home and spent the rest of the afternoon washing and pressing clothes. From the moment she had arrived in this slum, cleanliness had been a necessity, and her thoughts wandered back to those first terrible weeks. The basic sanitary facilities in the outhouse had horrified her, and the only means of cooking was a black stove in the scullery. There were only candles for lighting, but to her relief there was a sink and a water tap in the scullery. Everything was disgustingly dirty and she'd had no idea people lived in such horrifying conditions. When she'd shown her disgust, Bert had said it was all he could afford so she had to get on with it, and she had. What little money she had arrived with had been spent on strong cleaners and paint. After two weeks her hands had been raw, but the house was clear of vermin and dirt. Since then it had been a constant battle to keep it that way, but with hard work she had managed. Bert had continually jeered and insulted her about her high-and-mighty ways, but his taunts didn't touch her.

Her standards weren't going to be lowered just because he had brought her to this awful place, and when the children had arrived, she had been even more determined to do the best she could for them. They might have been living in the slums, but they had to be given every chance of a better life. That meant a good education, and she'd made sure they had that.

Over the years there had seemed no way out because she had been disowned and thrown out, so no one from her past would have lifted a finger to help her. Now they had a chance and she was going to damned well fight to see they succeeded.

Chapter Seven

'It's me, Granny.'

Dora smiled as Joe bounded into the room.

'Do you need any shopping? I can go now because dinner won't be ready for a while. Mum's had a busy day. She's got her first pupil.'

'That is good news.'

The boy nodded proudly. 'Our mum is very clever. She taught us more than the schools do. She even speaks French!'

'Then she has had an excellent education. Where did she go to school?' Dora probed carefully.

Joe shook his head. 'She never talks about herself, and always says that the past is not important. It's what we do now that matters.'

Dora smiled at him. 'None of us like to talk about ourselves. Now, if you have the time, I've run out of bread and a few other things. The list and money are in the shopping bag.'

Joe picked up the bag and nearly crashed into his brother at the door. 'Charlie's here to see you,' he called, then disappeared.

'Come in, Charlie.'

'Mum said you had a table that needs repairing. I've been doing a job for someone else, but I can do this for you now.'

'I would appreciate that. It's the small table in the corner.' She watched him closely as he examined it, and his love of wood and fine things showed in the way he ran his fingers over it.

'The workmanship on this is lovely,' he said, never taking his eyes off the piece of furniture.

'Yes, it is a favourite of mine, but I'm afraid to use it in case I do more damage. Do you think you can repair it for me?'

He nodded and then looked up. 'Do you trust me to work on this?'

'Completely,' she replied without a shadow of doubt. There was something about the young boy's manner that intrigued her. 'Do you need to buy anything for the repairs? Some glue, perhaps?'

Charlie looked at her with an expression of horror on his face. 'Oh no, I wouldn't use stuff like that. I'll just need a piece of wood to make new joints, and I've got a piece at home that might do. Can I take the table with me? I'll be very careful with it.'

'I know you will, and of course you can take it with you. And Charlie, I will expect you to charge me for the work.'

'I will, but it won't be much. I'll bring it back as soon as I can.'

She watched him leave and shook her head in amazement. That family desperately needed help and yet they all gave their time to help other people. She wondered how much he had been given for helping rebuild the fence and hoped he had charged a proper amount. The lad certainly wasn't work-shy.

Joe was soon back and unpacked the bag, showing her what he'd bought and what he'd paid for each item. Then he returned the purse so she could check that the change was correct.

'I picked out two lovely oranges for you,' he said, placing them in her hands.

'They are splendid.' She placed one in his hand. 'One for you and one for me.'

He immediately tried to give it back. 'Oh no, they are for you.'

Placing her hands around his and the piece of fruit she pulled him towards her. 'Joe, you are always giving and ask nothing in return.'

'I like to do it because it makes me happy,' he told her seriously.

'I know that, but you must learn to accept as well as

give. Would you deny me the same pleasure by refusing my small gift?'

He gave this some consideration before saying, 'I never thought of that. Would it make you happy if I took the orange?'

'It would make me very happy.'

He smiled then. 'All right, thank you, Granny. I'll share it with Mum and Charlie.'

Dora watched him putting the shopping away and then making her a pot of tea before leaving. She sighed when the door closed behind him. Jane Roberts might be living in the slums, but she was doing a marvellous job with her children. She was a mystery and Dora couldn't wait for Sunday to see if Ian had managed to find out anything about her.

'Where did you get that orange?' Jane asked her youngest son when he erupted into the scullery.

'Granny gave it to me. She told me I must learn to accept as well as give, and it would make her happy if I had it.' Joe looked uncertainly at his mother. 'Did I do right?'

'Of course you did, darling, and she is quite right. We must all learn to give and take. She appreciates what you do for her and that is her way of thanking you.'

Joe smiled then. 'We can all have a piece after dinner. What have we got?'

'The butcher let me have a nice ham bone and there is quite a lot of meat still on it, so I've made a ham suet pudding.'

'Oh, lovely. I'll set the table. Where's Charlie?'

'Upstairs, working on Mrs Jarvis's table. Nip up and tell him dinner's ready.'

The boy tore up the stairs calling out to his brother.

After enjoying the suet pudding and a piece of orange each, they cleared the table and sat around it for a business meeting, as they called it.

'First on the agenda is to tell you that I have had an interesting and successful first lesson with my pupil.' She then told them about Daisy. 'So, after spending on the glasses I only have four pence left, but it's a start.'

'I was given one shilling for helping with the fence.' Charlie put the money on the table. 'And now I have a table to mend.'

Joe looked at the money with a worried expression on his face. 'What can I do?'

'We need a bookkeeper, and I vote Joe does that job.' Jane glanced at her sons. 'All in favour raise their hands.'

All three hands shot up.

'That's carried,' Jane said in her best businesslike manner. The last thing they must do is let Joe think he wasn't contributing, and Charlie clearly understood that as well. She produced a small notebook and put it in front of Joe. 'What you must do is record everything we earn on one side and all expenses on the other. Date everything clearly, and at the end of each week we will have a meeting to see how we have done.'

The boy nodded and picked up the pencil. 'So, today Charlie earned one shilling.'

'That's right, and I made sixpence, but opposite my amount you must put the expenses for the glasses.'

He very carefully wrote everything down in his neat hand and then counted the money on the table. 'So the total left is one shilling and four pence.'

'Well done, Mr Bookkeeper.' His mother's praise brought a big smile to his face. 'Now, here is a small tin. I want you to put the money in it and find a safe place to keep it.'

'There's a loose floorboard under my bed. We could keep it there,' Joe suggested.

'Perfect,' Charlie declared. 'No one will find it there.'

No one questioned that remark because they all remembered seeing their father searching through Jane's purse and everyone's pockets trying to find money for a night at the pub.

When the boys were in bed, Jane sat quietly thinking things over. She had enough to just about get through the next two weeks, but they were going to have to earn a lot more than a few pence if they were to survive. She had been hoping to keep the money she had raised from the rings to help pay for the divorce, but it was clear that wouldn't be possible. The health and well-being of the boys meant more to her than anything, and they must come first, no matter how desperately she wanted out of this marriage. The spectre of the workhouse was always before her and she was determined not to subject the children to that shame. She hadn't seen her parents since that dreadful day when they had disowned her and thrown her out, but she would go to them begging on her hands and knees before she allowed that to happen. She wasn't concerned about herself, because her humiliation was already complete, and she didn't care what anyone thought of her. The children were the only good thing in her life and she must protect them – whatever it took.

'Don't worry, Mum, everything will be all right.'

She looked up, startled. 'Charlie, you should be asleep.'

'Couldn't.' He sat beside her. 'I'm thirteen now and can leave school, so I'm going to get a permanent job. I can earn a bit doing odd jobs and you might get a pupil or two, but that isn't going to be enough. We need time for your reputation as a teacher to spread so you can establish your school.'

Jane sighed wearily. 'I hear what you are saying, but calling it a school is ambitious, don't you think?'

'When Helen was here we talked about this and she insisted that even though we needed to earn money, we should also aim for something we would really like to do. You want to be a teacher, we've always known that, and it's something you are good at.' He grinned. 'Look at us, our level of education is way above any of the others around here. So, in Helen's words, go for it.'

That made her laugh. 'I can just picture her saying that. All right, I want to teach people to read and write, whatever their age or abilities, but what is your dream? Something to do with wood, I imagine.'

He nodded. 'I would like to be a carpenter and I'm

going to start looking for work in that line this week. It would make me unhappy to go against your wishes, so I need your blessing.'

'You have it, my dear. I will support you all the way.'

He leant over and kissed her cheek in a rare show of outward affection. 'Thanks, that means a lot to me.'

'Do you want me to come with you while you look for a job?'

'No thanks.' He stood up looking tall and confident. 'I'll be fine on my own. Get some sleep, Mum, and try not to worry. We'll get through this.'

Jane watched him leave the room and felt as if her heart would break. The last thing she wanted was Charlie looking for work at his age, but he was right, there wasn't any alternative. If he could find work, then that would mean two of her children were safe, leaving only Joe and nothing bad was going to happen to him. Nothing! She knew, of course, that custody of the children could become a battleground in a divorce, but she would fight with her last breath to see that Bert didn't take Joe away from her. It was unlikely, as he had never taken any interest in them, but if there was the slightest chance of that she would defy the courts and disappear with him. 'Please don't let that happen,' she whispered, praying that someone up there was listening.

Chapter Eight

The daily lessons with Daisy were a joy, and the girl made rapid progress now she had her spectacles. When Friday arrived, Jane was hoping the mother would want to continue with the tuition, and greeted Mrs Bowler with a smile when she arrived to collect her child.

Daisy excitedly showed her mother what she had been doing that day, and after praising her she turned and shook Jane's hand. 'I can't thank you enough for what you have done for our Daisy, Mrs Roberts. I've been to the school and explained about her not being able to see properly and they've said they will give her extra help to catch up with the other children.'

The disappointment was crushing, but Jane kept on

smiling. 'That is good news. I am sure Daisy will enjoy her lessons now.'

'She will. Daisy, thank Mrs Roberts for what she's done for you.'

'Thank you. Now I won't feel so daft.'

'I'm sure you will do very well. Listen to your teacher and work hard.'

'I will.'

When they were about to leave, Jane stopped the mother. 'May I ask a favour? Would you tell other people that I will teach anyone, any age, if they want help with reading and writing, or any other subject?'

'I've already told some what you have done for our Daisy and I'll do my best to spread the word. Thank you again, Mrs Roberts.' She placed some money in Jane's hand. 'That's to pay for the spectacles you bought, and it's amazing what a difference it has made.'

After they left, she opened her hand and saw four pence and guessed that had been a little extra to show her gratitude. She gave a wry smile. By discovering the child's problem and helping to correct it she had lost a pupil. Still, she couldn't be sorry about that.

Picking up her purse and shopping bag she left the house to see how much food she could buy for as little as possible.

It took a while, but she finally had enough to feed them over the weekend. Walking back home her mind kept going over and over the dire situation they were in. Charlie had been looking for work all week, and so far hadn't found anything. And she had just lost her only pupil after a week.

Still mulling over what more she could do she walked into the house and stopped dead when she saw Charlie sitting at the table. It seemed as if her heart skipped several beats as a picture of someone else doing the same thing flooded her vision. 'What . . . what are you doing?'

He glanced up. 'Mrs Jarvis asked if I could mend her clock.'

'But you don't know how.' Her voice was trembling slightly.

'I mended one at the school when it stopped working.' He frowned. 'Are you all right, Mum? You look awfully white.'

'I'm fine.' She struggled for composure and dredged up a smile. 'You didn't tell me about the school clock.'

'I didn't think about it. Look – isn't this beautiful? Mrs Jarvis said it had lovely chimes but hasn't worked for some time.'

'Well, be careful with it, dear. That could be valuable.'

'I thought that, and the table was high class too. Do you think she was once well-off but has fallen on hard times?'

'That's possible, I suppose.' Charlie had pieces of the mechanism spread out on the scullery table. 'Are you going to be able to get that back together again?'

He grinned. 'I have them all in the order I removed them, so I should be able to.'

She unpacked her shopping and began to prepare

a warming meal from the meagre items she had been able to afford. It was getting colder and they still didn't have coal for the winter fires. That was something to be dealt with soon.

Suddenly there was a musical chiming, something she had once been very familiar with, and Charlie gave a whoop of delight.

'It's working.' He was holding the clock up and gazing at it in awe. 'Isn't that a lovely sound, Mum?'

'Beautiful. Mrs Jarvis will be pleased.'

'I'll take it back to her now.' Holding the clock carefully he left the house.

Jane let out a ragged sigh and sat down. 'My goodness,' she murmured, staggered by what her son had just done. Taking a clock to pieces and making it work without any training was a difficult thing to do. With a skill like that perhaps he shouldn't be a carpenter after all, but widen his search for a job. That was something to think about.

Joe arrived home and immediately asked, 'Where's Charlie? Is he still out looking for work?'

'No, he's with Mrs Jarvis. He's just repaired a clock for her.'

A few minutes later Charlie came back. 'She was ever so pleased and gave me a whole shilling. I told her it was too much, but she insisted it would have cost a lot more to take it to a clock repairer.'

'She's quite right. Give it to Joe and here's the money Mrs Bowler gave me in payment for the spectacles. Get your book and tin,' she told her young son.

He hurtled upstairs to collect the things from their hiding place and he was back almost at once, still running. After entering the money in the book, he looked up. 'Any expenses?'

'We're going to need coal for the stove soon so we might have to use it for that, and I don't want us to be without a fire in the other room when it gets really cold,' Jane told them.

'We might be able to find some chunks of wood,' Charlie suggested. 'And if we went to the docks there might be something around there for fires.'

Jane didn't like the idea of them scavenging, but it would help if they could save in that way for a while. They had to do anything they could in this situation, and keeping a roof over their heads was paramount. 'We'll all go out on Sunday and see what we can find.'

Joe escorted Dora to church as usual and then ran back home. She enjoyed the quiet before the service, as this gave her time to remember all the good years spent with her husband, and vow once again that she hadn't given up on tracking down the brute that had caused his death. She saw Ian come in and sit well away from her. As far as anyone knew, he was a kind gentleman who escorted an elderly woman back home.

The sermon was all about forgiving those who had harmed us, but Dora was nowhere near being able to do that. Perhaps one day when he was behind bars she might feel differently, but she wasn't sure she could ever forgive such evil. Since moving to Fallon Street she had witnessed suffering as the people struggled daily to survive. And yet for all the suffering there was genuine kindness to be found as well, like the Robertses, for instance. Would Jane ever be able to forgive her uncaring husband for leaving her and the children without a penny to their name? She didn't know the whole story, of course, but you could see she had suffered because it showed on her face.

As soon as the service was over, she joined Ian and her immediate question was, 'Any news?'

'Oscar has managed to track down Roberts. He's living with a Mrs Hilliard in Bermondsey, and he also went to the church where he married Jane. He saw the records and the marriage was legal.'

'That lad is a treasure.'

Ian laughed quietly. 'I often think he should be in the police. They would welcome his investigative skills.'

'Did he also find out her maiden name?'

'He did.'

'Well, tell me,' she demanded when he didn't say anything else.

'You mustn't let anyone else know. I insist on that because we have no proof yet that she is connected to that family.'

'I give you my word.'

'It's Tremain.'

Dora stopped suddenly, a deep frown on her face, and then she looked up at him. 'You don't think . . . ?'

'As I've said, we don't know, but it isn't a common name.'

'No, indeed not.' Dora sighed. 'She is guarding her past, and if there is a connection then that is understandable. However, if the divorce goes ahead this will come out.'

'I am sure she knows that, and it's something she will face when it happens. From what you've told me she has brought up her children to be educated and well behaved. I believe she has the courage to do whatever it takes to see her children are safe and happy.'

'If she really did come from a wealthy family, then there is no doubt about that.' They continued walking. 'It must have taken great strength of character to survive slum conditions. I suspect that underneath that quietly spoken woman there is a strong person. Does she know what you have found out?'

'Not yet. I will be writing to let her know we have traced her husband, but I won't mention anything else at this point. Once we have enough evidence to proceed, Culver will want to meet her and let her know the situation at that time.'

Dora gave a rumbling laugh. 'I never took you for a coward, Ian.'

He grinned. 'I will be there as well.'

It had been quite a successful morning scavenging for firewood. They had decided to search along the banks of the River Thames and had found enough for a couple of good fires, and the boys were already planning to do this every Sunday.

'I'll put this in the coal shed to dry out,' Charlie said as soon as they arrived back.

'I'll help.' Joe disappeared with his brother.

Jane watched them with affection. They had taken this morning as an adventure, exclaiming proudly every time one of them found a suitable chunk of wood. It had been a degrading thing to do but she'd laughed and made it a fun time.

The front door opened and Helen walked in, making Jane cry out with pleasure and give her a hug. 'Oh, what a lovely surprise!'

'I've got the afternoon off, and Cook sent you some leftovers from a dinner party held last night.'

'That is so kind of her. Please give her my thanks, won't you.' She began to unpack the food, relieved and grateful for the gift.

At that moment the boys returned, and when they saw their big sister their faces lit up with huge smiles.

Helen gave them a puzzled look. 'You're filthy. What have you been up to?'

Joe laughed. 'We've been collecting wood for the fire. It was wet and muddy down by the river.'

Charlie was looking at the food now laid out on the table, and dragged his younger brother over to the sink. 'We'd better clean up or Helen won't let us have any lunch.'

'There's enough there to be able to make lunch for all of us,' Jane said. 'I've got some potatoes to put with the cold meat and that will make it more filling.'

The boys soon had clean hands and faces and began to tell their sister all the news. Suddenly there was a loud thump on the front door and it shot open.

'Where is he?' Fred Baker, the villain who lived at the end of the street, was standing there.

Jane's one thought was to protect her children from this bully, so she rushed over and pushed him out onto the street. 'Get out of my house!'

'It ain't your 'ouse, it's Bert's and if he's 'iding in there then I'm gonna find him. Come out here, Bert,' he shouted, trying to barge his way back in again.

Holding on to each side of the door Jane stood her ground and the children crowded behind her blocking his way in. 'He isn't here.'

'Don't lie to me, woman, or you'll regret it.'

'Mrs Roberts doesn't lie,' Dora said firmly, making the man spin round. 'He isn't here. What do you want him for?'

'None of your bloody business,' he snarled.

'What you do is very much my business, Fred Baker, and of every decent person. I heard all about you before I moved here. Now, stop threatening this family or I'll send for the police.'

He snorted. 'They won't come 'ere, or listen to you, so clear off. I got business with Bert Roberts.'

'We are still waiting to hear why you are looking for him,' Jane declared.

'He owes me two guineas, and I want it back now, as we agreed.'

Jane gasped. 'Two guineas?'

'That's right, and if he ain't here then you must pay.'

That was so ridiculous it made Jane burst out laughing. 'Where do you think I am going to get that kind of money from? He left us without a penny to our name.'

Dora moved forward until she was only a step away from the belligerent man, her gaze sweeping over him. 'How would a man like you be able to lend someone such a large amount of money? I doubt you've ever done an honest day's work in your life.'

'What do you know about it? You're new to this street.'

Dora's smile held no humour. 'It is common knowledge that you are a thief and don't care who you hurt in the pursuit of your crimes. I won't let you hurt my friends, so slink back to the hole you live in and don't come here again. If you do, then I promise that you will be the one who regrets it.'

He raised his hand to hit her but the walking cane she held came up with surprising speed. It hit his hand before it could connect with its target, making him yelp in pain.

Joe ducked under his mother's arm and ran to Dora, glaring up at Fred Baker. 'Don't you dare try to hurt Granny, or my mum. Dad isn't here any more.'

Dora put a protective arm on the child's shoulder. 'Bert Roberts has moved out, so if you want your money, then you had better go and find him.'

'Where's he gone?'

'We don't know,' Jane told him.

Without another word he turned and stormed off. Jane let out a pent-up breath, and then began to laugh quietly. 'Thank you, Dora. The man everyone is frightened of has been seen off by two helpless women and some children.'

'Ah, but bullies are always cowards. You call me if he comes round again.' She winked at Jane. 'He'll think twice before he confronts us again.'

'Won't you come in and share lunch with us?' Jane asked. 'It is cold meat Helen brought with her and we would be happy to share it with you.'

'Thank you. I would enjoy that.'

Chapter Nine

Sharing a meal with Jane and her family had given Dora a chance to get to know Helen. There was an air of strength and determination about her. It was a shame she was working as a maid, because it was clear she was capable of a better position. The sad thing was women were considered only suitable for menial tasks, and that made Dora angry. A great deal of talent was being barred from business, and it was time men changed their attitude towards women. Thankfully, there were some enlightened thinkers, and her husband, Alfred, had been one by involving her in the daily running of a successful business. Ian was another, and she had met a few men who didn't have shuttered minds where women were concerned. One day things would change, and as she gazed at the family around the table, she knew that it couldn't come soon enough.

Knowing the daughter only had a short time at home, Dora hadn't lingered, and left as soon as was polite. She settled in her chair, laid her head back and closed her eyes. Ever since moving in here she had looked for an opportunity to confront Fred Baker, and when she had heard the shouting it had been a chance not to be missed.

The first thing she had noticed was something he was wearing, but it was hard to see clearly so she had provoked him until he had lashed out at her, as she knew he would. The sharp crack across his hand had made him hold it up to see the damage, and that was all she had needed. There had always been doubt that he was the one they were looking for, but not any longer. Her husband's description of him had been perfect and he was definitely the bully who had broken into their home. She had proof, but was it enough to convince the police to take action? She would visit Ian in the morning.

The Sunday school hut was round the side of the church, almost hidden by trees and tall shrubs. Inside had been painted brown, with drawings by the children stuck on the walls, and was just large enough to accommodate around eight, including the teacher.

Jane settled down to wait, hoping the notice in the shop would bring her a pupil or two. She would come here between ten and twelve every weekday morning and knew it would be an anxious wait. Their situation was desperate and her mind was continually searching for a way she could earn money. To teach was Helen's idea, and truthfully it was something she wanted to do, but she couldn't waste too much time waiting around when there might be something else she could do. Charlie was out every day walking the streets looking for work, but hadn't found anyone to take him on yet.

A sharp knock on the door brought her out of her fretting and she looked up hopefully as the door swung open. A man pushed a boy in who was about the same age as Charlie, and then shut the door firmly behind them.

'You Mrs Roberts?'

'Yes, sir. How can I help you?'

'My missus heard what you did for Daisy Bowler and we wondered if you can find out what's wrong with our lad.'

She smiled encouragingly at the boy and then turned her attention back to the father. 'I'll do my best. What appears to be the problem?'

'Damned if we know. That's why I've brought him to you. We can only afford the same as you charged for Daisy.' He handed over sixpence, turned and, without another word, strode out of the hut.

She stared at the door in astonishment, and then at the boy who was studying her carefully, a slight smile on his face.

'Don't take any notice of him. He's always like that – impatient.'

The youngster's clear green eyes were glinting with amusement and Jane wondered what on earth they thought was wrong with their son. 'Let's start with your name, shall we?'

'Andrew Jones – but you can call me Andy.'

'Very well, Andy. Please sit down and we'll find out what you can do.'

He shrugged and did as he was told, waiting while she opened a book and put it in front of him.

'Read that page for me.'

He did, fluently and without any mistakes. She spent the next hour testing him on several subjects, and at the end of that time she sat back, perplexed. Not only was he good at everything, but he excelled in arithmetic.

'Why do your parents think you need extra help with lessons?' she asked.

'They don't understand me. I spend all my time doing this.' He began to write figures down, occasionally standing up and pacing the hut as if measuring it. When he'd finished he pushed it over to her. It was a diagram of the hut with all the measurements and angles worked out.

There was no way she could tell if they were correct, but instinct told her they were. 'Where did you learn how to do that?'

'I had a good teacher for a while and used to work after school with him, but he left and no one else seemed to understand what I wanted to do. I just see everything like that.' He grinned. 'Weird, eh?'

'Not at all. Do you want to be an architect?'

'Little chance of that for a kid from the slums.'

'You mustn't think like that, Andy. You have a talent and it should be used. Draw me something out of your head – like a house or building.'

'All right.' He gave her an assessing look. 'Daisy said you were nice.' Then he set to work. Within half an hour, using only a pencil and ruler, he had produced a design for a three-bedroom house with the top and lower floors set out separately in detail.

'That's beautifully done.'

His face shone with pleasure at the compliment, and he began to eagerly point to the calculations he had made. 'Could you help me with the arithmetic? I need to know more.'

'I will have to get hold of more advanced textbooks, but I will certainly try.' Now she knew why his parents didn't understand him. There was a touch of genius about the boy, and that wasn't a word she used lightly. Her thought flashed to the picture of her son repairing a clock without even being shown how to. It didn't matter where you were born because with a little encouragement talent always came to the surface. 'Will your father be coming for you at twelve?'

'No, he only wanted to make sure I came here. Why?'

'I want you to meet my son, Charlie. I think you will get along well together.'

'All right.'

Fortunately, her son was home when they arrived,

and Jane introduced Andy, leaving the boys to talk while she made a pot of tea and a sandwich for each of them.

'What's this?' Charlie asked as they studied one of Andy's drawings. He listened intently as Andy explained how the drawing was laid out.

Charlie understood a lot about angles and measurements from working with wood and his love of furniture design, but this was the first time he had ever seen it applied to a complete house and he was fascinated.

When she put cups of tea and a sandwich in front of the boys, they looked up briefly to say thanks, and returned to their discussions. Her instinct that they would get on well together had been correct; they both had enquiring minds.

She left them and crawled into the small space under the stairs where she kept her treasured textbooks. They were the only things she had managed to grab from the house after her parents had disowned her, and although in this crisis she felt they should have been pawned, she was glad now they were still here. They were well hidden because over the years Bert would have taken them to raise money for his drinking and gambling. Books were useless things, he would have declared.

It didn't take long to find the one she wanted, and after backing out of the cramped space she sat on the floor and opened the book, hoping it was advanced enough for Andy. It would help, she decided as she stood up and brushed the dust from her skirt. Her smile was wry as she wondered how long he would stay as her pupil. Not long, she guessed. If her assessment of him was correct, then he would soon outstrip her knowledge.

'Mum,' Charlie called, 'Andy's got to go and I'm walking a way with him.'

'All right.' She went to the door with them. 'See you tomorrow, Andy.'

'Today was fun. Thanks, Mrs Roberts.' He hesitated. 'Er . . . could you teach me to speak like Charlie?'

'Of course. We'll include that in the lessons.'

She watched the two boys walking up the street still chatting away, and so alike. It was good to see.

While she had been out a letter had arrived from the solicitor and Jane was reading it when Charlie arrived back.

'Who is that from?' he asked the minute he walked in. A letter was a rare thing and caused interest to the children.

'It's from the solicitor to let me know they have traced your father. He's living with a widow in Bermondsey.'

'Does that mean the divorce can go ahead?'

She took a deep breath and shook her head. 'They only say I will be informed of progress. Even though he has deserted me and is living with another woman it doesn't guarantee I will be granted a divorce. The law is mostly on the man's side, and if your father decides to fight, then it could prove difficult.'

'We'll fight back,' her son declared. 'He's in the wrong, Mum.'

'I know, dear, but I want you to know that it could get

nasty, and things about the past might be revealed that I would rather have kept secret.'

'We love you and don't care what happened years ago. All that concerns us is the future – a good future for us, and for that to happen you need to be free of him. He's held you back, Mum; he's held us all back.'

'That is so true, and you are right, we will fight.' She smiled then. 'I wouldn't be able to do it without the support of all of you.'

'You have it, never doubt that.'

Ian had been in court when Dora arrived at the offices, but she had waited, eager to tell him her news. The place held so many memories and they were all good. For many years she had worked here beside her husband, and in that time had learnt a lot about the law. One day these professions would no longer be male-dominated. Women were beginning to want more than being tied to the house, and if she were younger she would find a way to help push away the prejudices about what women were capable of doing.

'Dora.' Ian strode in, a deep frown on his face when he saw her. 'Is everything all right?'

'I have news and I couldn't wait to tell you.'

'That sounds intriguing. Oscar,' he called, 'any chance of tea? I'm parched from talking so much.'

'Kettle's already on the boil, sir.'

Ian sat down and sighed.

'Tough case?' she asked.

'Long, that's all. Ah, here's the tea. Thank you, Oscar.'

When the young man left them alone, Dora poured the tea and waited while he emptied his cup and held it out for a refill. She then explained about the encounter with Fred Baker. 'When I gave his hand a rap with my cane it made him hold it up to examine it for damage, and then I saw he was wearing Alfred's ring.'

'Was he now? I'll pass that information to the police.' He gave her a sympathetic smile. 'You know that still isn't enough. He could say he found it, or come up with some other excuse.'

She nodded as sadness showed in her face. 'The only witness to the crime was Alfred, and he is no longer alive to identify him, but he had lent Jane's husband two guineas and was wearing the stolen ring. It should be enough to make the police question him again.'

'I agree, and I'll do my best to make them take some action.'

'I can't ask for more than that. Now, any further news about Jane's divorce?' she asked, changing the subject.

'The case is progressing and that's all I can say. The law is slow to move on these things, as you know. How are the Roberts family getting on?'

'They are putting on a brave face, but their situation is dire. I know Charlie has been looking for work without success. Jane had one pupil for a week. Can that brute of a husband be made to support them, Ian?'

'Unlikely, and we've got to get him into court first.'

'Keep trying because I fear for this family. With

winter nearly here they have been out scavenging for firewood.' Dora shook her head in dismay. 'I keep trying to find a way to help them, but until this business with Fred Baker is settled and the man in prison, I can't draw too much attention to myself.'

'If you hadn't moved into Fallon Street you would never have known about them,' he pointed out. 'London has far too many areas like that, where families struggle against poverty and injustice, and you know that is why Alfred set up the business in this area. I do believe you are underestimating Jane Roberts. She loves her children with a passion and will fight like a lioness to protect her brood.'

'You are right. I saw that by the way she stood up to Baker. I'm starting to see that under that gentle exterior there is a strong woman, and I suspect that after years of being subservient she is just beginning to realise that for herself.' She tipped her head to one side and studied him carefully. 'You like her.'

He smiled and stood up without replying. 'Come on, we'll both go and see the police and then I'll take you out to lunch.'

The station was chaotic when they arrived, and a sergeant elbowed his way over to them as soon as they arrived. 'Hello, Ian and Mrs Jarvis, what can I do for you?'

'Mrs Jarvis has news about the man who broke into their house, and we thought you'd like to know.'

'Ah, yes, I know the case, though I wasn't involved in the investigation at the time. I believe your husband died soon after the burglary?'

'Yes, he had been ill, but was making a good recovery until he was brutalised by the intruder. He lived long enough to tell me he thought the man's name was Fred Baker, and give a description of him. He had seen him once coming out of court laughing and shouting that all coppers were stupid. He was fairly sure it was the same man.'

The sergeant bellowed across the room to a constable who came over at once. 'Get me the records of the Jarvis case.'

'Sir.' The man hurried off.

'Let's get out of this mayhem,' the sergeant suggested as he led them to a quieter room where they could speak without shouting above the noise. When the constable arrived with the records, he began reading, and after a while sat back. 'What information do you have, Mrs Jarvis?'

She explained what had happened and he made notes while she talked.

'Are you sure it was your husband's ring?'

'Positive. I bought it for him on our tenth wedding anniversary, and there is an inscription inside saying simply – "With love, Dora". So it will be easily identified. I want that man arrested and charged with murder.'

'So do we, but that bloody man is as slippery as an eel. Pardon my language. We have hauled him before a judge on three occasions, and each time he has walked free. We would need evidence that couldn't be disputed before attempting to arrest him again, especially on such a serious charge. Our case would have to be as solid as a rock.' He gave an exasperated sigh. 'Ian, you know we've got to have definite proof, and although everything points to Baker, we don't have enough yet to prove he is guilty without a shadow of doubt.'

'We are aware of that, George, but couldn't you make him confess?' The expression on Ian's face said that wasn't to be taken seriously.

The sergeant snorted with amusement. 'He might be a nasty villain, but he's not daft enough to put a noose around his neck.'

Dora could see the predicament the police were in. They had had a lot of trouble with Baker and had been unable to have him convicted of any crime. The only witness they had in this case was dead and there was only her word that the death was caused by Fred Baker. 'We'll get him somehow. I do not intend to give up, even if I have to live in Fallon Street for a long time.'

'You are living in that disgusting place!' he exclaimed in shock.

'It's the only way I could get close to him.'

'I have tried to stop her,' Ian explained, 'but she is determined.'

The sergeant leant forward in interest. 'If you find out anything, no matter how small, please let me know, Mrs Jarvis. In the meantime, I will have him watched and try to catch him in the act of a crime.'

'Thank you.' Dora was pleased they were going to do something. 'If you can get him behind bars, then I might be able to search his house.'

'Don't you dare!' both men exclaimed.

'You must leave that to us, Mrs Jarvis, or we could end up arresting you.'

She gave a wry smile. 'I know, but it might be worth it. I want justice for my husband.'

'If at all possible, you will get it.' He stood up and shook hands with both of them.

'George is a good man so please leave this to him,' Ian said once they were outside.

'I won't do anything silly.' She smiled up at him. 'I just wanted to shake him up a little.'

'You succeeded in shaking both of us up, so behave yourself.'

'When have you ever known me to do that?'

'Never.' He grinned. 'Forget I asked.'

Chapter Ten

It was halfway through the week and finding the kind of work he wanted was proving an impossible task, and he was now at the point where he would take anything. None of the cabinetmakers he had visited wanted an apprentice. Each day he had been to a different area, starting near the docks and working out from there. He had walked miles and worn holes in his shoes, but he couldn't give up. After being turned away from yet another workshop, Charlie stood on the street wondering what else he could do. He really needed to talk things over with Helen. In temperament they were much alike – both stubborn – and had always got on well together. His mother had insisted he have a couple of pennies in his pocket, so he decided to use one of those to go to the house in Chelsea where she worked, hoping he could see her for a moment.

When he arrived at the servants' entrance it had just started to rain and he realised this was a daft thing to do. His sister was probably too busy to spend time with him. He was about to walk away when the door opened and Cook looked out.

'You're Helen's brother, aren't you?'

He nodded. 'I wanted to see her, but I don't suppose that would be allowed. Will you tell her I called, please?'

'Don't go,' she said as he turned away, urging him into the kitchen. 'Come in before you get soaking wet.'

The warmth and smell of cooking food made him take a deep breath of pleasure.

'Have you had anything to eat?' she asked. Without waiting for a reply she handed him a slice of sponge cake. 'You eat that while you wait for your sister. She won't be long.'

'Thank you, Mrs . . . ?'

'Cook will do.' She studied him intently. 'What have you been doing? You look worn out.'

'I'm trying to find work, but no one is hiring at the moment. I'm so desperate I'll take anything.'

'Are things so bad for your family?'

There didn't seem any point in lying. 'We've got to earn some money soon or I don't know what we'll do. It's young Joe we worry about because he's only eight.'

At that moment Helen came in, dumped the heavy bucket of water she was carrying, and rushed over to him, alarmed to see him there. 'What's happened?'

'I wanted to talk to you because I've been looking for work and can't find anything. I wondered if you had any ideas.'

She sat beside him. 'Tell me what's been happening since I was last home first.'

By the time he'd finished explaining about their mother's lack of pupils, she had her head resting in her hands. 'Oh, I did hope for better news than that. I feel helpless living here and keep wondering if I should come home for good.'

'You mustn't do that,' he insisted firmly. 'We wouldn't be able to feed another mouth, sis. Mum's having a hard enough job as it is, and I've noticed she is eating very little to make sure we have enough.'

'This isn't right!' Cook had been listening and now she stormed out of the kitchen calling for the butler.

She soon returned with Mr Gregson. 'That boy and his family need help. He's looking for work. Can't we do something?'

The butler sat opposite Charlie and asked, 'What kind of work are you looking for?'

'I was hoping to get taken on as apprentice to a cabinetmaker because I like working with wood, but I'll do anything. I'm strong,' he added.

'I can see that, son, but the master isn't taking on any new staff at the moment.'

'Oh, sir, I didn't come here looking for a job,' he said quickly. 'I wanted to talk to my sister. I just don't know what to do next.'

The butler smiled and stood up. 'In that case you can have half an hour with her. Good luck, young man.'

'Thank you, sir.' Charlie turned to Helen, his expression worried. 'I've tried everywhere, sis, but there's nothing going and I'm at that point now where I'll take anything. Have you got any ideas? I must earn money soon. I'm the man of the house now and I feel as if I'm letting Mum and Joe down.'

'You mustn't feel like that. They know you are doing everything possible.'

'It isn't enough.' He clenched his fists in desperation. 'I've got to find a job – I just have to! The only option left is to go to the docks.'

'No, no, Charlie, that would break Mum's heart. You know she wants better for us and that's why she's made sure we had a good education.'

'Well, we're not living up to her hopes, are we? You are scrubbing floors and I'm being driven towards the docks for work.' The hitch in his voice showed how upset he was.

'I know,' she admitted, 'but I'm a woman and there isn't much available for us.'

He gave his sister a sympathetic glance. 'There doesn't appear to be much for young boys, either.'

'Damned thing!' The footman cursed as he came into the kitchen carrying an ornate mantle clock.

'Watch your language, Bob,' Cook scolded. 'What's riled you up?'

'This clock from the library. The master practically

threw it at me saying he was fed up with it going wrong. He told me to get the bloody thing fixed properly this time. His words, not mine, Cook.'

Charlie was already on his feet, his eyes fixed on the clock with interest. 'Would you like me to have a look at it?'

All eyes turned towards him and the footman frowned.

'I've repaired a couple,' Charlie explained, 'and one was similar to that. Does it chime the hours?'

'It's supposed to, but that part hasn't worked for some time, and it keeps stopping. We've sent it away several times and it has worked for a while, then starts messing around again.' Bob shook his head. 'I can't let you have a go at it because the master is very attached to the clock, otherwise it would have been replaced long ago.'

The butler had joined them. 'No harm in letting the lad have a look at it before we send it off for repair again.'

'If you say so.' Bob looked doubtful.

Charlie smiled his thanks and sat at the table, immediately setting to work.

The footman went over to Helen. 'Is he any good?'

'Well, he's always been interested in how things work.'

Everyone went back to their tasks while Charlie sat at the table in the corner of the kitchen. Mr Gregson sat close by, watching him work, but not interrupting as the clock was taken to pieces, cleaned and examined carefully, and then reassembled. Only then did he speak. 'You looked as if you knew what you were doing. Does it work, or is it beyond repair?'

Charlie carefully wound it up and sat back with a smile on his face as it began to tick. 'Whoever worked on it last didn't replace two small parts securely enough. One was loose and the other had fallen off, but fortunately was still caught in the works. It will be all right now.'

'What about the striking of the time?'

Charlie moved the hands to twelve o'clock and it chimed the time correctly.

The footman shot over to the table. 'Good gracious, he's done it. I'll take it back to the master and we'll keep an eye on it to see if it keeps working.'

'It will,' Charlie told him with confidence.

Bob laughed and patted the lad on the shoulder. 'Ah, the confidence of youth.'

'Where did you learn to do that?' the butler wanted to know.

'I've always wanted to see how things work.'

Helen smiled affectionately at her brother. 'Don't leave anything about or he will have it in pieces.'

Mr Gregson studied him with renewed interest. 'If you're looking for work why don't you try apprentice to a clockmaker, or better still the railways? That's growing all the time now and there could be a lot of opportunity for a talented young lad.'

'I never thought of that! Thanks, sir, I'll give that a try.' Charlie beamed at his sister, clearly excited.

'Good lad. Now, Cook, give this clever young boy something to eat, and we'll all have a nice strong cup of tea.'

'Right away, Mr Gregson.'

Helen helped set out the cups, and while they were preparing food and drink Cook whispered in her ear, 'I'll give Charlie a bit of food to take home with him.'

'That is kind of you and Mum will be very grateful.'

'I know you are worrying about them, my dear, and wish you could stay home with them.'

'I feel sick with concern at times, but if I go home it will be another mouth to feed.' Helen's eyes filled with tears and she wiped them away quickly. 'I should be doing more to support them by earning higher wages, but there is little on offer for young girls.'

'I know, and if it's any consolation to you, I believe you are doing the right thing by staying here. Your mum doesn't have to worry about you, does she?'

'You're right, of course, but it's so hard. They are struggling and I'm comfortable and well fed.'

'And knowing that must be a relief to your family. Now, you go and sit with your brother while you have a spare moment.'

Charlie was tucking into a huge roast beef sandwich when she joined him. 'What do you think of Mr Gregson's idea?'

He chewed the last of the sandwich and wiped his mouth before answering. 'Terrific. I've been concentrating on cabinet making or any menial job I could get, but he's made me see I must widen my search. The railways never occurred to me, but I'll certainly see if there is any possibility of work there.'

'What about a clockmaker? You're clearly very good at it.'

Charlie pursed his lips in thought. 'I enjoy doing it, but I think the railways would be a better job for me. One day there will be a station in every town across the country.' His eyes were shining with enthusiasm. 'If I can get in now, then there could be a good future in it for me.'

'I agree. Go for it.'

At that moment Bob swept back into the kitchen. 'The master is delighted to have the clock working and even chiming again. He gave me this for you with his thanks.'

Charlie gazed in wonder at the coins the footman had just put in his hand. 'That's two shillings!'

He laughed at the youngster's stunned expression. 'I'm only teasing. Here is more to go with it.'

'Four . . . shillings!' he gasped. 'Are you sure this is right? That's a lot of money just for making a clock work again.'

'I told you he was delighted. You should have seen his face when it struck the time. He said if it goes wrong again, we are to call on you. He wants you to have that as payment.'

Charlie studied the coins for a moment, then nodded and put them safely in his pocket. 'Please thank him for his generosity.'

'I will. Now, Cook, I can smell a cake baking in the oven. Any chance it could be ready yet?'

'You know very well it is.'

While everyone was busy making more tea and trying to cut a piping-hot cake, Charlie grabbed his sister's arm. 'Just wait till I give this money to Mum. That's enough for another week's rent and a little left over for food.'

'That will be a big help,' she told him. 'When you leave, wait outside for a moment and Cook will give you some food to take home with you.'

He patted the pocket with the money in it. 'I'm so glad I came here today, sis. We're going to make it through this, aren't we?'

'Of course we are,' she replied, confidently, praying this was true. This was a stroke of good luck, but they were going to need good fortune to smile on them for quite a while.

The lessons with Andy were proving a challenge, and at times Jane wasn't sure whether she was the teacher or the pupil. It was obviously a rare thing for him to receive praise, and as they discussed various subjects, laughing at times, she could see him growing in confidence. He was hard work, but she was enjoying their time together enormously.

She was concentrating on preparing a lesson for him when Charlie swept into the scullery and dumped a bag on the table. When she saw his animated face, she asked, 'Have you found a job?'

'Not yet, but look what I've been given. A bag of food and this.' He proudly put the money in front of her.

'Where did you get that?' she wanted to know, stunned by the unexpected bounty.

He told her about his visit to see Helen and what had happened while he'd been there. 'So you see, the master was very pleased and gave me all that money. The butler said that as I was good at things like that I should try for a job with a clockmaker or the railways. I think the railways are the best opportunity for a good job. They're expanding all the time and there could be a secure future there if I can get in now. I'm going to Victoria Station first thing in the morning.'

'In that case we had better make you look as smart as we can. I'll press your trousers and iron a clean shirt for you.'

Charlie grinned with excitement. 'I need to look older than thirteen.'

'You'll do that easily because you are tall and strong for your age.' She smiled and squeezed his arm, delighted to see him so happy. He had been rather down at his lack of success in finding work. 'They will take you on, I'm sure.'

'If they don't, then I will keep going to other stations until they give me a job. I really think this is right for me and I won't give up.'

Jane was up late that evening in an effort to make Charlie's clothes as clean and smart as possible. He was so eager for a job with the railways that she had to do everything possible to see he had a chance of being accepted. When Bert had walked out on them she had been frantic with worry, but so far they were managing – just. She was enormously proud of the way her children had gathered around her in support. They found themselves standing at a crossroad and had chosen the path they were going to take, but she had no illusions that the journey in front of them would be hazard-free. The biggest could be how Bert reacted when he was informed of her intention to divorce him, and she doubted he would just let it go ahead without protest. No matter what he did, though, she would stand up to him and keep fighting for what she wanted.

Chapter Eleven

Early the next morning Jane studied Charlie's appearance. His clothes were old, but after washing and pressing they were presentable.

'Do I look older than my age?' he asked.

'Yes, you do. Because of your height and build I would take you to be fifteen or even sixteen if I didn't know you.'

'Good. I know you don't like us to lie, Mum, but I'm going to tell them I'm fifteen.'

'I understand, darling, and you must do whatever you can to get the job you want.' She straightened his shirt collar and smiled. 'Don't make a habit of it, though.'

He laughed. 'I promise. Wish me luck.'

'You won't need that. Once they find out how clever

you are, they will employ you. You speak well and they will know at once that you are not some illiterate urchin looking for work.'

'More and more I'm beginning to understand why you insisted we had a good education and spoke well. It was to help us get out of this place, wasn't it, Mum?'

'That has always been my wish for all of you.' She smiled proudly at her eldest son and handed him a shilling. 'You'll need that for fares and food. Don't be afraid to spend it because I don't want you walking for miles and going hungry. Now, you had better be on your way.'

Joe tumbled down the stairs and stared at his big brother. 'Don't you look smart and all grown-up. I hope I'm going to be as tall as you.'

'I'm sure you will. Mum can hardly keep up with the speed you are shooting up. You are already growing out of my old clothes.'

'Good thing you weren't a girl,' Joe giggled, then rushed up to hug his brother. 'You'll get a job today, and I want to hear all about those big trains when you get back.'

He nodded, waved and strode out of the house.

Jane watched him for a while and marvelled at the difference in him since Bert had left. He had been worried and desperate at times, feeling he was now the man of the house and should be doing more to support them. However, the idea of working on the railways had appeared to lift that burden somewhat, and he was now looking more confident and very mature. She fervently hoped the day didn't end in disappointment for him.

She felt Joe catch hold of her hand and she looked down at him. The boys were very different in character. Charlie was a thinker, always interested in learning how things worked. He didn't often show outward signs of affection, but she knew he loved them all and cared deeply. Joe was the opposite. He was a hugger, needing that closeness, and had been like that from the moment he had been born. She had always felt more protective towards this sensitive child, but was becoming more aware that behind that bright smile and need to help others, there was an intelligent mind. From the time he could toddle she had prepared lessons for him every Saturday afternoon, as she had with the other two, determined to give them a chance in life. They were all bright, but Joe was different. He cared about other people and spoke out against injustice of any kind. That was a very surprising trait in someone so young.

He squeezed her hand bringing her out of her reverie. 'He'll get the job, Mum. They'd be daft to send him away.'

'They certainly would. Eat your slice of bread and then you must get off to school.'

As soon as her young son had left, Jane gathered her books and headed for the church hut, eager for the next lesson with Andy. With time before the boy was due to arrive, she settled down to go through the tasks she had prepared for him. Deep in concentration she didn't notice the time passing until she glanced at the clock. He was late, and that was unusual.

It was another hour before the door burst open and he rushed in, his face flushed with excitement. 'Sorry I'm late, Mrs Roberts, but I've got a job and start tomorrow.'

She had just lost another student, but she smiled, determined not to let her disappointment show. 'Sit down and tell me all about it.'

'Well, you've been so kind and encouraging about what I like to do, and when Charlie told me he was looking for work, I thought I'd try as well. There's this firm of architects in Greenwich advertising for an apprentice, so I went in.' He grinned. 'They are quite posh, so I tried to speak as you've been teaching me, and I showed them what I could do. They asked me who my teacher was and I said it was you. I hope you don't mind. These few lessons with you have given me the confidence to go for what I really want to do.'

When he stopped to draw breath she asked, 'Did you tell them you'd only had a very short time with me, and it was the teacher you had at school for a while who had helped you?'

He nodded. 'I did, and I told them it was your teaching that gave me the confidence to apply for the job as an apprentice.'

'What happened next?' She was relieved the boy had been honest with them.

'They asked me a lot of questions and I did one of my drawings for them. They said they would take me on if I was prepared to study hard. I told them I was.'

'That's absolutely wonderful, Andy. Do your parents know what you've done?'

'I told them what I was going to do, but they don't know yet that I've got the job. I came straight to you. I'll tell them tonight and they will be pleased.' He hesitated. 'Er . . . they seemed very interested and asked if you would give me a . . . reference, they called it. I'm to take it with me in the morning. Would you do that for me?'

'Of course. I have paper and an envelope with me so I'll do it right away. While I'm doing that you can look through the lesson I've prepared.'

'Thanks.' He sat down at another desk with the books.

Jane was delighted she had been able to give this gifted boy the confidence to make such a decision. She had only known him for such a short time and, to be honest, she knew the only thing she had been able to give him in that time was confidence. He had an unusual talent and she sincerely hoped this would open up a whole new world for him. Picking up the pen she began to write the required reference and when she went to sign it she hesitated, then did something unexpected. Her hand seemed to move on its own and her signature read – Jane Tremain-Roberts. It was the first visible step of claiming back her real identity.

After sealing the envelope, she handed it to the boy. 'Will you let me know how you get on?'

'I will, and I'd also like to keep in touch with Charlie. Is that all right?'

'Of course. He will be happy to see you at any time, and I'll tell him your good news.'

It was six o'clock and Charlie still wasn't home. She had expected him to be back by lunchtime or soon after, and couldn't imagine what was keeping him all this time. He could be going from station to station in an effort to find a job, of course, but it was dark now and she didn't like not knowing where he was.

'Should we go and look for him?' Joe suggested.

'I would, darling, but we don't know where he might be. He could be anywhere in London.'

Joe joined her at the window and they both gazed out at the dark street. Gas street lighting hadn't been put in this slum area yet. Suddenly her son rushed to the door and flung it open.

'He's coming, Mum.'

She stepped out into the street and was relieved to see her son's familiar figure striding towards them. 'Where have you been? We were beginning to worry about you.'

'I'll tell you if you let me get a word in,' he replied, stepping in and closing the door. 'Sorry I'm in such a mess but I've been working all day at the railway. They took me on, Mum, and showed me the engines. I've even had a ride on one, shovelling coal to keep the steam up. I've got to start at the bottom, but they said they will teach me how it all works.'

'That's wonderful. I am so happy for you, Charlie.'

This son was not a hugger, but she wrapped her arms around him anyway, and so did Joe.

When he disentangled himself from them, he said proudly, 'We don't have to worry about the rent now, and as soon as I get my first week's pay you can order some coal. We're going to be all right, Mum.'

Jane kept on smiling, although knowing her thirteen-year-old son had been forced to go out to work hurt so much. 'Thank you, Charlie. I'm very proud of you, and happy you will be doing something that interests you.'

'There's a good future on the railways, and I intend to learn all I can.'

'Will you take me to see one of your engines sometime?' Joe asked, holding his brother's arm in excitement.

Charlie laughed. 'They are not my engines – not yet, anyway.'

'If you take one to pieces don't lose any bits,' his young brother teased.

'I'll be careful,' he replied.

'You must be hungry so get out of those dirty clothes while I heat up your dinner. I'll wash them tonight. Oh, and I have exciting news about Andy.'

While Charlie was eating, she told him about Andy's job. 'He also said he would like to see you again.'

'That's terrific news, and I'll meet up with him as soon as possible. We'll have a lot to tell each other now we're both working.' His expression suddenly became serious as he looked at his mother. 'That means you've lost another pupil.'

'I can't seem to keep them,' she joked. 'However, I'm delighted for both of them, and Andy found the courage to apply for the job he really wanted. All either of them needed was understanding and encouragement.'

'They came to the right person, then. You'll soon get other students, but you don't have to worry if it takes time, now I've found work.'

'Thanks to you the pressure has been lifted, but helping people to have a better education is something I've always wanted to do. That dream was crushed over the years, but it is alive again. Living in this area has shown me just how desperate the need is.' The boys were staring at her in surprise and she sat back, a little embarrassed at having poured out her hopes and dreams.

'We've always known you enjoyed teaching so don't let anything stop you,' Charlie told her.

'We've got to tell Helen all this,' Joe declared, reaching for his mother's hand. 'Charlie's got a job with trains, and Mum's going to start a proper school.'

'I'll write a letter tonight,' said Charlie, 'and another to Mr Gregson, the butler. He was the one who suggested the railways.'

Later that night, when the boys were in bed, Jane scrubbed her son's dirty clothes, hardly able to believe what was happening. She had been frightened when Bert left, but it was turning out to be a blessing. The worry was still there, of course, because there were many hurdles yet to face. Two of her children would now be all right, but Joe was her main concern. She couldn't have carried on without seeking a divorce from Bert because it was the only way to be completely free of him. A divorce would cut the ties and then she would do all she could to climb out of this mess. A mess of her own making, and something she had every intention of putting right now she had the chance.

Chapter Twelve

'Helen,' the housekeeper called. 'A letter has arrived for you.'

Brushing the coal dust from her hands she took the letter and put it in the pocket of her apron. 'Thank you, Mrs Tarrant. I'll read it tonight.'

'Have you finished laying the fires in the bedrooms?' When Helen told her she had, the housekeeper nodded. 'Take a break and read your letter now. It might be urgent.'

Grateful to relax for a few minutes, she sat in the corner of the large kitchen and studied the envelope. There was no mistaking Charlie's bold hand, and she slit it open quickly. There was a two-page letter for her and another with the butler's name on it. At that moment he walked in. 'Mr Gregson, my brother has sent you a note.'

He took it and as he read a smile appeared on his

face. 'That is thoughtful of him. When you reply tell him I wish him all the best for the future.'

Helen hadn't read her letter yet, so she had no idea what he was talking about, but it sounded as if something good had happened. Without bothering to sit down again she began to read and almost cried out in relief at her brother's news.

The butler was watching her closely, and said, 'He's a good lad and I'm sure he will do well.'

She nodded, unable to speak as the implication of the news sunk in. With Charlie working it would ease their problems and give them a chance to reassess the situation. They had taken a jump forward and they mustn't falter. It was now time to consider how she could be of greater help, and that was a decision that needed a lot of thought. Jobs for women were very limited, and as much as she longed to do something else it would be foolish to leave this job without another one to go to.

'Why the deep frown?' Cook came over. 'Not bad news, is it?'

'No, my brother has got a job on the railways.'

'Then why are you looking worried? You should be smiling.'

'I am pleased and relieved. I was just thinking about something else.'

'Helen!' the housekeeper called.

'Ah, back to work.' She hurried off to answer the summons.

* * *

The family were entertaining that evening and it was late when Helen was finally able to retire for the night. She crawled into bed, tired but unable to sleep, her mind racing after Charlie's letter. He had sounded so enthusiastic, and she couldn't be happier for him. If he did well on the railways – and she had no doubt about that – then he could be set up for life.

While she was mulling this over an idea popped into her head, and she sat bolt upright. What was she doing working as a skivvy? Her mother had made sure she had a good education and spoke well. She grasped her knees and rocked back and forth as excitement rushed through her. Why not? She must talk this over with her mother. She would know what to do.

The next morning she knocked on the housekeeper's door and went in. 'I've finished all my jobs, Mrs Tarrant, and was wondering if I could have two hours off. I'll make up the hours.'

'We were all up very late last night so you may have the free time. Make sure you are back by twelve.'

'I will, and thank you.'

Knowing her mother was often at the church hut on a Saturday morning in case there were any enquiries, she went straight there and found her at one of the small desks reading a textbook.

'Helen!' She stood up and hugged her daughter. 'What are you doing here at this time of day?'

'I asked for a couple of hours free because I need to talk to you.'

'Well, I've got plenty of time, as you can see,' she joked, indicating the empty room. She pulled up another chair to the desk. 'Sit down and tell me what's on your mind.'

Helen smiled at the familiar words. Her mother had always encouraged them to sit down and talk over anything troubling them, offering advice and making problems seem like molehills instead of mountains. Only as she got older did she realise that her mother didn't have anyone to turn to for help and encouragement, although the problems she had with an uncaring husband were many. She kept all that to herself, and Helen recognised that had taken great strength of character.

Jane touched her hand. 'Whatever it is, I am sure we can sort it out.'

'Oh, sorry, I was lost in thought. I received Charlie's letter and am thrilled he has found a job he is enthusiastic about, and it set me thinking about my own position. I took that job because it was all I could get. I didn't want to leave you and the boys but felt it might ease things at home if I wasn't there. Dad tolerated the boys, but he never lost an opportunity to tell me I was useless, and every time that happened you stepped in to defend me.' Helen shook her head at the memory. 'That upset me and I had to leave as soon as I was old enough.'

'I know why you did it, darling, and it broke my heart to see you working as a servant.'

'Well, I want to change that now. Do you think I could apply for a job as a governess?'

'Yes, I do,' her mother replied without hesitation. 'It is what I intended to do, and I made sure you all benefited from the education I had received.'

'You were going to be a governess?' Helen asked, surprised.

'Yes, much to my parents' disapproval. I intended to do that until I could get a position as a teacher in a London school. I had already been offered a job with a good family when I met your father.' Jane passed a hand over her eyes. 'But that is a long story.'

'I'd like to hear it one day,' she told her mother gently, seeing the distress it still caused her.

'One day, but we are here to talk about you, not me. If you really want to do this, then we must put an advertisement in one of the London newspapers. I will see to that. The paper can send any replies to me and I will bring them along for you to see.'

Helen grimaced. 'If we get any.'

'We will.'

She laughed. 'I like your confidence. I haven't any experience, I am too young and not qualified for such a post.'

'You are more than qualified, darling, and not everyone wants an elderly, stern woman for their children. You are good with youngsters. Look how the boys love and respect you.'

'Do you think the boys will give me a reference?' she joked.

'No, but I will.'

'Er . . . will that be accepted?'

Her mother looked her straight in the eyes. 'It will be. Now, we'll put the advert in for two days to start, and if necessary a further two days after that.'

'Won't that cost a lot of money?'

'Not a great deal, but whatever it is we will find the money. I am happy you have come to this decision, and I'm sure it is the right one.' She grasped her daughter's hand. 'We'll make it happen.'

'Thanks.' Helen stood up and hugged her mother. 'You're marvellous, do you know that? Dad is a fool not to see what a treasure he had.'

Her mother brushed away the compliment. 'You'd better get back to scrubbing your floors – for the time being.'

'That's one job I won't be sorry to lose. See you when there is any news.'

Jane watched her daughter leave and noticed the spring in her step, excited now she was going to try and make a change in her life. Helen would make an excellent governess, and she was going to do everything possible to make it happen. She smiled and nodded in satisfaction. It was now time to start using the name she had kept hidden all these years. She had done that to protect her parents from the embarrassment of having a daughter living in the slums. They had turned their backs on her, and for that heartless act they ought to be ashamed, no matter how naive and rebellious their young daughter had been. That was something she could never do to any of her children. No matter what they did she would be by their side helping them through any mistakes they might make in life.

The time to hide was over!

She began to compose the notice to go in the newspaper, and when finished she felt a surge of relief as though chains had been binding her and had now fallen away. She'd signed Andy's reference Tremain-Roberts, and she now added that to her daughter's name. If it could help them climb out of this mess, she would shout it out loud, no matter what anyone thought.

There was a tentative knock on the door and a man peered in. 'Are you the teacher what put the notice in the shop?'

The man appeared very hesitant, so she stood up and smiled. 'Yes, I am. Please come in, sir.'

He took a couple of steps, cap in hand, and gazed down at his feet in embarrassment. 'I can't read nor write and I want to learn. A mate saw your notice and told me I should come and see you. Er . . . I'm twenty-two. Is that too old?'

'It's never too late to learn, and I'd be delighted to help you. Please sit down and tell me about yourself.'

'I ain't got any money,' he blurted out. 'I can only get labouring jobs now and again, but I want something better than that.'

'Then you are just the kind of pupil I am looking for. Don't worry about the money for the moment. You can pay me something when you get a decent job.'

'Really?' He did sit down then. 'I told my mate it was daft to come here cos as soon as you knew I was broke you'd send me on my way. I promised him I'd see you anyway.'

'I won't turn anyone away who needs help and really wants to learn,' she told him gently. 'Now, tell me why you can't read and write yet.'

'I only went to school for a little while, and then not regular.' He shrugged. 'After I was about six I couldn't go at all.'

'Why, were you ill?'

'No, not me. My ma was sick and Pa was a drunk, so I had to look after both of them.'

Jane was appalled. 'Didn't you have any older brothers or sisters?'

'No, there was only me.'

She was close to tears but didn't show her distress in front of this brave young man. 'You haven't told me your name.'

'Oh, sorry, it's Ted Randall.'

'Well, Ted, we will make up for those lost years of schooling. I will be proud to have you as a pupil. Just one more question. Where are your parents now?'

'Ma died six years ago, and Pa finally drunk himself to death six months ago. My mate said it was time I thought of myself.'

'He's absolutely right. Can you come every day?'

'I ain't got nothing else to do.' He smiled then, appearing more relaxed. 'Do you really think I can learn even though I'm older?'

'I'm not going to pretend it will be easy for you, but if you are willing to work hard and don't give up, then there's no reason why you can't learn.'

'I'll work hard. I'm used to that.'

'Right. I don't usually give lessons on a Saturday, but let's make a start right away, shall we?'

It was one o'clock before she sat back and smiled at him. 'Well done, Ted. If I give you homework, would you do it and bring it back on Monday?'

'I'll do my best, and thank you for taking me on. That was fun.'

'I'm glad you enjoyed it, and from what I have seen this morning, I am certain we'll have you reading simple stories in no time at all. One of the first things I am going to teach you next week is how to sign your name.'

'That would be good, Mrs Roberts. It's embarrassing just making a mark.'

'You won't have to do that any more. When you apply for a job you will be able to sign with a flourish.'

That made him laugh. 'I look forward to being able to do that. What homework do you want me to do?'

She handed him a couple of sheets of paper. One blank, and one with the letters of the alphabet on it. 'Copy those for me as many times as you can and say them out loud as we've been doing today.'

'All right.' He tucked the paper in his pocket saying that he would be back at ten o'clock on Monday.

She watched him leave and heard him whistling as he walked away. If any man needed someone to help him it was Ted Randall. What that boy must have gone through was unimaginable, and she was determined to do her best for him. The prospect gave her a feeling that, at last, she was doing something she was meant to.

Still smiling to herself, she read the notice through just to make sure it was all correct, and then hurried to the newspaper office. Helen was going to be puzzled when she saw it, but it might give her a better chance of being accepted.

There was still enough money in her purse to do some careful shopping. The little tin they had put the money in at the start was now empty and she still hadn't been able to buy enough coal to light a fire in the other room. Anything they had must be used for the stove in the kitchen or they wouldn't have any hot meals or water, and it was getting colder all the time. She gave a wry smile as she walked along. And she had just taken on a pupil who couldn't pay!

She had only been home for a short time when Joe arrived. He hugged her, as he always did. 'Any new pupils?' he asked.

'Yes, one young man came and I agreed to teach him. He can't afford to pay until he gets a job, but he needs help, Joe, so I couldn't turn him away. He's had a terrible time and was deprived of schooling.'

'He'll soon learn with you, Mum, you're the best teacher in thc world.'

She ruffled her youngest son's hair in amusement. 'My goodness, such praise.'

Patting his hair back in place he grinned. 'I wonder how Charlie's getting on?'

'Thoroughly enjoying himself with all that machinery around, I expect.'

'They'll have to watch him or he'll have their beautiful engines in pieces to see how they work. Have I got time to see Granny before dinner?' he asked, suddenly changing the subject.

'Plenty of time. We will be eating later tonight in the hope that Charlie will be home by seven o'clock. If he isn't, I can keep his dinner warm for him. So off you go.'

'It's me, Granny.'

Dora smiled at the face peering round the door. 'Come in, Joe.'

He bounded in. 'Are you all right? Do you need any shopping?'

'Not today. I had to go out, so I picked up a few things then. There's fresh tea in the pot if you could stay and talk to me for a while.'

'I don't have to rush off,' he told her, busy pouring two cups of tea before settling on a stool in front of her chair. 'We'll be having dinner later because Charlie won't be home very early now he's got a job on the railways. When he went to see if they would take him on they showed him the engines and he even had a ride on one. He had to shovel coal in to make it go. He's ever so happy about it, and so are we.'

'I'm sure you all are. He's a clever boy and should

do well. Has your mother had any more pupils yet?'

'One man came today and she's going to teach him even though he can't pay anything. She said he hasn't had much schooling and needs help.'

'That is very kind of her, and I think you must have inherited her desire to help others.'

He nodded, his little face serious for a change. 'It's always been important to her that everyone should have a good education. Helen said Mum tried hard to help Dad, but he thought it was a waste of time.'

'That was foolish of him.'

Suddenly there was a loud bang on the door and it shot open. Fred Baker stepped in, obviously furious. 'You set the coppers on me!' he bellowed. 'What I do is none of your blasted business, you interfering old cow!'

Dora was on her feet and facing him calmly. 'I don't know what you are talking about. And how dare you burst into my home like this.'

He took a step towards her, his fists clenched. 'It had to be you. One of my mates saw you coming out of the coppers' shop with some posh bloke, and then they started on me.'

'Then your mate was mistaken,' Dora declared, making sure her dismay didn't show in her face or voice.

'No, he wasn't. We know everyone that lives around here, and 'Arry don't make mistakes like that.'

After hearing the commotion Jane arrived and pushed past the furious man to stand with Dora and put a protective arm around her son. 'If the police are after you it's because you have been up to no good. They don't waste their time pursuing innocent people.'

'Found your voice now your old man's left you, have you?' he sneered.

'What exactly have the police done?' Dora wanted to know, relieved Jane had stepped in to help keep Joe safe.

'Stopped me in the street and searched me. Didn't find nothing, though,' he said smugly.

That remark was disappointing and Dora glanced at his hands. He wasn't wearing the ring. 'This hasn't anything to do with us, so get out, and don't you dare come here again. If you are in trouble with the law, then that is your own fault.'

Still red in the face he glared at Jane. 'I still haven't found Bert. You must know where he is.'

'I wouldn't tell you if I did. You'll have to find him yourself to get the money back.' She gave a mirthless laugh. 'But I wouldn't hold out much hope of that if I were you.'

'Bloody women,' he growled, then spun round and stormed out.

'Granny, you ought to lock your door,' Joe told her with concern.

'I'm not going to let that bully frighten me.' She patted Joe on the shoulder and smiled at Jane. 'I think we all need a nice strong cup of tea after that, don't you?'

Chapter Thirteen

Charlie arrived home at seven o'clock that evening and didn't stop talking about his day.

'Did you have a ride on a train?' Joe asked as soon as his brother stopped chewing for a moment.

'No, at the moment I am just following two men around who have been showing me how everything works. It isn't only the engines and tracks I've got to learn about, but also the daily running of the station.' He cleared his plate and sat back, a smile on his face. 'I'm going to like working there, Mum. The men don't mind me asking questions, and they said I could have a good career there.'

'That's wonderful,' Jane said as she removed his empty plate. 'If you are still hungry, I've got half a loaf of bread.'

'I'm fine, thanks.'

She knew this wasn't true. He'd had a long day and was obviously hungry.

He saw the worry on her face. 'It's all right. The men shared their lunch with me. They had plenty, and we'll soon be able to buy more food. When I get paid, we'll put the rent aside and you can go out and have a good shop.'

'That will be lovely. However, I must give you something to take.'

'A couple of dripping sandwiches will be fine, if you can manage it. Now, tell me how you got on today. Any new pupils?'

Jane told him about the man she had agreed to teach without payment. 'I know we need the money, but I couldn't turn him away, Charlie.'

'Of course you couldn't.' He sighed. 'What tragic lives some people have. It isn't right. Doesn't anyone care?'

'Many with comfortable lives probably don't even know, or don't want to know, but things will change one day. They have to. Education is part of the answer, and I'll help in any small way I can.'

'That's all any of us can do.' Charlie turned his attention back to his younger brother. 'And what have you been up to today?'

'Just school, but when I went to see Granny, Fred Baker burst in and accused her of telling the police about him.' Joe then told him everything that had happened.

'I don't like the sound of that, Mum, so be careful

because I won't be around much now. I'll only get Sunday off, and if there is an urgent job to be done then I will sometimes have to work then as well.'

'Don't be concerned. Dora and I can handle that bully,' she joked. 'He's still after your father, so he hasn't found him yet.'

Charlie snorted in disgust. 'He was stupid to borrow money from Baker and not pay it back. I expect he wanted a bit to flash around to impress his new woman.'

'I'm sure that's what it was.' Jane changed the subject. 'Now, you boys had better get to bed.'

After church on Sunday Dora told Ian about the confrontation with Baker and he was alarmed. 'You really must leave that place and return to your own home. There isn't anything else you can do, and it could be dangerous living there. That man is suspicious about you now, and you know how violent he can be.'

'I do admit to being concerned, not only for myself but for the Robertses. He's after Jane's husband and insists she must know where he is.'

'Dora,' he said gently, 'they are not your responsibility. Living in a place like that they have probably had to face many unpleasant incidents. Now Baker knows you have been talking to the police you must get away from there.'

'I understand you are worried, but I am not prepared to move out just yet. You say the Robertses are not my concern, but I must disagree with you. I like them and adore young Joe. I am watching their struggle to survive and my heart aches for them. The eldest boy has gone out to work in an effort to stop his family being thrown out on the street. It isn't right that people should have to live like that. I feel like storming up to those politicians, banging their heads together and telling them to bloody well do something about the slums. They ought to be dragged out of their comfortable homes and from their tables groaning with food and made to visit these areas.'

Ian stared at her in amazement. 'My goodness, I have never heard you speak so passionately before, not about anything.'

'Living in Fallon Street has opened my eyes. Some are rough and no doubt turn to crime, and for the most part I believe it is the harsh conditions that make them like that, but there are also many decent law-abiding people caught up in that kind of life. All many of them need is a helping hand, and Jane knows that. In spite of her own desperate plight she is still reaching out to try and help a few.'

'That isn't surprising because if she is who we believe, then she has seen both sides of society.'

Dora sighed deeply and patted his arm as they walked along. 'I do hope you can help to free her from that disastrous marriage.'

'We will do everything we can, but we have strayed from the point. I firmly believe it is too dangerous for you to remain in Fallon Street.'

She shook her head. 'I know you think I'm being reckless, but I won't leave yet. We were never blessed with children, and I feel as if the Robertses are now my family. I won't abandon them, and I promise to be very careful.'

'All right,' he agreed reluctantly, 'but if you have any more trouble with Baker then you must reconsider.'

'You have my word on that.' She looked up at him and there was a hint of mischief in her eyes. 'When this is all over, I want you to gather together politicians, and anyone in authority, and I will give them a lecture they will never forget.'

'That is an excellent idea. I'll put them in a room and lock the door so they can't get out.'

They were laughing as they parted.

'We have a busy night tonight,' the housekeeper told the assembled staff. 'There is to be a dinner for eight guests.'

'Tonight!' Cook exclaimed. 'That is very short notice and they never entertain on a Sunday.'

'This is a special occasion, I was told, and four courses will be sufficient.'

Without further comment Cook turned and began barking out orders. The kitchen instantly burst into life as the staff began to prepare for this unexpected dinner.

With the kitchen staff in full flow, the housekeeper handed Helen a list of the guests. 'Make the place names in your best writing.'

This was her usual job and she settled down immediately to the task. Although the Daltons were not a titled family, they were immensely wealthy and carried a lot of influence in society, so it wasn't unusual to have lords and even a duke dining with them. This was the first time, though, there had been a general on the guest list.

Every member of the staff was needed to help prepare a function at short notice, and it was eleven that night before they could breathe a sigh of relief.

Cook mopped her brow and gave a satisfied smile. 'That went well.'

The butler appeared with two bottles of wine. 'The master said that the evening has been a great success and thanks Cook for an excellent meal, and all the staff. He said everyone must have a drink and he's given us his best wine.'

There were murmurs of approval as the glasses were handed round. Helen wasn't used to alcohol, so she had only a small amount, but the bottles were soon empty. She yawned and was about to retire when she saw a Sunday newspaper on a chair. Her mother had sent word to say her advertisement would appear today, so she picked it up. 'Does anyone mind if I take this?'

The footman waved his glass at her. 'You can have it, Helen, I've finished with it.'

'Thanks.' She went to her room at the top of the house, hardly able to keep her eyes open, and tossed the paper on the bed while she undressed. Determined to stay awake long enough to check for the notice she propped herself up and began to turn the pages. She soon found it and began reading eagerly to see what her mother had put in the advertisement. After a moment she put the paper down and frowned. Her mother had stated that she was a young girl, and that was good because most families wanted an older person, so that would save unnecessary replies. Her name was also there, but it wasn't correct. It plainly said that Miss Helen Tremain-Roberts required a position as governess. That couldn't be right; her mother would never make a mistake like that. Tremain? Where had she seen that name? She shot out of bed, her tiredness forgotten as she remembered the guests. One of them had been General Charles Tremain! She had served him and his wife. He was a tall, impressive man, and at the time she had a feeling that he reminded her of someone, but had been too busy to dwell on it.

Hastily dressing again, she tumbled down the stairs intent on finding the list again. She was mistaken – she must be.

Everyone had retired by now and the kitchen was empty, but the list was where she had left it on a small table by the wall. The name was exactly the same spelling as in the advertisement. How bizarre. Clutching the list to her she tried to remember everything about the general and his wife, but to be truthful they were just guests to be given unobtrusive service. The woman had been attractive and had even smiled at her once, but she couldn't remember anything else about her. The general, on the other hand, had an unmistakeable air of authority about him, and it had briefly crossed her mind that he wouldn't stand any nonsense from anyone. That had been clear in his hazel eyes that seemed to flash green at times. No wonder she had thought he seemed familiar. Her brother Charlie was the only one with the strange, beautiful eyes, the rest of them were just hazel.

Good gracious, she was letting her imagination run away with her just because she had found a mistake in a newspaper. Nevertheless, that was something that must be put right, and she had to find time to see her mother tomorrow and show her the error.

Her mother was just finishing the lesson with her student when Helen arrived. She waited outside until he left and then went into the hut. After greeting her mother, she said, 'I haven't got much time, Mum, but I just had to see you.'

'Sit down and tell me what has brought you here in such a rush.'

'There's a mistake in the newspaper advertisement. My name is incorrect.'

'No, it isn't, darling. Tremain is my name and we are going to use it when we need to.'

She stared at her mother in astonishment. 'But why?'

'Because I am going to use everything I have to get my family a better life, and the name that is rightfully mine will, hopefully, help us. I've stopped hiding.'

'Why have you been hiding?' she asked her mother gently.

'I did not wish to embarrass my parents more than I already had when I defied them. I was wrong, but so were they. I was turned away with nothing but the clothes I was wearing. Over the years they have never once reached out to me, although I did send letters, but they were never answered. In the end I gave up.'

'So they knew where you were and didn't even check to see if you were all right?' Helen was appalled by this story. 'How could parents do that to their child, no matter what they had done?'

'It's hard to understand. I would never turn my back on any of you, no matter what you had done. My father is a hard man who expects his orders to be obeyed without question, and my mother would not go against him. His word is law. I believe he was always disappointed I was a girl. If I had been a boy, he would have put me in the army as soon as I was old enough, but he didn't know how to deal with a wayward daughter.'

'General Charles Tremain.'

Jane glanced sharply at her daughter. 'How do you know that?'

'They were guests we had last night. I served him and was struck by Charlie's likeness to him.'

'Yes, your brother does resemble him in looks, but not in temperament, thank heavens.' Jane clasped her daughter's hands tightly. 'I don't want the boys to know about this – not yet, anyway. Will you promise to keep this just between us for the time being?'

'Of course.' Helen laughed quietly. 'I was so shocked when I read the advertisement I thought I was imagining everything. If I had known this at the time, I would have spilt soup over him and said, "So sorry, Grandfather."'

'I long for the day when he will look at the three of you and regret his actions all those years ago.'

'Will that day every come, Mother?'

Jane shook her head. 'Most unlikely. He made his decision at the time and I doubt he has ever had a moment of regret.'

Chapter Fourteen

The next morning Jane was disappointed to see that no one had replied to their advertisement, but they would come she was sure. This had only been the first time and she wasn't going to be disheartened.

There was a spring in her step as she made her way to the church hut, and she smiled when she saw Ted already waiting for her, but he wasn't alone. There were two more men with him, all propped up against the hut. 'Good morning, gentlemen.'

This caused some merriment and one said, 'We've never been called that before.'

'I was telling some mates how I'd found this kind lady who was teaching me to read and write,' Ted explained. 'We wondered if you could help a few more.'

'Of course. Come inside and you can all tell me what you need in the way of extra education.'

First, she sat Ted on his own to study the lesson she had prepared for him and then got into a huddle with the other two. One, Peter, could write his name and make out simple words; the other, Derek, could read and write, if somewhat laboriously. They clearly needed help.

At the end of the discussion she nodded. 'Can you stay and begin lessons straight away?'

They agreed and the eldest of the two looked concerned. 'We know you're not asking Ted to pay anything cos he ain't got nothing, but what about us?'

'Do you have jobs?'

They both shook their heads.

'Then you don't have to pay me anything either.'

'That's generous of you, Mrs Roberts, but it don't seem right you are doing this for nothing.'

'When my daughter and I decided to reach out and help anyone who needed help in this way, we knew many in this area were struggling with poverty and wouldn't be able to pay for lessons. We know because we live in Fallon Street and have the same problems as everyone else.'

The men gaped at her in surprise. 'You don't sound like you come from here.'

'That's because I've had an excellent education, and I want to use that to help others. We agreed that it would depend on the circumstances of each pupil, and in cases like yours I don't expect payment. I won't turn anyone away who genuinely wants to improve their lives with a better education. Now, let us start the first lesson.'

It had been a good morning and she had thoroughly enjoyed having three pupils who were clearly eager to learn. However, it appeared that she was going to end up with a class of people who couldn't afford to pay anything. Still, that was only what they had expected and, to be honest, she felt good about helping in this way. She wouldn't turn them away.

That week sped by. Her three pupils had different needs and had to be taught separately, but they had made good progress in just a few days, and she was really enjoying the challenge. For so long she had felt useless and just struggled through each day, but now she was using the talents she had. It was a good feeling.

Another thing adding to her contentment was seeing her son go off to work each day with a smile on his face. He was happy, and that was a great relief to her. Now she wanted to see her daughter settled into a job that made her happy too.

She had paid for the advertisement to appear again, and fervently hoped this would bear fruit because it wouldn't be possible to keep doing this. If nothing came of it, they would have to find another way. The small amount of money they'd had in the tin was almost gone.

Much to her relief she had received one reply from a family she had heard about and it looked promising, so she went straight to her daughter, wanting her to see this immediately.

Luckily, Helen was on her lunch break so she was able to come outside where they could talk privately. When she had read the reply she looked at her mother. 'What do you think?'

'Reply at once to Lady Grant. I know of the family and it could be just what you are looking for. If you've got time to do it now, I'll wait and see it in the post for you. Put this as your address, and if you have an interview don't mention Fallon Street. It has a bad reputation and will ruin your chance straight away.'

'I can see that. Will you come in and wait while I compose the letter?'

'No, I'll stay here. Keep it short and to the point, darling. All they need to know is that you are willing to be interviewed by them.'

'I'll show you the letter before sealing the envelope.'

When her daughter went inside Jane wandered round the side of the house and looked at the garden, noting the vegetable patch, several fruit trees and flower beds, now devoid of colour. It wasn't very large, and that wasn't unusual in London, but it would be a lovely place in the summer. She had liked spending time in the garden, but those days seemed like a lifetime ago now.

Helen was soon back and handed Jane the letter to read. 'Perfect. I'll send it on its way at once. If they want to see you don't be intimidated by their status. The only difference between them and us is that they have money.'

'I'll remember that.' She laughed and hugged her mother. 'I've just heard some gossip. It seems that the unexpected dinner party last Sunday was to celebrate a special occasion. General Charles Tremain is now General Sir Charles Tremain.'

Jane's laugh lacked humour. 'So he's done it at last. Well, I doubt he is going to be pleased to have a daughter emerging from the slums of London.'

'Is that what we are doing, Mum?'

'Yes, darling. It's going to take time and won't be easy, but we will have a damned good try.'

Later that evening when the boys were asleep, Jane wrote a letter to Lady Grant in the form of a reference for her daughter. She spelt out her education to show she was qualified to have tutored Helen. Reading it through she had to admit it was impressive, and what it brought home, not for the first time, was what she had thrown away by insisting on marrying Bert. Looking back the sheer stupidity of it took her breath away. She had believed herself in love, and although Bert came from a lowly background, she had convinced herself he could be helped up the ladder of society. She gave an inelegant snort of disgust. That illusion had soon been shattered.

'Mum.' Joe came in and sat down at the table with her. 'I can't sleep. I'm hungry. Have we got anything to eat?'

'Only a slice of bread and dripping, darling. Will that help?'

He nodded, and she cut a slice from the small amount

of loaf left, being careful to save enough for the boys' breakfast. 'Want salt on it?'

'Yes, please.'

She watched him devouring the bread and her heart felt as if it would break. They were all hungry and she longed for the day when she could return home from shopping with a basket full of good food. The rent had to come first because if they slipped behind with that the landlord wouldn't hesitate to throw them out, and the thought of that turned her cold with fear. Not for herself; she had long ago stopped caring what happened to her, but she had to keep her youngest son safe. That dread would ease somewhat with Charlie's regular wages, but it was still going to be a struggle. If only she could get paying pupils, but she knew that would be almost impossible in this area.

Joe finished every crumb and smiled at his mother. 'I think I can sleep now. My tummy was rumbling so much I thought it might wake Charlie.'

'I doubt that, darling; he's had a busy day and is very tired.' She kissed the top of his head. 'You'd better go back to bed now.'

'So should you, Mum. It's late.'

'I'm coming up now.' She followed him up the stairs and tucked him in, then went to her own bed. He was right. She should try to get some sleep, but the night-time was always the worst as fears and doubts rushed in.

* * *

Helen waited anxiously for the postman, and on Monday afternoon she managed to catch the post when it arrived. Shuffling quickly through the letters she found one addressed to her, and she slipped it in her pocket before anyone saw it. She didn't like hiding her intention to find another position because it might come to nothing and she needed this job.

It was another hour before she had the opportunity to go to her room and read the letter. She gave a little whoop of delight. Lady Grant wanted to see her tomorrow at two o'clock. Perfect. That was her afternoon off so she wouldn't have to ask for extra free time.

She spent the evening washing and pressing her clothes and polishing her shoes until they shone. She certainly wasn't the height of fashion, but at least the clothes would be clean and pressed. Then she washed herself from head to toe, using a small piece of scented soap she had been carefully hoarding for a special occasion. Finally, her hair was washed, dried and brushed until the dark brown shone with a hint of gold in places. Satisfied that she would look clean and presentable she settled down to sleep.

The next day she was at the Grants' home in Park Lane well in time for the appointment, and as the lady of the house had sent for her she went to the main entrance instead of the servants' door at the back. There had been so much to do that morning and she hadn't had time to see her mother first. Taking a deep breath to steady her nerves she knocked firmly on the door.

It was opened immediately by the butler and she held out the letter. 'I have an appointment to see Lady Grant.'

After checking the letter, he stepped back to allow her to enter. 'Please wait here. I will let Her Ladyship know you are here.'

'Thank you.' Left alone she studied the elegant entrance hall and instead of sitting down she wandered along looking at the many paintings. Most of them were of long-past Grants, but there were a few landscapes. These she liked the best.

'Her Ladyship will see you now.'

She followed the butler to an upstairs drawing room, telling herself there was no need to be nervous. If nothing came of this, then there would be others, because she had no intention of giving up now she had decided this was what she wanted to do.

The butler announced her and she stepped inside the charming room furnished in a soothing pale green. The young lady waiting to see her was dressed in a beautiful soft rose-coloured gown that emphasised her blonde hair and pale complexion.

Helen curtsied carefully. 'Thank you for seeing me, Lady Grant.'

She inclined her head and indicated a chair opposite her. 'Please sit down. I have ordered refreshments we can enjoy while we talk.'

The door opened and a maid wheeled in a trolley. Once she had been dismissed, Helen stood up and served Her Ladyship.

Over the next hour Lady Grant explained what she wanted for her only child – a daughter aged six by the name of Victoria. 'I know it is usual to have someone more mature for this position, but I would want you to be not only governess, but her teacher and friend as well. I had a very strict, regimented upbringing and I don't want that for my child. I have interviewed four applicants so far, but did not feel any of them suitable for my daughter.' She paused and studied Helen carefully. 'Do you think you could fulfil my wishes and be a good companion to Victoria?'

'I am sure I could, Lady Grant. I have two younger brothers and have always loved children.'

'In that case, Miss . . . may I call you Helen?'

'Of course.'

'Well then, Helen, I can offer you the position and would like you to start in two weeks' time, if the terms of employment are agreeable to you.'

They then talked over working conditions and salary, and Helen was overjoyed.

'Splendid. That seems very satisfactory,' Lady Grant declared when everything was agreed. 'Now, before you meet Victoria there is another matter I wish to discuss with you. I have received a letter from your mother giving details of her education and I was interested to see she attended a school we are considering for our daughter when she is older.' She paused. 'I would very much like to meet your mother. Would you ask her to come and see me tomorrow at ten o'clock?'

'She holds her classes every morning, but I am sure she would like to come in the afternoon, if that would be convenient for you.'

'Classes?'

'She is teaching anyone who is in need of help with reading and writing, whatever their age. Many from the slums are lacking a good basic education.'

Lady Grant leant forward, her eyes questioning. 'And your mother is trying to do something about it?'

'Yes, she is.'

'How interesting. Please ask her to come and see me tomorrow afternoon at three o'clock, then. I would very much like to hear about her endeavour.'

'I'll see her when I leave here, Lady Grant, and I'm sure she will be delighted to meet you.'

'Thank you, Helen. I shall look forward to that immensely.' She picked up a bell and rang it, requesting that Victoria be brought in to meet her new governess.

Helen adored the child at once, and they were soon laughing together, much to Lady Grant's satisfaction.

After leaving them, Helen couldn't wait to see her mother with the good news. She had been at the interview for two hours so her mother would certainly be home. After waiting a long time for the omnibus and then a long walk after that, she tumbled through the door, flushed with rushing. Without waiting to greet her she poured out the good news. At last pausing for breath she sat down and grasped her mother's hands. 'I don't know what you said in the letter you sent her, but she wants to see you tomorrow at three o'clock. She said something about a school you attended.'

A slow smile spread across Jane's face. 'I will see her as requested.'

Her mother wanted to know every detail of the interview and they lost track of time until Joe erupted into the house and launched himself at his big sister. When the boisterous greeting was over, he had to be told the good news, which caused more celebration.

'Joe, I have to go out tomorrow afternoon, so will you ask Granny if you can stay with her after school until I return?'

He tore off, a wide smile on his face, eager to tell Granny the good news, and Helen turned to her mother. 'Just what kind of an education have you had, Mum?'

'A privileged one for a girl, but that is another long story that will have to wait for another day when we are alone,' she added as her young son appeared again.

'Granny said it is all right for me to stay with her.'

Chapter Fifteen

Jane liked Lady Grant on sight, and they talked for some time about Jane's effort to improve the education of the underprivileged.

'What you need is to advertise over a larger area,' she suggested after hearing of the difficulty in attracting pupils.

'I agree, but it would cost more money than I have,' she replied honestly. 'Word is beginning to spread, though, so I have hope more will come along.'

'It is a much-needed project and deserves success.' Lady Grant called for more refreshments, which appeared almost at once. After urging Jane to have another dainty sandwich, she sat back. 'My husband is a politician and has been campaigning for some time to get something done about the appalling conditions many have to endure. Would you mind if I told him what you are trying to do? He would be most interested.'

'Of course you may tell him.' Jane smiled wryly. 'I cannot imagine that my small effort would be of much interest to him, though.'

The lady laughed. 'There you are mistaken. He is passionate about the subject. Do you hold lessons in your home?'

'No, the vicar of a local church is kindly allowing me to use his Sunday school hut.'

After enjoying another cup of tea, she took her leave and walked for quite a way. She had thoroughly enjoyed the visit and was sure her daughter would be happy and secure there. Her two eldest children would now have respectable jobs, and that was a blessing, although it had been upsetting to see Charlie forced out to work, but he was happy, and that was the main thing. There was one burning desire that couldn't be accomplished until she obtained a divorce. She had to be completely free from this marriage before there was a chance of succeeding.

Continuing her walk she took a deep breath. *Step carefully*, she urged herself. *You acted without thought all those years ago and you mustn't make the same mistake again. Let this new development unfold and see where it leads.* She then used a couple of her precious pennies for the rest of the journey home.

She knocked on Dora's door and opened it to see her youngest son sitting and chatting away, as he always did.

'Mum.' He leapt to his feet. 'Granny's been telling me

about the seaside and how blue the water is, and there is lovely golden sand you can walk on with bare feet. It sounds lovely.'

'It is, darling, and one day we will all go and see it.'

'You've seen the sea?' he asked in awe.

'Yes, and I've been on a big boat.'

'Oooh, how big?'

'Well, there were about forty passengers and the crew, of course, so it was quite big.'

Joe's eyes were huge as he listened. 'Where were you going?'

'We were sailing for London Docks. We were coming home,' she said softly, remembering the excitement of that moment. 'Now, young man, we have taken up enough of Granny's time, and there is a meal to prepare. Charlie will be hungry when he gets home.'

He was already heading for the door when he turned back. 'Thank you for letting me stay, and telling me all those lovely stories.'

'I enjoyed it as well.' When he nodded and smiled, Dora looked at Jane. 'Was your afternoon successful?'

'Yes, it is a lovely house and Lady Grant is intelligent and charming. I'm sure Helen will be very happy there.'

'I'm pleased to hear that. If there is anything I can ever do for you, please ask.'

'Thank you, Dora. I'll keep that in mind, and thank you for keeping an eye on Joe for me.'

'That child is a joy to have around, and I love his company.'

Later, with Charlie home and the dishes cleared away, she told the boys about her visit with Lady Grant, and they were very excited to know their big sister was going to a good house.

Charlie looked thoughtful. 'With Helen and me earning better money, we might be able to find somewhere else to live. I know that's what you want.'

'It is, but we mustn't act in haste. I think at this point we can just be happy we are going in the right direction. I must write to Helen now and tell her about my visit.'

Her three mature pupils were doing well, and she praised every step forward they made, encouraging them to concentrate on the lessons, although they often found it hard going. They were happy to have found someone who was sympathetic to their plight and prepared to help them. The small room echoed with teasing and laughter at times as they urged each other on as each one tried to do better than their mates. Jane saw this good-natured competition as useful to their progress and joined in the banter at times. The men thought this was fun, and that was what she wanted.

At the end of Friday's lesson each one presented her with a small gift. One gave her two carrots, one a large potato and the other an onion.

'It ain't much,' Ted explained, 'but we wanted to give you something for being so kind to us. We know you have a job feeding your kids, and yet you still spend your time with us for nothing. There ain't many around who'd do that.'

There was a lump in Jane's throat as she accepted the gifts. They might only be small, but they were given out of their poverty with gratitude, and to her they were of more value than bars of gold. 'Thank you, gentlemen. I am grateful to have been given such useful gifts.'

They all smiled then, pleased she was happy, and were laughing and joking when they left.

She was just tidying up when she saw a man standing in the doorway. One glance told her he wasn't looking for lessons. His beautifully cut clothes pointed to wealth and position. 'Can I help you, sir?'

He stepped inside, closed the door and gave an elegant bow. 'I wish to talk with you if you can spare me the time. Allow me to introduce myself. I am Lord Grant.'

She managed to hide her surprise that a man of his standing should come to such a deprived area. This was to be her daughter's new employer, and she hoped there wasn't a question about that. 'I have a moment now, Lord Grant. Won't you sit down, please?'

He inclined his head and waited for her to sit before doing the same. 'Are the three men I saw leaving your pupils?'

'They are. For one reason or another, the schooling they received has been inadequate, and they now want to put that right so they can do better in life.'

He gazed around the humble hut, then back at the vegetables on the table.

She saw him frown and decided to explain. 'That is a show of gratitude for a week of lessons. Beautiful gifts, My Lord, given out of their poverty.'

Anger blazed in his eyes for a moment, and then it was gone. 'My wife told me what you are doing, and I wish to discuss this with you. I am a Member of Parliament and have been trying for a long time to get legislation passed that will improve the lot of those living in the slums, without success. Then my wife tells me of one woman who is trying to do this on her own. That is an impossible task, surely?'

'I agree, but if I can help just a few, then it is worth doing. I have already seen two young pupils move on. One, a very talented boy, has gained an apprenticeship with a firm of architects, and a girl the teachers had given up on has been able to return to school.'

'That is good, but there are hundreds who need help.'

'I am well aware of that, Lord Grant, but I am only one person, and many are reluctant to admit their lack of education. However squalid the conditions they live in, they do still have their pride.'

He stood up and began to prowl around the hut, looking at the children's religious drawings adorning the rough walls, then he spun back to face her. 'I admire what you are trying to do and agree that even one person whose life is improved is a victory.'

'That is how I feel,' she replied, wondering where this was leading.

He returned to his seat. 'Would you permit me to become involved in your excellent scheme?'

This wasn't what she had expected, and she paused, rather wary. 'In what way?'

'The first thing is the opportunity for further education should be widely advertised.' His gaze swept around the hut. 'You need a larger space to hold the lessons, and a good supply of all tools and materials needed. I could supply that, and as the pupils increase there will be a need for more like-minded teachers. The hours need to be extended to accommodate pupils who cannot attend in the mornings, and we could—'

'Lord Grant!' Jane interrupted, stopping him in mid flow. 'I appreciate your interest, but what you are suggesting would not be practicable, and make people afraid to approach me.'

'Tell me why.'

'I have lived in the slums for the last sixteen years and, like everyone else, I have struggled to bring up my children, keep a roof over our heads and food on the table.' She noted his startled expression, but continued. 'If we make the changes you are suggesting, then the people I want to help will not come. This simple hut by the local church is something they see every day, and so they are more likely to come in and ask for help. Also, they know the teacher comes from Fallon Street and is one of them.'

'But you are not!' he exclaimed. 'You are a genteel lady who has been educated in the best schools. Surely you are from the esteemed Tremain family? I can see the resemblance.'

'That is so,' she admitted freely, no longer trying to hide who she was. 'I made a very bad mistake by defying my family and was disowned.'

'And you ended up here?'

She nodded.

He ran a hand through his hair in agitation. 'What could be so terrible that a family would abandon their child to a life of deprivation? I could never do that to my daughter.'

'Neither could I, but that was my father's way, and he had every right to do as he did.'

'Do you not hate him?'

She thought for a moment, and then smiled. 'That is too strong a word. What I feel is sadness. They have three lovely grandchildren to be proud of, and they don't even know.'

'Yes, my wife told me your daughter is a charming girl with beautiful manners. You have taught her yourself, I believe.'

'My children all attended the local schools, but I extended their education because I wanted to give them more of a chance in life. That is what I am now trying to do here, and I firmly believe that by keeping this small and informal is the right way at this time. Do you understand?'

'Yes, I do, and as eager as I am to rush in and change what you have started, I see the wisdom of what you are saying. Will you, at least, allow me to support you?'

'In what way?'

'I could see that word is spread to other areas, and you must need books and materials for the pupils. I would supply those and I would also like to make it known that they can attend lessons free of charge. I would support you financially with a payment of a guinea a month.'

Jane actually gasped. 'That . . . that is very generous of you, but I couldn't possibly allow you to do that. This idea of mine might not be successful in attracting more pupils, and you would be wasting your money.'

'I would not consider it in that way. It could benefit me in my work. You say you have helped two youngsters so far, and you now have three men who want to improve their lot in life.'

'That is so, and I am delighted with their enthusiasm and progress.'

'Splendid. Let me help you in the way I have suggested.' He smiled eagerly. 'If we work together, we might be able to knock some sense into those in authority. I give you my word that I will not interfere with what you are doing here. If the day comes when changes are needed, then we shall do it together.'

After only the briefest of hesitations, she knew that this was an opportunity she would be a fool to refuse. She had met Lady Grant and liked her immensely, and her husband was clearly a man who cared about other people. Whatever good fortune had brought the Grants into their lives could not be ignored. She must grasp every opportunity that came along. She held out her hand. 'That's a deal, Lord Grant.'

Chapter Sixteen

Although they were just into November, Lord Grant had insisted on paying her in advance for the entire month. There was a cold wind blowing so the first thing Jane did that afternoon was to order a small amount of coal, then she went shopping. They were going to have a good nourishing meal tonight. She didn't know if this bounty would continue, but if it did, then the future could be given some consideration.

Returning home with a basket of food she set about preparing the evening meal. Charlie always came home ravenous, and tonight he would have enough to satisfy that hunger.

Joe arrived home from school, telling her what he had done that day, then he ran off to see that Dora was all right.

As soon as Charlie came home, she dished up the meal and sat down with them, watching carefully to see their reaction. Her youngest son dived straight in, and after the first mouthful began to study the plate.

'There's three vegetables on the plate!' Joe's eyes were wide. 'Mum?'

'And there's meat in this pie,' Charlie declared.

Jane kept a perfectly straight face. 'Eat up. There's stewed fruit and custard when you've finished that.'

'What's happened?' Charlie wanted to know.

'Eat first, and I'll tell you later.'

No more was said until the plates were cleared and every scrap of food gone.

'My goodness, these plates hardly need washing.' Jane set about making a pot of tea. 'Let's take this into the other room.'

'It's cold in there,' Joe protested.

'Not tonight, it isn't. Bring the tray in, Charlie.'

The boys went straight up to the blazing fire and held their hands out to the warmth, and then Charlie turned to face his mother. 'What's happened, Mum?'

'Sit down and I'll tell you. Something extraordinary happened today.' She then told them about the visit from Lord Grant. 'So the first thing I did was order coal and have it delivered right away, then I went shopping and bought food we have not been able to afford before. I must add a note of caution,' she said, when she saw their faces alight with excitement. 'We must be careful until I see how this is going to work out, but I wanted us to have a treat tonight. I still have a little left over for Joe to put in the tin for another day.'

Charlie leant forward, hands on knees. 'Let us assume Lord Grant will continue to support you, and with me and Helen working in decent jobs, what are your plans for the future, Mum?'

'I think we should save as much as we can, and then in the new year, if things are still going well, we might be in a better position to move. But we mustn't forget that I am going to divorce your father, and that could get unpleasant if he tries to oppose me. So, let us enjoy this step forward, and deal with any problems as they arise.'

Joe had a broad grin on his face. 'Can I tell Granny, or is it a secret?'

'Lord Grant told me he has been trying to get Parliament to do something about the slums, so he intends to use my efforts as an example of what can be done to help some of those in deprived areas. He is passionate about it, so there is no way it is going to be a secret. Of course you can tell Granny.'

Jane arrived at the hut early on Monday to give her time to prepare for the morning's lessons. She had only been there a few minutes when there was a commotion outside, a thump on the door and a face peered in.

'We've got a delivery for the teacher. Is this the right place?'

'Yes, it is. Bring it in, please.' She watched in astonishment as two men brought in a bookcase, two desks, chairs and several large boxes. 'What's all this?'

'The items I promised you.' Lord Grant stood in the doorway and began to give the men orders to get everything unpacked.

'But the hut belongs to the church, My Lord.'

'Not any more. It is now yours, and I am building the church another Sunday school. We may have to extend this as the number of pupils increases.'

'Can you do that? It is still on church property.'

He smiled. 'Don't worry about that. I had a long talk with the vicar on Saturday, and we have come to a mutually beneficial arrangement.'

Jane sat down, not sure her legs would hold her any longer, and watched as the bookcase was filled with books, paper, pencils and many other items a school might need. The last item to be unpacked was a blackboard with chalk and a rubber to clean it. He had thought of everything.

When the workmen left, Lord Grant looked round with satisfaction. 'We can get another two desks in, I think. Is there anything else you need?'

'More pupils,' she said, slightly out of breath from shock.

'They will be coming quite soon. My campaign is already under way.' He perched on the edge of one of the desks. 'In view of what you told me the other day, do you have any objection to me using your name? I have been thinking it through and feel it would be of some advantage to let everyone know who you are.'

'I have also been giving that some thought, and if it will help you get something done about the slums, then you have my permission.'

He bowed his head in acknowledgement. 'That is gracious of you, and I am sure it will be a tremendous help. I also have another favour to ask, but please do not hesitate to refuse. I believe your story should be told. You come from a background of wealth and privilege to living in the slums. The culture shock must have been unimaginable, and yet you have survived and not lost your dignity. I have prepared a speech I would like to give to the House.' He handed her several pages written in a bold and confident hand. 'Would you read that and give me your opinion? If there is anything you object to, I will remove it.'

In the beginning the speech focused on the plight of those living in deprived areas. Then it went on to point out that one concerned lady was attempting to reach out and help those who lacked basic reading and writing skills. There was quite a long piece about her bringing up her children and educating them to a high standard so they had more of a chance in life. A slight smile appeared on her face at the final section and she couldn't resist reading it out loud. 'When you sit down in your warm homes and a table groaning with good food, give a thought to the many who have little or nothing to eat. One compassionate lady is helping a few while we wallow in comfort. We should be ashamed. I know I am and, therefore, I urge this House to do something about finding a way to improve the conditions and education for these people. After all, that is why we are here, is it not?'

Lord Grant chuckled when she finished. 'I think that speech would be more successful if you gave it instead of me.'

'Oh, I doubt they would listen to a mere woman but, hopefully, the day will come when women are no longer considered only good enough for the home and children.'

'I too hope that. It will eventually happen, I am sure, but not for a very long time.' He took the papers back from her and frowned. 'Your parents are bound to hear what you are doing. Does that concern you?'

'I have kept in the background in order not to embarrass them, but I can no longer do that. I have always wanted to see my children better themselves and leave poverty behind, and now they are older that time has arrived. My parents' feelings now come quite low down on my list of concerns.'

He slapped his hand against the side of the desk in anger. 'One day they will be proud to call you "Daughter" again.'

'Ah, but will I ever be able to be their daughter again? Not only did I marry a man they objected to, but I am now seeking a divorce, which they will consider scandalous.' She shook her head. 'I doubt very much they will ever acknowledge me again, and I am nothing like the young person I was all those years ago.'

'I don't suppose you are. You have had the privilege of seeing both sides of life.'

'Privilege?' She laughed. 'That is not how I would have considered it, but one thing is sure, if I had remained in that sheltered background, then I would now be very different.'

He stood up and bowed slightly. 'You can be proud of what you have become.'

'Thank you, Your Lordship, and I hope your speech shakes up the other members.'

'It might if they stay awake.'

They were laughing when the pupils arrived and glanced, hesitantly, at the posh man talking to their teacher.

'Gentlemen,' she said the moment they walked in. 'May I introduce Lord Grant. His Lordship has generously stepped in to help us, and we now have books and plenty of writing materials.'

'Thank you, sir.' Ted was the first one to speak.

Much to their surprise, Lord Grant stepped forward and shook their hands. 'My pleasure, and well done for seeking help. I shall be interested in your progress.'

He then bowed gracefully to Jane and walked out, leaving behind three stunned men.

Ted quickly shot out of the door, and returned shaking his head. 'That bloke's walking along the road as if he's in Park Lane. He's even stopping to talk to people. Don't he know he could be set upon for all that gold on his waistcoat? How'd he know what you were doing?' he asked Jane.

'My daughter is going to work as governess to their daughter, and during the interview with Lady Grant she told her how I was prepared to give lessons to anyone who needed help with reading and writing. It seems Lord Grant is a politician and is trying to get something done to improve conditions in deprived areas.'

'Really?' Pete didn't look as if he quite believed that.

'Some people do care,' she told him, 'but unfortunately not enough. Anyway, we can be grateful for his interest because we now have plenty of writing materials. Now, who has homework to show me?'

Two weeks later she had six pupils ranging from the ages of ten to thirty. For one reason or another they had all slipped through the net with regard to basic education. Lord Grant hadn't visited again, but she thought he must be doing something because people were coming to her from different areas now. Helen was settling in her new job and loving it. Lady Grant had given her an allowance to buy suitable clothes, and it was a joy to see her daughter smartly dressed. Both of her working children insisted on giving her most of their wages, only keeping what they needed for each day. When Charlie had spare time he would go to meet Andy, and they had become firm friends. With their unselfish generosity and the money from Lord Grant, their worries had eased considerably, but she wasn't being complacent. She was only too aware that things could change in an instant, but for the moment they were hopeful of a better future.

Later that afternoon Joe hurtled through the door. 'Mum, there are policemen everywhere down the end of the street.'

She had to lunge to grab hold of him before he disappeared again. 'Where are you going?'

'I want to see what's happening.'

They were outside the door now and she could see what he was so excited about. There were policemen by Fred Baker's house and an angry crowd had gathered to shout abuse at them. Her son was wriggling to get free, but she held on tightly. 'No, Joe, you mustn't go down there. It looks as if things are getting nasty and it's too dangerous, darling.'

He stopped struggling and gazed up at her. 'Looks like they're arresting Fred Baker for something. I'd better see if Granny's all right.'

'We'll both check on her.'

Joe knocked on the door, opened it and called out as he always did. 'It's me, Granny.'

When there was no reply they went in, but she wasn't in her chair. 'Check upstairs, Joe.'

He ran up and soon clattered down again, a worried expression on his face. 'She isn't there.'

'I expect she's slipped out for a moment. We'll come back later.'

He nodded and followed his mother back to their house, lingering outside for a moment to see what was happening at the other end of the street. Then he came in and sat at the scullery table. 'What do you think he's done, Mum?'

'I really don't know, but it is well known that he is a crook, so they were bound to catch him sometime.'

'There's loads of policemen down there so it must have been something bad.'

She nodded. 'I expect we shall find out soon enough.'

'Wonder where Granny's gone. If she needed shopping she knows I can get it for her after school.'

'She's probably visiting someone, and will be back soon. Will you peel the potatoes for me?'

He jumped down, always eager to help.

Half an hour later the police walked past their house with Baker in handcuffs, and an angry crowd following. Jane made sure the door was locked and the curtains drawn so no one could see inside. There was no telling how long it would take for that mob to calm down, or what they would do once the police left. They would probably go to the pub, get drunk and then run riot, causing all kinds of trouble. Without the protection of Bert in the house now, who was one of them, they were vulnerable, and incidents like this only made her more determined to get her family away from here.

Chapter Seventeen

'Dora, you promised me.' Ian paced up and down the office. 'You can't go back there. The police told us there was a mob trying to stop them arresting Baker and search his house. By the time they've been to the pub and have plenty of beer inside them, there's no telling what will happen.'

'I'll be all right until the trial begins, then I will move out, but I can't go back to my house. After what happened I don't think I could live there again.'

'Come and stay with me. You know it's only me and the housekeeper, so I have plenty of room.'

She shook her head. 'That's kind of you, but I'll stay where I am for as long as possible. How quickly can we sell my house and buy another one?'

'Are you absolutely sure that's what you want to do? That house must hold many happy memories for you.'

'Not any longer.' Her face clouded with sadness. 'I'll never forget the scene after that brute had broken in, and it would be a constant reminder if I lived there again. I can't go back, Ian, you must understand.'

'Of course I do.' He sat down and gave a tired smile. 'At least he's going to pay for his crimes this time. They found a room full of things he'd stolen, and many of them can be identified as belonging to you. We can't understand why he held on to them. If the police hadn't found anything they wouldn't have been able to arrest him.'

'Perhaps he knew the person he attacked had died so he was waiting for things to settle down before selling them.'

'I think that is probably the reason. You will be called as a witness. Does that worry you?'

'I'm not looking forward to the trial, but I'll do what has to be done to see that man punished. Now, I had better get back because young Joe will be wondering where I am.'

His sigh was one of resignation and he called Oscar into the office. 'We are both going to escort Mrs Jarvis back to Fallon Street.'

'That isn't necessary,' Dora protested, but when she saw Ian's expression, she relented. 'Very well, if you feel it is necessary.'

To be honest, she was glad of the company. The dark,

dingy street seemed menacing and the house even more squalid. They insisted on coming in with her to check no one was hiding in there.

They had hardly arrived when there was a knock on the door and two worried faces peered in.

'Are you all right, Granny?' Joe called, looking at the two men with concern as he edged in. 'Charlie's with me.'

'I'm fine. Come on in, boys, I want you to meet some friends of mine.'

Charlie towered over his younger brother now, having shot up over the last couple of months. He was a tall, strong lad, and she knew he had come to protect his brother in case there was trouble.

Joe looked up at them and smiled, then held his hand out politely. 'We're pleased to meet friends of Granny, sirs. My name is Joe and this is my brother, Charlie.'

Ian was taken aback by this introduction and shook the boy's hand. Their mother had obviously done a wonderful job of bringing them up in such awful conditions. 'I'm Ian and this is Oscar.'

'It was kind of you to walk Granny home,' the youngster told them seriously. 'There's been trouble down the road and it isn't safe to be out tonight.'

'We are aware of that.' Ian turned to the elder brother. 'Will your family be all right? It could get rough when the pubs turn out.'

'We will lock the door, sir, and Mum said Mrs Jarvis can stay with us if she doesn't want to be alone.'

'That is very kind of her. You should do that, Dora.'

'Thank you, Charlie,' she replied. 'I would like to spend the evening with you.'

'Shall I make a pot of tea for your friends?' Joe asked her.

'That would be welcome. Please sit down everyone.' She looked pointedly at Ian. 'When we've had our tea you two had better be on your way before the pubs close. I don't want you around here then; it could be dangerous.'

Both men laughed and Ian said, 'We are supposed to be looking after you, not the other way round. I could stay here as well.'

She waved away the offer. 'We will be quite safe with Charlie to protect us.'

'That's right, sir. We've had plenty of trouble here and we know what to do. Mrs Jarvis will be all right with us.'

'I'm sure she will, and please thank your mother for being so thoughtful.'

'I will, sir.'

When Joe handed round the cups, Oscar took a sip and said, 'My goodness, this is a good cup of tea, Joe.'

He flashed his smile. 'Granny says I make the best tea she's ever tasted.'

They chatted for a while and when the men left the boys escorted Dora to their house.

'I could hardly believe I was listening to boys born and bred in the slums,' Oscar told Ian as they walked along the dark, foreboding street.

'Quite remarkable, isn't it? From what Dora told me, their mother has brought them up to be gentlemen in the hope of giving them a better chance in life.'

'I understand her reasoning, but they don't fit in here and can't have many friends. The young ruffians from this area probably make fun of the way they speak and behave.'

'No doubt, but it doesn't appear to bother them.'

Oscar peered into the darkness, keeping a sharp look out for any trouble, and shuddered. 'Lord, but this is a disgusting place, and once people find themselves living like this it must be nigh impossible to get out. Mrs Roberts might want better for her children, but what chance do they have?'

'Sadly, not much, but with luck and help from others, she might find a way.'

'She's a nice lady.'

Ian nodded and, seeing the lights ahead of them they lengthened their strides, eager to get away from the dingy area.

They smiled at each other when they reached the street lit with gas lamps, and nodded to a policeman walking his beat.

'Evening, gentlemen.'

'Good evening, Constable,' they replied.

It took another twenty minutes to reach the office and Ian unlocked the door. 'Come in for a moment, Oscar. I could do with a drink.'

'That's an excellent idea.'

* * *

Later that night there was a lot of shouting when the men staggered out of the pub, but nothing worse than they had heard many times, and by eleven o'clock all was quiet.

Jane had insisted that the boys go to bed at their usual times, leaving the two women downstairs, and Dora saw this as a good opportunity to let Jane know she would be moving quite soon. 'Please don't tell Joe yet. I will let him know when I have found somewhere else to live.'

'He will be disappointed, but I expect you'll be pleased to get away from here. Have you any idea where you are going?'

Dora shook her head. 'Not yet, but now Baker has been arrested I can't stay.'

'Oh.' Jane was puzzled. 'What has he got to do with you moving?'

'Everything. However, I won't tell you yet because it's better you don't know the details at the moment. Your family has been the one bright thing about living here. I consider you my friends and I hope we can keep in touch.'

'Of course we can. Joe will insist we do.'

'Ah, that dear boy. When I came here I was distraught and consumed with anger, but he helped me to see that there was still good in this world.'

'I agree. No matter how worried I am, when he smiles at me I feel as if everything is going to be all right.'

'It will be, my dear. You probably don't know it yet, but you have friends who are looking out for you. I suspect you feel as if you are fighting this battle on your own, but you are not.'

'In the beginning I did feel like that. When Bert left, taking what little money I had, I was frightened, but my children made me see this was an opportunity and not a disaster. Then that kind solicitor, Mr Preston, agreed to help me with a divorce, even though I could only offer him a small amount of money, which he refused to take at that time, and then along came Lord Grant to support my teaching. And we have met you, so I'm aware luck has been on my side up to now, and I feel as if I am surrounded by friends.'

'Luck has nothing to do with it. You're a giver, like Joe, and what you give comes back to you in abundance.'

'That's what the nuns used to tell us, but I'm not sure we believed it.'

'You went to a convent school?'

'My father moved around a lot and I went to quite a few, but one of them was a convent school. It was very good, and I think I was happier there than at some of the others.'

Dora studied her intently. 'From the little you have been prepared to talk about, I can see you don't belong here.'

'Neither do you.'

'True.' She laughed quietly. 'In that case we had better see about returning to our rightful places.'

'That isn't going to be easy for me, but I have every intention of doing so, if at all possible.'

'That's what I like to hear.' Dora stood up. 'It doesn't seem as if there is going to be trouble tonight, so it's time I returned to my house. Thank you for inviting me to stay with you, Jane, I have enjoyed talking to you. Remember, you are to call me if you need anything at all. We might both be in our wrong places, but we can at least help each other through the rough times.'

'That's a comfort. Sleep well, Dora.'

Dora went to the office and was pleased to see Culver there. 'What are you doing about Jane Roberts' divorce?' she demanded the moment she saw him. 'She has to be free from that man, so for heaven's sake get a move on.'

He held up his hands in surrender, grinning. 'And it's good to see you as well, Dora. Ian and I are discussing that very case now.'

'Well, stop discussing and do something. That divorce is hanging over her head, and she won't be able to move on until it's granted.'

'If.'

It was her turn to laugh. 'When have you ever lost a case?'

'Not often,' he replied with a satisfied smirk, 'but you know the courts favour the man.'

'Then it is your job to convince them otherwise. That is what you are being paid for.'

He raised his eyebrows at Ian. 'Am I being paid?'

'Not a penny.'

'You get her that divorce and I'll pay you.'

'That isn't necessary, Dora. I've agreed to take the case gratis, and I intend to have that court crying in their beer. I promise.' He was thoughtful for a moment. 'You all appear to be very fond of the lady. I'd better have a talk with her to see what is so compelling about her.'

'Yes, you should.'

'I can't waste my time chatting when there is so much work to be done, however diverting the conversation.' He stood up, shook hands with Ian and kissed Dora's hand, his eyes glinting with amusement. 'Have no fear, for I will excel even my most impressive performance in the case of Jane Roberts.'

When he'd gone, Dora chuckled. 'He's a cocky sod, isn't he?'

'I see you have picked up some of the local language since you've been living in Fallon Street, but I do agree with you. However, he is the best, and Jane stands more chance with him representing her.'

'That's true, and you must have been very persuasive for him to agree. It isn't his kind of case.'

'No, but Fred Baker is. That's the main reason he was here today.'

She gasped. 'He's not going to defend, is he?'

'He wouldn't defend a man who has caused you such grief. No, he's the prosecutor, and that man won't get away this time. With you testifying, the case against him is solid and our barrister friend can't wait to get in court. It's some time since I've seen him so excited.'

'That's a relief.' She let out a huge sigh of relief. 'I can now start to look to the future. A lonely one, unless . . .'

'Unless what?'

'Never mind, it's just an idea of mine. Would you have time to help me sell my house and find another?'

'I'll always find time to help you, Dora, you know that. Alfred was my friend and I want to see justice done as much as you. What are you looking for, and where?'

'Somewhere away from the heart of London, but not too far out. The house doesn't have to be large, but I would need three bedrooms and a good sized garden – overlooking the river would be pleasant.'

'What about somewhere like Putney or Mortlake? I could find out if there is anything suitable in those areas.'

'That sounds perfect.'

'Leave it with me. How much do you want for your house in Kennington?'

'I want that settled quickly, so get what you can for it.'

'I know it's none of my business, but are you all right for money? Houses by the river could be expensive.'

'Thank you for your concern, but Alfred left me well provided for. I can afford a fine house.'

'In that case, I'll get on it straight away. I'll only relax when you have moved out of that slum.'

Her smile was tinged with sadness. 'Surprisingly, it will be hard for me to leave. I went there full of rage and grief, thinking there was only evil in the city, and do you know what I found? Kindness and gentleness from a young boy, and friendship from his family. I don't regret my time there at all. I accomplished what I set out to do, and it has turned out to be a blessing.'

Chapter Eighteen

In the weeks since Bert had abandoned them their lives had changed for the better. Helen and Charlie had jobs they loved, and had both insisted on contributing to the everyday expenses like rent and food. And although she hadn't seen Lord Grant again, he had sent a servant to enquire whether there was anything she needed and an envelope with the promised money for this month. He had also engaged men to enlarge the hut and instal a wood-burning stove, so they were warm now the weather was cold. He had also fulfilled his promise to the vicar and was building a new Sunday school for him which would be far superior to the one he had before, so the church was delighted with the agreement.

She gazed at the pupils with their heads bent over

their lessons, and smiled to herself. There were eight now, and it made her so happy to see their progress and growing confidence.

Preparing lessons for their various needs was keeping her busy, and Ted had taken it upon himself to be her helper, which she appreciated. He came in early each day and made sure the fire was alight and everything ready, and now they had the stove they could make a hot drink halfway through the lesson.

What a difference to the time she would sit here on her own hoping someone would come along. Lord Grant's visit had changed all that, and she often wondered how his speech was received. Did they stay awake? she thought with amusement.

When she arrived home, there was a letter waiting for her and she opened it quickly, knowing who it was from. Mr Preston requested her presence for a meeting the next day at two o'clock. It was a very formal letter, not giving any indication as to why he wanted to see her. It could only be for one of two reasons, she guessed. Either to tell her there wasn't a chance of obtaining a divorce, or they were going ahead with the case and needed more information from her. She fervently hoped it was the latter.

She was at the office on time and the young man, Oscar, showed her immediately to Mr Preston's office. When she walked in, two men stood up, much to her surprise. She hadn't expected anyone else to be there.

Ian shook her hand. 'Thank you for coming. May I introduce Barrister Culver.'

A barrister? Another surprise, but she held her composure and smiled while shaking his hand. 'I am delighted to meet you, sir.'

'The pleasure is all mine.' He held a chair for her. 'Please sit down.'

She sat and waited, but before anything could be said, Oscar wheeled in a trolley with refreshments, and then took a seat slightly away from them with a notepad in his hands.

Ian poured the tea himself and handed it round, then sat behind his desk. 'We have been fortunate to obtain the services of Mr Culver who has agreed to take your case.'

Jane almost gasped, but managed to stifle it. She couldn't afford a barrister.

'With him you will stand a much better chance of obtaining a divorce,' Ian continued. 'You don't need to be concerned about the cost of his service because he has agreed to represent you free of charge.'

Now she was stunned, and looked the barrister straight in the eyes. 'I do not wish to appear ungrateful, sir, but why would you do that? I am sure a man of your standing does not take on divorce cases.'

'You are quite right, I don't, but Ian is a friend and he was very persuasive.' He smiled and leant forward. 'However, when he told me about your circumstances, it caught my interest. The more I looked into it, the more I wanted to help you.'

'Do you believe a mere woman can win against male prejudice?' she asked bluntly.

'Oh, you underestimate yourself. From what I have learnt you are no mere woman, and together we will get you that divorce.'

She studied him carefully. This man was very sure of himself, and there was an aura of power about him, but she doubted his motives. What was he doing wasting his time with something like this? What was in it for him?

His smile widened. 'I can see you have doubts about me. I'll lay my cards on the table, shall I?'

'Please.'

'Very well. Briefly, you were brought up in wealth and privilege, but after making an unfortunate marriage found yourself in the slums, but being a well-brought-up girl you stuck by the man, bearing him three children. Now he has deserted you for another woman, leaving you penniless. That is one hell of a story, and I need to know how much of it you will allow me to use in court.'

'You may use anything that will get me the divorce, Mr Culver,' she replied without hesitation.

'Does that include your family name of Tremain?'

'If you feel it is necessary.'

He slapped his knee in delight and turned to Ian. 'You're right. She has courage.'

'You do realise that this could get unpleasant?' Ian looked concerned. 'With such a story, the newspapers are bound to get hold of it, and we don't know how your husband will react to a public case with a noted barrister representing you.'

'Whatever storm this unleashes I will ride it out. You have engaged Mr Culver on my behalf, believing it will give me the best chance of success, and I trust you, Mr Preston. My greatest concern is for my youngest son. The two eldest are working and my husband can't touch them, but Joe is only eight years old, and I want him protected at all costs from his father.'

'If he tries anything, then let me know and I'll see he has no right to the child.'

'Thank you, sir.'

'Now, I know only a part of your story, and I would like you to tell me about yourself. It is always helpful if I have a complete picture, even if the information is not necessary to the case. Oscar will make a record of what you say, and you have my assurance that this will not go outside this office until the divorce proceedings. I may need to use some of it, or none of it then. Do you understand?'

Jane nodded and took a deep breath. 'Where shall I start?'

'From the time you were born. I need to know everything, because I don't like surprises thrown at me in court.'

Painful as it was, she made herself turn her thoughts back, and slowly go through her life. She did, however, hold back a few details, believing such information had no bearing on the case. It took about an hour, and she was drained by the time she had finished.

The two men looked grim, and Ian handed her a small

glass of brandy. 'Drink that, it will make you feel better.'

She sipped gratefully. That had been very hard.

The barrister finally spoke. 'My dear lady, we have got to get you out of this mess and back where you belong.' He stood up. 'I have work to do. Send me the transcript when it is ready, Ian.'

'You will have it by the end of the day.'

Culver bowed to Jane, and kissed her hand. 'I am proud to be representing you.' Then he strode out.

'Are you all right?' Ian asked after Oscar had left the room as well.

'Not really, but I will be if I can sit quietly for a moment.'

'Take your time.' He gave a wry smile. 'Our barrister friend is rather overpowering, but he is the best. Once he gets his teeth into something like this he never lets go. You can trust him, Mrs Roberts.'

'After pouring out my life story to you, I think you should call me by my first name.'

'Thank you, Jane, and please use my first name as well. Now, you sit there while I have a word with Oscar. Then I will walk you home.'

He insisted on escorting her right to the door, and she was surprised when Joe ran out of Dora's. She hadn't realised so much time had passed.

The boy skidded to a halt and smiled up at Ian. 'Hello, sir. Have you come to see Granny again?'

'I have walked your mother home, but I will go in and see her while I'm here.'

'She'd like that.' He turned to his mother and hugged her. 'You weren't in when I came home so I went to Granny. She didn't mind.'

'That was kind of her.' Jane gave her son a puzzled frown. 'Do you know Mr Preston?'

'Oh yes. He's a friend of Granny's.'

'That's right.' Dora came out of her house and smiled at Ian. 'I think we have some explaining to do. Jane looks completely confused.'

'That's hardly surprising. We have just had a meeting with Culver,' he told her.

Dora tipped her head back and laughed. 'That's enough to scramble anyone's wits. Come in and Joe will make us all a nice cup of tea.'

The youngster tore off to carry out his task, and Jane allowed herself to be led into the house, thinking that this was turning out to be a very strange day.

When they were all settled, Dora asked Jane, 'What did you think of our esteemed barrister?'

'Knows what he wants and will stop at nothing to get it.'

'You've summed him up perfectly, but if you want the best legal help possible, then you go to him. He gets results, doesn't he, Ian?'

'Without a doubt.' He smiled kindly at Jane. 'Have you quite recovered from the meeting yet?'

'Not really. I'm thoroughly confused. How do you know Dora? Is she one of your clients?'

His chuckle was deep and amused. 'No, she's my boss.'

'Pardon?'

'I'm not,' Dora declared, her eyes shining with amusement. 'You run the firm and I don't interfere. Well, not much.'

'You own fifty-five per cent of the business, so you are technically the head of the firm.'

'Not any more. After Alfred died, I transferred ten per cent of that over to you.'

He turned sharply to face her. 'Why didn't you tell me?'

'I was saving it as a surprise Christmas present, but now I'll have to get you something else.'

'Dora, you shouldn't have done that.'

'Nonsense, you deserve it, and I haven't been much use to you since that man broke into our house and changed my life completely. It is what Alfred intended to do, but didn't have time to change his will before he died after Baker's attack.'

Jane gasped and looked from one to the other. 'Excuse me, I know it's none of my business, but I don't understand what is going on.'

'I'm sorry, my dear. The firm of solicitors you happened to engage was founded by my late husband, Alfred Jarvis. A few years after that, Ian joined him and they changed the name to J & P Solicitors, wanting to keep it simple so it didn't frighten people from asking for help. My husband always believed that the law was for everyone, not only those with money, as I expect Ian told you.'

Jane nodded.

'Some months ago, my husband became ill and had to retire, and with rest he was improving, though still weak. I stayed by his side, only going out when necessary, but one afternoon I was at the office when someone broke into our house and treated Alfred so roughly that he died two days later. Before he died, he had a lucid time when he was able to tell me he believed the man was Fred Baker. He had seen him at court once, and he never forgot a face or a name. The police had hauled Baker before a judge on several occasions, and he walked free every time. They were naturally reluctant to arrest him again without solid proof he had committed the crime. They only had my word that Alfred had identified him, you see.' She wiped moisture from her eyes, and then continued. 'I was consumed with grief, and furious they couldn't do anything about him, so much against Ian's wishes I moved in here, determined to find the necessary proof. It wasn't going to be easy, and I knew it could be a waste of time, but we had some luck. When Baker came looking for your husband, I saw he was wearing Alfred's ring. There was no mistaking it because I had had it specially made to celebrate our tenth wedding anniversary, and he never took it off from that moment. It was missing when I found my husband, along with other items of jewellery. We gave the police this information and they moved in. He is now in prison awaiting trial.'

'Oh, Dora, I'm so sorry.' Jane had listened to the story with mounting horror, and was lost for words. What could you say to someone who had endured such pain and loss?

Joe was sitting on a stool in front of Dora and, sensing her distress had taken hold of her hands, gazing up at her with compassion. This was a rare quality in one so young, but he had always been sensitive to the emotions of those he loved. 'He'll go to prison now, Granny.'

She smiled down at him, the affection between them mutual. 'Yes, he will, Joe, and that is where he belongs so he can't hurt anyone else.'

'What will you do now?' Jane asked.

Ian took over the conversation. 'Dora will be called to give evidence at the trial, so it will no longer be safe for her to remain here.'

'Are you leaving?' Joe's expression showed that news upset him.

'I will have to, but I will expect you to come and visit me a lot. When I have found somewhere suitable to live, I would like you all to visit as often as you can.'

'We would like that, wouldn't we, Joe?'

He nodded at his mother, looking happier at that prospect. 'Where are you going to live?'

'I don't know yet, but I thought a nice house in a quieter area, and perhaps by the river.'

'That sounds lovely.'

'It does, and when you come to see me, we can have a boat ride. Do you think you would like that?'

'Oh yes. I've never been on a boat.' Joe was smiling happily now.

'We will have to put that right then, because everyone should go on the river.' Dora reached across and grasped

Jane's arm. 'When I am settled, perhaps I could help you with your pupils. I've had a good education, and will need something to do other than pester Ian,' she teased.

'Please do let her help you,' he joked, making them all laugh.

'I would be glad of any help you can give, of course.'

Dora became serious again. 'I am aware it is going to be a wrench leaving here. You have become like family to me, and I don't want us to lose contact.'

'You won't,' Jane assured her. 'My son would never allow us to do that. You are his granny, so we are family now.'

'Thank you, that means a great deal to me. Once Baker is in prison and your divorce comes through, we can all start a new life.'

'I look forward to that, but we mustn't forget that the next few months are going to be hard, for both of us.'

Dora gave a wry smile. 'Yes, but we can handle it, can't we?'

'Without a doubt.'

Chapter Nineteen

Pulling the drapes aside to let in the light, Dora turned and looked around the room, her gaze resting on the chair her husband always sat in. She hadn't been back here since that terrible day, but had known it was something that had to be faced before she could move on with her life. Her eyes filled with tears and she brushed them away quickly. 'Stop that, you silly old fool,' she told herself sternly. 'Alfred wouldn't want you to keep on grieving, making yourself unhappy.'

As she wandered from room to room it was almost as if he was following her and saying, 'This was always a happy home, so make it one again.'

She nodded. The modest house in Kennington had been their first and only home. They had intended to move to a larger place as the children arrived, but that had, sadly, never happened, so they had stayed in the house they loved. Now someone else needed to love it and be as happy here as they had been.

Halfway down the stairs she stopped and looked back at the four doors on the landing. There were three bedrooms and one bathroom, which Albert had had modernised to the latest plumbing a year before he had died. She could just imagine what delight such facilities would cause.

Hurrying down the stairs there was a smile on her face. Yes, she would see it was a happy home again. Pausing by her husband's chair she straightened the cushions. *I'll see there is laughter in this house again, my darling*, she promised silently.

There was a variety of transport in London at this time, but she preferred the horse-drawn cab to the train or omnibus. It didn't take her long to find one, and she was soon on her way to the office, hoping Ian was there.

He was and greeted her warmly when she walked in.

'I have just come from the house, and hope you haven't promised it to a buyer yet,' she said the moment she arrived.

'I've had a couple of enquiries, but nothing definite. Why, are you going back there?'

'No, but I don't want it sold to strangers, after all, because I have had a better idea.' She gave him rather an embarrassed glance. 'I've been talking to Alfred and he wants it to be a happy home again.'

'I see.' He kept a serious expression, trying very hard to keep his smile at bay. 'And did Alfred tell you how to go about this?'

'He did. I'm going to offer it to a nice family I know.'

'Ah, and might I know this family?'

'Guess.'

'The Robertses.'

'Right first time.' Dora sat down. 'I can't leave them in that awful place.'

He settled behind his desk. 'Have you thought how they are going to be able to pay the rent?'

'I'm not going to rent it to them, they can buy it. The repayments will be the same as they are paying now for that hovel.'

'Dora, Jane is an intelligent woman and will know that is ridiculous for such a lovely house. She will never agree to those terms.'

'Then we will have to convince her.'

'We?'

'Of course.' She smiled smugly. 'Ask Oscar to put the kettle on. I'm parched.'

Shaking his head in bewilderment, he stood up and went to the other office. When he returned he sat down again with a resigned expression on his face. 'All right, what are your plans?'

'First, I must find myself another house, and we haven't got much time. Baker's trial starts in early January, so I want to be out of Fallon Street by then. Have you found anything suitable yet?'

He pulled a couple of leaflets from his desk drawer and handed them to her. 'There are two in Mortlake you can have a look at.'

After studying them for a moment she pushed one back to him. 'This could be worth a visit. It's right on the river and not too large. Can you spare the time to come with me now?'

He glanced at the clock and nodded. 'Oscar can handle the next appointment.'

The young man found them a cab and they were soon on their way. It was a cold but bright day and it felt good to be doing something positive again, she realised. It was almost as if she had been living in a bad dream since Alfred had died, the only thought in her mind had been to do everything in her power to see Baker punished. That short time at Fallon Street had been difficult, and if it hadn't been for that lovely boy, Joe, and his family, she didn't know how she would have survived. They had given back her sense of perspective by showing that no matter how awful the conditions, there was still good to be found in the most unlikely places. It had caused her sleepless nights knowing she would be leaving them in that dreadful place. Now she had the solution, and all they needed to do was convince Jane to take over the Kennington house. She knew well enough by now that wasn't going to be easy. That family would work for anything they needed, and the slightest hint of charity would be refused – politely, there was no doubt.

The traffic was chaotic, but once out of the busy area the road cleared and they made good time.

Arriving without an appointment it was doubtful whether they would be able to see inside, but fortunately the owner was there and was pleased to let them inspect the property, inside and out.

When they had seen everything, Dora stood outside and watched the River Thames. It was soothing and she sighed contentedly, relaxed for the first time in months.

'What do you think?' Ian came and stood beside her. 'Do you want to have a look at the other one while we are here?'

'No reason to look at anything else. I could be happy here, and still get to the heart of London easily. Let's have a talk with the owner.'

An hour later they got back in the cab and smiled at each other.

'You are a fine negotiator,' she told him. 'We got that for a reasonable price.'

'It was easy. He needed a quick sale because he's going to live with his daughter. I'll get someone to clean and paint the place, and then you can move in. I can also have the paperwork settled in a couple of days.'

'How long will the redecorating take?'

'A week at the most.'

'Splendid. All we have got to do now is move Jane and her family to Kennington.'

'Ah,' was all he said.

When they arrived back, Oscar handed Ian a

newspaper. 'Something you ought to see, sir. I've marked the article.'

'Thanks.' Ian took the paper and opened the office door for Dora.

When she sat down and gave a deep sigh, he asked, 'Tired?'

'It has been an unsettling time and I have forgotten how to relax. Also, my legs haven't been too good since I fell.'

'Once you are in your new home you will feel better. The sound of the river can be relaxing, I am told.'

'I'm looking forward to it, but I will only be really content when Baker's trial is over and he is in prison. I must know that my family are safe, as well, and then I can start to put this distressing business behind me.'

'Family?'

'The Robertses, of course. Joe calls me "Granny", so I have adopted all of them. What's in that paper Oscar found so interesting?' she asked, seeing it still on his desk, unread.

Ian picked it up then and began to read, and after a few moments he whistled softly through his teeth. 'Oh damn. This could cause trouble.'

'Let me see.' Dora took the paper from his hands, read it and then looked up, rather puzzled. 'It's a very good article about Jane's effort to help people from the slums to read and write. Why are you concerned?'

'If her husband should see that, he could become difficult and oppose the divorce.'

'He can't read.'

'Someone could read it to him.'

'I suppose they could.' Dora was silent for a while, and then nodded. 'We have to get them out of that place. Bert Roberts has too many friends around there who could also become nasty. I'll take them to the house on Sunday afternoon. Are you free to come with us?'

'Yes, of course. Let's hope that between us we can convince them to move there. I doubt it will be easy, though, because Jane knows there's no way they can afford to buy it from you.'

'They can with an extended loan for twenty years.'

'And where is the loan coming from? You know in their precarious situation no one will advance them money.'

Dora sighed. 'Ian, they don't have to get a loan. I've already explained they can pay me a monthly amount until the price of the house has been paid.'

He gave her an exasperated look. 'And you think you are going to live for another twenty years?'

'Of course not, but I'll change my will. Once I'm gone the house will be Jane's without further payment.'

He shook his head. 'You'll never get Jane to agree to that. She expects to pay her way in life. When I said she didn't have to pay me more than she could afford for the divorce, she offered to come and clean the offices until the fee was settled.'

'I know, but I believe she can be persuaded to do what is the best for her family.'

At that moment the door opened, and Oscar looked in. 'Mr Culver is here to see you, sir.'

'You don't need to announce me.' The barrister strode in carrying a newspaper. 'Have you seen Lord Grant's article?'

'We have,' they both answered.

He sat down and stretched out his legs, a smile tugging at the corners of his mouth. 'This is good. We'll be able to use this to our advantage. With someone of such high standing praising her, it will show she isn't just an ordinary housewife from the slums trying to get rid of her husband.'

'It could also make her husband take notice and fight the case,' Ian pointed out.

Culver waved away the concern. 'I'll deal with him if he does. That man's chances are diminishing by the day. Will you let the dear lady know we shall probably be using this?'

'I'll do that.'

'Good.' He stood up. 'Roberts will be receiving notification of the divorce on Monday. This is going to be fun.'

They watched him leave, and Dora murmured under her breath, 'I'm sure Jane won't think of it as fun.'

Ian was reading the article again. 'I hope Lord Grant told Jane he was going to do this. It will certainly come to the notice of the family who disowned her. I wonder what they will think.'

'I hope they are bloody well ashamed of themselves.'

He gazed up at the woman sitting opposite him. 'The sooner we get you out of Fallon Street, the better. Much longer there and you'll have a cockney accent to go with the bad language.'

She was chuckling as he helped her out of the chair. 'Come on, I'll walk you home, and then see Jane to let her know Culver's plans.'

When they arrived and knocked on the door it was opened by Jane, who smiled in welcome when she saw them.

'Can we talk to you for a moment?' Ian asked. 'We have news for you.'

'Of course, please come in.'

It didn't take long to let her read the newspaper article and tell her what Culver intended to do.

'If you have any objections, then tell me now and I'll make sure our barrister friend behaves himself.'

Dora snorted at that remark. 'No one can do that, Ian, not even me.'

'It's all right,' Jane told them. 'I gave Lord Grant permission to do this if it would help his campaign, and if Mr Culver thinks it will aid in the divorce, then he can go ahead. I am well aware things could get rough, but I am prepared for that.' She gave Ian a steady look. 'I have never expected this to be easy or pleasant, but I must be free of this marriage now.'

'Your parents are bound to see this article, as well,' he pointed out. 'How do you think they will react?'

Jane gave a slight shrug. 'They will probably deny I am anything to do with them, but I can't worry about that any more. I have my children to care for, and they come first.'

'Quite right,' Dora declared. 'Now, I want you all, including Helen, to come with us on Sunday afternoon because we need to show you something.'

'That sounds intriguing. What would that be?'

'You'll have to wait and see,' Dora teased.

'As it happens, Helen will be free that day.'

'Perfect. We will collect you at two o'clock, then.' Without giving Jane a chance to refuse, she took Ian's arm and led him quickly out of the house, calling back, 'See you on Sunday.'

Chapter Twenty

'Where are we going?' Joe asked.

'I don't know. It's a surprise.' Jane ushered her children out of the house where Dora and Ian were waiting.

There were two cabs at the end of the road, and the luxury caused much excitement as Charlie and Helen got in one with Ian, and Jane, Dora and Joe got in the other one.

Joe leant forward to watch where they were going as they began their journey. After a few moments he wriggled back to sit properly and gazed at Dora. He was clearly bursting with questions. 'I've never been in one of these before, Granny.'

'Do you like it?'

He nodded and ran his hands over the plush seat. 'It's

very comfortable and the horses are lovely. Er . . . are we going far?'

'No, but it's too far to walk, and Ian and I wanted to make this a special treat for everyone.'

'He's a kind man,' the youngster noted.

'Yes, and he's also a good friend.'

The view outside was hard to resist and he edged forward again so he could look out, exclaiming at the things he saw.

Jane watched her son with a lump in her throat. He would be nine in March of next year, and he'd seen very little of London, let alone anywhere else, while at that age she was moving around all the time. She felt Dora touch her arm to draw her attention.

'He's enjoying this.'

'Yes, and I wish you would tell me what this is all about.'

'You'll soon see. I want to show you something, and I asked Ian to come along because I hope we are going to need his expertise regarding the legal application of what I have in mind.'

'Now I'm even more intrigued.'

Dora smiled. 'All will soon be revealed, so just sit back and enjoy the ride. We've asked the drivers to take a scenic route.'

When they came to a halt and got out of the cabs, they gazed at the building in front of them.

'What a charming house,' Helen declared, 'and in a nice area of Kennington.'

'I'm glad you like it.' Dora led the way and opened the front door, urging them all inside. 'I want you all to have a look around, inspect all the rooms and tell me what you think of it.'

'Are you buying this?' Charlie asked.

'No, I already own this house. Go on, all of you, and explore.'

Helen took hold of her mother's arm. 'Let's look at the kitchen first.'

The boys ran upstairs and they could hear whoops of delight about something. Charlie suddenly appeared and looked over the banister. 'Mum, Helen, you've got to have a look at this. There's a bathroom up here and the plumbing is fantastic.'

'Trust Charlie to notice that.' Helen laughed, as they made their way up to join the boys.

With the inspection finished they returned to the lounge to find Dora and Ian waiting for them with pots of tea and a feast of luxury cakes.

The youngsters were too busy eating to ask questions, but Helen was looking thoughtful, and turned her attention to Dora. 'You said this house was yours, so are you moving back here now?'

'No, I won't be living here again. My husband and I bought this house just after we were married. We planned for it to be only temporary until the children arrived, but sadly they never did, so there was no need for a larger house. We loved this place and they were happy years.' She sighed. 'I want this to be a happy home again for a family who would care for it.'

'Are you going to rent or sell it?' Jane asked.

'Sell, to the right person, of course.'

'Well, you won't have a shortage of prospective buyers. It is a really lovely house.'

'I have already decided who I want to live here.' She looked Jane straight in the eyes. 'I want you and your family to have this house.'

There was a shocked silence for a moment before Jane recovered enough to speak. 'Dora, you know I could never afford to buy this. We have enough trouble finding the rent for that hovel we live in now.'

'I've considered that and have a solution. Ian will draw up an agreement where you pay me ten shillings a month over the next twenty years, and then the house will be paid for.'

Ian watched carefully, and could see Jane working this out in her head. He had already warned Dora she would never accept a proposal like that.

She was shaking her head. 'That amounts to around a hundred and twenty pounds. This house is worth a lot more than that. You can't do that. It's beautiful and standing on a sizeable plot of land.'

'I don't need the money, and I want you to have it. It would make me so happy to know you and the boys were here caring for the home Alfred and I were so happy in.'

Jane straightened up. 'I understand what you are saying, Dora, but I can't possibly accept such a proposal. You have had a hard, emotional time, and as much as I would love to live here, I couldn't take advantage of that. It wouldn't be right, so please do take time to think again.'

'I don't need to think again. My mind is made up, and I know what I am doing.'

'I couldn't accept for many reasons. Suppose I couldn't keep up the payments? A house like this is well beyond our means.' Jane gazed around the elegant room. 'And if by some miracle we could afford it, how on earth would I furnish it? Our belongings are meagre, and I certainly couldn't bring what few pieces of shabby furniture we have into this lovely house. No, it just wouldn't be possible, but I am touched by your generous offer.'

'Let's deal with those points, shall we? If you fall behind with the payment it would just take you longer to pay off the amount agreed. And the furniture comes with the house. I will only be taking some of the smaller items.'

'Dora, that is even worse. You are practically giving us the house and contents, at a considerable financial loss to yourself. I would not be happy about that.'

There was silence for a while, and Dora glanced at Ian, clearly disappointed with the refusal. He raised his eyebrows as much as to say, 'I told you so'. A way to get this family living here had to be found. Eventually she turned back to Jane. 'All right, I know you don't like that idea, but there is another way. I will rent you the house and contents for the same amount each month. If you fall behind with the rent at any time you will still be secure because you will never be turned out. All you will need to do is come to Ian or myself and we will give you time to get through whatever the crisis might be. Is that proposal more acceptable to you?'

'Take it,' Helen urged her mother quietly.

Jane stood up suddenly. 'I'm going into the garden.'

Helen went to follow her mother, but Dora caught hold of her arm. 'She needs to be alone for a moment.'

'Yes, of course.' She sat down again.

The boys hadn't said a word while this had been discussed, but Joe couldn't contain himself any longer. 'Are we going to live here, Granny?'

'That is up to your mother.'

'It's what she has always wanted.' Charlie glanced at his sister. 'We must convince her we can afford it.'

'The problem is your mother is well aware of the value of this property, and she is reluctant to accept such a generous offer in case Dora regrets it later,' Ian explained.

'Which I will not. Ian, I have done all I can, now you go and talk to her.'

'I will see what I can do.'

He found Jane at the end of the substantial garden with her hands resting on an apple tree, head bowed. Approaching quietly, he stood behind her and said her name. He saw her take a deep breath before turning to face him, and when he saw the tears running freely down her face, he wanted to take her in his arms and comfort her, but of course he couldn't do that. She was still a married woman.

'What am I to do?'

'That is your decision, and no one is going to pressure you into doing something you feel is wrong. Before you decide, let me tell you more about Dora. She lived here with her husband all their married life, and they were very happy together. When Alfred had a heart attack she came to the office regularly to help with the work. On one of those days she returned home to a horrific scene.'

Jane nodded. 'That was when Fred Baker broke in.'

'It was, and as you know, Alfred died shortly after. Without him as a witness the police did not have enough evidence to arrest and charge Baker with the crime. Dora was distraught and determined to do something about it herself. Much against my advice, she found out where he lived and moved into the same street, posing as an elderly lady down on her luck. She was so grief-stricken I couldn't reason with her, and honestly I feared for her well-being. Then she met your delightful, caring boy, and the rest of you. I saw her begin to heal. Meeting you and your family was her salvation, and for that we will always be grateful.' He handed Jane a clean handkerchief to wipe her face, and smiled gently. 'The desire to see you in this house is her way of repaying your kindness. Joe has always called her "Granny", and as she doesn't have a family of her own, she has adopted yours. This house means a lot to her, and she wants people she loves to live in it.'

The tears had begun to flow again, and she turned away. When she faced him again she was composed. 'I value your opinion. What do you think I should do? I don't want to upset Dora, but this is a huge step to take for me, and I would hate to think I was taking advantage of her grief.'

'I know this is a silly question, but would you like to live here?'

'Oh yes.'

'If the thought of being offered it at too low a price troubles you, then accept it as a rented property. That will remove your concern that sometime she will regret letting the house go for such a low price, as it will still be hers. The terms will be drawn up legally, so you will never be in danger of losing your home, no matter what your situation. You can trust Dora, and you can trust me.'

'I would certainly feel easier with such an arrangement.' She gazed around the garden. 'Joe would love playing out here, and I'd be a fool to turn Dora's generous offer down. It was such a shock that I couldn't seem to take it in at first. I needed this moment to clear my mind.'

Ian gave a silent sigh of relief. He wanted this lovely woman and her family to be safe and happy. 'If you have decided, then I think we should get out of the cold and go in and let everyone know the good news.'

'Yes, they must be anxious to know.' She placed a hand through his arm and smiled up at him. 'Thank you. I bless the day I walked into your office.'

'As do I.'

When they returned, all eyes fixed anxiously on Jane. She walked over to Dora, bent over and kissed her cheek. 'I will rent this lovely house from you, and I accept your generous gift with gratitude and love.'

The room erupted in celebration and Joe began running around to hug everyone.

'Bring out the champagne, Ian,' Dora called to him above the noise and laughter. Then she walked over to him and whispered quietly in his ear. 'Well done.'

They all toasted a happy future with the champagne, and even the boys had a little drop.

Giggling at the bubbles, Joe pushed his brother. 'Chase you to pick the best bedroom.'

They tore up the stairs, shouting and shoving each other and could be heard laughing as they sorted out who was going to sleep where.

Dora had a tear in her eyes as she listened and smiled at Jane. 'Thank you, my dear. I am so happy to hear that laughter, and so would Alfred have been. He would thoroughly approve of you living in this house. Ian will make sure everything is done legally.'

'Yes, he has explained.'

'Good. Now, when I move to my new home in Mortlake, I will take the few things I need, then have this house cleaned and decorated. You should be able to move in after Christmas.'

'You don't need to go to that expense. I can do it myself.'

'No, my dear, you are busy enough with your pupils

and family. I want you to move in with it in good order.'

'There is no point in arguing with her,' Ian pointed out. 'Goodness knows I have tried hard enough to do so over the years, but once her mind is made up you will not succeed.'

Dora laughed. 'There is a man who knows me. But you must agree, Ian, that the house needs some attention. With Alfred being so ill, everything has been neglected, including the garden.'

'You are right, of course, and while we are at it, I think we had better have someone look at the roof. I saw a couple of loose slates up there.'

The boys tumbled down the stairs and Joe rushed up to his mother. 'We've picked one each and left the big room for you.'

'That is very kind of you, but what about your sister? Where is she going to sleep when she comes to visit?'

Joe thought about that for a moment. 'She can have my room and I'll go in with Charlie. There's loads of room.'

'Darn it,' Charlie explained. 'And I thought I was finally going to get rid of him.'

Joe launched himself at his big brother, clambering on him as he sat in the chair. 'You know you like me. Admit it!'

'All right, I admit it. You're the best brother anyone could have,' he said as he tried to dislodge him.

'Behave yourselves, boys,' Jane called. 'This isn't your home just yet.'

With that reprimand order was restored and Helen

stood up, motioning to her brothers. 'Let's have a look at the garden.'

She winked at her mother as she led the boys away.

'I'm sorry about that, but they can get a bit boisterous when they are excited.'

Dora held up her hands, smiling happily. 'No need for apologies. It does my heart good to hear laughter and see the happiness on their faces. Helen didn't say much, but I can see she is pleased.'

'Helen is what I would call a thinker. Everything is considered very carefully before any action is taken. She is a steady influence and we all look to her when we need advice or help. She was the one who made us face up to that difficult time when my husband left us. Her sound common sense made us see that it could be turned to our advantage. And she was right.'

'If you don't mind me saying, Jane, but considering who their father is, you have three bright and sensible children.'

'I count that a very great blessing. Bert never took an interest in them, and complained constantly when they were babies and cried. Their upbringing was left entirely up to me.'

'You've done an excellent job under dreadful conditions. Now,' Dora turned to Ian, 'I believe you have papers for us to sign.'

He opened a bureau drawer and took out the documents.

'You have them prepared already?' Jane exclaimed.

'I wanted everything settled today,' Dora explained. 'A small change from buying to renting must be made, but Ian will do that, and we will all sign the alteration.'

'But I might have refused.'

'Then we would have had to destroy them, but I had no intention of letting you refuse.' She gave an impish smile. 'Anyway, I was sure reason would prevail and you would see the offer was too good to turn down. I need you to have this house, and then once Baker is in prison, I shall be happy, and able to make a new life for myself. In all the grief and loss I have found something very precious – a kindness that asks nothing in return. Now, read that and sign it, so we can all start a new life.'

She read it with care, as Ian had instructed, then took the pen he was holding out for her and signed it in the appropriate places, watching as Dora and Ian added their signatures to the document. With the business finished she could hardly believe how much her life was changing in such a short time.

'These are now yours.' Dora handed her the keys.

'But the agreement states that I don't start paying until the first of January.'

'That is so, but you have access to the house the moment you signed.'

Jane ran a hand over her eyes. 'I don't know what to say. "Thank you" seems so inadequate.'

'Thank you will do nicely. Ah, the children are returning from their inspection of the garden.'

Joe ran up to Dora, his cheeks glowing from the cold. 'I like your garden. It's ever so big.'

'I'm pleased you like it, but it's your garden now. The

house has just been signed over to your mother, and you will be able to live here after Christmas.'

He glanced at his mother, and when she held up the keys he jumped up and down in excitement, and then clearly decided this momentous news deserved another hug for everyone. No one was left out, and when he reached Ian he was lifted up and swung around, giving a squeal of delight.

Helen and Charlie were more subdued as usual, but were smiling and clearly happy with the arrangement. As she watched, it became apparent that her youngest son needed a man in his life, someone who would talk to him and show affection.

Helen came and sat beside her mother, speaking softly. 'Joe likes him, doesn't he?'

'Joe likes almost everyone, but yes, he does seem drawn to him. You and Charlie were always self-sufficient and in control, but he was different from the moment he was born. He needs love, affection and friendship in his life.' She sighed. 'We have always been thought of as different, and I know it has been hard for all of you to make friends in such a rough area. There has been so much lacking in your lives, and I've tried very hard to give you what I could.'

'We know that and love you for it, but it is now time to think about yourself and leave the past behind.'

'I won't be able to do that until I have been granted the divorce, but we have all taken huge steps forward since he left.'

'I told you it would be for the best, didn't I?'

'I remember, but what is happening is beyond my wildest dreams. Did you ever imagine that you and Charlie would be in good jobs, I would gain the support of Lord Grant for my teaching, and we would be offered a lovely house like this to live in?'

Helen shook her head. 'Not for a moment.'

'Mum.' Joe towed Ian over to her. 'Mr Preston said he'd show me how to grow things we can eat. Nothing will grow until the weather gets warmer, though. When it does, he said he'd dig me a vegetable patch, if you don't mind. Can he, Mum?'

She saw her son's animated face and smiled up at Ian. 'That is very kind of you, and if you can spare the time, we would like that very much.'

'My pleasure.' He took hold of Joe's hand. 'Come on, young man, let's go and pick a spot and decide what we are going to grow.'

They disappeared with the young boy chatting away in his usual manner.

Chapter Twenty-One

Ian had been urging the men to finish the work on the Mortlake house. It had taken longer than expected due to some unexpected work that needed doing. The same was happening at Kennington, and that must also be finished before the weather turned to snow and ice, then work would come to a stop. But at least this one was finally ready for Dora to move into. He was watching the men pack up and breathed a sigh of relief as Oscar came and stood beside him.

'I closed the office early to come and see if I could help. Hope that was all right?'

'That's fine. They've just finished, and with Baker's trial starting on Monday we have got to get Dora out of Fallon Street today. Once word gets around that she is testifying against him she won't be safe.' The anxiety he was feeling showed on his face. 'I tried to persuade her to stay in a hotel until this was ready, but I was wasting my breath, as usual.'

Oscar smirked. 'I can imagine. What about the items she wants from her old house?'

'I've already dealt with that. Now all we have to do is move her out of that slum. Come on, Oscar, I will need all the help I can get.'

When they arrived, Dora went to put the kettle on to make them tea, but Ian stopped her. 'There isn't time for that. Gather your possessions together because the house is ready and you are moving in now.'

'What, this minute?'

'Yes, and don't argue, Dora. Once Baker's mates find out what you're doing, this place won't be safe for you.'

'I don't like leaving Joe and his family here. Can't we move them now as well?'

'The Kennington house is a shambles at the moment because we found that the hall floor has to be replaced, and half the roof is missing. I'm pushing the workmen as hard as I can, but the wet weather doesn't help for the outside work.'

Dora made a sound of exasperation. 'Why the blazes did they have to bring Baker's trial forward?'

'That was Culver's doing. He believes that getting him in court quickly will give them a better chance of success. The man is evidently furious and shouting abuse at everyone, and if he does that at his trial it will show what a violent person he is. Our barrister friend knows what he's doing.'

She sighed. 'I suppose so. It's put us in a rush, though. Still, it will be a blessing to get that out of the way.'

'Without a doubt.' Ian saw how concerned she was and smiled kindly. 'Oscar's here to help, so what do you want to take from here?'

'Not much, but I must let Jane know I am leaving.'

When they walked in, Joe was thrilled to see them. Helen was there as well, and when Oscar was introduced to her, he couldn't take his eyes off her, clearly liking what he saw.

'We've come to let you know I am leaving right now. Baker's trial has been moved forward and begins on Monday. Ian insists it isn't safe for me to stay here any longer.'

'He's quite right, and sensible to do it while it's dark,' Jane agreed. 'Can we help you?'

'No thanks, my dear. I'm only taking some of the smaller items with me and Ian has a cab due to take me to Mortlake.' She glanced down at Joe, the excitement wiped from his face at the thought of his granny moving. 'I want you all to come and spend Christmas Day with me. Will you be able to come as well, Helen?'

'Lord and Lady Grant are going to the country to stay with friends, so I shall be free.'

'That's wonderful. Please do come. Hopefully Baker's trial will be over by then and we can have a lovely time together.'

'I'll come and collect you, and we can all go together,' Ian suggested.

Jane glanced quickly at her children who were all nodding, especially Joe. 'Thank you, we would love to come.'

'Splendid. I shall look forward to us all being together. I must insist that you don't bring anything with you,' she added sternly. 'This will be my present to you for being so kind while I have been here.'

'You have already shown your gratitude by renting us your Kennington house – at a ridiculously low price,' Jane pointed out.

Dora waved her hand in dismissal. 'You are doing me a favour. I couldn't let strangers live there because Alfred would have objected.'

They all laughed, as she had intended.

'Well, we certainly can't have that.' Jane ushered them out of the cramped scullery and into the other room. 'Please stay and have a cup of tea with us.'

'I'll help.' Joe leapt into action. 'I know just how Granny likes her tea.'

Dora sat in a chair by the fire and looked at Ian, nodding slightly towards Oscar who was talking to Helen.

He raised an eyebrow to let her know he had noticed, and then stood up. 'I'll go and help Jane bring in the tea.'

When he left the room, Dora turned her attention to Charlie. 'Do you like working for the railway?'

'I love it, and I'm learning a lot. They are already letting me work on the engines.'

'That's good. If you do well, it could set you up for life. It is giving people a chance to travel, and many have never been able to do that before. It is something that is here to stay and will keep on growing until it covers the entire country. That is exciting, isn't it?'

He nodded enthusiastically. 'With training I am hoping to become an engineer one day.'

'I'm sure you will. Ah, here comes our tea.'

Soon after that the cab arrived, and they watched the few precious possessions Dora had brought with her being tied securely on the top. They waved, sad to see her go, but they knew she couldn't stay now the trial was imminent.

Back inside they washed the cups. Nothing matched, and Jane couldn't help remembering the fine china her mother always used. It had only ever been the best for the Tremains, and she had no doubt that was still the same. It was a shame their daughter hadn't lived up to their high ideals, she thought as she dried a chipped cup.

Dora was quiet on the journey to Mortlake, and Ian touched her arm in sympathy. 'They will be all right. I won't let anything happen to them, and they will soon be out of there as well.'

'I know I should be rejoicing. I have achieved what I set out to do when I moved to Fallon Street. Baker is going to trial for his crimes and I have found a good family to take over the house we both loved.'

'But?'

She sighed. 'I have a feeling of foreboding I can't shake off, as if trouble is lurking round the corner ready to pounce. I need you and Oscar to keep a watch out for any trouble, and help them if it is needed.'

'We will, Mrs Jarvis,' Oscar replied immediately.

'You can rely on us to step in if they need assistance for anything.'

'I know.' She squeezed Ian's arm and gave a weary smile.

They reached the new house, and by the time everything was unloaded and in place, Dora was so weary in body and mind, she hardly had the strength to climb the stairs. Fortunately, she slept well in her new home.

The next morning she went outside and, despite the cold, gazed at the river and found it comforting. She was going to miss her usual Sunday services at the little church with Joe insisting on seeing her safely there, though. Once settled she would find another church to attend. Strength was what she had to have to get through the next week or two. This was something she could do for Alfred. He had devoted his life to the law, and it was unthinkable that it would not be brought against the brute that had made him suffer. She would see it through, no matter how unpleasant. Once Baker was found guilty – and Culver was certain he would be – then Alfred could rest in peace, and she could get on with her life. A life she had once believed was going to be lonely, but not any more. She had found friendship from Jane and her lovely family in that dreadful place. That was a blessing.

* * *

When Jane arrived at the hut on Monday, she found more pupils waiting for her. She now had twelve in the class, and realised that if any more came she was going to need help. However, Ted had taken it upon himself to help her in any way he could. He was doing so well, and she was immensely proud of him.

'Have you thought about finding a permanent job?' she asked him. 'Your reading and writing skills are improving all the time.'

'I've been looking, but I don't want to stop my lessons just yet.' He gave a boyish grin. 'I'm picking up casual work and earning enough to keep me going, but I want to wait until I can find work I will enjoy.'

'Any idea what you would like to do?'

'Not really.'

'My eldest son has a job with the railways and loves it. Why don't you think of something like that? There are all kinds of jobs going, and the prospects are good as they keep expanding.'

'Thanks, Mrs Roberts, I'll think about it. Where is your son working?'

'Victoria Station – the Great Western Railway, but there's London Bridge and others as well.'

He nodded, glanced at the clock and took his seat in class.

Jane studied the pupils in front of her. 'If any of you have concerns, or need advice about anything at all, do come to me and I will talk to you privately, if that is what you wish.'

It wasn't until later that day that she had time to

wonder how Dora was getting on, and if she had been called to testify against Baker yet.

The next day she had her answer. Charlie was telling her about his day when shouting could be heard and breaking glass. The boys were immediately on their feet, but she managed to stop them from running outside to see what was happening. Rushing to the front door she locked it, blew out the candle and pulled the curtains aside just enough to see out.

'What is it?' Charlie asked.

'There's a crowd outside Dora's old place. They are kicking in the door and breaking the windows. Thank goodness she's no longer there. Ian was right when he said she had to move.'

Charlie joined her at the window and peered out, then stepped back and closed the curtains. 'Better push the table against the door, Mum, just in case they decide to run amok. No one will be safe if they do.'

'The police will come,' Joe declared confidently.

'Let's hope so.'

They sat in the dark listening to the destruction going on, and waited. The mob had obviously got inside now and were wrecking the place, making the rickety structure of their house shake. It was some time before they heard police whistles blowing and the sound of running feet as the men tried to get away.

When the commotion had died away there was a sharp knock on their door. Jane quickly lit the candles again and called out, 'Who is there?'

'Police.'

Charlie moved the table and opened the door a little.

'We're checking to see if you are all right,' the constable told them.

Jane stepped into view and opened the door wider, and before she could speak her youngest son had slipped in front of her.

'Did you catch them, sir?' he asked.

'Most of them, son.' The man smiled at him, and then turned his attention to Jane. 'They've done a lot of damage. Do you know who is living there?'

'No one. Mrs Jarvis moved out at the weekend.'

'Ah, that's all right, then, only the place ain't fit for anyone to live in now.'

Jane gave a dry laugh. 'These places are not fit to live in anyway, Officer, but the people round here haven't any choice. It's either this or the workhouse.'

He looked startled at her genteel accent, but said nothing. She was used to that kind of reaction.

'Ah, yes, well, I just wanted to check you haven't been harmed.'

'No, all the drunken anger was on the one house. Thank you for coming to check, though.'

'Just doing our job, madam.' He turned to go and then looked back. 'If I were you, I'd keep your door bolted.'

'We will.'

'Good thing Mrs Jarvis moved when she did,' Charlie declared when the policeman had gone and the street was quiet. 'They must have found out she is giving evidence against Baker at his trial.' He gave a quiet laugh. 'When she came here, we thought she was an elderly woman down on her luck. Then we find out she has that lovely house, and wants us to have it. Now she's involved in the trial of a villain like Fred Baker. That's quite a story.'

She looked at her sons' faces flushed with excitement. 'Get the cups out, Joe. We need a hot drink before going to bed.'

Chapter Twenty-Two

Ian studied Dora, a worried frown on his face. She shouldn't have to face this ordeal after all she had been through, but her determination to see justice done for her husband was holding her together. However, today was going to be the hardest because she faced cross-examination by the defence, and he wished he could save her this as he knew how brutal it could be. The evidence against Baker was solid, but the defence would try every trick in the book to get him released.

'Culver is tearing Baker to shreds,' Dora commented, as she waited to be called. 'If he wasn't such a nasty brute, I could almost feel sorry for him.'

'He's doing a good job, and with luck it could be over soon.'

'I didn't expect him to try for a murder charge, though. Alfred died two days later.'

'That's true, but if he can prove his death was due to the treatment he received at the hands of Baker, he might be successful. The thought of the hangman's noose has panicked Baker, so I expect that is our barrister friend's intention.'

Dora nodded and glanced at the clock. 'They are taking their time about it this morning.'

He turned the conversation round to business in the hope of taking her mind off what was waiting for her in that courtroom. 'Oscar and I are spending a lot of time out of the office, and with our workload increasing we need another solicitor. I have taken the liberty of speaking with Howard Chapman. You know him.'

'Ah, yes, he's a good solicitor. Would he be interested?'

'The firm he's been working with for over ten years closed down, and being in his fifties it's difficult to find another position. He's very experienced, and shares our sympathy for those in deprived circumstances. He would jump at the chance to work with us, so do you agree we should ask him to join us?'

'Yes, he would fit in very well. Contact him with an offer.'

'I've already discussed terms with him, and he's quite happy to accept. Howard badly wants the chance to start working again.' He motioned Oscar over who was talking to someone across the passage. 'Run and tell Mr Chapman he has a job with us, and could he come as soon as possible, please.'

'Yes, sir.' Oscar smiled. 'It will be good to have him with us. He's a friend of my father's,' he told Dora. 'You won't regret your decision.'

'I know we won't.'

He hurried away, and they could hear his rapid footsteps on the marble floor, eager to tell his father's friend the good news.

'It won't be long before Oscar sits his final exams. Will he pass?'

'Without a doubt, and he will be a great asset to the firm.'

Dora nodded. 'We were fortunate to find such a fine young man. However, you are going to need someone to replace him.'

'I'm aware of that, but let us get through this first, and then we can think about reorganising the business.'

The time passed, two, three hours, and she was still waiting to be called. Yesterday had been easy, but she knew this session would be hard as she faced the defence counsel for Baker. Ian had slipped in to see what was happening, and she looked up anxiously when he returned.

'It's chaos in there. Baker is terrified and shouting abuse. They have had to take him out for a while to calm him down, and that is the cause of the delay. He's back now, so it shouldn't be much longer.'

Ten minutes later she walked into the court, and on the way to the witness stand she glanced at Fred Baker, and saw a terrified man in fear for his life. To her, at that moment, it was justice enough, and she hoped he would just be facing a lengthy stay in prison, instead of the death penalty.

The questions came quickly, one after the other, and although it was an ordeal, she managed to keep her composure, speaking clearly and identifying the objects taken from her home.

When dismissed she was grateful to find Ian waiting at the back of the court, offering his arm to lead her out to a seat in the passage.

'Thank heavens that is over!' She let out a ragged sigh and looked at him. 'It is over, isn't it?'

Before he could answer, the courtroom door swung open and Culver strode out, a wide smile on his face. 'Dora, you were magnificent – the perfect witness. Thank you.'

More people were coming out now, and she watched, frowning. 'What's going on? Has the trial ended?'

'It has, and now we wait for the verdict.' Someone called his name and he went over to them, smiling and shaking hands.

'I would have thought it was early for congratulations,' she said to Ian, while studying the scene. 'I hope he isn't being too confident.'

'Culver's an expert at judging the mood of the court, and he has no doubt about the outcome. Baker will be convicted.'

'But what will he be convicted of?'

'Ah, for that we will have to wait and see.'

'How long will it take? Do we leave now and come back later?'

Culver swept back to them, having heard Dora's question. 'It won't take long. A guilty verdict is a foregone conclusion. I have ordered refreshments while we wait.'

'That would be welcome.' She allowed them to help her stand and they went to a private room where refreshments were already waiting for them.

It was a relief to get away from all the noise and bustle, and her hand shook a little as she took the cup handed to her.

The barrister sat down next to her. 'I am sorry I had to put you through such a lengthy ordeal, but your testimony was the final nail in his coffin – so to speak.'

She looked up sharply. 'Do you really believe that is going to be the sentence, if he's found guilty?'

He pursed his lips for a moment, as if giving it thought. 'I am certain he will be found guilty of his crimes, especially the one against you and Alfred, but what the sentence will be is anyone's guess.'

'You mean you don't know?' she teased, beginning to feel better.

'Not the faintest idea.' He laughed, then changed the subject. 'Ian, you briefly mentioned you were considering taking on Howard Chapman. I've worked with him many times. He has a fine legal mind and will be an asset to you.'

For the next hour they chatted about many things to help pass the time. Then there was a rap on the door and a man peered in. 'Sir, the verdict is in.'

Culver swept out of the room to return to court, and Dora was already on her feet, wondering what they should do.

Ian took her arm. 'We can slip in the back.'

They found seats and waited until the judge had taken his place, then Dora clasped her hands tightly together, forcing herself to breathe slowly. This was the culmination of months of anguish, and no matter how sure Culver was, she was afraid they might fail. She didn't believe she could survive that.

The turmoil inside her was so great she didn't hear what was being said. It wasn't until Ian grasped her hands, his face wreathed in a smile that she realised she had missed the verdict. 'What? What?'

'Guilty and sentenced to life imprisonment.'

Something seemed to shatter inside her, and for the first time since that dreadful day, silent tears ran down her face.

'Let's get you out of here, my dear.' Ian helped her up and led her out of the courtroom.

There were always cabs outside, so they had no difficulty finding one. On the way back to the office, Ian remained silent, knowing she didn't want to talk.

After a while she gave a shaky smile. 'I'm sorry, Ian, that was silly of me.'

'No, it wasn't. You've been through so much and it's quite understandable. Since Alfred died you have had only one thing on your mind, and that was to see the man responsible pay for his crime. You've achieved that, and now it's over.'

She laid her head back and closed her eyes. 'Yes, it's over and that brute will now spend years locked up. Years for him to reflect on the grief he has caused, and in my opinion that is a more just verdict than the death penalty.'

'I agree.'

'We should have stayed to thank Culver.'

'Don't worry about that. He'll understand and come to see us when he can get away from those wishing to congratulate him.'

She laughed then, and Ian smiled at her. 'Feeling better?'

Nodding, she straightened up and wiped the moisture from her face. 'Oscar will be anxious to know the verdict, and we must welcome Howard to the firm.'

They hadn't been back long when Culver swept in, champagne in hand. Oscar and an older man followed, and while Oscar introduced Howard Chapman to Dora, glasses were handed round. 'You should have been there,' the barrister was telling Howard. 'Dora was magnificent. She won my case for me.'

She coughed on a sip of champagne. 'What do you mean, your case? I went to live in the slums to get close to that man and find proof. You wouldn't have had a case without me,' she teased, then laughing she raised her glass to Howard. 'Welcome to the firm. Thank you for coming so soon, and that is the only time you will hear Culver giving anyone credit for winning a case for him.'

Culver kissed her cheek and refilled her glass. 'Don't take any notice of Dora, gentlemen, she's had a tough couple of days.'

'That I will not deny, but now it is over, and I shall expect you to concentrate on a certain divorce case. No hanging about.'

He raised an eyebrow. 'Madam, I never hang about. Notice has been sent to the husband, but we haven't had a reply from him yet.'

'He can't read or write.'

'So I believe, but someone should be able to read it for him. However, if there is no response within the next week, I will send someone to explain it to him.'

'Better make that two people capable of handling a difficult man.'

'Ah, like that, is it? In that case I might even go and read it to him myself.'

Ian smirked. 'That will really terrify him.'

'Never!' he declared. 'I'm as gentle as a kitten.'

'With very sharp claws,' Howard pointed out, clearly enjoying this banter.

'Of course. They are necessary for hunting.' He tipped the bottle up and found it empty. 'I should have brought a case of this stuff, but never mind, it was enough to toast our success and welcome my old friend, Howard, to this excellent firm.'

'Yes, indeed. You are greatly needed,' Dora told him. 'I am afraid I have taken up a lot of Ian's and Oscar's time, and they must be falling behind with their own work.'

'Your ordeal is over now.' Culver stood up and took Dora's hand, his expression serious for a change. 'You have put your own interests aside to see that man pay for what he did. Now you must move on with your life.'

'Easier said than done,' she admitted, 'but I've taken a few steps forward.'

'So Ian told me. I wish you much happiness and peace in your new home. Now, I must be on my way. I have an important divorce to deal with.'

He left them then, and Dora turned to Oscar. 'Would you find me a cab, please? I would like to go home now.'

'You must be very tired.'

'Yes, I am feeling quite drained, Ian. Will you do one more thing for me? Go and tell Jane what has happened.'

'I'll do that as soon as we close up for the night.'

'And I'll see you safely home,' Howard told her.

'Thank you both.' She let Howard help her out to the waiting cab. 'I will be pleased to have company.'

Once on their way, Dora sighed with relief. 'I'm glad that is over. For the last few months I have lived with a burning desire for revenge, and those feelings do not make for a tranquil life. I must say, though, that our barrister friend has been efficient and supportive.'

'I have always suspected that under that brash exterior there is a man who cares deeply,' Howard remarked. 'He usually only takes the most high-profile cases, so I was surprised to hear he is working on a divorce.'

'Not his usual line of work,' Dora agreed, 'but Ian managed to persuade him, and once he learnt the unusual nature of the case, he became enthusiastic.' She went on to tell him about Jane and her family.

He listened with great interest, and when she had finished, he said, 'Now I understand why he has taken it on. What an extraordinary lady.'

'Ever since she married that man she has been living in the slums but has not let her standards slip. Her three children speak beautifully, and she has seen they have had a high standard of education.' Dora smiled. 'Her youngest son is a treasure, and I can honestly say he saved my sanity when I moved to Fallon Street.'

'I look forward to meeting them sometime, and I would like to know more about the school she has set up.'

'I'll take you there one day, if you are interested.'

'Thank you. I would very much like to see how she is going about such a difficult task. Teaching adults to read and write cannot be easy.'

'I agree, but there is a great need for someone to care enough to try. The number of pupils is increasing, so I feel she will need help soon. I have also had a good education and I intend to help her when I can. I am going to need something useful to do, and I can't keep turning up at the office and disrupting things. You gentlemen are quite capable of running the business without me interfering,' she added with a smile.

They talked of many things during the journey, finding they had a lot in common.

When they arrived at the Mortlake house, Howard wouldn't come in, but just saw her safely inside and then left. It was only when she was alone, she realised just how exhausted she was, but it had all been worth it.

Justice had been done.

Chapter Twenty-Three

It was nearly seven o'clock when Ian reached Fallon Street, and when Jane opened the door to him there was a worried expression on her face.

'Is Dora all right?'

'She's tired after her appearance in court, but apart from that, she's fine. She asked me to come and let you know what has happened.'

She smiled then, and stepped back to allow him to enter.

'Mr Preston.' Joe immediately greeted him. 'Do you want a cup of tea? We've just made a fresh pot.'

'Thank you, that would be most welcome. It's a cold evening.' He slipped out of his coat and placed it over the banister before following Jane into the scullery. It was warm from the stove they had to keep burning for cooking and heating water, and the place was spotlessly clean. He couldn't help wondering how Jane managed to keep it like that. By sheer hard work, he guessed.

'I'll light the fire in the other room. It's more comfortable.'

'Please don't bother. This is fine.' He smiled at the boys who were gazing at him expectantly, waiting for news.

'If you're sure, then please sit down. We are anxious to know about the trial.'

He settled at the table, took a sip of his tea, and then gave them a brief outline of the court case.

Joe edged his chair closer to Ian, the usual smile missing. 'It was good you made Granny leave here. Men came and broke all the windows and kicked in the door. They messed up the place, and she would have been hurt if she had been there.'

'I know, but you needn't worry about her now because she is safely in her new house, and Baker will be in prison for a very long time.'

'Good,' Charlie declared. 'This street will be safer without him and his group of ruffians. The police caught a few of them, and I don't think those that got away will dare come around here again for a while.'

'You won't have to put up with this for much longer.' He sat back and smiled at Jane. 'The house will be ready for you after Christmas. Dora has insisted that the entire place be redecorated to remove any lingering signs of what happened when Baker broke in. You understand?'

'I do, but it wouldn't have mattered, as I would have been quite happy to do it all myself.'

'I know that, but there is also some structural work to be done, which we didn't find until the men began pulling the place apart. She wants everything to be new and fresh for you.'

'That is so kind of her, and I don't know how I can thank her enough. Getting my family out of the slums has been a dream of mine and, to be honest, at times it seemed impossible.'

'I have been told that sometimes dreams do come true if we wish hard enough.'

'Oh, I wished hard – very hard.' She laughed.

'There you are, then, that's what it takes.' He turned to the boys. 'How is the job going, Charlie?'

'Wonderful! I love it, and I'm being taught a lot about engines and the general running of the railways.'

'That will help you with getting promoted once you are older. What about you, Joe? Have you decided yet what you want to do?'

'Well, I thought I'd like to be a policeman because they help people.'

'A policeman? If you are interested in helping people, you could train to become a solicitor like me. We help people all the time.'

'Like you're helping Mum?'

'That's right.'

'Mum?' Joe swivelled round in his chair. 'Do you think that would be better than a policeman?'

'Much better, darling. As a policeman you would have to patrol the streets in all kinds of weather, and deal with some nasty people at times.'

'Hmm.' That information took a little thought, then he turned back to Ian. 'What would I have to do?'

'When you reach the age of thirteen you could come and work with me to be trained. It will mean a long period of study before you become qualified, but the work is interesting, and I believe you would enjoy it.'

They could almost see his mind working as he thought this through.

'I'm nearly nine. Will you wait for me to grow up?'

'Certainly. The day you reach thirteen you can come and work with me.'

'You mean it?'

'Absolutely, and I'll even put it in writing for you to keep.' Ian held out his hand. 'Is it a deal?'

The youngster smiled and shook his hand. 'It's a deal.'

'Splendid, I'll get the letter sent to you tomorrow.'

That was all Joe needed and his excitement erupted. He jumped off his chair and hugged everyone, including Ian, and then he laughingly pushed his brother. 'Now I've got a job, as well.'

Charlie dodged another exuberant shove. 'Not until you're thirteen and you don't go hugging your boss,' he teased.

'I don't know, I think it should be a mandatory requirement.' Ian joined in the fun.

'Mandatory? Mum, I don't know that word.'

'It means compulsory, darling. Something that must be done.'

'Oh, I see.' He sidled up to Ian. 'I like learning new words.'

'That's good, because there are lots of long words in the law books.'

He nodded. 'Will you tell me some of the things you do, please?'

Jane watched her two boys in deep discussion with this gentle man, and her insides clenched with regret at what they had been missing by having an uncaring father. Now they were older they needed a man to talk to. She'd done her best to fill that gap, but it wasn't enough. It was different with Helen. They had always been able to talk things through, growing to be more like friends than mother and daughter. But the boys needed a man they could talk to.

She was so lost in thought that the firm rap on the door made her jump, and she stared in astonishment when she opened it. She peered around Culver and saw a couple of unsavoury characters watching him with interest. Catching hold of his arm she pulled him in. 'Come in. You shouldn't be around here in the dark.'

'Don't be concerned. I can take care of myself, Jane. May I call you that?'

'Of course.'

Ian was on his feet, as surprised as she was to see the elegant barrister in Fallon Street. 'What on earth are you doing here, and dressed in your finest clothes? Couldn't you at least have put on an old coat?'

'I don't possess such an item.' He smiled at the boys who were studying him with interest. 'You must be Charlie and Joe.'

'Yes, sir,' they both replied.

Joe tipped his head back and looked up at him. 'How tall are you, sir?'

'Six feet two inches.'

'Wow. I thought Mr Preston was tall, but you're bigger than him.'

'Only by about two inches, I believe.' He turned to Jane. 'I hope you don't object to me calling on you, but I wanted to see where you live so I will have a clear picture of your circumstances when the time comes. Also, I have news.'

'You are welcome. Would you like tea? I'm afraid I don't have anything stronger.'

'Tea will be lovely, thank you.'

'Please sit down, sir.' Charlie held out a chair for him.

Jane filled the kettle and placed it on the stove, while the boys found enough cups for all of them.

'Have we got enough milk?' Charlie whispered.

'Just about, but I'll take mine black.'

'So will we,' Joe told her quietly.

'Thank you, that will help.'

With the tea made they all managed to squeeze round the scullery table. The place seemed small for such big men, but it was too late to light the fire in the other room, and there wouldn't have been enough seats for everyone in there, anyway.

'You said you had news,' she prompted.

Culver glanced uncertainly at the boys, and Jane said, 'You can talk openly in front of my children. They know I am going to divorce their father, and are quite happy about it.'

He nodded. 'Your husband was informed officially about your intention to seek a divorce. As he hadn't replied I decided not to wait any longer and went to see him myself. I read the notification to him and made sure he understood. He told me he knew because someone had read it to him, but he had thrown it away. I gave him another copy, and explained everything to him again.' He paused and held her gaze. 'I must tell you that he wasn't pleased, and that is putting it mildly. He threw words at me I had never heard, and my repertoire of bad language is extensive.'

'Is he going to make trouble?' Ian asked.

Culver sat back, his expression serious. 'I can't answer that, but I did warn him he would see the inside of a prison if he acted violently towards his wife and children. He is an unpleasant character – if you will excuse me saying so, Jane – so it behoves us all to be vigilant.'

'You are to come to me at the first sign of trouble,' Ian told her.

'I will, and thank you for your concern. It is probably all bluster on his part, though.'

'Let us hope so. However, as Ian has suggested, you

are to go to him with any problems, and he will let me know. I will deal with it if he steps out of line.'

'I am grateful to both of you for your kindness and consideration. Especially as I am not paying either of you,' she told them with a frown on her face.

'It is our pleasure,' Culver replied. 'We do not expect payment from our friends when they need help.'

That remark jolted her. Did they consider her a friend, or was he just being polite to make her feel better about the situation? It was hard to tell, but she was determined one day, somehow, to find some way to repay their kindness, even if it took her years to do it.

Culver had turned his attention to the boys. 'While I'm here, I would like to get to know your sons. Tell me about yourselves.'

Jane stood up and cleared the crockery from the table, leaving the four of them to talk – all men together. She wasn't a fool, and was well aware that the barrister had come here to warn her after meeting her husband. There had always been a lingering worry about how Bert would react when he knew about the divorce. She had hoped, of course, that he wouldn't make trouble by opposing it. Culver was a good judge of character, as he had to be in his line of work, so for him to come here was an ominous sign. A sign she would do well to heed.

There was a lot of laughter coming from the men around the table, and that brought a smile to her face, wiping away some of the concern. Soon they would be out of here and living in a nice house. She would be watchful, but was doubtful Bert would have the courage to go against that powerful man's warning.

Having convinced herself, she put the freshly washed crockery away, and sat down to enjoy the lively conversation. It was such a treat for her and the boys.

After a while, Culver stood up. 'I must be on my way. Thank you for a pleasant and entertaining visit, Jane.'

'I'll come with you.' Ian also stood up.

'I don't need protecting, my friend.'

'I'm not protecting you, it's the other way round,' he replied drily.

'In that case I will be glad of your company.'

They took their leave and walked away, laughing together.

'I liked him,' Joe told her, eyes shining with excitement. 'He told us what happens in a court of law. I definitely want to do something like that when I grow up.'

'Well, when you get that letter from Mr Preston, you must make sure you keep it in a safe place. Chances like that don't come along often.'

'I'll find a nice safe place in our new house. How do you become a barrister?'

'Only after years and years of studying the law, but a solicitor is just as important. They are usually the people you go to first with your problems.'

'It was kind of Mr Culver to come and see you,' Charlie said, and then smirked. 'Tough-looking man, isn't he? I believed him when he said he could look after himself. Only a fool would try to rob him.'

'He is an impressive man, I agree, and a very successful one, I understand.'

'As Fred Baker found out,' Charlie remarked. 'I was sorry to hear about Mrs Jarvis's husband. It took courage to move here to try and get evidence against him.'

'Granny will be happy now.' Joe nodded wisely.

'And so will we when the divorce is granted.'

Charlie chewed his bottom lip and looked at his mother. 'Do you think Dad will cause trouble?'

'I doubt it,' she told him brightly. 'Mr Culver was just doing his job by warning us about his meeting with your father.'

'You're probably right. After leaving us in a mess, I don't suppose he'd have the nerve to show his face here again. Unless he has a few pints inside him, of course,' Charlie added.

'I've dealt with him many times in that state, and I'm sure I can manage it again, if necessary.'

Charlie grinned. 'So we've heard. You only ever raised your voice when talking to him when he was drunk.'

'I had to. The drink seemed to make him deaf as well as incapable. I used to take that opportunity to go through his pockets and take any money he might have left.'

They all laughed at that memory. Although unpleasant at the time, knowing it was in the past made it seem funny.

Chapter Twenty-Four

'This arrived for you today.' Jane handed her youngest son the letter with his name on it when he returned home from school.

He stared at it in wonder. 'For me?'

'Yes, it is addressed to you. I expect it's from Mr Preston. He did say he was going to put your agreement in writing for you to keep.'

He read the letter carefully, and then he waved it at her. 'It is from Mr Preston. It says the firm of J & P will employ me to train as a solicitor when I'm thirteen, if I still want it at that time. It's signed by Granny as well as Oscar Strathern and Ian Preston. See, you can read their signatures quite clearly.'

Strathern? That was the first time she had heard

Oscar's surname. 'That is an official document and you must send a reply to let Mr Preston know you have received it, and to thank him.'

'I'll do that.' He folded the letter carefully and put it back in the envelope, looking thoughtful. 'Mum, he said he would employ me, so why doesn't it say that?'

'The firm has been quoted to cover all eventualities. It will be some time before you are old enough and there could be changes there by then. He obviously wants to make sure the agreement stands, even if for some reason he is no longer working there.'

'Oh, I hope he is, but it was kind of him to think of that.'

'He's a very kind man, and still young enough to be working there by the time you are ready to join them, so you don't have to worry about it.'

The door opened and Charlie walked in, earlier than expected. 'I've been given a bit of time off because we worked on Sunday,' he explained.

Joe waved his letter in front of him. 'Look what I've got. It's addressed to me – Mr Joseph Roberts,' he told his brother proudly, handing it to him. 'Be careful, don't make it dirty.'

After reading it, he patted Joe on the shoulder, a teasing smile on his face. 'You do realise that you will have to call Mr Preston "sir", when you work there, don't you?'

'Of course I do. I expect you call your boss "sir", don't you?'

'Yes, we show him the respect his position requires,

but they are quite friendly, though, and don't mind me asking lots of questions. When I apologised once, they told me it was all right because that was the way to learn.'

'I'll remember that. I'll put this in the tin under my bed after I've written the reply, as Mum told me. It will be safe there until we move, then I'll find somewhere else for it.'

'That's a good idea. How much money have we got in the tin, Joe?'

'There's enough for two weeks' rent, and two shillings and three pence spare,' he said without hesitation, taking the responsibility of keeping a record seriously.

'Will you bring me down sixpence, darling, because I am going to need that tomorrow.'

'All right.' He turned and ran up the stairs to get the money.

'No sign of Dad yet?' Charlie asked quietly.

'No, thank goodness. I think he took Mr Culver's warning seriously or we might have seen him by now. I think we can relax.'

'Hmm. I don't trust him. If he does come while I'm not here, promise me you will go straight to Mr Preston, as he told you to.'

'I promise.'

'And keep the door locked. I just walked in today, and he could do the same. Have you got a spare key I could have?'

She opened the drawer and took out the key Bert had thrown down before he left. 'You are right. I'll try to remember to keep the door locked at all times until we move.'

Charlie took a deep breath. 'I can't wait to get away from here. Do you know when the house will be ready?'

'I'm going there tomorrow, after class, so I'll find out then.'

She was just closing after the morning lessons for that week when Lord Grant's servant arrived. 'Lord Grant would like to see you, madam, right now, if that is possible.'

'Of course. Is he at home?'

'No, madam. I have the carriage waiting at the church gate to take you to him.'

The sight that greeted her was a surprise, but she managed to keep her expression dignified, instead of bursting into laughter, as she was tempted to do. Standing there was a magnificent black carriage, bearing the Grant coat of arms in gold. Two magnificent black horses were stamping, anxious to get moving.

She was helped in, and when the door closed she was alone in plush elegance. Running her hand over the dark gold velvet seat she allowed herself a wry smile. For the early part of her life this kind of luxury had been an everyday thing, but after being in the slums for many years it almost took her breath away, making her conscious of her shabby clothing.

The carriage moved off smoothly and she sat back to enjoy the ride. She had half expected the servant who had helped her in to join her, but he had taken a seat next to the driver. Considering his dress and manner, she guessed he wasn't a house servant, and could possibly be a secretary who helped Lord Grant with his parliamentary work.

It was a while before they reached their destination, and there was another shock awaiting her when she alighted from the carriage.

'If you will come with me, madam, I will take you to Lord Grant's office.'

'Thank you.' There was a temptation to exclaim in pleasure and stop to admire the beauty of Westminster Palace, but she managed to retain her composure.

They walked for a while, turning one way and another, until she had no idea where she was. It would be so easy to get lost.

Finally, the man stopped, rapped on a door, opened it and walked in. 'Your guest has arrived, Your Lordship.'

Lord Grant was immediately on his feet, smiling broadly and shaking her hand. 'Thank you for coming. I hope I haven't inconvenienced you.'

'Not at all, Lord Grant.' She gave an amused smile. 'I enjoyed the ride.'

Giving a deep chuckle he held out a chair for her. 'Please sit down.'

It was warm in there so she removed her coat, which was taken from her by the servant who was still in the room. Ah, she thought, as she watched him settle in the corner of the room, notebook in hand, she had been right. He was a secretary, not a servant.

'I will get straight to the point,' His Lordship declared. 'I am going to ask if you will do me a very great favour. I have arranged a meeting with a group of gentlemen who I am hoping will support my efforts to get something done about the conditions and education of those living in deprived areas. Any changes will, of course, take years to implement. More houses need to be built where land is available, and the slums demolished. Then there is education. That, I believe, is the key to helping people help themselves, and I know you understand that better than anyone.'

'It is a move in the right direction, but there is much more that needs to be done, as you have mentioned.'

'You are right, and what you are doing is only a very tiny step, but all great achievements have begun in that way. I believe that with your help we can take another step forward.'

'In what way can I help?' She had no idea where this was leading.

'I want you to come to the meeting and tell them what it is like to live in the slums, and explain why many cannot even read and write. Then explain your views on education and how it can help some people make a better life for themselves. An example or two would be helpful.'

This was the last thing she had expected and she was stunned for a moment. 'You are asking me to give a speech at your meeting?'

'Exactly.'

'But won't they be offended to have a woman give her views on such a subject?'

'Perhaps, but I'm sure it will be enough of a shock to keep them awake. Will you do this for all those unfortunate people who need someone to care about their plight? I believe you to be more than capable in convincing them that action is urgently needed – now, not tomorrow or the next day, but now!'

Taking a deep breath to control the excitement rising in her, and running the implications of this request through her mind, she paused for a few seconds. However, she already knew this was an opportunity not to be missed. All right, they might demand she leave the room and refuse to listen to her, but there was always the chance they couldn't defy a man as powerful as Lord Grant, and would listen to what she had to say. It was worth a try. She lifted her head. 'Thank you, Lord Grant. I am honoured to have been asked to do this. Would you like to see what I am going to say before the meeting?'

He was on his feet, eyes gleaming with pleasure. 'No, you are an intelligent, well-educated lady, and I have no doubt you will impress the gentlemen.'

She laughed. 'I wish I had your confidence, but we shall see. Will you tell them beforehand that a woman is going to talk to them?'

'No.' He smirked. 'I'll leave that as a surprise.'

'Where is the meeting to be held, and what time, please?'

'Here. Wednesday evening at seven o'clock.'

'That doesn't leave much time to prepare a speech, but I should be able to have it ready by then if I work on it over the weekend.'

'Excellent. I'll send a carriage for you.'

'He won't want to come down Fallon Street, so I'll meet him at the end of the road.'

'Nonsense,' he protested. 'My driver will go where I tell him.'

She didn't try to hide her amusement. 'There is one more thing I must point out. This is the only decent frock I have, and it is quite old. Will it offend your gentlemen to have a woman dressed in such a poor way?'

'Certainly not. They would pay little attention to a lady expensively dressed in the latest mode, and would immediately assume she didn't know what she was talking about. Your natural charm will overcome your simple outfit.'

'You are too gallant, and have mastered the art of flattery to perfection.' She stood up, sketched a curtsy she had learnt as a child and said jokingly, 'Ah, see, I haven't forgotten how to do it.'

They were both laughing and he bowed. 'Thank you for agreeing to do this for me. My driver is waiting to take you home.'

'Thank you, but I am going to Kennington now. I have to find a new school for my youngest son.'

'Why Kennington?'

'We are moving there after Christmas. Mrs Jarvis is letting us have her house at a price we can afford.'

'That is splendid.' He frowned. 'Where have I heard that name before?'

Jane then explained, briefly, about Baker's trial. 'So you see, she doesn't feel she can live there again, but wants someone who will make it a happy home once more.'

'That's right. I read about the trial. A sad business, but I am very happy for you and your family.'

'Thank you, My Lord. There is just one thing I haven't mentioned. May I bring my two sons with me? I don't want to leave them alone, and they are well behaved.'

'Of course. We can find something with which to keep them occupied while you address the gentlemen.'

'If they don't all leave the moment they see me,' she joked.

'Curiosity will keep them in their seats, I assure you.'

She held out her hand. 'I look forward to it, My Lord.'

'As do I.' He beckoned his secretary over. 'Tell the driver to take Mrs Tremain-Roberts wherever she wants to go, then wait and return her to her home.'

'That isn't necessary,' she protested. 'I can catch the omnibus.'

'I have taken up a deal of your time and won't hear of it.' He bowed his head. 'Until Wednesday.'

Knowing it was useless to refuse, she walked out with the secretary to the waiting carriage. The driver was given his instructions, and they were soon on their way. Jane's mind was already working on what she would say to the gentlemen, and couldn't help smiling. In her last year at school she had often been chosen to stand up before everyone and give speeches or announcements because of her clear voice that carried easily to the back of the room. She hoped she hadn't lost that skill. It was incredible to think that she was riding in luxury with an invitation to do something like that again. She could almost feel as if the past years hadn't happened, but of course they had, and had made her what she was today – someone who knew what it was like to live on both sides of society, and a mother with three lovely children. There were no regrets about that, and now it seemed as if she was on her way to giving them a better chance in life.

The carriage came to a stop and she was helped out in front of the Kennington house. 'Thank you. I'll be as quick as I can, because I have to get back before my son comes home from school.'

The house was full of workmen, and from what she could see, it was being transformed. Dora really meant it when she'd said they were to remove every sign of what had happened here. She was about to talk to one of the men when she heard her name called.

She turned. 'Ian, how lovely to see you.'

'I am checking to see that all is progressing smoothly.' He smiled. 'Want to have a look round?'

'I'd love to, but I can't stay. I wondered if any of the men know of a good school near here? It must be a free school, of course.'

'There's one about half a mile from here. Come outside and I'll give you instructions.'

When they walked outside, he stopped suddenly when he saw the waiting carriage.

'Do you like my transport?' she asked, trying not to burst into laughter at the stunned expression on his face.

'You came in that?'

She quickly explained about her meeting with Lord Grant, and the speech he had asked her to give.

He gazed at her with respect. 'What an opportunity,' he exclaimed. 'You are going to do it, aren't you?'

'Yes, but goodness knows what will happen. However, it's a challenge I couldn't refuse.'

'Oh, I wish I could be there. You must tell me all about it.'

'I will, but now I must hurry. I don't want Joe to come home and find the house empty. He hasn't got his granny to go to any more. Where is this school?'

'Follow this road and turn left at the end, then take the first right, and it's halfway down that road.'

'Thanks.'

'Good luck on Wednesday,' he called.

The school looked clean and well cared for, and the headmaster was easy to talk to. He told her Joe would be welcome there when they moved to the area, and she left, well pleased with her day.

Chapter Twenty-Five

The carriage that arrived for her was not the one emblazoned with the gold coat of arms, but the unadorned black one was still enough to cause interest in Fallon Street.

Jane and the boys settled inside, ignoring the rude remarks coming from some of the residents.

Joe was so excited he couldn't stop smiling. 'Tell me again where we're going, Mum.'

'Westminster Palace.'

'Does Queen Victoria live there?'

'No, darling. It's where the politicians govern the country.'

'Ooh, I can't wait to see it.'

She smiled at her eldest son, who was taking all of this with his usual calm manner.

'Are you nervous?' he asked.

'Yes, I am. Not about giving the talk, but how the gentlemen will react to a woman addressing them. They will either go to sleep or throw me out,' she joked.

'Or they will listen to you.'

'They might, but I think Lord Grant is taking a chance on his career as a politician by asking me to do this.'

'I'm sure he knows what he's doing. He obviously chose you because he believes it will help his cause to see reform. They'll be hanging on your every word, Mum. After all, you know what you are talking about.'

'Thank you, Charlie. That has settled my nerves somewhat.'

'Will we be able to hear you?' Joe asked.

'I don't know about that, darling, but we'll ask Lord Grant if it will be possible.'

The rest of the journey was quiet, and she was pleased because it gave her time to go over her speech one more time in her head. The written copy was with her, but she had been over and over it until she knew it by heart.

When the carriage came to a halt and the door opened to let them alight, the boys stared at the building in front of them.

'It looks so much bigger when you're up close,' Joe remarked.

The secretary came towards them and bowed politely. 'Please come with me. Lord Grant is waiting for you.'

'Who is that?' Charlie whispered, as they entered the building.

'His Lordship's secretary.'

They were taken to a small room, comfortably furnished, where their host was waiting to greet them. He rose to his feet and smiled broadly. 'Welcome. I trust the journey was pleasant. And these are your sons.'

'Yes, My Lord. May I introduce Charlie and Joe.'

'Thank you for allowing us to come, Lord Grant,' Charlie said and gave an elegant bow.

Joe was watching his brother and did the same.

'It is my pleasure to meet you.'

'Sir . . .' When Charlie nudged Joe, he quickly corrected himself. 'Lord Grant, would it be possible for us to see and hear our mother give her talk? We would be very quiet,' he assured him.

'Well, let me see.' He called his secretary over and pointed to a screen standing in the corner of the room. 'Do you think we could put that by the door and two chairs behind it?'

'Yes, My Lord, and it would not appear too out of place because there is an alcove to the side of the door.'

'Splendid. See to it, please.'

He picked up the screen and disappeared into the adjoining room, then came back for the chairs.

'Now, gentlemen, you will be able to hear what is going on, but not able to see. I must ask you not to move about or make a sound of any kind. Can you do that for me?'

'Yes,' they both answered together.

The secretary arrived again. 'Your guests have all arrived.'

'Everyone?'

'Yes, Your Lordship. No one has declined the invitation,' he said, the corners of his mouth twitching in amusement.

Lord Grant rubbed his hands together and laughed. 'Oh, this is going to be interesting. See the boys to their hiding place.'

Jane received a hug from both children, even Charlie, which showed how excited he was.

Lord Grant turned to Jane. 'Ready?'

'Looking forward to it.'

'As am I. Now, what will happen is this. I will go in first and warm them up, so to speak, then I will announce our speaker, not giving your name, then you enter. They won't know you are a woman until you come in.'

'Then there will be a stampede for the door,' she remarked, drily.

He gave a slight chuckle. 'No, I believe they will stay out of curiosity, and if they leave, they will miss out on the sumptuous meal I have promised them after the event.'

'Ah, bribery, that is clever thinking, My Lord.'

They were both laughing when the secretary appeared again. 'It is time, My Lord.'

Giving Jane an encouraging smile, he told her, 'You will be magnificent, I just know it.'

She watched him stride out, and stood by the door, which was left slightly open so she could hear what was being said. It didn't take her long to realise that he was an expert orator, and soon had the assembled gentlemen laughing and relaxed.

He touched briefly on the need for dealing with slum areas and helping the people who lived there. Then he told them he had asked someone to speak to them – someone who had first-hand knowledge of the deprived areas, and was wholly qualified to talk on the subject. He turned towards the door. 'Gentlemen, please welcome our special speaker for this evening.'

She stepped onto the small platform, smiling confidently, and ignoring the murmuring and shuffling of feet. 'Thank you, Lord Grant.' Then she turned to face the audience, her expression serious now. 'I am well aware of the honour bestowed upon me by being allowed to address such a distinguished audience.'

The muttering had already ceased, and they were all paying attention, waiting to hear what she had to say.

The transcript of the talk was on the lectern in front of her, but she stepped away and moved to the front of the platform. For the next thirty minutes she explained what it was like to live in the slums, and how hard it was for people to move out of that environment once they were trapped there. She also explained how many had missed out on basic education. Without mentioning names, she gave examples of some of those who had come to her, and when she outlined Ted's tragic story there wasn't a sound in the room. Walking along the platform to make them feel she was talking to each one personally, the years of struggle melted away, and she was back at the finishing school. With every minute her confidence grew. They were listening.

While composing the speech she had been tempted to throw in a challenge or two, but had decided that it would only offend the men, and it wasn't what Lord Grant wanted. Her job this evening was to inform, and leave everything else to His Lordship. From the little she had heard before he introduced her, he was more than capable of challenging them to action.

At the end she paused briefly and smiled. 'You have been very attentive, and I thank you, gentlemen.'

Turning, she curtsied gracefully to Lord Grant, and he bowed, joining in with the applause.

Back in the other room again she let out a pent-up breath. It had been a challenging experience, but she had enjoyed it.

The secretary actually smiled. 'You did well, madam. His Lordship will be pleased.'

'Thank you. I'm afraid I don't know your name.'

'People just refer to me as the secretary.' He gave a lopsided smile. 'But my name is Tennant. Now, I had better retrieve your sons from their hiding place.'

A moment later the two boys slid quietly into the room, and the moment the door was closed, rushed to their mother. Joe hugged her, but Charlie was studying her with a question in his eyes.

'Where did you learn to speak like that, Mum?'

Seeing he wouldn't be satisfied with brushing away the subject, she said, 'I went to a finishing school where they taught us how to speak in public. I also went to one run by a teaching order of nuns. My father thought this would be a good place for a rather difficult daughter, but he didn't know the nuns were determined to change us into independent women.' She gave a quiet laugh. 'We learnt there how to make our opinions known. What did you think of the speech?'

'It was terrific,' Charlie replied. 'I wish I could have seen the audience. They were very quiet.'

'They were either listening intently, or they were asleep.' Jane smiled when the secretary laughed out loud.

'They were certainly awake, madam, because I watched them carefully.'

At that moment Lord Grant entered the room, all smiles. 'My dear lady, you were magnificent. That was very clever of you to begin by complimenting them by referring to their status. Your speech was exactly what was needed to hold their attention.'

'Our mum is clever,' Joe told him seriously.

'Indeed, she is, young man, so is Helen and all of you, I am convinced. Your mother has told me you will be moving to a smart house soon. Congratulations, that is splendid news. Now, are you hungry?'

Joe nodded, still gazing at the imposing man in front of him.

'Now I must feed the gentlemen, and I'm truly sorry you can't all join us, but I have arranged for you to be served the same meal. Tennant will look after you, and then see you safely home.'

The boys thanked him, excited about the prospect of a special meal in luxurious surroundings.

Lord Grant bowed to Jane. 'I must leave you now, but I am indebted to you for giving such an informative and stirring speech.'

'It was a pleasure and an honour.'

He acknowledged the compliment with a slight tilt of his head, and then turned to his secretary. 'Look after my guests, and see they have everything they want.'

'I will, My Lord.'

'Excellent. Now if you will excuse me, I must see the gentlemen are well fed before I begin demanding that they take action by supporting me in this endeavour. Enjoy your meal.'

He left with a determined expression on his face, and she watched the door close behind him, highly impressed. If anyone could get something done it was Lord Grant. He was clearly a force to be reckoned with.

'If you will come with me, please.' Tennant took them to another room set up for dining, and held a chair for Jane to sit on. The boys had the other two chairs opposite her.

She noticed her sons studying the array of cutlery, and when Joe looked up, puzzled, she said, 'Remember what I told you. You start from the outside, but if in doubt watch me and do the same.'

They nodded and waited expectantly.

She knew this was a completely new experience for them, but didn't have any doubt they would handle it perfectly.

A door opened and the staff arrived with the food in covered silver dishes. For the next two hours they worked their way through six courses. Considering the boys had never tasted many of the dishes and all the various sauces before, they cleared their plates with obvious enjoyment. The only thing they weren't sure about was the strong coffee at the end of the meal, but one of the waiters kindly brought them tea.

Charlie sat back and grinned. 'I'm so full I won't be able to eat for a week. It's hard to imagine that some people eat like this all the time.'

Joe was already looking sleepy, so Jane thanked everyone for a wonderful meal, and the secretary saw them to the waiting carriage.

Their house seemed dingy and even smaller after spending time in the beautiful surroundings, but it wouldn't be for much longer.

Chapter Twenty-Six

'Look at this, Mum!' Charlie burst through the door after work the next day waving a newspaper at her. 'You're famous.'

She spread the paper on the scullery table so they could read it by candlelight.

'Second page,' he told her excitedly.

Joe knelt on a chair to get a better look as she opened it at the right page, and he exclaimed, 'That's you!'

She read the article and all she could think of saying was, 'My goodness.'

'Did you know there was someone sketching you?' Charlie asked.

'I wasn't aware of it.' She studied the picture of herself and Lord Grant standing on the platform. 'I think that was at the end, and I was so relieved to have got through it I didn't notice what was going on at the time.'

'I told the men that that was my mother,' Charlie straightened up proudly. 'And we were at Westminster Palace with you.'

'I hope Granny sees this.' Joe ran his fingers gently over the picture, and then smiled at his mother. 'It was very exciting, and I've never tasted food like that before.'

'Neither have I.' Charlie put his head on one side and studied his mother. 'You have, though. I could tell it wasn't new to you.'

'No, it wasn't, but it's been a long time since I've been served a meal like that.' She placed an arm around each of her sons. 'But if my plans work out, that will be normal for you one day.'

'What plans?' Joe wanted to know.

'Ah, I'm not telling.' She ruffled his hair. 'We have a long way to go before that can happen.'

Her eldest son was intrigued. 'You say we have a long way to go yet, but I would say we have travelled quite a way already. Helen and I have decent jobs, we will soon be moving to a nice house, you are helping people with their education, and becoming famous by doing it. How much further can we go, Mum?'

'Quite a way, my darling boys.' They didn't understand what she was talking about, of course, but every step they had taken since Bert had left them increased her confidence and determination to regain at least some of what she had lost. She had always felt it was her duty to see they had a better life than this. For years that had seemed impossible, but now there was a glimmer of hope.

Charlie folded the paper carefully, and tucked it in his pocket. 'I'm seeing Andy tonight, so do you mind if I show him this and tell him about last night?'

'Not at all.' She began to dish up their simple meal of sausages and mash. Nothing like the sumptuous dinner they'd had the night before, but it was plentiful and an improvement on the meagre food she had been able to give them only a few short weeks ago.

'Mum, can we go and see Granny at the weekend?'

'I expect she's busy and still getting settled in her new home, but I'll go and ask Mr Preston if it would be all right for us to pay her a short visit.'

'Thank you. I miss her.'

'I know you do, darling, and I'm sure she misses you, but you know she couldn't stay here any longer, don't you? Would you like another sausage?'

Both of her sons had healthy appetites and nodded, holding out their plates.

'How is Andy getting on?' she asked Charlie.

'Very well. You wouldn't recognise him now. He's all smart in his new clothes and looking quite the gentleman, but he hasn't forgotten what you did for him. He said you were the only one who understood what he wanted to do. Without your encouragement he doubted if he would have had the courage to apply for that job.'

It was good to hear about the success of someone she

had helped, and that made her smile. 'What do his family think of him now?'

'I met his parents, and they told me they are very proud of him.'

'Good. Support from family is important.'

Charlie nodded and smiled at his mother affectionately. 'It is, as we well know.'

The moment the plates were empty, Charlie was on his feet, eager to meet his friend.

'Do you need money for the omnibus?'

He patted his pocket. 'I still have enough left until payday.'

'Are you sure? I don't want you walking miles in the dark.'

'Andy doesn't live miles away, Mum.' Giving a wave he headed for the door.

The next morning two more new pupils arrived. One was a girl of ten, and the other a man of around forty. The class had grown so much it was difficult to fit them all in, even after the hut had been enlarged. The only way was to sit two of a similar age at the same desk. It was becoming a squeeze, but she would find room for them somehow. However, with such a variation in ages, the workload on her was becoming heavy.

She was with the new arrivals to sort out what their particular needs were when Dora walked in.

'My goodness!' she exclaimed when she saw the crowded hut. 'You look as if you could do with some help. I've come to offer my services.'

'Which I accept with gratitude.' Jane stood up. 'Can you spare the time, though?'

'Of course, my dear. You tell me what I can do.'

'Each pupil is at a different stage of learning, and the only way to deal with that is to sit with each one and give personal tuition.'

'Hmm, quite a task. Where would you like me to start?'

'The older ones, please.'

'Right.' Dora removed her hat and coat, ready for action.

Jane called attention and introduced Dora, explaining that she was going to help with the class.

It was a busy morning and she was relieved to have Dora's help. She appeared to be enjoying herself, and the pupils were chatting and laughing with her now and again.

At the end of the lesson and when the pupils had left, Dora sat down and said, 'I enjoyed that. It is good to feel useful again.'

'Thank you for coming and you will be welcome any time.'

'I was hoping you would say that. I can't promise to come every day, but will make it as often as I can. I will tell you in advance when I'll be here. Would that be acceptable, my dear?'

'That would be wonderful.' Jane smiled with relief. 'I do admit that with so many pupils now it is becoming hard to give each one the time they need.'

'Have you thought what you are going to do if more pupils arrive?'

Jane sat down next to Dora and shook her head. 'I honestly didn't expect this many. I thought some of the older ones would have found work now their reading is improving, but work is hard to find, as you know.'

'I think there is another reason they are still here, my dear. They like and admire you, and love coming to the classes. Everyone here is in the same situation and they don't have to feel embarrassed about their lack of education. I spoke to some, and they are all delighted you have been in the papers, and proud they had been able to read a lot of it themselves. Your lessons are adding to their self-esteem.'

'That is what I am aiming for, and I can't turn anyone away, no matter how crowded we get. I had better try to see Lord Grant at some time and let him know we have more pupils.'

'Ah, that reminds me. I am giving a little party on Sunday to celebrate moving into my new home. I would love you all to come.'

'That would be lovely. Joe was only asking me last night when he could see his granny again. I'll find out if Helen is free, because I know she would love to come.'

'Good. I would like all the family there.' Dora put on her hat and coat and gave a mischievous smile. 'Now I am going to pester Ian.'

The moment Dora walked in and saw Ian and Oscar sorting through mounds of paperwork, she stood there with a frown on her face. 'Ian, you really have to get more help. You have been putting it off for too long.'

'I know.' He ran a hand through his hair. 'I just haven't got around to it.'

'Tell me what you need.' She sat down, not going anywhere until this situation was dealt with.

'Well, Oscar will be fully qualified in January, so we will need someone to take over his work, like running errands, delivering documents to various places, and help with the general running of the office.'

'Hmm. I have just spent the morning with Jane and her pupils, and there is a young man there who might be just what you are looking for. He told me about himself, and he has had a tough life, but he's a nice lad and not at all bitter about what has happened to him. He went to Jane unable to read or write, but he's eager to learn and has made excellent progress in a short time.'

'Sounds interesting, but are his reading skills sufficient for us?'

'I believe so. However, he would still need tuition. If Jane can't do it, then I will. Would you be willing to see the lad?'

Ian sat back and frowned. 'I would have to do that before I could give an opinion on his suitability.'

'Of course.' She turned her attention to Oscar. 'Would it concern you to have someone in the office who would need extra help at times?'

'Not at all, Mrs Jarvis. I would be happy to guide him through anything he needs to do. Your husband set up the business to help the underprivileged as well as others who can't afford legal fees. I think he would approve of giving a job to the young lad.' He glanced at Ian. 'If Mr Preston agrees, then I would be happy to welcome him and help in any way I can.'

'I have no objection, but I must interview him, as I would anyone else. When can I see him?'

'Why don't you come to the class on Monday? You will also be able to see what a huge task Janc has on her hands.'

'I'll do that. Has she had any trouble from her husband since he's been notified of the divorce?'

'Not a word.'

He nodded in satisfaction. 'That is good news. I told her she is to come straight to me if he turns up, but I'm not sure she would.'

'Maybe not. She has been used to dealing with problems on her own, and is now becoming more independent by the day.' Dora pointed to the littered desk. 'Is there anything I can help you with while I'm here?'

He picked up a few documents. 'I'd appreciate it if you could check these for mistakes, then Oscar can deliver them for us.'

She had done this many times in the past, and settled down to the task, knowing how important it was that all the documents were in perfect order.

Towards the end of the lesson, Ian walked in. Jane immediately went up to him, a concerned expression on her face. 'Is everything all right?'

He laughed. 'Good morning, Jane.'

'Oh, I'm sorry not to have greeted you in the correct

manner, but the moment I saw you, I thought you needed to see me urgently for some reason.'

'The last I heard from Culver was that everything about your case is proceeding smoothly. I am here because Dora believes one of your young men would be suitable to work for us.'

'Really? Which one?'

Dora then came over with Ted in tow. 'Ian, this is the lad I told you about. Ted, meet Mr Preston. He would like to talk to you.'

He shook Ian's hand politely, looking puzzled.

'What is your full name?'

'Ted Randall, sir. Are you a policeman? Have I done something wrong?'

Jane stepped forward and gave him a reassuring smile. 'You are not in any trouble, Ted. Mr Preston is a solicitor and he needs to talk to you, that's all. The pupils are just leaving so why don't you sit at the back where you can discuss things in private.'

They settled down and were soon in deep discussion, so Jane made a pot of tea for all of them. After handing the cups round, she sat with Dora. 'What do you think?' she asked softly.

'They appear to be getting on well, but Ian will only take him if he is sure he can handle the work.'

Eventually Ian stood up and came over to them with a stunned young man beside him. 'Ted is coming to work for us, but we have one more detail to settle. He will need to continue with his lessons, Jane, so is there any way you can do this? I would be happy for you to come to the office twice a week for an hour, and teach him there. We will pay you for this, of course.'

The pleading look Ted gave her was enough to make her agree at once. 'I'm sure I could manage that. What time and when?'

'I thought perhaps Monday and Thursday. I leave the time to you.'

'One o'clock, then I could come straight from here.' She smiled at Ted who was now so excited he could hardly stand still. 'I shall be giving you extra homework as well.'

'Oh yes, as much as you like.'

'That's settled, then. Come with me now, Ted, and I'll show you where you will be working. Oscar will be relieved to have help.'

'Thank you, sir.'

'Good luck, Ted,' she told him quietly as he turned to follow his new employer, and the smile he gave her was enough to brighten anyone's day.

Left alone, Jane took hold of Dora's hand. 'Thank you for doing that. If anyone needs some kindness and luck in their life, it is that young man.'

'I liked him, and Ian desperately needs more staff. That young man will be a big help, and you can be sure they will look after him.'

'I know, and each time I see a pupil move on to something better, it makes all the hard work worthwhile.'

'And now you've got extra work by continuing to give Ted his lessons.'

'That will be a pleasure.' She glanced around the now-empty hut. 'We will be able to fit in another pupil now, but I will miss Ted. He's been a big help with the class, but I am so happy for him.'

'You should be proud as well,' Dora told her. 'Without your help that poor lad wouldn't have stood a chance in life. It's another victory.'

'Yes, it is. I wish I could save them all, but that isn't possible, is it?'

'No, and that's why we need men like Lord Grant. Help on a large scale needs to come from social reform, and that means by the government.' Dora made a sound of disgust. 'What they need are a few women in their ranks to shake them up.'

'That's a long way off, I'm afraid, but I can just imagine you in Parliament.' She chuckled.

'One day that will happen. Not in my lifetime, but perhaps in yours. Now, I must be on my way.'

'Thanks for your help. This has been a lovely start to the week. When will you be able to come again?'

'I'll be here on Thursday. Give my love to Joe, and don't forget you are all coming to me on Sunday. Come in the morning and we can spend the day together.'

'We will look forward to it.' Jane watched her walk away, her cane tapping on the ground. What a wonderful surprise that had been, and what a kind and caring man Ian was.

Chapter Twenty-Seven

It was quite a gathering at Dora's that Sunday, and although it was cold the sun was shining, the rays brightening the river. Jane loved the house, and it had been furnished simply but with elegant taste. Although Dora had only been there a short time, she had engaged a cook and a maid who lived locally and came in when needed.

The party consisted of Jane and her children, including Helen who had been able to get the day off, Ian, Oscar and the new solicitor, Howard. They had all enjoyed an excellent meal and Jane was outside watching Joe with Dora and Howard, feeding the ducks. Her son's excited chatter could be clearly heard.

'Joe is happy to see her again, isn't he?' Ian came and stood beside her.

'He has missed her. It's remarkable to see the bond between them when you consider the big difference in their ages.' She smiled up at the tall man beside her. 'Howard is a nice man and Joe is certainly enjoying his company as well.'

'I believe that isn't the only friendship that has been formed.' He nodded towards two by the river, standing apart from the others. 'Oscar is quite taken with your daughter. When he knew she was coming nothing would have kept him away. Do you mind?'

'Helen is rather young to form attachments, but she's sensible, and I am sure he is.'

'Yes, he's a fine young man, and has good prospects. He becomes a solicitor in January and will be an asset to the firm.'

She nodded and, watching them together, was pleased to see a friendship blossoming. 'I know she will come and discuss with me any relationship she might have. She needs someone. Although she loves where she is, the job of governess is not an easy one. They are neither a servant nor a member of the family, and it can be quite lonely at times. She misses sitting round the table with the other servants at mealtimes, and dines alone when her charge is with her parents. She waves it off and tells me she is getting used to it, and it is better than scrubbing floors. It is a step up for her and she was well aware of what it would mean in regard to working conditions.'

Everyone was getting cold, so they went back inside

for a warming drink. The afternoon ended with a lovely tea of special pastries and cakes, made by the new cook.

Ian and Oscar escorted them home, while Howard remained behind as he didn't live far away from Dora.

They stayed up talking for a while, but the boys soon went to bed.

'Want a cup of tea?' Jane asked her daughter.

'I'll make it.'

It was too late to light the fire in the other room, so they sat in the scullery where it was warm, and Jane asked, 'When do you have to go back?'

'Tomorrow morning. I've only been given the one day off.'

'Ah, well, it was lovely you could come. What did you think of Dora's house?'

'It's lovely, and I'm sure she will be happy there. I can understand her not wanting to live in the other house after what happened. She's done the wise thing and she will also be near Howard. They seem to like each other, and it will be good for her to have a friend living not far away.'

'Yes, I agree. It has been a lovely day and you were getting on well with Oscar. He's a nice young man.'

Helen looked her mother straight in the eyes. 'He's asked me to walk out with him when I have time off, and I've agreed. I know I'm still young and he is older, but we talked this over today. He is about to be qualified, but knows it will take a couple of years to become established, so he doesn't want a serious attachment at the moment. As we seem to get along well together, we have agreed to be friends and meet up when we can.'

Jane gave a silent sigh of relief. She hadn't really been worried, but it was good to know exactly what was going on between them.

'Do you mind?' her daughter asked.

'Of course not, darling, but thank you for telling me what you have decided. I like Oscar, and I trust you to be sensible. You can always come to me if you are concerned about anything – you know that, don't you?'

'It's what we have always done.' Helen squeezed her mother's hand. 'I'm so happy things are working out for all of us. I told you Dad leaving could be for the best, and we would be able to move on. Well, look how far we have come.'

'I agree it's remarkable, and I sometimes wonder if it's just a dream. There is a way to go yet,' she cautioned.

'I know the divorce is hanging over you, Mum, but you will get it. How can you fail with such experienced men helping you?'

Jane nodded. 'I bless the day I walked into that office, and know how fortunate I am, but these things take such a long time. Still, as you say, we have made good progress. Now it's time we got some sleep.'

It had been wonderful to have the children all at home for a change, and it was always hard to see her daughter leave. She was so young, but wise beyond her years, and it had been her decision to go into service as a way to help the family. And, as always, she had been right. At times it had been hard to buy enough food for them, and they were hungry, so she had left. Jane didn't know what she had done to deserve such kindness and understanding from her children, and now Dora, Ian and Lord Grant. It was strengthening to have people around who cared what happened to them, and for the first time in many years she didn't feel as if she was struggling on her own.

It was a good feeling, and she entered the hut for the morning class with a smile on her face. At least she was giving back some of the kindness she was receiving by helping others less fortunate.

The sense of achievement stayed with her later in the morning as she made her way to see Ted. When she walked into the office Oscar was bending over explaining something, but when he saw her, Ted stood up, a wide smile of welcome on his face.

'My goodness,' she exclaimed. 'Don't you look smart.'

He ran a hand over his jacket, appearing a little shy at the compliment. 'Mr Preston gave me one of his suits, and Oscar gave me the shirt and tie.'

'That was kind of them, and you look like a posh businessman now.'

Oscar grinned at Ted. 'You have your lesson now, and we'll finish this later.'

Ted was thrilled with the job, and even more determined to become proficient with his reading and writing.

At the end of the lesson she asked him how he was managing with the work.

'There is so much to learn, but everyone is very patient.' There was a glint of determination in his eyes. 'I've been given a chance beyond my wildest dreams, and I'll hold on to it tightly. Please give me lots of homework.'

'I intend to,' she told him, handing over the work she had prepared for him. 'I'll be here on Thursday, and will expect to see that completed.'

'It will be. Thank you.'

'It's a pleasure to teach you, Ted.'

Oscar came back then, asking if she would like tea before leaving.

She glanced at the clock. 'Thank you, but I can't stay.'

He nodded. 'I'll tell Mr Preston you came. He is in court today.'

'I'll see you on Thursday,' she told them as she hurried out. First there was shopping to get for an evening meal, and then she must be home before Joe arrived from school. He didn't have Dora to go to now if she wasn't there.

She had only been home a few minutes when the door crashed open and Bert strode in. One glance told her he had been drinking already and was in a belligerent mood, looking for trouble. She braced herself for the onslaught but, surprisingly, this time she was quite calm.

He tossed a newspaper on the scullery table, his face contorted with rage. 'Doing all right for yourself, ain't you, Madam High and Mighty. I've come for my share of the money.'

'What money?'

'Don't give me that. You ain't doing all this for some lord for nothing.'

He moved so quickly she didn't have time to react, and he was emptying her purse. She watched as he pocketed the two pence that fell out.

'Where's the rest?' he demanded.

'That's all there is. Now get out of my house.'

'This ain't yours, it's mine.'

'Not any more. When you left I had my name put on the rent book. You've got no right to be here now.' Her hand wrapped around a cast iron pot, determined to defend herself if he became violent.

He took a step towards her. 'Tell me where you're keeping the money, or you'll be sorry. I kept you for all these years and I want some of that money back now.'

'I've told you, there isn't any money. Now get out!' To her horror, at that moment Joe arrived. Still holding the pot she stepped past Bert and shoved her son towards the stairs. 'Go up and shut yourself in. Push something against the door so he can't get in.'

'Mum?'

'Do it, Joe!' After another shove he disappeared, and she spun round to face the irate man, who was trying to get past her to get hold of Joe. Blocking his path to the stairs she held up the pot. 'Leave him. This is between you and me, and I'll use this if I have to.'

'Do anything to protect your precious kids, won't you? Well, you needn't think you are going to get rid of me. I'm moving back now you've become famous. There's money to be had in what you're doing, and I'm going to get it.'

'Spent all your new woman's money already, have you? Well, that's too bad because you are not coming back here. We don't want or need you, and once the divorce is finalised you will no longer have a claim on us.'

He actually laughed. 'You won't get a divorce because you're a woman, and I won't let you.'

She heard Joe dragging furniture against the bedroom door, and smiled, knowing he was safe. 'I've got two powerful men representing me, and if you object, they will show the world what a greedy, mean-spirited man you are.'

He lashed out, but she managed to block his fist with the pot, not moving from the foot of the stairs. He was very drunk and she knew from experience how nasty that could make him. Her heart was thumping loudly, but whatever happened she was not going to let him win this battle. In the past she had stepped away from confrontations like this, but not any longer. He was out of their life, by his own choice, and there was no way he was coming back. There had to be some way to make him leave – and then it came to her.

'I'm surprised you dare show your face down this street again after borrowing money from Baker and then disappearing. He was not pleased, to say the least.'

'That don't matter now he's in prison.'

'He might be, but his mates are still here and looking after his interests. I expect you've seen the damage they've done to the next house. They took their fury out on someone who helped with the arrest. They came here looking for you, so you'd be wise to run and never come down here again, or I might tell them where to find you. In fact, I expect news has already reached them that you are here.'

Panic showed on his face and he headed for the door, pausing briefly to shout, 'You ain't heard the last from me.'

The moment he had gone Jane's legs gave out and she sat on the bottom stair with a thump. She'd lied about Baker's friends looking for him, but it had worked and she prayed it would keep him away.

'Mum?'

'It's all right, darling, you can come down now. He's gone and I don't think he'll be back.'

There was the sound of things being moved, and then footsteps coming down the stairs. Joe sat beside her, his face white with worry. 'Are you all right? Did he hurt you, Mum?'

'No.' She held up the pot and gave a shaky laugh. 'I threatened to hit him with this.'

'What did he want?'

'Someone must have told him what was in the newspaper, and he wanted any money we had.'

Joe nodded. 'I've got that safe. Does he know we are moving soon?'

'No, and we will keep that a secret.' She took a deep, steadying breath before standing up. 'We had better put this pan to good use and get dinner ready. Charlie will be hungry when he gets home.'

The young boy was still subdued when his big brother arrived home and didn't greet him with his usual enthusiasm.

Charlie frowned, looking from Joe to his mother. They were both still tense and pale. 'What's happened?' he demanded.

'Eat first, and we'll tell you later.'

'No, Mum, I can sense something bad has happened, and I want to know now.'

Tears welled up in Joe's eyes. 'Dad came and threatened Mum. I had to hide upstairs.'

'It's all right, darling.' She hugged her youngest son. 'We weren't hurt, and we sent him away.'

He gulped. 'He shouted and wanted any money we had, but he didn't get it.'

'Damn!' Charlie swore. 'I really didn't think he'd come back. Tell me exactly what happened.'

She then explained, leaving nothing out, and when she'd finished her eldest son looked grim. 'That was good thinking to tell him about Baker's mates looking for him, and fear of that should keep him away from here.'

'Of course it will.' Jane began to dish up the meal.

'You should tell Mr Preston, though, Mum. He told you to, didn't he?'

'I will mention it next time I see him, but I doubt we have anything to worry about now.'

'Hmm,' was Charlie's only response.

Chapter Twenty-Eight

For the next couple of days Jane was on edge wondering if Bert was going to turn up again, but as the week progressed she began to relax. They were all looking forward to spending Christmas with Dora, even Helen, who wasn't needed by the Grants. They were staying with friends in the country and Victoria would join the children under the charge of their governess. It was good news, and everyone was delighted.

On Thursday she was on her way to give Ted his lesson, and hoped to see Ian for a moment. She really ought to tell him about Bert's visit.

When she walked into the office Ted's face lit up with a bright smile. He was so happy, and she was very proud of him.

'Hello, Ted, I'm early so I'll be with you in a minute. Oscar, I need to have a word with Mr Preston. Is he available?'

'He's just arrived so I'll tell him you are here.'

Ian came out to greet her, and they went back into his office. 'Jane, I hope everything is all right?'

'I don't think it's anything serious, but you did say I was to let you know if my husband showed up.'

'You've seen him?' When she nodded, he said, 'Tell me about it, and I want every detail.'

He listened intently while she explained what had happened, and was looking concerned when she finished.

'I'll pass this on to Culver, but you should have come to me immediately,' he reprimanded gently. 'Even if I am not around you can tell Oscar or Howard. Promise me you will if anything else happens.'

'I will do that, but he hasn't been back again, so I don't think he will.'

'Maybe, but I wish we could move you to Kennington right away. Unfortunately, the roof needs more work than anticipated and bad weather is delaying completion.'

'Please don't worry.' She smiled to allay his concern, and changed the subject. 'Helen is home for a week over Christmas, and we are all going to Dora's. Joe is very excited.'

'I'm sure he is. They have formed quite a friendship.'

'They have, and it's been good for both of them.' She stood up. 'Thank you for seeing me, but now I must give Ted his lesson. He seems happy, but can you tell me how he is coping with the work?'

'Remarkably well. He's bright, obedient and willing to learn. With someone like that we don't mind taking the time to go through everything until he fully understands. We are happy with his progress.'

'That is good to hear, and it is very kind of you to have given him this chance.'

'He's a fine lad and deserves it.'

'He certainly does.'

The moment she walked back to the other office, Ted was waiting at the desk they used for the lessons. 'I've done all the homework.'

She sat next to him. 'Let's have a look at it together before we begin, shall we?'

'It's getting easier, so you can give me more than that if you like. I enjoy doing it.'

'I don't want to load you with too much work.' It was encouraging to see such enthusiasm, and a quick look through showed very few mistakes. 'I believe you can move on to reading books now. Would you like to try that?'

'Oh, please. Do you really think I could read proper books now?'

'I do, as long as it is something easy to read. It will be a while before you can handle Shakespeare,' she joked.

An amused snort came from Oscar. 'It will be a while before a lot of us understand his works.'

Laughter filled the office and Ted swivelled round to

face Oscar, grinning broadly. 'I'm determined to read Shakespeare one day soon.'

'I'm sure you will,' Oscar told him. 'Tell you what, the day you finish reading one of his plays and tell me you understand it, then I'll take you to see one of them performed.'

'That's a deal.' Ted was on his feet, and the two of them shook hands to seal the agreement.

As Jane watched, the tension of the last few days dissolved. The joy of seeing one of her pupils beginning to make a good life for himself was beyond price.

'Helen, come and help me,' Lady Grant called. 'I'm in my dressing room.'

Hurrying along the landing she found Her Ladyship with clothes thrown everywhere. They were draped over chairs and even tossed onto the floor in large heaps.

The moment she saw Helen, she sighed with relief. 'Give me a hand to sort through these gowns. They are far too old and out of fashion for me to wear again.'

'What are you going to do with them?' Helen couldn't believe her eyes. The room was like a flower garden of many colours. The gowns were of the finest silks and satins, and the petticoats beautifully soft.

'Perhaps we can find someone who would want them. If not, I suppose we could always ask the servants to burn them.'

'Burn them?' Helen was horrified. 'Oh, My Lady, that would be a terrible thing to do.'

Lady Grant retrieved another gown from the rack, grimaced, and then tossed it onto a heap on the floor.

Helen instinctively reached out to rescue it. 'This is new. I remember it being delivered.'

'I don't like it and will never wear it.'

She ran her hands over it lovingly. How could someone just toss this away without a thought? She looked up to see Lady Grant watching her.

'I know what you are thinking, Helen, but you must understand my position. My husband is a prominent, well-respected man, and when we are seen in public I must appear beside him fashionably dressed.'

'I know, and you always look beautiful, but I have grown up in poverty and this seems to me a terrible waste. The materials could be used for making other clothes.'

'Could they?'

'Oh yes. When we were growing up nothing was ever thrown away. My mother used every scrap of material she could find to keep us clothed. It was no easy task for her, and now my youngest brother is wearing hand-me-downs from his older brother.'

'She's good with a needle, then?'

'Very good, or we would have been walking around in rags like many of the other children on our street.'

'I liked your mother, and my husband admires her greatly.' Her Ladyship gazed at the mountain of clothes for a moment. 'Do you think she could do anything with some of these?'

'I'm sure she could.'

'Splendid. Let us sort out what you think she would like. You have two brothers so she could probably use clothing suitable for them, as well. I'll see what I can find.'

Helen watched her leave the room in amazement. Was she going to raid her husband's wardrobe now?

When she appeared again, she was followed by a maid who had her arms overflowing with clothing. 'Would these be of any use to your mother?'

One look was enough to tell her they would. 'She could make clothes for my brothers out of those, but won't Lord Grant be upset to discover you've given them away?'

'No, no, he can't wear these again. They are quite out of fashion. Now let us find some more items for your mother.' She dismissed the maid and sighed as she surveyed the clothes littering the room. 'You take what you want, and I'll get the servants to dispose of the rest.'

The elaborate ballgowns were put aside, and Helen chose two day-dresses and several plain petticoats. There was also a large woollen shawl in navy blue, which she knew would make a warm coat for Joe. She added that to the pile and looked up. 'Would it be all right if I took these, My Lady?'

'Is that all? You have hardly taken anything. What about this?' She held up a gown in oyster satin. 'It doesn't have much decoration on it so the material might be useful. Oh, and this also.'

She was holding up a long piece of exquisite lace, some ten inches wide and about three feet in length. 'We purchased this an age ago, but my dressmaker never used it.'

'Thank you,' was all she could think of saying as the items were gathered together.

'Annie,' Lady Grant called, and the maid hurried in. 'Ask the housekeeper to get this mess cleaned up and to get rid of the clothes any way she can.'

'Yes, My Lady.' She disappeared quickly.

'As Victoria is with her aunt today you might as well take these to your mother now, Helen.'

Left alone, she began to gather up the clothes, making it into something she could carry. After a struggle she had two large bundles, but she was determined to get them home in one trip.

She was puffing with effort by the time she walked into the house, nearly obscured by the heap of clothes. She dropped them on the floor with relief.

'What have you got there?' Jane declared, jumping to her feet in surprise at the unexpected arrival of her daughter.

'Lady Grant is turning out her dressing room and insisted I give these to you.' She sat down, taking deep breaths. 'I've had a struggle getting them here.'

She looked at her daughter with a smile on her face. 'I imagine you did.'

Having now got her breath back, Helen stood up and began to untie the bundles, watching as the clothes unfolded in a billowing mass. 'She's throwing these away and she even raided her husband's dressing room. I thought you could do something with all this material.'

Jane was already sorting through and nodding as she held up every garment. 'I can make this suit fit Charlie, and the other one can be cut up to make something for Joe – long trousers, perhaps.'

Helen laughed. 'He'd like that. What about the gowns? They are too small for us, but the material is lovely.'

One gown was quickly turned inside out to check the seams. 'There is plenty of material to let out the seams, but it will still be too short for you.'

'What about this?' Helen held up the lace.

'Oh my.' Her mother sighed. 'Was she going to throw that away as well?'

'Yes, and even threatened to have it all burnt if they couldn't be disposed of in any other way.'

'That would have been a terrible waste. How long can you stay? I'm going to need help.'

'I have to return by five o'clock when Victoria comes back from her aunt's.'

'That gives us three hours.' Jane quickly cleared the large scullery table. 'We'll get some of the cutting out done now.'

They were still busy when Joe arrived home from school, and was fascinated to watch the cutting, measuring and pinning together of new items of clothing.

Helen had to leave then, and Jane began to prepare the evening meal. When Charlie came home, she explained how the clothes had been given to Helen, and showed him the dark charcoal suit. 'I'm going to make this fit you.'

He examined it and raised his eyebrows. 'But it's in perfect condition. How can anyone throw out such a quality garment?'

'They have a position to maintain, and if something is not in the height of fashion they cannot wear it.'

'By the time you've finished it will be perfect.' He grinned at his mother. 'Goodness, I'll look as smart as Andy in a suit like that. Thanks, Mum, but what about Joe? He's shooting up so fast he's in desperate need of new clothes.'

'There is another suit, so I'll be able to make him something out of that. There's also lots of lovely plain cotton so I can make shirts for both of you.'

'Can I have long trousers?' Joe asked.

'Of course you can, and I might be able to squeeze out a jacket, if I'm very careful.'

Charlie was examining the gowns. 'Don't forget you and Helen. You both need something decent to wear, especially as we are going to Mrs Jarvis for Christmas. If you wash and press your one decent frock again it will fall to pieces.'

'I know, but you and Joe come first.' She smiled fondly at her two handsome sons. 'You are quite the young gentlemen now. However, I will make something for us girls, so we don't let you down in company,' she joked.

Over the weekend she worked tirelessly, and made good progress with the clothing for the boys. The suit had to be completely taken apart, because although Charlie was tall for his age, he didn't yet have the stature of Lord Grant.

On Sunday Charlie had gone out with Andy, and Joe was doing his best to be helpful, a thoughtful expression on his face.

'Is something worrying you, darling?' she asked.

'Hmm. I wish I could give Granny a present for Christmas. That is what people do, isn't it?'

'It is, but we've never had enough money to do things like that.' When one of the children mentioned something like this it always felt as if a knife had been plunged into her. They had spent so many a bleak Christmas, often without enough to eat, while Bert went and spent what little there was at the pub with his mates. She picked up one of the satin petticoats and the lace. 'Shall I make you something pretty to give Granny?'

His eyes lit up. 'Can you?'

'I'm sure I can.' She had intended to keep the lace for an idea she had for Helen, but if she was careful there should still be enough. She cut out a few of the roses and laid them aside.

Joe was kneeling on a chair and resting his elbows on the table, watching intently. 'What are you going to make?'

'Something she can keep her gloves in.'

'Oh yes, she always wears gloves.'

An hour later the finely stitched glove case was completed, along with two delicate handkerchiefs. She laid them out for Joe to have a look at.

He touched the lace roses stitched on in the shape of a heart, and the same symbol embroidered on the handkerchiefs with the word 'Granny' as well.

'She'll like these.' Her son launched himself at her for a hug of gratitude. 'Thank you, thank you.'

She handed him a piece of paper she had saved from a delivery of notebooks Lord Grant had sent for the pupils. 'Wrap them up in a nice parcel, and I've got a piece of stiff paper you can make a card out of to go with the present.'

He nodded and cleared a space on the table for him to work on, a happy smile on his face.

Chapter Twenty-Nine

Monday was a busy day with a full class, and the extra lesson for Ted. Dora was now coming in most days and her help was a blessing.

Well pleased with the way things were going, she hurried home, eager to get back to her sewing. Christmas was on Saturday and she was determined to have everything finished in time. She smiled to herself. Dora wouldn't recognise them.

So absorbed in what there was to do in such a short time she hadn't taken note of the time passing, and was shocked when she saw it was almost five o'clock. Where was Joe?

She rushed around, calling him in case he had come in and not wanted to disturb her, but there was no reply.

He wasn't in the house. Now she was worried. He always came straight home from school.

Frantic, she grabbed her coat and almost ran to the school. It was closed up and appeared empty, but she banged on the door. When no one came she kept knocking and also shouting, praying someone was around to hear her.

Eventually a man appeared at the door, and to her relief it was the headmaster. 'My son, Joe Roberts, hasn't come home. Is he here?'

'Calm down,' he told her sharply. 'Your son is quite safe. His father came and took him out of class this afternoon. It was an urgent matter, he assured me.'

The bottom fell out of her world, and she was tempted to hit the man standing in front of her. 'You damned fool. You've never seen his father, so how do you know it was him?'

'Your son called him Dad, so I assumed it was all right.'

'You assumed!' she shouted. 'If my son has come to any harm, I will see you lose your job.'

'Don't you threaten me, madam.'

'I'll do more than that. Did you ask where they were going?'

'I did not.'

She spun round and began to run, tears streaming down her face. Her husband knew the only way to hurt her was through her children. He couldn't touch Helen or Charlie, and that left young Joe – her darling, gentle boy. Why hadn't she been more careful?

She lifted her skirt and increased her speed, desperate to get to Ian before they closed for the day.

The door was still unlocked and she crashed into the office, ending up in a heap on the floor. She could hear anxious voices and someone helping her into a chair.

'Jane! Talk to me. What has happened?'

Something was held to her mouth and she took a gulp, gasping when the strong liquid hit her stomach, but it revived her enough to be able to speak. 'Joe. He's taken him. I should have been more careful. Everything's been going so well I got careless. I should have known he would do something like this. It's my fault. Why did I let it happen?'

'Jane, stop rambling and tell us exactly what has happened,' Ian demanded, taking hold of her hands.

The strong hands holding her gave her a gentle shake, bringing her back to what was happening. When she looked up there were four men standing around her all very concerned. Taking a deep breath, she realised this was no time to fall apart. She had to keep a clear head. 'When Joe didn't come home on time I ran to the school. The headmaster told me his father came and took him out of class. He said he knew it was his father because Joe called him Dad.'

Ian surged to his feet, his face like thunder. 'Oscar, go to Culver's chambers and tell him what has happened. If he isn't there, then leave a message. After that go to Lord Grant's and let Helen know what has happened. Howard, report the abduction to the police. Ted, you come with me. We know where he's been living and that's the place to start.'

'I'm coming with you.' Jane was a little unsteady when she stood up.

'I want you to go home and stay there,' Ian told her. 'I'll get you a cab.'

She lifted her head defiantly. 'No, I need to be with you. Joe will be frightened. I won't be a nuisance, I promise.'

'Very well, then,' he agreed, knowing that nothing was going to keep her away from the safety of her child. 'Let's get going. There's no time to waste.'

Ted had already obtained a cab and they were soon on their way to Bert Roberts' last known address. Suddenly, Ian made the driver stop and jumped out of the cab to talk to a policeman.

There was only one thing on Jane's mind and that was to get to the address where her son might be. 'What's he doing?'

Ted slid over to her. 'He wants the help of the policeman. It will give us a better chance of getting your son back.'

'Of course. Thank you, Ted. I'm not thinking straight at the moment, but I wish he'd hurry.'

'We'll find him,' he told her confidently.

Whatever Ian had been telling the policeman, it had been successful because the officer joined them, and they were once more on their way.

The house was in a slightly better area than Fallon Street but not much, and it crossed her mind that he had left her and the children for this. It didn't make sense.

The policeman and Ian knocked loudly on the door, and when no one answered, the policeman called out, 'Open up! This is the police.'

Ted stayed by her side, holding her arm to make sure she kept out of the way.

After more knocking the door eventually opened, and Jane tried to move forward, but was held firmly in place. The woman who had answered the door was quite attractive and appeared to be in her fifties or even older. 'I need to talk to her,' she protested.

'Let them handle it,' Ted told her quietly. 'They know what they are doing.'

'What's all this noise?' the woman demanded. 'The whole bloody street must know you're here by now.'

'We are looking for Mr Roberts, madam,' the policeman informed her. 'We understand he has been living here. He has his young son with him. Are they here?'

'No, they're not. I won't have no kids in my house. Can't stand the noisy buggers. I'd like to know where he is as well. He left yesterday and took my bracelet and some other bits of jewellery, and I want them back.'

'Was the jewellery valuable?' the policeman asked, making notes in his book.

'Not very, except for the bracelet. That's gold and belonged to my grandmother.'

'Do you wish to charge Mr Roberts with theft?'

'I certainly do. He ain't gonna get away with that. I was about to go to the station when you arrived.'

'Please do that, madam.'

'Do you have any idea where Roberts might have gone?' Ian asked.

Jane could stand it no longer and pulled herself free of Ted's restraining grip. 'Please tell us if you know where he might be. I must get my son away from him.'

The woman eyed her curiously. 'And who might you be?'

'I'm his wife.'

'What? The crafty bugger told me he wasn't married. Said we could get married any time I wanted to.'

'Did you?' Ian wanted to know.

'I was thinking about it, but just as well I didn't. He would have been a bigamist as well as a thief and liar.'

Ian now had a notebook in his hands and smiled encouragingly at her. 'I don't know your full name.'

'It's Betty Hilliard.' She returned his smile. 'And who might you be?'

He held out his hand. 'Ian Preston, solicitor for Mrs Roberts.'

She shook his hand and stared at Jane. 'You sure come with impressive help. Why did that rat leave you?'

'I really don't know,' she replied sharply. 'Do you know where he is?'

'Well, let me see.' She pursed her lips in thought. 'He's got a mate who lives in Bow, and another in Stepney. He might be at one of those, I suppose.'

'Addresses?' Ian asked.

'Hang on a minute and I'll see if I can find them.'

She disappeared and Jane could have cried out in frustration. This was taking too long, and there was no telling what her son was going through.

When Betty returned, she thrust a piece of paper into Ian's hand. 'Can't be sure those addresses are correct, but that's all I got.'

'If you do hear from him, madam, please inform the police at once.'

'Oh, I will, make no mistake about that.'

After thanking her they all climbed back in the cab and headed for the address in Bow.

The next two hours were a nightmare as they went from place to place without success. No one knew where he was and many when they saw the policeman denied even knowing him.

They returned to the office, weary and even more worried.

'There isn't anything else we can do tonight,' Ian told her. 'I'll take you home. Charlie will be concerned you are not there.'

She nodded miserably, knowing he was right. They had followed up every lead, but the thought of leaving her son at the mercy of an uncaring father terrified her.

Before returning to the station, the policeman had assured them that the search would continue.

Ian thanked everyone for their help and said their search would resume at first light the next day.

'Shall I go and tell Dora what has happened?' Howard asked. 'She'll want to know.'

'Yes, please, and I'll stay with Jane for a while.'

Charlie was pacing up and down in the street when they arrived, and he rushed up, helping his mother out of the cab. 'What's happened? Why are you so late? Are you all right?'

Ian ushered them all inside after dismissing the cab.

'Tell me!' Charlie demanded. 'Where's Joe?'

'Your father has taken him. We've been searching all over the place, but haven't found him.' Jane's voice broke with emotion.

Charlie swore, and then hit the door with his fist. 'Damn him! What's being done to find him?'

'Calm down,' Ian told him firmly. 'You are upsetting your mother even more.'

'Sorry.' He sat down, trying to control his fury. After a few moments, he said, 'Tell me exactly what has happened.'

'Let's make a strong pot of tea first,' Ian told him. 'We could all do with it.'

At the mention of tea Jane broke down. She could almost hear her youngest son saying 'I'll do it'.

'It's all right, Mum.' Charlie sat next to her and grasped her hands. 'He won't hurt Joe, and that little devil is tougher than we think. We'll find him.'

'I'm so afraid for him. He's out there somewhere with an angry, vindictive man and probably calling for us.' She stood up and grabbed her coat. 'I can't stay here. I must do something.'

Ian caught her as she made for the door and led her

back to the chair. 'There's nothing you can do tonight. The police are looking for him, and if they have any news they will come here. I know it's hard to stay at home, but you must,' he told her firmly.

'It isn't your fault, Mum. You couldn't have watched Joe every minute. If he'd made up his mind to do this, then he would have found a way. I expect he's shocked you've got the nerve to divorce him, and wants to get back at you. He'll soon get fed up having a young boy with him. It will interfere with his drinking time.' Charlie made an attempt at a feeble joke, but no one was in a laughing mood. 'Once he thinks he's frightened you enough, he'll let him go.'

She lifted her head and grasped her son's hand for comfort. 'I expect you're right, but it tears me apart to imagine Joe alone with him and afraid.'

'He won't be happy, that's certain, but you know Joe. Wherever they are he has probably tidied up and made tea to calm him down.'

'I hope so.'

'Let me get you both something to eat.' Ian walked over to the stove and began to see what food there was.

Jane was immediately on her feet. 'Oh, Charlie, you must be very hungry. I'm so sorry.' She moved Ian out of the way. 'I'll see to the meal. It will give me something to do.'

Concentrating on something as ordinary as preparing a meal helped to calm her down, and although it was difficult to eat anything, she forced it down.

As soon as the dishes were washed and put away she dredged up a smile. 'Ian, thank you for your support today. I don't know how I would have managed without you – without any of you. I am so grateful, and you're right, there isn't anything we can do tonight, so you must go home and get some rest.'

'Are you sure? I will be happy to stay.'

'No need. We'll be all right now.'

He stood up, shook Charlie's hand and kissed Jane on the cheek. 'Try and get some rest. We'll find Joe tomorrow.'

'Of course we will.'

Chapter Thirty

It had been a long, sleepless night, and first thing in the morning she went to the offices. Charlie had wanted to stay with her, but she'd insisted they had plenty of help and she didn't want him to miss a day at work. The moment she walked in, she asked, 'Any news?'

'The police didn't have any luck last night,' Ian told her. 'But his lady friend has filed a complaint against him for theft, and with the kidnapping as well the police are eager to catch him.'

Ted was hovering, looking rather uncertain. 'Sir, can I make a suggestion?'

'Go ahead.'

'Well, my old dad was a villain and everyone knew it. They also know me, being one of them, you see, so if I went around asking questions they might talk to me, whereas they wouldn't to anyone else, especially the police.'

'He's right.' Oscar joined them. 'If I wore old clothes, I could go with him.'

'I would be better on my own.' Ted's smile was apologetic. 'They'd spot you for a gent a mile off.'

'Ted's right,' Ian agreed. 'Get out there and see what you can uncover, but if you do find Roberts you mustn't confront him on your own. Come straight back here and we'll take the police with us.'

'Understood, sir.' He stooped down by Jane. 'I owe you a lot, so don't you worry, now. I'll find your son for you.'

'Thank you,' was all she could say. Fear for Joe and lack of sleep had drained all the life out of her, or so it seemed.

'Oscar,' Ian said after Ted had left. 'Where the hell is Culver?'

'He's still tied up with a difficult case and in court most of the time. I did leave a message, though, and thought we would have heard from him by now.'

'Go and see if he's around yet. He should know what's going on.'

Oscar slipped on his coat and left at once.

'There isn't anything else we can do at the moment,' he told Jane. 'Why don't you go and take your class? I'll send for you the moment we hear anything at all.'

She glanced at the clock. They would be waiting

for her, and she couldn't let them down. It would keep her mind occupied and she knew it wouldn't help anyone if she sat around here. They were all working hard to find Joe, and she had to trust them, as hard as that was. Her instinct was to go out searching the streets, though she knew very well that would achieve nothing. She nodded agreement.

When she arrived, Dora was already there and talking to the pupils. She stopped the moment Jane walked in. 'I'm so sorry, my dear. Is there any news?'

'Nothing yet. I'm so pleased to see you here. Ian told me to come, but I'm not sure if I'm up to teaching this morning.'

'I understand, and that is why I came today. You can go back to the office, if you wish, and I'll continue with the class for you.'

'No, I'll only be in the way there, and I need to keep busy. The thought of Joe out there somewhere and frightened terrifies me.'

'He'll be all right, my dear. That little boy has a fine head on his shoulders, and he won't do anything to antagonise his father. He'll find a way to get away from him, if he can.'

'Everyone keeps telling me he will be all right, but how do we know? Bert is clearly desperate to go to such lengths to hurt me, and there's no telling what he will do.'

They had been talking quietly, but the pupils were all watching with interest as they discussed the situation, so Jane straightened up and pinned a smile on her face, determined to get through the morning. These people had come to her for help, and she had to do the best she could for them, regardless of whatever crisis was happening in her life.

The moment the lessons were over, Dora insisted they went and had something to eat before going to the office. 'You've got to eat, my dear. You are already too thin, and Joe wouldn't want you to make yourself ill. There's a small restaurant not far from here, and the food isn't bad. Alfred and I used to eat there quite a bit when we were both working at the office.' She took Jane's arm, giving her no chance to refuse.

She let Dora order, not caring what she had, and somehow she managed to clear her plate.

'That's better. Now, let's go and see what is happening.'

The office was quiet, and there was no sign of Ted or Oscar. Jane felt panic rising inside her. She should be out there searching, not sitting around doing nothing.

At that moment the door swung open and Culver swept in, followed by Oscar. He went straight up to Jane. 'My dear lady, you must be out of your mind with worry, but we will find your son. The stupid man has just blown any chance he had of opposing the divorce. Now, someone tell me what is being done to find the boy.'

Ian explained the situation and the barrister looked grim. 'So what you're saying is we have no idea where Roberts might be.'

'Not yet, but Ted is out there in the hope people will talk to him.'

'That's a possibility. First sight of anyone in authority and most people forget how to speak. I know the man in charge at the station well, so I'll go and have a word with him.'

'That would be a help,' Ian told him. 'Can you spare the time, though?'

'I can always find time for my friends, and we must find the child. He mustn't have to endure another night in that man's hands. That he should subject Joe to such an ordeal is despicable, and what makes it worse is he is doing this to his own son.' Anger showed clearly on his face. 'My son is about the same age and I would never harm him; no decent man would. Roberts will pay for this, you have my word.'

The furious man strode out and Oscar whistled softly through his teeth. 'I've never seen him so angry. He's always very composed.'

'It's because a young boy is involved,' Ian pointed out. 'He adores his son, and this has clearly touched a nerve with him.'

'He'll sweep into the police station like a thundercloud, demanding to know what they are doing about this.' Dora gripped Jane's hand, then looked at Ian. 'Is there anything we can do to pass the time? You must be falling behind with your own work.'

'We are, but once Joe has been safely returned to his mother, we have all agreed to work extra time to catch up.' He watched Jane with concern. She had a haunted look in her eyes, seeming oblivious to what was happening around her. 'Would you like a brandy?'

'Hmm?'

'I asked if you would like a brandy.'

'No, thank you. I would rather have tea.'

'A nice strong pot of tea for all of us is coming up.' Oscar disappeared to the small kitchen at the back.

Several cups of tea later they still waited. The light was beginning to fade and still there was no news.

Jane was frantic and kept walking outside in the hope of seeing Ted or the police coming along the road. When Dora came out and tried to guide her back inside, she said, 'Why don't you go home and get some rest?'

'I'll rest when we've found our boy, and not before. Don't you worry about me, my dear, but you must stop pacing up and down. Come back inside.'

Half an hour later Ted arrived back and everyone shot to their feet, desperate for news. He was dirty, dishevelled and had been running. It took him a moment or two to get his breath back, and then he said, 'I've found him.'

'Where?' everyone demanded at once.

'He's by the docks on the Isle of Dogs. There's a piece of rough ground with a fence around it. It was once used by the docks and there's a small building on it. He's in there.'

'You're sure?' Ian asked.

He nodded. 'A vagrant told me he'd seen a man go in

there with a young boy. He told me he usually slept there but didn't like the look of the man, so he's had to find another place to sleep.'

'Oscar, go and tell the police we know where Roberts is hiding.'

'No need, sir. I went there first and they are already on their way.'

Jane grasped Ted's hand. 'Thank you so much. Please take me there.'

'We'll all go.' Ian rushed outside to find transport of any kind.

It was completely dark by the time they reached the place, and much to their surprise Culver strode up to them.

'How did you get here so fast?' Ian wanted to know.

'The police sent a message and I came here immediately. We've made an opening in the fence away from the windows. We mustn't do anything to alert Roberts that we've found him, so please keep very quiet.'

'Where are the police?' Ted asked.

'Trying to find a way to get in the building, but they want to discover where Joe is before they burst in.'

'Please, I must be there when they find him,' Jane pleaded.

'Of course. He will need to see you because I expect he's frightened. Come with me. There is an overgrown area close to the building and we can hide there while the police do their job.'

All was quiet for a while, and suddenly there was shouting and crashing as the police broke in. This was too much for Jane, and before anyone could stop her, she was running towards the noise. The men took off after her, afraid she was running into danger, but fear for her son had given her a speed they couldn't match.

By the time she rushed through the open door, two policemen were sitting on Roberts, having subdued him after a struggle. The room was lit with a candle and there was no sign of Joe. 'Where is my son? What have you done to him? Joe! Joe!'

The men arrived and helped the police with the struggling prisoner.

'Be quiet,' Culver shouted. 'I hear something.'

The silence was immediate as everyone listened. Then Ian picked up the candle and began to search the room until he came to a tall cupboard with a wooden crate against it. He dragged it away and wrenched open the door.

Jane cried out in relief. Sitting inside was her son, blinking at the candlelight. She rushed to him, gathering him in her arms and letting the tears run freely down her cheeks. 'It's all right, my darling, we are all here. Has he hurt you?'

He didn't speak, just held on to his mother, shaking badly from fright.

Dora came over and took hold of Jane. 'Come, my dear, let's get him out of here.'

Ian stepped in and swept the traumatised boy up in his arms. 'You're safe now, son.'

Joe wrapped his arms around Ian's neck and whispered, 'Home.'

'That's where we are going.'

'Is he hurt?' Culver wanted to know. 'Do we need a doctor?'

'We don't know yet, but he's asked to go home, and that's what we'll do.'

'I have my carriage round the corner. It will only take a moment to get it.'

Oscar and Ted had gone with the police to see Roberts safely delivered to the station.

All Jane wanted to do now was get her son safely home.

Charlie was pacing up and down outside when they arrived, and concern for his brother was etched on his face. 'You've found him. Is he all right?'

'We don't know yet. Please light the fire in the other room. He's very cold.'

'Right away, Mum.' He ran inside the house, leaving the door open.

Still carrying Joe, who was now asleep, Ian walked in, followed by everyone else, and laid him on the couch. The fire was just beginning to take hold and Charlie tore upstairs to find a blanket to put over his brother. Tucking it around him, he then knelt beside him and rested his hand on his brother's brow. 'He's in a mess. What has that man done to him?'

'He had him locked in a dark cupboard,' she told him, fighting back the tears.

Her eldest son made a noise something like a growl. 'If I get my hands on him he'll be sorry.'

Culver sat on the arm and gazed down at the sleeping

child. 'I know how you feel. If it hadn't been for the police being there, I would have knocked him senseless, but never fear, he is now locked up.'

'Can I do anything?' Dora asked Jane.

'We can start boiling water. I want to get him out of these filthy clothes and into a bath, but I will have to wait until he wakes.'

'I'll get the tin bath and put it by the stove.' Charlie stood up. 'Then I had better go and let Helen know Joe's home.'

At that moment Oscar and Ted arrived back from the police station.

'I'll do that,' Oscar offered at once. 'Your brother will need you when he wakes up.'

'Thanks. I'll write the address down.'

'I already know it, thanks.'

'If you are able to see her, say that as soon as I know how he is I will send word. Thank you for everything you've done.'

'I've been pleased to help, and relieved it has ended in his safe return.'

When he'd gone, she gazed round at all the concerned faces. 'I don't know how to thank all of you. Without your help I don't know what would have happened to my son – and Ted, you deserve a special mention. You found Joe when all our efforts had come to nothing. I am deeply grateful. If there is anything I can ever do for any of you, then please ask. I owe each of you a huge debt of gratitude.'

'You don't owe us anything,' Ian assured her. 'The law is our business, and we spend our lives seeing justice is done.' He glanced at the barrister. 'Isn't that so?'

'Most certainly. There is one thing I will not tolerate and that is cruelty to children. I could not do anything other than help in this case.' He brushed a strand of hair from the sleeping boy's face, and said softly, 'Poor little soul. It is reward enough to see him safely restored to his family who love him.'

Charlie came back. 'Everything's ready for when he wakes. I've also made a pot of tea, if anyone wants it, and I've put that vegetable soup on to heat through, Mum. He'll be hungry, I expect.'

'He's bound to be.' She was holding his limp hand in hers and rubbing gently. 'He's a bit warmer now.'

'Did he say anything when you found him?'

Jane shook her head, already worried about this. 'All he uttered was one word, and that was – "home".'

'Probably too frightened and exhausted to talk, but he'll soon be chatting away, as usual.'

Her eldest son was doing his best to keep positive, but she knew he was just as worried. 'I think the best thing we can do is let him sleep.'

'I agree.' Dora stood up. 'We are all tired, and there isn't anything we can do here except get in the way. Jane, don't worry about class tomorrow. I'll take it. You stay with Joe.'

'Thank you, Dora.'

'Don't worry, they know me well enough now, and I'll give them all homework.'

Culver stood as well. 'Allow me to take all of you home.'

After everyone had left, Jane and Charlie sat with Joe, wanting him to see them when he woke, so he wouldn't be frightened.

Chapter Thirty-One

It was the early hours of the morning before Joe opened his eyes. They had kept the fire burning and several candles alight so he wouldn't wake up in the dark. Being shut in that cupboard must have been terrifying for him.

With a cry of distress he shot straight up and fixed his eyes on his mother, but said nothing. She caught hold of his hands. 'It's all right, darling; you are home and safe now.'

Charlie leant over him, a smile on his face. 'You've been asleep for hours, and I bet you're hungry. We've got some lovely vegetable soup for you.'

They watched in dismay as silent tears ran down his dirty face, and she gathered him in her arms. 'That's right, you let it all out.'

'I'll go and warm up the soup.' When Charlie began to stand up, his brother grabbed hold of his arm and held on tightly. He sat on the edge of the couch again. 'I'm only going to the scullery,' he told him gently. 'You must eat something, Joe. I don't suppose you've had much, have you?'

Joe shook his head, reluctantly releasing his grip, watching his brother walk out of the room. He then examined his dirty hands, his filthy clothes, and held out his hands to his mother.

Seeing he'd noticed the mess he was in, she asked, 'Would you like to have a good wash before you eat, darling? We've got the tin bath in front of the stove and it won't take long to heat the water.'

He nodded, got off the couch and went straight to the scullery and began to take off his clothes.

The water was still warm, and Charlie began to fill the bath. 'Leave this to me, Mum. I'll see to him.'

She handed him a bar of soap. 'I'll keep the hot water coming. Wash his hair thoroughly and check to see he isn't hurt anywhere.'

Filling the big pot with more water she hoisted it onto the stove. Joe was nearly nine now, and very independent, so he wouldn't like his mother washing him as if he was a baby. Charlie knew that, and also how important it was not to upset him at this moment. They had no idea what he had endured because he still wasn't talking to them.

'This water will be hot enough when you want it,' she

told her eldest son. 'I'll get him a clean nightshirt.' She went upstairs sick with worry. Normally, when they had the bath out, the boys would be shouting and laughing as they took turns to splash about, but apart from the soft murmuring from Charlie, there was silence.

Once Joe was scrubbed clean of the filth, she dished up bowls of soup for all of them. None of them had eaten for hours.

Clean, and with food inside him, they tucked him up in his bed, but stayed with him until he was fast asleep.

'Did you see any sign of damage on him?' she asked quietly. This was the first chance she'd had to ask.

'He's got a bruise on his arm and another on his back, but nothing else and I looked carefully.'

'I wish he'd talk to us.' She ran a hand over her tired eyes. 'You'd better get some sleep, Charlie. It's three o'clock, so it will be a short night.'

'You need sleep as well. I'll be here if he wakes. Leave the candle burning so there is some light. I don't think it would be good if he woke in a dark room.'

Jane reluctantly left her son's side and collapsed on her bed, not bothering to undress. All the doors were open, so she would hear the slightest sound.

She was still on top of the bed when she woke, and with a cry of alarm she rushed to the boys' room. Both beds were empty, and then she realised what had woken her. It was the sound of activity coming from the scullery.

Not bothering to put on her shoes, she ran down the stairs. The boys were both washed and dressed. 'I'm so sorry I overslept.' She put an arm around Joe and smiled. 'How are you this morning, darling? Are you feeling better?' When he only nodded, she glanced at Charlie and mouthed, 'Has he said anything?'

He shook his head, before saying out loud, 'I found Joe's clean clothes, and we've both had a slice of bread, but I must go now, Mum. Will you be all right?'

'Yes, off you go, and thank you. I don't know what I would have done without you.'

Much to her surprise her eldest son hugged her briefly, and then hurried out, anxious to get to work.

'I'll get you something else to eat in a moment, Joe. I must wash and change my frock first.'

She had just finished tidying herself up when there was a knock on the door. Ian had arrived carrying a fresh loaf of bread and a package.

'How is he?' he asked the moment he was inside.

'I honestly don't know, and I'm worried sick. He hasn't said a word.'

'He's still in shock, I expect.' He walked to the scullery and sat next to Joe. 'Do you like strawberry jam?'

The boy looked at him, puzzled.

Ian produced a jar out of the package. 'I do. It's my favourite. Where's your bread knife, Jane?'

She handed over the knife, wondering what he was doing. He cut three thick slices from the loaf and spread them with a generous helping of jam. Placing one in front of each of them, he continued talking to Joe in a relaxed manner. 'Doesn't that look good? There are whole strawberries in the jam. You've got four on your slice.'

Joe looked, and then picked up the bread and began to eat with obvious enjoyment. Jam was a luxury in their house.

Ian motioned to Jane to do the same, still chatting away. 'We can grow strawberries in the garden, and you'll be able to go out and pick them when they're ripe. I've already started digging over the vegetable patch. We can have one for winter vegetables, like cabbage, carrots and onions, and another for summer foods. Have you got a favourite you'd like to grow?'

There was silence for a moment, and Jane thought her son wasn't going to answer.

'Rhubarb,' he said quietly.

'That's a good idea. We can easily grow that. I'll add it to the list.'

Joe had finished his bread and was studying the jam jar.

'That was good, wasn't it? Shall we have another slice?'

'Save some for Charlie.'

Jane had to turn her head away then so he couldn't see the tears in her eyes. That sounded more like the son who always wanted to share any good thing they had.

Ian reached into the package and retrieved another jar. 'I wouldn't forget Charlie, so I brought another jar as well. How about another slice?'

He looked up at Ian, a slight smile on his face. 'Yes, please, sir.'

Jane quickly got up to make another pot of tea in an effort to hide her emotions. She hadn't known what to do for her young son after his ordeal, but Ian did, and she wanted to kneel at his feet in gratitude.

By the time they had emptied one jar, Joe picked up the other one and put it in the cupboard they used as a larder to make sure it was safe for his brother.

'Now we've all had a good breakfast, I've got another surprise. Put your coats on and come outside.'

Joe gasped in surprise when he saw the splendid carriage Ian had engaged. He caught hold of Ian's arm, beaming with delight. 'Are we going to have a ride in it?'

'Of course. I need to see how the men are getting on with your new house, and as it's a dry day we can have a look at the garden and decide what else we'd like to grow.' He turned to Jane. 'Is that all right, Mum? I believe Dora's taking your class today.'

'She is, and I'd like to see the house again.'

'Splendid.' He lifted Joe up and put him inside, and then helped Jane in.

Jane was eager to see the house and couldn't wait to move in. To have proper plumbing instead of a tap in the scullery and a hut at the bottom of the garden would be such a relief.

Ian spent a while talking to the workmen and then came over to them. 'They assure me all will be finished in a couple of days, so you will be able to move in at the beginning of January.'

'That will be wonderful. Everything looks perfect now, except for the dust and debris from the work.'

'That will all be cleared soon.' He laid a hand on Joe's

shoulder. 'Let's go in the garden and have a look at the vegetable patches, and we can decide where to put things.'

She watched the two of them discussing plans for when the weather was warmer, and was overjoyed to see her son chatting away again. He was rather subdued, though, and that was understandable, but Ian was marvellous with him.

Joe saw her at the window and waved. She waved back, and knew she wouldn't be able to feel easy again until she saw the return of his bright smile. It was worryingly missing at the moment.

They didn't stay out there for long because it began to rain, and with the business finished, they were soon on their way to the office.

It was lovely and warm in there and they quickly shed their coats, and then Ian stooped down to the boy. 'We've come here because I want you to meet the people who helped to find you. Would you like that?'

Her son nodded and Jane took a deep breath when she realised what Ian was doing. The breakfast and the morning's outing had been to get Joe to relax and begin to act normally again. Now was the most important part – her son had to talk about what had happened to him, for that burden would rest on him until he released it. She found it hard to talk about the circumstances of her unfortunate marriage to Bert and knew that bottling things up inside was unhealthy and stopped you from moving on. It had taken her sixteen years, and she didn't want that kind of torment for her son.

With a hand on Joe's shoulder, he guided him towards the men in the office. 'You haven't met Ted yet. We all searched everywhere, and even with the help of the police we couldn't discover where you were. It was Ted who finally found you.'

'Thank you, sir.'

'Your mother has done a lot for me and I was happy to be able to repay that kindness.' Ted grinned. 'I've never been called "sir" before, and I'm honoured to meet you – sir.'

A hint of a smile touched the boy's face. 'What did my mother do for you?'

'She taught me to read and write so I could get a job like this.'

'I'm going to work here when I'm thirteen.'

'Are you?' Ted exclaimed. 'You'll love it, and we'll all look forward to you joining us.'

The smile was hovering, but was not quite there yet, as he glanced around at everyone, then back to his mother. 'Where's Granny?'

'Here I am.' Dora walked in and gave Joe a big hug. 'It's wonderful to see you. You have been so brave, sweetheart. Are you feeling better now?'

'Yes, thank you. We've been to the house and marked out where we are going to grow food.'

At that moment the barrister swept in. 'Ah, there's our boy. I'm delighted to see you looking so well.'

Jane saw the look that passed between Ian and his friend, and knew Culver wasn't here by chance.

He turned his back on Joe, then, and stood close to her, speaking quietly. 'I need your son to tell me exactly what happened. Do we have your permission to see if he will talk about it? I assure you we will not frighten him. At the first sign of distress, we will stop.'

'You may try, Mr Culver, but please keep that promise. He has improved, but has not yet fully recovered.'

'Trust us, my dear. Ian and I are used to this kind of situation, and know how to handle it without causing harm. He likes and trusts Ian.'

'Can I be with you, as well?'

'No, it would be better if you weren't. He might not want to talk, knowing it would upset you.'

'I understand. In that case you have my permission, but I will be right outside the door if he needs me.'

He patted her arm, and then turned to Ian, nodding.

'Want to come and see my office, Joe?'

'Yes, please, Mr Preston.'

He followed Ian quite happily, with Culver right behind him.

When the door closed behind them, Oscar told her, 'They will be very careful, and not force him if he is unwilling to talk about it yet.'

Dora stood up and put her coat and hat back on. 'Come with me, Jane, and I'll buy us both lunch. We can eat while I tell you about this morning's class.'

'I don't think I should leave. What if Joe needs me?'

'I doubt that will happen, but if it does, then Ted

will come for us. We will only be at the cafe a couple of doors away.'

'I will be there at once if you are needed,' Ted assured her.

She gazed at the closed door, and then turned, reluctantly, away. Dora was right to try and distract her, or she would have to constantly fight the desire to burst in and protect her son from being hurt again.

They talked about the pupils, while Jane kept an eye on the door, expecting Ted to burst in at any moment, but he didn't, much to her relief. However, she was on edge and anxious to return to the office. The moment the meal was over she was on her feet and heading for the door. When they walked in, all was quiet and Joe was still in with the two men.

'Haven't they finished yet?' she asked Ted, walking up to the door as if to enter, then turning and pacing back.

'No, but don't worry,' he told her with a smile. 'They are enjoying a plate of lovely cakes, and I've heard lots of giggling going on.'

She let out a pent-up breath at that piece of news, and was about to sit down when the office door opened. The three of them walked out, and Joe was carrying a paper bag which he handed to her.

'There's a cake in there for you and Charlie.'

'Thank you, darling. We will enjoy those, but what about you?'

'I've already had two.' He fished in his pocket and held out a pen for her to see. 'Mr Culver gave me that.

See, it's got his name on it – A. A. Culver, Barrister.'

It was a beautiful silver pen with the name etched in gold. 'That is a precious gift. What does the A. A. stand for?'

A slow smile crossed her son's face and he turned to the man in question, pulling him down to his level so he could whisper in his ear.

Culver whispered back, and Joe burst into laughter. He glanced back at his mother. 'I can't tell you because it's a secret, but I know.'

'Really? And why is it a secret, Mr Culver?'

Standing to his full height there was an amused glint in his eyes. 'I never use my given names.'

'So I've noticed. Everyone refers to you as Culver, or Barrister. Now, why would that be?'

Her son was still giggling, and when she looked at everyone else they all had smiles on their faces. Whatever this was about it was making her son laugh, so she joined in the game, relieved at the change in him. 'Hmm, well there can't be many names beginning with A, so I expect I can guess.'

'You won't be able to. I've never heard the names before,' Joe told her gleefully.

'They are unusual, then.' She glanced at Ian. 'Do you know?'

He nodded. 'We were at university together, and it was there he decided to just be called Culver, and abandon his other names.'

'Why would you do that, Mr Culver? They can't be that bad, surely?'

'They are old family names, and my parents, in their infinite wisdom, decided to give me both of them.' He smirked. 'They have always had an odd sense of humour.'

'I see, and have you kept up the family tradition with your son?'

'Certainly not! His name is Frederick, or Freddie, to the dismay of my parents.'

Laughter rang through the office, and Joe walked over to Ian, standing beside him with a smile on his face, clearly enjoying seeing his mother trying to find out the names.

Culver stepped close to Jane and lowered his voice. 'Your son is a brave lad and has told us the whole story. It took a while, but once he began to talk it tumbled out. He might have a nightmare or two, but he is well on the way to recovery. He has given me all the facts I need.'

She nodded. 'Should I talk to him about it?'

'No, just act normally, and leave it to him. When he is ready, he will tell you what happened.'

'I'll do that, and thank you for what you have done. I was so worried and at a loss to know what to do.'

'Mum.' Joe had hold of Dora's hand. 'Mr Preston is going to take us home in the carriage.'

Joe insisted on seeing Dora safely inside, and while he was gone Jane asked Ian, 'Why doesn't Culver like his names?'

He laughed quietly. 'Don't let Joe know I've told you, but his names are Ashton Algernon, and at university they called him Ashy, which he didn't like. After some . . . persuasion, they soon changed it to Culver.'

'I can imagine,' she remarked, hiding her amusement as Joe returned.

Once back in Fallon Street and preparing the evening meal, with Joe's help, she didn't think she could be any happier. It had been a difficult day, but a good one. She had her young son almost back to normal, and she loved those two men for knowing what had to be done to heal a traumatised young boy.

Chapter Thirty-Two

When Charlie arrived home that evening, Joe rushed up to his big brother, bursting to show him the treats he had for him. First the jar of jam came out, and then the cakes.

'My goodness,' Charlie exclaimed. 'Where did you get these?'

Joe told him about their visit to the house and garden, then tea and cakes at the office. He didn't mention talking to the men about his kidnapping, but he did, proudly, show the pen he had been given.

'He said I must keep it for when I'm a barrister like him.'

'A barrister! Ah, well, why not aim high.' Charlie examined the pen carefully. 'What does the A. A. stand for?'

'Can't tell you. It's a secret.'

'Evidently he has unusual names and doesn't use them. That's why everyone refers to him as Culver,' Jane explained. 'Joe knows, but he's been sworn to secrecy.'

He handed the pen back to his brother. 'In that case, we won't ask. You had better keep that in a safe place. It looks valuable.'

'I will.' He tore upstairs to do just that.

Charlie turned to his mother. 'What a change in him. What happened today?'

'I'll tell you about it when he's in bed. Culver said we mustn't ask him what happened, but to let him do it in his own time. Ian and Culver took him into the office alone, and when he came out he was more like himself.'

'Did he tell them about it, though?'

'Evidently he gave them a full account of the kidnapping, and he's much happier now he's talked it over with them.'

Joe was tired and soon after dinner went up to bed and was fast asleep in no time at all.

Jane sat with Charlie and told him in detail everything that had happened that day.

'Seems to me they knew what they were doing.'

'They did, and what have we done to receive such kindness, Charlie? It is as if your father leaving has opened up a whole new world for us. It's hard to grasp, isn't it?'

'Not really. Dad held you back and tried to hold us all back, but you made sure we had a good education and were brought up decently, in spite of our surroundings.

He didn't like that. What he wanted was to see us sink to his level, and I think he hated us all for not allowing ourselves to do that. When he left, that influence was removed, and Helen was the one to recognise it could be a blessing.'

'She was right, and we have all done remarkably well, but the road ahead isn't clear yet,' she cautioned. 'When I decided to divorce your father, I was not concerned for you and Helen. You are both grown-up and he would not try to get to me through either of you, but Joe has always been my concern and, as it turned out, I was right to be worried.' She studied her eldest son. He was wise for his years and had changed a lot since he'd started working. He was turning into a tall, good-looking young man, with an air of confidence about him. It didn't take imagination to see he was going to go far in life. She had seen pictures of her father as a young man, and Charlie's resemblance to him was unmistakeable.

'Time you got some sleep, Mum. You are exhausted.'

'Time for us both to retire, and it's been good to talk to you like this. It helps, doesn't it?'

He nodded, and they walked towards the stairs. 'It's nearly Christmas and we will all be together. I wonder if Mrs Jarvis will decorate her home? Joe would like that.'

'I'm sure she will, and it will be the first proper Christmas we've had.'

Charlie gave a quiet laugh. 'And we won't have to put up with Dad coming home dead drunk, having spent every penny he could scrape together.'

'Another blessing, and they are mounting up.' At the top of the stairs she turned and hugged him. 'Sleep well.'

'And you, Mum.'

The next morning there was a letter from Lord Grant to let them know Helen had told them about Joe's safe return home, and how relieved they were to hear the good news. They all agreed it was kind of His Lordship to take the trouble to write, then they all enjoyed the other jar of strawberry jam on their bread, and Joe saw the empty paper bag on the table.

'Did you like the cakes?' he wanted to know.

'We did, and thank you,' Charlie told him. 'We had them after you went to bed and they were delicious, weren't they, Mum?'

'A real treat,' she agreed. 'We would have shared them with you, but you were too tired to stay awake.'

'They were for you. I had lots yesterday.'

'And you were given a silver pen.' Charlie ruffled his brother's hair, making him laugh and duck. 'We'll have to watch him, Mum, he's getting spoilt.'

'I'll keep a very sharp eye on him.'

Charlie grabbed his coat and cap. 'See you tonight.'

When he had gone, the smile left Joe's face, and he nervously pushed his plate around.

'What's the matter?' she asked, alarmed by the sudden change.

'Um . . . do I have to go to school today?'

'No, darling.' She sat beside him and took hold of his

hands to keep them still. 'You are never going back to that school again.'

Relief flooded his face. 'Never?'

'We shall be in our new house soon and I have found you a good school quite close to where we will be living. I've talked to the headmaster, and he was very nice. You can start there in January.' She gave him a mischievous look. 'You can't go back to that old school, because when I found out the headmaster had let you go with your father, I called him a fool and an idiot.'

Joe's eyes widened in amazement. 'You didn't.'

She nodded. 'I might have called him worse than that, but I can't remember exactly. Anyway, he slammed the door in my face.'

They were grinning at each other now.

'You can come with me today and meet my pupils. Granny will be there, as well. She is helping now because we have quite a large class.'

He was delighted with this news and was eager to get to the church hut.

Dora held out her arms for a hug when she saw Joe. 'Have you come to help us?'

He nodded, and looked around with interest at the hut prepared and waiting for the pupils to arrive. 'I can't go back to my school because Mum swore at the headmaster, and he slammed the door in her face.'

'Is that all? If I'd seen him, he would have had a black eye as well. The man is a fool.'

That made Joe grin. 'I'm glad I don't have to go back there

again. Mum's found me a new school for when we move.'

'I know it well, and you will love it.'

The pupils began to arrive and gather around the stove to warm up for a few moments before taking their seats. Many had inadequate clothing for the winter months and Jane knew what that was like. Her own coat was too flimsy, but she made sure her children didn't suffer from the cold too much.

She smiled at the ten who had arrived. Sometimes it was less and at other times more. Not everyone who came attended regularly, and there were many reasons for this. They might have found temporary work, disappear, and then turn up again when they were unemployed again. For others it would be family pressure, or they simply found it too much for them. Jane always assured them they could come and go as they pleased, and was careful not to put any pressure on them. She gave everyone the same encouragement, whatever their abilities, but the most satisfaction came from the pupils who stuck to the task with determination, like Ted. Seeing one of them move on and improve their life gave her the greatest joy.

'Good morning, ladies and gentlemen. I must apologise for my recent absence, but Mrs Jarvis has assured me you all did well.' She pulled Joe forward. 'I know you were told why I wasn't here, and I would like you to meet my son, Joe, who is now safely home with us again.'

They all clapped and called out encouraging words to him, making him smile in response.

She bent down to Joe. 'Will you go and sit with Dan and help him? He's new and rather shy. Most of the pupils are older than him.'

He went and sat with the boy his mother had pointed out, looking pleased to be helping.

Dora and Jane then went from one to the next checking any homework they might have done. When it came time for a break, Joe was immediately helping with the tea, and chatting to everyone, including Dan, who now looked more at ease.

They were about to begin lessons again when the door opened, and Lord Grant came in. 'Forgive me for intruding, but I had to come and enquire about Joe.'

She beckoned her son over. 'Joe, you remember Lord Grant. He's kindly come to ask about you.'

'Good morning, Your Lordship,' he said, sounding very grown-up.

'Good morning, young man. Have you quite recovered from your unpleasant ordeal?'

'I have, thank you.'

'Splendid, I am pleased to hear it.' He stooped down in front of him. 'Your sister has been very worried, and if we had known at the time, we would have sent her home.'

'Will you tell her you've seen me and I'm fine, and helping Mum with her class?'

'I'll do that.' He stood up and rested a hand on the young boy's shoulder in a protective gesture. Then he swept his gaze over the pupils. 'Is there anything you need?'

'We could do with more notebooks and pencils. I don't believe you have met Mrs Jarvis. She is kindly helping out now we have more pupils.'

'I am pleased to make your acquaintance, Mrs Jarvis. It is most generous of you to give your time.'

'This is a much-needed venture, Your Lordship, and I am happy to be doing something useful. I have seen for myself how inadequate education is in some of the deprived areas. Your interest is much appreciated, and we could wish for more like you.'

He bowed his head at the compliment. 'I am managing to whip up a flicker of interest, but there is much to be done yet. Now, I have taken up enough of your time, but I had to see you to confirm that Joe was unharmed.'

Before leaving he bent down, spoke softly to Joe and pressed something into his hand. Then with a smile to everyone, turned and left.

The young boy was studying what was in his hand, and then held it out to his mother.

When she saw what it was, she curled his fingers around the gift. 'My goodness, that's half a crown. Aren't you a lucky boy to be receiving another present?'

'You have it, Mum,' he said, trying to give it to her.

'Certainly not. That was given to you, not me. Keep it, darling. You can buy yourself something with it.'

He glanced down at his feet. 'My shoes have holes in and are too tight for me now.'

'I'm sure Lord Grant would be pleased to know you

had bought new shoes with his gift. We'll go shopping this afternoon, shall we?'

He smiled and slipped the coin in his pocket, then took his seat again for the second part of the lesson.

'I'll come shopping with you,' Dora said, 'and we'll have something to eat while we are out.'

'I can't do that,' Jane admitted. 'Joe desperately needs shoes and I might have to add more money to afford a decent pair.'

'The meal is my treat. Let's call it a celebration for getting our lovely boy back safely. I know you have your pride and don't like taking from others without being able to repay them, but doing something as simple as buying you both a meal will give me great pleasure. Would you deny me that pleasure?'

'Dora, I suspect you are well practised in getting your own way.'

'Of course I am, my dear. Now, let's finish the lesson and then we can get something to eat.'

Knowing it was useless to argue, Jane gave a resigned smile and returned to the task at hand.

Later that evening Joe excitedly showed his brother his new shoes. 'Lord Grant gave me the money, and Mum said I must buy something for myself. My other shoes were too small.'

'Then you had to have new ones.' Charlie dutifully examined them, expressing admiration, then turned his head to glance at his mother. 'I told you he's getting spoilt.'

Joe tried to hit his brother, who ducked expertly out of the way just in time. 'I'm not sure I'll give you the present I bought for you.'

'What is it?'

Jane watched her sons laughing and teasing each other. Even though there was a good few years between them, they had always got on well.

Shrieking with laughter, Joe hurtled up the stairs with his big brother on his heels. After much banging and shouting, Charlie appeared with a big grin on his face and holding up a new pair of socks.

'Just what I need, Mum. The ones I'm wearing won't stand any more darning.' He lifted Joe up and spun him round. 'Thanks, little brother.'

The young boy was glowing with pleasure at Charlie's obvious delight in the gift.

Jane couldn't be happier. The smile and laughter were back, showing Joe was recovering well from his ordeal. She had been so afraid he might be damaged in some way by her husband's cruelty, but because of everyone's concern and kindness that wasn't happening.

How was she ever going to be able to repay the people who had gathered around her with help and support since Bert had walked out on them? Thanks were inadequate, but that was all she had.

Chapter Thirty-Three

After removing the last of the pins, Jane sat back on her heels and looked up at her daughter. 'How does that feel?'

'It fits perfectly. How did you manage that, Mum? Lady Grant is petite, and I am nowhere near her size.'

'Whoever made that gown left a generous amount of material on the seams, and I used the lace at the hem to make it longer.'

Helen did a twirl, laughing in delight. 'And you've put lace around the neck to make it look as if it was made that way. You are so clever. It is the best gown I've ever had.'

'That shade of green brings out the colour of your eyes.' Jane studied her daughter, and then nodded in satisfaction. 'You look beautiful. Let's go and show the boys.'

When she walked downstairs, her brothers stared at her in astonishment. They had never seen their sister looking so grown-up and elegant.

'What do you think?' she asked, when they didn't say anything.

'You look very posh,' Charlie told her.

'And lovely,' Joe added.

'So do you two. My goodness, Charlie, you are quite the gentleman in that suit, and so are you, Joe.'

He beamed and looked down at his first pair of long trousers. 'Mum's been sewing every night to get everything finished so we'll look smart enough to go to Granny's.'

Helen saw her mother standing with a smile on her face, and frowned. 'What about you, Mum? Haven't you made yourself something new to wear?'

'I didn't have enough material left, but I'm fine. I've washed and pressed my frock. It's old but clean.' She glanced out of the window. 'Come on, it's time to leave. Ian has just arrived with the carriage.'

Dora's house was decked for the festivities, and there was even a tree in the sitting room, brightly decorated.

'That's pretty.' Joe was entranced while he inspected it in detail.

'I am pleased you like it, and don't you all look smart in your new clothes. Helen, that suits you perfectly.'

'Thank you. Lady Grant was turning out her dressing room and she gave me some of the clothes, including a couple of her husband's garments. Mum's been working hard to make these for us.'

Dora looked across at Jane who was talking to Ian, noting she was still wearing the same old frock.

Helen said quietly, 'She never thinks of herself, and I wish she would. We always come first, and I know there have been many times in the past when we have eaten and she hasn't.'

'Is that why you went into service, to ease the burden on her?'

'One of the reasons. At least my going made one less person to feed, and although the pay was poor, I could help out with leftover food at times.'

'Hopefully things will change when she's free of her husband. She's still a very attractive woman.'

'Yes, she is. With less worry and a bit of care and attention she could be quite beautiful again.'

Joe was waiting patiently for his mother to stop talking, and then tugged her arm, making her bend down so he could whisper, 'When do I give Granny my present?'

'After lunch.'

'Have you got it?'

'Yes, it's in my handbag. I'll give it to you at the right time.'

Satisfied with that he went to have another look at the tree.

Howard arrived then, laden with parcels, and after stacking them around the tree with the many others already there, he kissed Dora on the cheek, and shook hands with everyone else.

Jane glanced at the stack of parcels with some

concern. She had seen Ian do the same when they had arrived, and was hoping they were just to make a colourful display.

'Don't look so worried,' Ian told her. 'This is a time for giving.'

'I know, but I have nothing to give, and I feel awful about that.'

'You are quite wrong. You are giving us the joy of sharing your delightful family. We couldn't ask for more than that.'

'That is gracious of you.' She smiled sadly then. 'This takes me back to when I was a child. My mother loved Christmas and we always had a house full of guests. This is the first time my children will have experienced anything like this,' she told him sadly.

'This is the first of many because your life is changing now.'

She nodded, but said nothing. Her life was changing in remarkable ways, but she was well aware that difficulties lay ahead. A woman divorcing her husband would not go unnoticed and society would be scandalised. She would probably be shunned and her future lonely, but she was prepared for that. Two of her children were already making a life for themselves, and Joe would do the same as soon as he was old enough. Then her job would be done. They were not responsible for the mess she had made of her life, and her one aim had always been to set them on a path out of the slums and poverty.

Dora clapped her hands to gain their attention. 'Everyone, please take your places in the dining room.'

The long table was beautifully set with two candelabra alight with flickering candles. There was much laughter as they took their seats, and Jane abandoned all thoughts about what kind of a future might be awaiting her. Whatever it was she would deal with it and survive. That was something she had learnt how to do over the years. Ian was right: this was the first of many times like this for the children, and it made her happy to see that long-held desire coming to fruition.

Dora had hired a cook and staff to prepare the meal, and when they had all eaten as much as they could, Jane thought that even her mother would have been proud to serve such a splendid meal.

The presents were given out later in the afternoon, and although rather embarrassed, she accepted the gifts with obvious pleasure, relieved they were small and not expensive. That was thoughtful of them.

Joe gave Dora her gift and when she exclaimed in delight, he was happy. Ian had given her a fine pair of leather gloves, and they fitted in the case perfectly. Jane and Helen received a warm shawl each and some scented soap, and Charlie a book on railway engines, and also a small model engine. He was thrilled. Joe had a gardening book and a couple of small tools, as well as a box of lead soldiers and horses.

Just as the light was beginning to fade, Jane wandered

over to the window and gazed at the river, taking in the tranquil scene.

'Lovely, isn't it?'

She nodded at her daughter who had just joined her. 'It seems so peaceful in the half-light.'

'This has been a special day,' Helen remarked. 'Charlie is quite grown-up now and talking easily with the men. Also, if Joe had any lingering fears about what happened to him, then I suspect today has banished them.'

Jane turned her head to look at her young son. He was sitting on the floor near the fire with the soldiers lined up, and chatting away to Dora, who was making him laugh. 'Yes, he will be all right now, but being the youngest I have taken the precaution of protecting him as much as I can. I have registered him at the new school as Tremain-Roberts.'

Helen looked startled. 'I know you used that as a reference for Andy and to help me get the governess job, but why use it again for Joe?'

'When the divorce goes through, and Culver is certain it will, then it will most likely cause a scandal by appearing in the newspapers. I don't want Joe to be shunned or treated badly. I know you and Charlie will be able to handle it, but Joe is still young and I don't want to see him hurt any more.'

'Mum, I'm sure you are worrying too much. We all know it will be a difficult time, but not as bad as you fear, I'm sure.'

'I hope you are right, but I'm trying to prepare myself for every eventuality.'

Helen slipped her hand through her mother's arm and smiled at her. 'Once it's over you will be able to make a new life for yourself. You're still a lovely woman and eligible men will be queuing up to meet you.'

She gave a startled laugh. 'That won't happen. I will be a woman who divorced her husband and no respectable man will have anything to do with me.'

'I don't believe that. What about the men here? They know you have applied for a divorce, and they are happy to call you a friend. And let's not forget Lord Grant. They are not going to turn away from you in disgust. Women's voices are now being raised against the injustice they face, and many will congratulate you. You can't really believe you are going to lose everything you have worked so hard for, and the friends you have made along the way. That will never happen, Mum!'

'I have faced so many bitter struggles over the last sixteen years, and perhaps I am afraid to hope things will turn out well. If they do, then I shall be ecstatic, but I still feel I have to prepare myself for the worst.' She patted her daughter's arm now gripping tightly on her own. 'Don't be concerned, my dear. I must sever the past before we can truly be free, and my only thought is to protect all of you as much as I can.'

'But . . . but . . .' Helen stammered, shocked and dismayed. 'You took that step believing it would condemn you to a bleak life?'

'I condemned myself to that when I married your father against my parents' wishes. I have talked to you frankly because I wanted you to be aware of how unpleasant the divorce could be, and what impact it might have on your lives. However, this is just between us; I don't want the boys to know.'

'I'm confused, Mum. Why bother to do this if you believe it could be so traumatic?'

'Because I have plans for the three of you, and I don't want Bert Roberts to have any claim on you. The only way I can do that is to divorce him.'

'What plans?'

Jane turned away from the window, a smile on her face. 'I can't tell you yet. Smile, now, we mustn't be sombre on such a lovely day.'

It was an effort, but Helen managed to join in the celebrations again, though she didn't believe she was all that successful in hiding the shock she was feeling. She'd had no idea her mother was feeling so pessimistic about her future after the divorce.

Ian came over to her. 'Are you all right? You are looking rather pale.'

'Am I?' She smiled brightly. 'Perhaps it was the cold coming off the window. We stood there enjoying the scenery for quite a while. The river looks beautiful in the half-light.'

'Hmm.' He didn't appear to be convinced. 'You know you can come and talk to me any time if something is troubling you, Helen. I'm a good listener,' he added.

'That is kind of you, and I'll remember that if I have a need to talk to someone.'

He nodded, giving a concerned glance at Jane before walking away.

He was a very perceptive man, she realised. They had been quite a way from everyone in the room, so their conversation could not have been heard, but he clearly had a suspicion that it had been a troubled exchange between mother and daughter. She wished she could tell him what her mother believed, but didn't feel that would be right. Their conversation had been confidential. Anyway, nothing her darling mother feared would happen. She was just preparing for the worst possible outcome. It would all go smoothly and without any fuss. It would. It had to. Her mother deserved some happiness in her life.

Chapter Thirty-Four

On the first of January they all walked out of the Fallon Street house, and as Jane closed the door behind her the sense of relief was enormous. She had dreamt of this moment, but deep down she had never believed it would ever come. All they were taking with them were a couple of bags of clothing because after years of living from hand to mouth they had little in the way of personal possessions. The larger items had been given to neighbours and smaller things had been pawned to raise a little extra money. Fortunately, Dora was leaving behind all china, cooking essentials and bedding, as well as the furniture.

Ian and Oscar had offered to help them move, but she had insisted it wasn't necessary. With Helen still at home she wanted them to settle in the new house without anyone else there. For her this was going to be an emotional day, and one to be shared only with her family.

It was a cold day and a few flakes of snow were falling when they arrived at Kennington. They stood outside for a moment and then, with great ceremony and anticipation, Jane opened the front door. The children let her go in first, and when the door closed behind them, she wasn't the only one with a tear in her eye.

'I'll get the fires going,' Charlie declared, shrugging out of his coat.

'I'll help.' Joe followed his brother.

Helen took hold of her mother's hand and smiled. 'We made it. A new year and a new life, but I know it isn't going to be easy. Our financial situation is better, but still precarious, and it will need all of us to work together, as we have been doing. We never got behind with the rent at Fallon Street, even in the worst times, and we won't here.'

'I considered this very carefully, and I agreed to the move because of my trust and respect for Ian and Dora. Also, it would have been madness to refuse such a generous offer. It was our chance to get out of the slums at last, and whatever the difficulties we will deal with them, as we have always done.'

'And this time we have a sympathetic landlady,' Helen reminded her.

'And what a relief that is.'

'Mum, Helen.' Joe ran up to them. 'The fires were already laid in all the rooms, and there's a load of coal and wood in the shed. It's lovely and warm in the kitchen now, and we've made a pot of tea.'

'Just what we could do with,' Jane said as they followed Joe along the passage. The old house had been flimsy and draughty, but this was solid and cosy. 'I'll have a cup of tea and then go and do some shopping.'

'No need,' Charlie informed her, opening the pantry door. 'There's enough food in here to last us several days.'

Jane couldn't believe her eyes. The shelves were laden with everything they could need. 'Oh my goodness! Who on earth did this, and how are we ever going to be able to pay for it?'

'There's a note.' Charlie handed it to her.

It was from Ian, Oscar and Howard, saying that the food was a gift to welcome them to their new home.

'There's something from Granny, as well,' Joe said, pointing to a large tin on the table.

It was a lovely iced cake with the words 'Welcome Home' on the top, and when she turned round, Charlie was already holding out a knife for her to use.

'That will go nicely with our cup of tea,' Helen said, as they admired the cake. 'It seems a shame to cut it, though.'

There was a chorus of 'No, it isn't' from the boys and, laughing, Jane cut them all a generous slice.

'Is this as nice as the Clapham Common place you dreamt about?' she asked her youngest son.

'It's much, much better,' he told her before taking a large bite of the cake.

After that they spent the rest of the day settling in, and by nine o'clock that evening they were all tired out with the excitement.

Before Christmas she had sent her pupils home with lots of homework and stopped the lessons until the second week in January. She wanted to spend as much time as possible to see Joe settled in his new school, and although his father was in prison awaiting trial, she knew he might still be uneasy. For the first week she would take him and collect him every day.

Helen went back to the Grants two days later, and the next day Jane received a note from Ian asking her to call at the office.

She went straight away and after thanking Oscar and Howard for their wonderful gift of food, she was shown into Ian's office.

'How are you getting on in your new home?' was the first question he asked.

'It's lovely.' She laughed. 'Actually, it is heaven, and the thoughtful gifts from all of you made it a very special day. Thank you.'

'We wanted to make it as happy as possible for you. My apologies for not coming round to see you, but we have been very busy and Dora said we must leave you alone for a while to get used to the place.'

'That was very thoughtful of her, and she was right.'

'She usually is,' he remarked drily. 'Now, down to business. As you know, your husband has been charged with theft, and the police would like to add holding Joe against his will, but if they do, it will mean you have to appear in court. Would you be prepared to do that?'

Jane had already given this a lot of thought, so she answered straight away. 'No, it could cause problems, not only for Joe, but also the divorce. There will probably be enough bad newspaper reports at that time, and I don't want to make things worse. Let him be charged with theft. That will be punishment enough.'

Ian sat back, studying her intently. 'Are you sure?'

'Positive. If at all possible, I don't want the kidnapping to be mentioned.'

'You are letting him off lightly.'

'I don't see it that way.' She leant forward. 'Ian, he must have been desperate to take Joe away, and couldn't have been thinking straight. True, he did it to get at me, but it was a stupid, thoughtless way to do it. I know I am hurting his pride by seeking a divorce, but I have no desire to burden him with more shame. Please tell the police that I will not speak against him.'

'Will you sign a statement to that fact?'

'Yes.' She gave a slight smile. 'You think I am a fool.'

'On the contrary, you are one of the most sensible women I have met. I understand your reasoning, and as much as I would like to see the man pay for the trauma he caused young Joe, I respect your wishes.' He had been making notes all the time and called Oscar, asking him to prepare the statement.

'What is going to happen to him now?' she asked.

'He will probably serve a short time in prison for theft.'

She sighed and shook her head. 'He's thrown away everything by going to live with that other woman, hasn't he?'

'I'm afraid so.' Ian frowned. 'Are you still in love with him, Jane?'

'No,' she replied, startled by his question. 'My love died the moment I realised he had only married me because I came from a wealthy family. I was hurt and angry with myself for falling for his charm, but when my father disowned me he reverted back to his true self. He took me to Fallon Street and told me to get on with it, so I did. There wasn't a choice. I didn't have anywhere else to go. I had been brought up to always honour my obligations, so as I had married him I stuck by him.' She gave a sad smile. 'It was a spoilt, naive girl who fell into that trap, but she doesn't exist any more.'

'No, she doesn't,' he said quietly.

Oscar returned with the prepared statement and she signed where needed.

When she left, it was as if a burden had been lifted from her shoulders. It surprised her she had spoken so freely to Ian about her past, but it had helped. So much had been locked up in her for years, and it was good to have found someone she could talk to easily. He was a good man, and one she had become very, very fond of. Whatever Bert had done after he had left them was his concern, not hers, but she was relieved the incident with her son would not be mentioned at his trial. She had Joe back, safe and sound, and the next important thing was to obtain the divorce. If it had been just for herself, she doubted she would have taken this course of action, but she had three children, and that made all the difference. They deserved better, and she was well on the way to giving them that. Bert leaving had broken the daily grind of just trying to exist. It was a way of life she had accepted, but now that distant dream of a better life was becoming a reality.

The week slipped by, and the next one, and soon it was February. Joe had settled quickly at his new school, Charlie had taken a step up with a small increase in pay, Helen was meeting Oscar when they had time, and a fine friendship was developing between them. Bert had received a three-month sentence for theft, and she was glad that was over. After the first week they had begun to receive visitors. Dora, Howard, Ian, Oscar and Ted came regularly, and she was fully occupied with her pupils again. If it hadn't been for the divorce hanging over her, she could have been completely happy. They still had to be careful with money, of course, but Charlie and Helen were helping, as was Lord Grant with his continued support. They were paying their way and even putting a little aside for more coal when they needed it. The children were better clothed now because she had managed to buy some offcuts of material from a garment manufacturer down by the docks, and her two boys were looking quite respectable. Helen kept urging her to make herself a new frock, and she would later, but didn't feel she needed new clothes yet. The old ones were still washing up all right.

With a final press with the flat iron, Jane held up the finished shirt and surveyed it with satisfaction. Charlie was getting quite broad across the shoulders and often came home with a tear in his shirt, so she was trying to make him a couple of new ones. His cast-off ones she would alter to fit Joe. Her two sons were going to be quite big men, and handsome, she thought proudly. Charlie was looking more and more like her father, which she found rather disconcerting. Still, that might be an advantage when the time came.

There was a knock on the door and, singing quietly to herself, she went and opened it, breaking into a huge smile when she saw Ian and Culver standing there. 'How lovely to see you. Please come in.'

They followed her to the kitchen, and Culver picked up the shirt she had just finished.

'Did you make this?' he asked, looking at the sewing materials on the table.

'Yes, I make all our clothes. It's cheaper, and I can reuse the materials for Joe.'

'You are an excellent seamstress. Where did you learn such a craft?'

'At the convent school I attended in Switzerland for a while.' When she saw his surprise she added, 'As you know, my father moved around a lot and I went to school wherever he was stationed.'

'When you told us about yourself you failed to mention you lived in other countries.' Culver leant on the table, eyes full of interest. 'How many countries have you been to?'

'We were mostly in India, but my father was determined I should have an education to the standard a boy would have received. I always felt he was disappointed I was not the son he wanted. It wasn't easy finding schools that would take females, so I had a private tutor in India, and lastly I went to a fine finishing school near Paris.'

'Did the convent you went to take students of any denomination?'

'Yes, they were teachers, and their purpose in life was to educate girls, whatever their beliefs. We did, of course, have to obey their rules and attend all their religious services.'

'How many languages do you speak?' Culver continued with his cross-examination.

'French, a little German, and I studied Latin in France.'

Ian let out a breath of surprise. 'Latin? Would you be willing to give Ted lessons in Latin? We will pay you an additional fee, as it will be of benefit to the firm.'

'I would be happy to, but I will need books. I left all mine behind when I married.'

'No problem, we have everything you could need.' He smiled. 'Thank you. He doesn't need extensive knowledge, but Latin words are sometimes used in official documents. Oscar has been trying to help Ted in that way, but we haven't the time, and he's no teacher. He will be delighted to hand that task over to you.'

Jane was delighted. 'Would you like me to come to the office, or Ted could come here after work, if that would be more convenient for you?'

'I'll ask him.'

Culver grinned at Ian. 'I'm afraid we have been rather sidetracked, but Jane is a constant surprise. I do have more questions, though. Do your children know French and Latin?'

'No, I gave them the choice, but they were not enthusiastic, so I didn't push them.'

'Very wise. Now, the purpose of our visit. We have been to see your husband in prison and had a talk with him. He is grateful you didn't press charges against him for taking his son without you knowing, and is sorry for the distress he has caused. He will not oppose the divorce.'

Jane had been holding her breath and let it out with a sigh of relief. 'That is good news!'

Culver sat back looking smug. 'He will keep his word because I warned him that I will make the incident public knowledge if he causes trouble. You will have your divorce.'

'Thank you. How long will it take, now?'

'Should be within the next three or four months. You will be free by the summer.'

Jane bowed her head, hiding the moisture gathering in her eyes. It was nearly over.

Chapter Thirty-Five

It was agreed Ted should come to the house two evenings a week, as it would cause less disruption to the work of the office. When she opened the door to him, he was standing there with a broad grin on his face, and balancing a pile of books in his hands.

'Mr Preston said you were to have these.'

She grabbed the top book as it wobbled. 'My goodness, you must have brought everything they had at the office. Come in, Ted.'

He followed her to the kitchen, dumped the books on the table and then gazed around. 'What a lovely house.'

'Yes, we've been lucky.' She began sorting through the books to find one suitable for their lessons, then looked up and smiled at him. He was wearing a smart suit with shoes polished to a high shine. His hair was nicely cut, and because he was standing straight, he appeared taller. There was also an air of confidence about him that hadn't been there before. The boy was happy, and she was overjoyed for him. He had come a long way in a short time, and it showed what a difference help and encouragement could make. She was proud to have played a part in his transformation.

'Sit down. We'll work at the table.' She watched as he opened his jacket to reveal a matching waistcoat. 'That's a smart suit, and you are looking quite the gentleman now.'

'Ah, well, I have to look smart for the office, and I'm living in a nice house now, just like you.'

'Are you? Tell me about it.'

'Oscar has been looking after me. He chose the suit, sent me to his own barber, and even found me digs with a family he knows who take in lodgers. I've got a lovely room, big and ever so clean. The landlady's kind and every evening there's a fine dinner waiting for me.' He sat up proudly. 'Mr Preston said I'm becoming a real asset to the firm, and has even given me an increase in wages. I'm saving up to get a place of my own one day. None of this would have happened if I hadn't come to you, and I bless that day.'

'You deserve everything you've got because you worked, and continue to work, hard. Without that determination you would still be living in the slums.' She opened the book and gave a quiet laugh. 'And now you are going to work even harder.'

He turned his head as Joe came quietly into the room. 'Hello, Joe, how are you?'

'I am well, thank you.' He inspected one of the books and sidled up to his mother. 'Can I stay for the lesson? I won't say anything or make a noise. I'm going to work for Mr Preston, so I'll need to know some of the words, won't I?'

'It will be up to Ted whether you stay or not. This is his lesson.'

'You won't even know I'm here,' he pleaded.

'Of course you can stay. You can help me with the words if I get stuck.'

The youngster jumped eagerly onto his chair, opened the notebook, and waited for the lesson to begin.

He was as good as his word and didn't make a sound to distract Jane or Ted, but she saw him writing things down, his mouth moving silently as he tried to grasp the strange words.

Charlie had been out with Andy and brought him home with him just as the lesson was ending. Ted and Andy began to exchange stories about how their lives had improved since coming to Jane for help. Joe joined them, listening intently while she made them all a hot drink. From the laughter coming from the boys it was clear they were getting on well.

Charlie picked up his brother's notebook and exclaimed, 'You're not trying to learn this as well, are you?'

'I joined in with the lesson, and it was fun.'

She laughed when she saw the look of horror on her

eldest son's face. 'I gave you all that chance when you were young, but each of you refused.'

'I'm still refusing. Everything I'm doing with engines is in English, thank goodness, so that's all I need to know. What about you, Andy?'

'I haven't come across it in my work.' He glanced at Jane. 'It's not a very useful language, is it?'

'It's only used now in a few professions, but if you boys ever want to have a go at another language, then I'll be happy to help.'

That received definite shakes of their heads. It was another half an hour before Ted and Andy left, still chatting away.

The next three months were the happiest Jane could remember. Helen had settled in her job as governess. The Grants were good to her and even had a cake made for her sixteenth birthday at the end of May. Her friendship with Oscar was thriving. They liked the same things, and perhaps in time it would blossom into a closer relationship, but Jane was happy with the way things were going. Charlie loved his work and was growing in stature and confidence all the time, often arriving home greasy but ecstatic about the things he was learning. Joe was still Joe, and the bright smile also told her he was happy. He had never talked much about the time his father took him away, and she had never pushed. He was back to his normal self and did not appear to be at all bothered by the incident any more.

As the weather improved, Ian kept his word and spent every Sunday with Joe in the garden. Dora was still helping with the pupils and enjoying going out and about with Howard. Jane was happy she had found a companion after all she had gone through.

She took each day as it came, and enjoyed the tranquil months, knowing there were still a couple of hurdles to face, but for the moment she pushed all of that out of her mind. Sundays were the best, like this one. Dora and Howard were coming for afternoon tea. Ian was already here working in the garden, and with the back door open she could hear the chatter and laughter. Ian appeared to enjoy his time with Joe, and her young son adored him.

Charlie was spending the day with Andy and his family, so she had enough food to invite Ian to stay for lunch. He had joined them a few times and didn't seem to mind the simple offerings. Over the months her feelings for this gentle man had grown, and she had fallen in love with him. It was foolish, of course, because he would never be interested in a divorced woman with three children. She couldn't help but wonder what it would be like to be married to him, though. Ah well, it was nice to dream . . .

She wandered outside. They were both on their knees, dusty and enjoying what they were doing. 'The pair of you love to get messy, don't you?'

Two heads turned and they scrambled to their feet.

'Don't let me stop you. I have only come to ask if you would join us for lunch, Ian.'

'That would be lovely. Thank you.'

Joe beamed, pleased to have his gardening friend stay. 'Everything is growing, Mum, and you'll soon have lots for cooking.'

She took her time admiring the rows of carefully planted vegetables, and nodded. 'It will be a real treat to have something fresh from the garden. Lunch will be in an hour.'

They went straight back to work, and when they came to the table, minus the dust, she smiled. Ian always wore old clothes for working in the garden, changing into a suit after they had finished, and Joe had put on his long trousers and a clean shirt.

'My goodness, what a difference,' she teased, as they sat at the table.

Later when Dora and Howard arrived Joe took them outside to show them what he had been doing in the garden, leaving Jane and Ian together.

'While we have a moment alone, I want to make something clear.' Ian made her sit down. 'Helen came to me the other day and told me you fear everyone will reject you if there is unpleasant publicity about the divorce.'

That surprised her. 'I told Helen not to say anything.'

'I know, but she was greatly troubled and came to me. I'm pleased she did, because you are completely wrong. Over the last months we have formed a firm friendship with you and your children. Nothing – and I repeat, nothing – is going to change that.' He gave her a look of affection. 'You are stuck with us, whether you like it or not.'

'Oh, I like it.' She gave a shaky smile of relief. 'I have been happy since we moved in here, and do you know, in the years since I married Bert, I have never had a friend. Now I have many, and I was so afraid I would lose it all once the scandal of the divorce was made public.'

'Did you really believe we would abandon you?'

'I didn't know for sure, but I was preparing myself for the worst, because the pain would be great if it did happen. You must think I am very foolish, but the change in our lives has been enormous, and lingering at the back of my mind is a voice telling me this can't be true, and I could lose it all again.'

He sat beside her and took hold of her hand, giving it a reassuring squeeze. 'We have been with you from the time your husband left you, and we'll all still be here no matter what happens. Anyway, you are underestimating Culver. Now your husband has agreed not to oppose the divorce, our barrister friend will do his best to see the divorce is granted without any fuss or adverse publicity.'

'I know he's well respected in his profession, but I can't believe he can influence the newspapers.'

'He can and will try, Jane. Now stop worrying, and look forward to a better future for you and your family.'

'I promise I'll try, but I'm having a difficult time convincing myself that the bad times are really over.'

'They are, my dear, and you will soon be a free woman.'

The sound of the others returning put a stop to their conversation, but she just had time to grasp his hand in gratitude, and put a smile on her face as Joe burst back, face glowing with pleasure.

'You are turning our boy into an expert gardener, Ian,' Dora said.

'We enjoy working out there now the weather is better, and I've always loved growing things.'

'I know Alfred came to you for advice, and I never understood why you stayed in that flat without a garden.'

'I never intended to stay there so long, but somehow the years slipped by.'

'And your work came first, but you are not getting any younger, and it's time you thought about yourself,' she admonished.

'I fully intend to now Howard has joined us. Oscar has qualified, Ted is efficiently taking his place, and Joe will be old enough to train in a few years, so I will be able to relax more.'

'Good. Since Alfred retired you have shouldered the burden, now it's time for you to have fun.' She smiled at everyone. 'We should all have fun, so let's start with a cup of tea and a large slice of the cake my cook baked for us.'

Dora and Howard didn't stay long and Jane understood that. It couldn't be easy for her to come to the house holding so many memories, good and bad, but there was no doubt she did it for Joe. He missed her and loved it when she visited.

Ian left at the same time and Joe went back to the garden again, giving her time to think over what he had said. To be assured that their friendship wouldn't end had come as a great relief. She could see that the pessimistic view she had been holding on to was a way to protect herself if things did go terribly wrong. Helen, with her usual good sense, had gone to the right person, sensing it would be the loss of Ian's friendship her mother would find the most devastating. It was foolish to have become so fond of him when nothing could ever come of it, but she would happily settle for his friendship and support. To keep that meant the world to her, she admitted to herself.

Her days were busy and challenging, but she loved seeing some of her pupils making progress, and the effort was worth it. The number of pupils fluctuated, but it was clear the need was so great that something had to be done. She had sent a message to Lord Grant asking if he could spare time to discuss the dilemma, and much to her relief he turned up the next day just as the pupils were leaving.

'Thank you for coming, Your Lordship. I'm struggling to cope with the demand, and I need your advice.'

He nodded and sat at one of the desks. 'I knew this day would come, and I have a solution, though I am not sure you are going to like it.'

'Oh?'

'I have been approached by several gentlemen with

a suggestion that we set up a larger further education centre in the East End. There are retired teachers who would be grateful to help and feel useful again. You would, of course, still be involved, but with others to help you.'

'That sounds wonderful, but why do you think I might not like it?'

'It isn't the idea you might disagree with, but one of the gentlemen who wishes to join in helping to finance such an undertaking.'

She frowned.

'It's General Sir Charles Tremain.'

'What?' She shot out of her seat in shock. 'That can't be.'

'I admit to being stunned when he approached me, but after talking to him I believe he is sincere in his desire to help.'

She sat down again, not sure her legs would hold her. 'Why would he do that?'

'Perhaps as a recompense for the harsh way he treated you all those years ago?'

'Never.' She was shaking her head. Was he even trying to take this away from her?

As if reading her thoughts, Lord Grant leant forward. 'It was the general who insisted that you be consulted to make sure the school continued to help those in need. You started this on your own, but it is becoming too big for you to handle. You need to be free to take on just one or two special pupils if you want to. Terms for the new venture will be drawn up to include your original plan. I believe this is a step forward and we must grasp it. It is a logical next step.'

Taking a deep breath and then blowing it out quietly, she nodded. 'You are quite right, and I mustn't let my personal feelings influence me in any way. If at last someone is taking an interest, then I mustn't stand in the way of a school that could help a lot more people.'

'It would be helpful if you could attend the meeting. Your views and experience would be appreciated.'

'No. If my father wants to help you set this up, then that is up to him, but I will not meet him. How does he know what I am doing, anyway?' Or care, she nearly added.

'You don't know, do you?'

'Know what?'

'You are becoming famous.'

She gave an inelegant snort. 'Oh, and I'm going to be even more famous when the divorce is made public knowledge. My father will be horrified, so you had better be prepared for him to withdraw his offer.'

'He already knows.'

'I can't believe that.' She rested her head in her hands. 'He must have some ulterior motive, so watch him, Lord Grant. He's never cared about anything but himself and his career.'

'People change,' he pointed out gently.

'Yes, they do, and I'm being unnecessarily harsh in my judgement, but I have the spectre of a young, foolish girl being disowned and left to live in the slums.

But you are right, and I believe your idea is a good one. If men are offering backing, whoever they are, then I am happy. Please go ahead.'

He stood up. 'Thank you, Jane. We'll make it work. I'll be in touch.'

Chapter Thirty-Six

Handing over her pupils to others was going to be hard, but she was well aware it had to be done so more people could be helped. There was a limit to what she could do on her own.

Jane paused outside the office. Another thing coming to an end was Ted's English lessons. He had made remarkable progress and was becoming quite the scholar. He still came to her for Latin, but he only needed a basic working knowledge of that, and in her opinion he had already grasped enough to help with the legal work. Ian could also decide to stop them at any time now.

Ted greeted her with a huge smile when she walked in. 'Mr Preston wants to see you. I'll let him know you are here.'

When she walked in, he got to his feet and held out a document for her.

'What's this?' she asked, taking it from him.

'Your decree nisi. As from today you are no longer married to Roberts.'

Stunned, she sat down and stared at the papers in her hand. 'I thought I would have to go to court.'

'No, your application was unopposed, and with Culver handling it everything went through smoothly.' He stepped towards her, frowning. 'Are you all right, my dear?'

'I'm not sure. This is turning out to be quite a day, with one shock after another. However, I am overjoyed the divorce has been granted, and with so little fuss. It is more than I could have hoped for. Do you know if Bert is still in prison?'

'He was released a week ago and is working at the docks. Ted checked on him and he has found somewhere to live and is happily out drinking with his mates again, and gambling, no doubt. He's all right, Jane, and getting on with his life, which is what you must do now that worry has been lifted from you.'

'Thank you for finding that out for me; it makes me feel easier. I am very grateful for all you and Culver have done for me. You must let me know how much I owe you. My financial situation is slightly better now, and I could pay you something each month.'

'No payment is required.'

'Of course it is, Ian. We agreed in the beginning a fee

would be decided when the divorce was granted.'

'I remember, but you left out one important point to that agreement. I said it would depend on what you could afford to pay, and in my opinion that is nothing.'

Her head dipped in acknowledgement, and was shamed by that fact. 'You are right because I will soon be losing the money from Lord Grant.'

'Why?' he asked sharply.

'He has the backing of several gentlemen, and they are taking over the school to set up a larger one in the East End.'

'Oh, my dear, that will be upsetting for you.'

She nodded. 'It's a good plan and I was having a hard time managing the number of pupils coming to me now. It's good to know the publicity has made some aware of the desperate need. I know Lord Grant has worked hard to gain support.'

'Who are these men, do you know?'

'I don't know all their names yet, but one of them is my father.'

He drew in a deep breath, and then he reached out, taking hold of her hands and pulling her out of the chair. 'I'll take you out for lunch and you can tell me all about it.'

'But Ted's lesson?'

'He doesn't need those any more.' He guided her out of his office. 'Look after everything, Ted. We are going out for lunch.'

'Yes, sir.' He smiled and held the door open for them.

'When we've had lunch there is a fine art gallery nearby. Do you like art?'

'Yes, very much.'

'Good, we'll spend an hour or two there and then have afternoon tea somewhere. Do you like classical music, or more modern?'

'Er . . . classical.'

'So do I. Would you like to go to a concert one evening?'

She gave him a startled glance.

'Don't look so surprised. You are a free woman now, so is there any harm in asking you to enjoy a concert with me?'

'I suppose not, but it's rather sudden, and I've hardly had time to realise I am no longer married.'

'I have waited for months for your divorce to come through, and I don't intend to waste another moment. As Dora pointed out, I am not getting any younger, and it's time I had something in my life other than work. The moment I saw you I knew it was you I wanted.' He slipped her arm through his. 'I hope that is all right with you – and Joe needs a father.'

'Ian!' She was laughing now. 'Is it my son you are interested in, or me?'

'Oh, you, my dear. The children come as a welcome extra. I know I am probably speaking too soon, but I want you to be aware of my feelings for you. Now we can take things at leisure and enjoy each other's company. I am here to help you in any way I can, as I have been from the moment you walked into my office for the first time.'

'My goodness!' she exclaimed. 'What a day, and this is the last thing I expected.'

'I expect it is, my dear. I wouldn't have been so open with my feelings if I didn't believe you are fond of me as well. We have formed a close friendship over these months, and now you are a free woman, I want it to be more. I hope I'm right in my assessment of your feelings towards me?'

'You are, and I'm so happy you told me, but I still have one more thing to do, and need a little time to deal with it.'

'You can have all the time you need, as long as it doesn't take more than six months. I have plans also.'

'It won't take me that long. I intend to deal with this task within the month.'

'Excellent. Care to tell what it is? I might be able to help.'

'I will tell you, but it is something I need to do on my own.'

They spent the entire afternoon talking, and by the time she returned home it was as if a huge burden had been lifted from her. It had been a shock when Ian had made known his feelings for her immediately the divorce papers had come through, but he had evidently been waiting until she was free. During the months when he had been spending time with Joe in the garden and sharing their lunch, she had fallen in love with him. Believing it could not possibly come to anything she had hidden her feelings, but he had obviously sensed the affection growing between them.

Joe rushed through the door, hugged her and then shot out to check on his garden. Once Charlie was home, she would tell them the divorce had been granted, and about the proposed new school. She wouldn't mention her father's interest, though, or what had passed between Ian and herself. That would come later.

It was a week later Lord Grant called her to his home to let her know about the plans being made for the new school. She hadn't expected to hear so quickly, but he clearly was a man who made things happen.

She had managed to buy some material cheaply and had made herself a new frock, so she didn't feel quite so shabby.

He greeted her warmly the moment she was shown into the library. 'Thank you for coming. I am pleased to see you looking so well, and your gown suits you perfectly.'

She laughed. 'You flatter me again, Lord Grant.'

'I only tell the truth,' he stated, his mouth twitching in amusement when she raised her eyebrows. 'You believe politicians are incapable of being truthful?'

'Oh no, My Lord, I wouldn't dare to judge.'

He tipped his head back and laughed. 'One day I believe we shall have women in Parliament, and you would make an excellent politician.'

'We must be given the right to vote first.'

'That will come; it has to, but not for some time yet.'

That surprised her. 'You are very liberal in your views.'

'Indeed, and I often get shouted down in discussions, but I love a good verbal fight. There's nothing better, and do you know, sometimes they listen. Now, to the reason you are here. I promised to let you know of progress, and things are moving rapidly. Would you care for refreshments while we talk?'

'Tea would be welcome.'

He rang a bell and a maid wheeled in a trolley almost immediately. After serving them she left the room quietly.

'Now, I have formed a committee of enthusiastic gentlemen – four in all, with myself as chairman. A suitable venue has been found within walking distance of the church hut you have been using. It is a large abandoned house in need of renovation. This is already well under way, some inside walls have been removed to make classrooms – two downstairs and another upstairs. There will also be a kitchen and toilet facilities. Two retired teachers have offered their services and the wives are willing to prepare meals for those in need.'

'How have you managed that in such a short time?'

'The gentlemen working with me have influence and are eager to see the project up and running. Your example has woken some to the desperate need of many living in squalid conditions. We are also considering setting up a kitchen where the homeless and destitute can be given something to eat. We intend to arrange fundraising events amongst the wealthy to pay for the kitchen, but the school will be paid for by our committee.' He sat back. 'What do you think?'

Truthfully, she was lost for words. It was hard to grasp that her desire to help those who couldn't read or write had grown into this. 'I am overwhelmed, Lord Grant, and of course, wholeheartedly agree with such a scheme. I do have one concern, though. Can you assure me that the school will continue to meet the educational needs of the pupils attending, and it will be open and free to all who need help?'

'I can, and that is why our committee is maintaining complete control of the school. We hope you will also come regularly to talk to the pupils, and take a class from time to time. If you see any deviation from your original plan you are to come to me, and I will deal with it. This will also be put in writing, which everyone will sign as a guarantee. I know you are friends with Mr Preston, who is a reputable solicitor, and you can ask him to check and witness the signatures, if you prefer. Is that acceptable?'

'It is. I will ask him to be my representative as I would not attend a meeting of your committee. You understand?'

'I do, and I thank you, Jane,' he said sincerely. 'None of this would have come about without you, and I am ever in your debt for the help and opportunity you have given me to bring this deplorable situation to public notice. Now you are here, would you like to see your daughter?'

'May I?'

She was shown up to the nursery and Helen jumped to her feet in pleasure when she saw her mother. 'I knew you were coming, but I didn't know if I would be able to see you.'

'Lord Grant has been kind enough to let me come up, but I can't stay long. Joe will be coming home soon, and I must be home in time.'

'Of course.' She hugged her mother, then stepped back to study her. 'I'm pleased to see you have made yourself a new frock at last. It looks lovely.'

'I had to.' She gave a rather shy smile. 'I didn't want to embarrass Ian when we went out together.'

Helen did a little dance of joy. 'Oh, that's wonderful. I guessed a while ago how he felt about you. I have also been searching all the newspapers and haven't seen anything scandalous about the divorce, so your fears were groundless.'

'Yes, thank goodness, and Ian had a talk with me after you had been to see him, making it quite clear nothing was going to change the friendships we have made over the last months.'

'I know you asked me not to tell anyone about your fears, but I just had to.'

'You did the right thing, as always, darling.'

Helen studied her mother's happy face, and asked, 'Now the divorce is through, am I going to be able to call Ian "Father" soon?'

'Oh no.' Jane held up her hands. 'We are not rushing anything. I did that once in my life with disastrous results. We have agreed to take time to get to know each other well, and you're the only one I have told so far.'

Helen chuckled. 'I bet the boys have already guessed, and they will be as thrilled as I am.'

'Things are happening so fast now my head is spinning.' Jane glanced around the empty nursery. 'Where's your charge?'

'Victoria is having her afternoon nap, but she'll be awake soon and wanting her tea.'

'I must go now, anyway, but I have one more thing to ask. Will you be able to get a Sunday off soon?'

'I expect so, but why a Sunday particularly?'

'That is the only day I can have you all together. Let me know when you can arrange it, and I'll tell you all about it then.'

'That sounds mysterious.'

Jane grimaced. 'It is not something I am looking forward to, but it must be done for everyone's sake.'

When Ian came round that evening, Jane explained the situation to him, and he readily agreed to deal with the committee for her. 'I'll see everything is done legally. I expect you will be sad to see someone else take over your pupils.'

'Sad and pleased. These men are in a position to accomplish more than I can on my own, and it would be selfish of me to refuse. What the people living in deprived areas need is someone who cares. Well, Lord Grant and the men he has with him do care enough to do something about the problem and, hopefully, that will make others take notice. I will still be able to attend the new school and keep in touch with the pupils.'

'And make sure they are running things properly,' he added.

She tipped her head to one side and studied the man beside her. 'You haven't expressed an opinion about this scheme. Do you believe I'm doing the right thing?'

'Yes, I do, my dear. You have worked hard to highlight the plight of those living in the slums, and you can count this as a success. It was getting too big for you, and this is the right way to go.'

'That's how I feel, and I'm glad you approve.'

He took her hand. 'We need to celebrate. It's a lovely afternoon, so why don't we have tea somewhere, and go for a walk in a park?'

'Oh, I can't. Joe will be home soon.'

'He comes with us, of course.'

The words were no sooner said when the boy burst through the door, delighted to see Ian there, and even more thrilled about a ride in the carriage, tea, and a visit to a park.

Chapter Thirty-Seven

Within a week the papers for the new school were approved by Ian and signed. They also visited the house being renovated, and then she went back to the hut, sat down with her pupils and explained the proposed changes. There was some concern at first until they knew Jane would still be involved, and then they were happy with the arrangement. The new teachers also came to the hut so they could get to know everyone, and it turned out to be a happy and productive meeting.

It was a hectic few days, but she was pleased with the way things were going.

Another two weeks and she closed the hut for the last time, its ownership reverting back to the church on Lord Grant's instructions. There was a tear in her eye as she walked away, but she brushed it away. The way this had worked out was more than she could have ever dreamt of, and it was not a time for sadness.

When she arrived home, there was a message from Helen to say she would be home next Sunday, and that would give her a few days to do some checking to make sure she was choosing the right time. She had already asked Charlie to keep his Sunday afternoons free for a couple of weeks until they heard from his sister.

Ian was extra busy and didn't arrive until the boys were in bed.

'How did it go?' he asked, kissing her before sitting down.

'Very smoothly.' She ran a hand over her tired eyes. 'It's been a busy and emotional time, but I am happy my pupils will be receiving a high level of teaching and care.'

'Good. Now we can spend more time together and make our plans for the future.'

'As you know, I have one more task before I can put the past completely behind me. Helen has this Sunday off, so I will take the children then. I need to do this, Ian. It may turn out badly, but I must try.'

'I understand. Maida Vale, isn't it?' When she nodded, he said, 'I'll take you there.'

'That is kind of you, and as much as I would love your support, we can go on our own. It might be unpleasant.'

'That's all the more reason for me to be there for you and the children. I can see why you want to do this, my dear, but do you really feel it is necessary? You can't keep blaming yourself, and the children certainly don't.'

'I know they don't, and I promise you that if no good comes out of this, then I will walk away and never think about it again. I've always felt that my foolish actions denied my children the life they should have had. I've got to stop carrying this burden, and I believe this is the only way it can be removed. If I don't try, then it will always be with me.'

'If you feel so strongly about it, then you must do it. However, I insist you let me come with you. I will take you there and stay out of the way, and I promise not to interfere in any way. You and the children will deal with this on your own, as you wish, but I will be there if needed.'

'Thank you, darling. It will be a comfort to know you are close by.'

'Have you told the children what you are trying to do?'

'No, I won't explain until we are there.'

'Are you sure that's right? It could come as a nasty shock.'

Jane gave a mirthless laugh. 'It will be a shock for everyone.'

Helen arrived home on Saturday evening, and they were all curious about this mysterious outing the next day. Ian also arrived and helped Jane keep them intrigued without mentioning where they were going, or why.

She was grateful for his solid, calm presence, because she felt sick, and was desperately trying not to show how worried she was. Suppose it was like last time? Should she be exposing her children to something like this? But even though doubts were filling her head, she knew it had to be faced, or she would never be able to put it behind her. It wouldn't be fair to Ian or the children.

'Shall I wear my long trousers?' Joe asked the next day when they were getting ready.

'Yes, darling, I want you all to look very smart. Charlie will wear his suit and Helen her best frock.'

She was being bombarded with questions, and breathed a sigh of relief when Ian arrived with the carriage.

'Are we going far?' Charlie asked Ian.

'Not far.' He looked at the eldest boy, so tall and grown-up now. 'It's a pleasant day for a ride.' They set off and Ian kept up a light-hearted conversation until they reached their destination.

The house was set back from the road and had a sweeping driveway up to the front door.

'Stop here,' she told Ian. 'We'll walk the rest of the way.'

He did so, helped them all out, and watched as they walked up to the house.

'Why are we here?' Charlie asked. 'Who lives in this place?'

'I am going to introduce you to people you have a right to know.'

Helen pulled a face, indicating she had guessed what this visit was all about. 'But are they going to want to know us?'

'There's only one way to find out.' When they reached

the door, Jane took a deep breath, hoping her enquiries had been correct and they would be at home. 'I don't know what our reception will be. We might have the door slammed in our faces, and if that happens, we will simply walk away. Since your father left us, we have come a long way, and this is the last step to clear the road for our future.' She moved Joe to stand between his brother and sister, then knocked firmly and waited, head held high. She wasn't coming back grovelling for forgiveness, but as a mature woman who didn't need their approval.

The person who opened the door wasn't a servant as expected, and she lost all colour when she saw who was standing on the doorstep. She didn't move or speak.

'Who is it?' a man demanded.

Jane heard the firm footsteps as he came to stand beside his wife. She looked him straight in the eyes. 'I've brought your grandchildren to meet you. This is Helen, the eldest, who is governess to Lord and Lady Grant's child. Charlie is the next and is working on the railways. He is a marvel with anything mechanical. And the youngest is Joe, still at school, and will be training as a solicitor when he is thirteen. They are well educated and I am very proud of them, as you should be. I have brought them here today so they can see who their grandparents are.'

They hadn't said a word while the introductions were made, but they hadn't shut the door either.

Charlie was studying his grandfather with narrowed

eyes, hostility coming from him in waves. Her father also had his gaze locked on the boy, and it jolted Jane to notice the resemblance between them, not only in appearance, but in manner as well.

Her parents still hadn't uttered a word, so she gave the children a wry smile. 'It seems we are not welcome, but at least you now know who they are.'

She had turned away, taken one step when her father barked, 'Stop!'

'Did you wish to say something?' she asked with polite dignity.

'Come in . . . please,' he added.

'My children can, if they wish, but I will not.'

Her mother was near to tears as she looked from her daughter to Helen. 'I've seen you before.'

'Yes, I served you and your husband once.'

She nodded. 'You are the image of your mother and it gave me quite a shock when I saw you. Please come in and talk to us.'

Joe hadn't said a word, but now he turned to his mother, obviously confused. 'I've already got a granny.'

Mrs Tremain stepped forward and took hold of Joe's hand. 'We are your mother's parents, therefore you are our grandchildren.'

He pursed his lips. 'Why haven't we seen you before, then?'

'Because we didn't know about you until quite recently.'

Charlie gave a snort of disgust, but held his tongue – just.

'Why didn't you know?' Joe persisted.

'It's a long story, lad, and not one we are proud of.'

That remark shocked Jane. To hear her father admit he might have done something unkind or wrong was unheard of. When she looked up, he was staring at her.

'You have turned a disaster into a triumph. When you started using the name Tremain again, I had a devil of a job trying to explain how I had suddenly acquired a daughter. After all these years everyone thought we were childless.'

She dipped her head to hide her amusement. It would have been wonderful to be a fly on the wall when he'd tried to talk his way out of that. Fixing her gaze on him again, she said, 'You still do not have a daughter, but you do have three fine grandchildren. Are you going to disown them as well?'

'No!' Her mother stepped forward. 'Please come in, all of you.'

'As I have said, I will not. The only reason I am here is to show my children who their grandparents are. They have a right to know.'

Charlie tore his gaze away from his grandfather. 'I'm not sure about this. What do you want us to do, Mum?'

'Your grandparents want to get to know you, but the decision is yours. I will not ask you to do something you don't want to. This is part of your family, and you can talk to them, or walk away. I hope you will get to know them.'

The three of them considered this for a moment, and then Helen stooped down to Joe. 'Do you want to go in and talk to them?'

He nodded.

'Charlie?' his sister asked.

After giving the general another withering look, he shrugged. 'It's what Mum wants, so all right.'

Relief flooded through Jane. 'I'll come back for you in an hour.'

'Please, Jane,' her mother pleaded.

'Not today, Mother. This isn't the time to settle our differences. Get to know your grandchildren.'

With a look of resignation on their faces, Charlie and Helen took hold of Joe's hands and walked through the door.

Jane turned and began making her way back to where Ian was waiting, hearing the door close behind her, just as it had done all those years ago. But this was different; it was her choice. It was done and now she was content.

Ian saw her coming and went to meet her, placing a comforting arm around her. 'How did it go?'

'Better than I expected, though Charlie clearly wasn't happy to meet them. He is so like my father, and from the way they were glaring at each other, I don't think the general will find it easy to win him over.'

'Didn't they ask you to stay as well?'

'They did, but I'm not ready to do that just yet. I'm going back for them in an hour.'

'Come and sit down, my dear, you look quite drained.'

'I expect I do. It wasn't easy to face them after all these years, but I feel good now I have.'

They settled to wait, and Jane lifted her face to the warm sun, relaxing. They were talking quietly when Ian tensed, and got out of the vehicle.

Thc tall figure striding towards them was unmistakeable, and Jane got out and stood by Ian's side.

'Ah, thank you for bringing our daughter and grandchildren to meet us.'

'My pleasure, sir.' Ian shook his hand.

The general studied his daughter for a while and actually smiled. 'They are fine children and a credit to you. It couldn't have been easy bringing them up to be well educated and polite, living as you did.'

'We managed,' was all she said.

'I'm not going to apologise.'

'I don't expect you to. I know insubordination was a serious crime to you, and you acted as you thought right. The punishment was harsh, but I expected no mercy from you. However, I did attempt to maintain some link with you, but my letters were ignored, so I gave up in the end.'

'I never read them. They went straight on the fire.'

'If you thought they contained pleas for forgiveness and help, then you were wrong. I didn't ask for, or expect, anything from you. All I yearned for was that you didn't forget me. A little word of kindness would have helped to ease my despair at that time, but when there was no answer, I turned my back on you and fought to survive. I am only here now because my children have a right to know who they are related to.'

He nodded, then changed the subject. 'The eldest boy is very protective of you. He doesn't like me and isn't afraid to show it. I showed him some of my clocks and that caught his attention. Takes after me, I think.'

'Yes, like the son you always wanted, but he has a quality you have lacked – compassion. Did you ever consider what you were doing to mother with your harsh, unbending rules?'

'At the time, no, but I hope I have mellowed with age. I can't undo the past, but perhaps we can be friends in the future.'

'Perhaps.' Jane looked up and smiled at the group coming towards them. Joe was chatting away to her mother, just as he always did with everyone.

'Ah, there you are.' The general smiled at the youngsters, then asked Jane, 'Will you allow us to see our grandchildren again? It has been a pleasure to meet them, and we have a lot of catching up to do.'

'That will be entirely up to them.' She handed him a piece of paper. 'That is our address should you wish to keep in touch by letter. The children will let you know if they want to see you again.'

'Thank you for coming,' her mother said, still holding Joe's hand.

After handshakes all round they drove away, and Ian asked, 'Well, what do you think of your grandparents?'

'I liked them,' Helen said.

'So did I,' Joe told them.

'Charlie?'

'They're all right, I suppose.'

Jane smiled to herself. That was a better verdict than she had expected from her eldest son.

Chapter Thirty-Eight

Later that evening when the youngsters were all in bed asleep, Jane and Ian sat at the kitchen table talking quietly.

'You look more relaxed now,' he told her. 'Though, to be honest, I thought you were making a mistake by taking the children to see your parents.'

'I've made many mistakes, and that could have been another one, but it's a relief it turned out so well. I shouldn't have gone against my parents' wishes, but in my ignorance I thought I could change Bert into the kind of man I pictured in my mind. I was wrong. I soon discovered that his only interest in me was what he could get out of a family with wealth and position. When my father disowned me, Bert changed – no, that isn't correct – he reverted back to the man he really was, but was also determined to hang on to his "posh wife", as he bragged to his mates. Not all the blame for our unhappy life together rests with him, though. When the children arrived, I was determined they would have a good education, which I could give them, and be brought up to speak and act properly. This infuriated him and we had many heated rows about it, but even if we lived in dirt, I wasn't going to lower my standards. I was going to give the children every chance to get out of the slums, even if I couldn't. If I hadn't done that, perhaps he would have been a better father and husband. The children were born, and I took them away from him by turning them into something he couldn't love or understand.' She gave a ragged sigh. 'I shouldn't have done that, but neither could I condemn my children to a life of poverty. I had to give them a chance to get out, didn't I?'

'You did what you felt you had to do, and without a thought for yourself. No one can blame you for that.'

'Maybe not, but the thing I have learnt, though, is we have no right to try and change someone into the image of what we want them to be.'

'That is very true. It is a road to disaster.'

She nodded and looked at him curiously. 'I have never asked you, but why haven't you married?'

'I was going to many years ago. We had begun to plan the wedding when she received a better offer. He was titled, and in her opinion that was too good to turn down.'

'Then she was a silly girl.'

He sat back and smiled. 'I'm glad you think so. After that, I concentrated on my career, and never found anyone else until you walked into my office. First, I was intrigued by you, and as I got to know you I soon realised that I was in love with you.'

'I felt the same, but hid my feelings, believing it was impossible.' She grasped his hands. 'I would have settled for friendship.'

'Not a chance,' he told her. 'We are meant for each other.'

'Yes, we are.' She gave him a teasing smile. 'But you don't only get me. I come with three children.'

'I know, and how lucky can a man get?' he said, as Jane joined in his laughter.

Six months later, Ian had purchased the Kennington house from Dora, and they were married on Christmas Day. At the registry office her parents had been beside them, smiling with pleasure. The children were thrilled to know Ian was now their father. Dora and Howard came as a couple, and although there was no sign of them marrying, they were inseparable.

Oscar and his family came, as did Andy and his parents. Ted arrived looking resplendent in a new suit and with a young girl on his arm.

Lord and Lady Grant and their young daughter

took time out from family festivities to be present.

The reception was being held in the largest room of the new school, and Jane was delighted to see her first ever pupil, Daisy, waiting outside with her mother to cheer the couple. She insisted they also come in and enjoy the food.

'Just look at that.' Ian pointed across the room.

Joe had decided that Daisy and Victoria needed looking after, and the two girls were sticking close to him.

'That boy is going to play havoc with the females when he gets older. We are going to have to keep an eye on him.'

She laughed. 'He's already getting in plenty of practice.'

'The relationship between the children and your parents has grown stronger over the last few months. You are easier with them now, as well.'

'Yes, and I do believe it's good for everyone.'

'Especially your mother.'

Jane's gaze rested on her for a moment. 'I feel sad for them. They have missed seeing them grow up.'

'So, have you forgiven them now?'

'I don't feel there is anything to forgive. Each of us did what we felt was right then, and it was a long time ago. We have all changed.'

She gazed around at the people enjoying the celebration, and then smiled at her husband. 'When we found ourselves facing a crossroad, not knowing which way to go, I never dreamt it would have such a happy ending.'

'I'm so pleased you took the road that led you to me, Mrs Preston.' Laughing, he pulled her to her feet. 'Come on, we must mingle with our guests.'

BERYL MATTHEWS was born in London but now lives in a small village in Hampshire. As a young girl her ambition was to become a professional singer, but the need to earn a wage drove her into an office, where she worked her way up from tea girl to credit controller. After retiring she joined a Writers' Circle in the hope of fulfilling her dream of becoming a published author. With her first book published at the age of seventy-one, she has since written over twenty novels.